The Threat From Within

White Nationalism

by Gilbert Lewis

The contents of this work, including, but not limited to, the accuracy of events, people, and places depicted; opinions expressed; permission to use previously published materials included; and any advice given or actions advocated are solely the responsibility of the author, who assumes all liability for said work and indemnifies the publisher against any claims stemming from publication of the work.

The names, characters, places, and incidents in this book are from the author's imagination and are purely fictional. Any resemblance to actual events or persons, living or dead, is entirely coincidental. Throughout the book, several types and methods are described in conducting physical or electronic surveillance. The author has dedicated his professional career to these types of methods and techniques. Great care has been taken in this book to ensure that these methods and techniques are fictional and currently do not exist. Should a technique described in this book exist, it is coincidental.

Dorrance Publishing Co
585 Alpha Drive
Suite 103
Pittsburgh, PA 15238
Visit our website at www.dorrancebookstore.com

ISBN: 978-1-6461-0500-7
eISBN: 978-1-6461-0599-1

Acknowledgments:

I would like to acknowledge several friends who were instrumental in the publication of this book: Scot who provided the initial advice and inspiration that I write my first book and continues with advice and assistance. Special thanks to Owen who did a great job in the design of the cover and providing advice on the overall theme of the story.

In the completion of this book, I had four beta reads who read the final manuscript and provided excellent comments on the continuity of the story and making sure that what was said in the closing chapters was consistent with what was said the opening chapters.

Jason reviewed the action sequences and recommend that I included more details on the surrounding. Rick reviewed the sections on the hologram and the drones and ensured some degree of believability. Juanito reviewed the entire book and provided excellent advice on the technical areas and the firefight scenes. Bob, who said, "You went into detailed descriptions to make it interesting for the geeky types of readers - and also for the non-geeky types."

To my editor Alicia, who read every sentence and corrected my grammar and ensured that the storyline flowed in the proper sequence. Alicia was most helpful in the development of the main antagonist, Wolf.

To my editor Jefferson, who did a great job in editing the manuscript and his words of encouragement that the story needed to go to print. Following is a direct quote from him, “For me, the heart of the story is the cat-and-mouse game between Wolf and Rose, and they give each other a run for their money throughout. What makes it work, though, is Wolf himself. He is exactly what you want your antagonist to be: capable, deadly, and cunning, but also complex. While his racism is abhorrent, his “origin story,” where his father is killed, makes you feel for him in a way. And if you were to ask him, he would say that he is the good guy of the story. In other words, he a horrible person, but he’s not just a monster He has depth, and that makes him interesting. I look forward to seeing it in print!” Jefferson.

A Note from the Author

This book, *The Threat from Within*, is the second in a series about the heroine, Rose Mathews. The first book, *Hidden in Plain Sight,* establishes the bona fides of Rose and the American company White Mountain Analytics (WMA). The following story does stand on its own. However, the reader is encouraged to read the first book to provide the full content of the battle that the heroine has with the ISIS terrorist organization. Rose is a member of British MI6 and has been transferred to the CIA. In the first book, the CIA, FBI, and WMA uncover a plot by ISIS to destroy the Indian Point nuclear plant in Buchanan, thirty-five miles upstream from New York City. The destruction of the plant will result in New York City being uninhabitable for thousands of years, like the Chernobyl incident in Russia.

I truly hope that you enjoy reading these books as much as I have enjoyed writing them.

Prologue:

SUMMARY OF THE FIRST BOOK, "HIDDEN IN PLAIN SIGHT."

ISIS terrorists are holding six hostages for ransom. The ISIS high command has ordered that all Western hostages held by ISIS be brought to a safe central location. These hostages will be used to extract a ransom from the Western allies. The allies have assembled to watch a video recorded by ISIS. The six hostages are placed in a row, and as each hostage has the black hood removed from their head, a voice in English with a heavy Arabic accent says, "State your name and nationality." After each hostage does so, his or her head is again covered. All ISIS fighters are wearing khaki pants, short-sleeve black shirts, and heavy belts with ammunition clips and sheaths with KA-BAR knives, and they are all holding AK-47 Kalashnikov automatic rifles. They are also wearing balaclavas. ISIS demands ten million in bitcoins, or one of the hostages will be executed. After forty-eight hours, when ISIS does not receive the money, a reporter from the *New York Times* is beheaded. The combined forces of Great Britain and France assemble a special operations team. After a significant firefight, the British-French team successfully rescues the remaining hostages.

After the unsuccessful ransom demand, ISIS now turns to wealthy Arab jihadist supporters for funding. Before receiving any funds from the grandson of Osama bin Laden, ISIS needs to prove that they can successfully carry out an attack on US soil. ISIS plans and successfully carries out an attack at a US football stadium. Thousands are killed. The US now assembles a combined team from the CIA, MI6, FBI, and WMA.

The antagonists continue to plan for more devastating attacks on nuclear power plants, bridges, and tunnels in the United States. The protagonists are working just as hard, investigating every lead as they attempt to determine what ISIS is planning. The story offers a very realistic sequence of events that takes the readers to such places as Saudi Arabia, Pakistan, France, Switzerland, Mexico, El Paso, Los Angeles, Maryland, and New York.

ISIS has training camps in Pakistan, Chechnya, and Mexico, and the organization forms an alliance with a Mexican drug cartel. The cartel lends assistance in moving the terrorists and weapons to the US The team is always one-step behind. Based on electronic intelligence, raids are carried out on the training sites in Pakistan and Mexico. At the end of the story, the US team is successful in decoding the ISIS communications and determines the location of the attacks. The US team successfully counters the ISIS attacks and prevents the destruction of the nuclear power plant. The ISIS teams that are to place the explosives at the bridges and tunnels detonate their explosives before reaching the target. Several ordinary citizens confront the terrorists and prevent the destruction of the intended targets.

Chapter One

US Congress Senate Intelligence Committee

Washington, DC

ISIS has attacked the United States. The Senate Intelligence Committee is holding hearings to determine what went wrong and how to prevent future attacks. Senator Meacham of Virginia is the chairman of the committee. After the opening statements, the first witness is Mr. Hector Calvanese, FBI director. He says, "On Monday, March 28, elements of the terrorist organization ISIS attacked the United States. A total of twenty-six terrorists infiltrated the United States through legal ports of entry at several major airports. The infiltration of the terrorists was made possible due to them having passports from Western nations. All terrorists were killed or committed suicide. When the attacks occurred, the terrorists were wearing suicide vests. We also have an uncorroborated incident where four possible terrorists crossed the Rio Grande and infiltrated through the mountains in the Big Bend area of West Texas."

"The attacks occurred at the Indian Point nuclear power plant in Buchanan, New York, and ten seaports. All attacks were successfully detected and all attacks were unsuccessful. However, we did incur a number of fatalities at the nuclear power plant and all of the seaside entry ports."

Mr. Calvanese describes the investigation and how the terrorists were detected at the entry points. Then he explains how the terrorists assembled in Las Vegas during the Consumer Electronics Show. After his opening comments, questions are now directed to him.

A senator from South Carolina asks, "Director Calvanese, are you certain that the terrorists entered the country through US airports?"

"Yes, sir."

"What proof do you have that the terrorists entered through US airports?"

"Sir, we have photos of the terrorists entering Los Angeles, New York, Miami, and other airports." The director then says, "If you look at exhibits D, E, F, and G, you will see the photos of four terrorists entering the country."

The senator's face turns red with anger. "So, why the hell did we not arrest the terrorists at the airports?"

"Sir, these photos were obtained and analyzed after the attacks. All terrorists entered with valid passports from Western countries. These were Western terrorists who left their countries to join ISIS. They were likely radicalized using the internet. As was stated in my opening remarks, these terrorists were hidden in plain sight."

"Are you sure? You stated that there was circumstantial evidence that four terrorists infiltrated across the border in the Big Bend area of West Texas."

"Yes, sir, Border Patrol has a report of four persons, who appeared to be non-Latin American, entering the country by crossing the Rio Grande. The report states that the persons crossing the border surprised the Border Patrol agents, tied them up, and stole their four-wheel-drive vehicle. Since the agents were not hurt, it is unlikely that these persons were terrorists."

"So, what evidence do we have?"

"Only the word of the agents."

"So, where they entered, there was no wall. Is that correct?"

"Yes, sir, it appeared that was the case."

Half of the senators on the committee break into small groups and low whispers. "The president is right; we need the wall."

A senator from California now asks, "Director Calvanese, if we had a wall from the Pacific to the Gulf of Mexico, would we have prevented the attack?"

"No, not in my opinion."

"Why not?"

"Sir, the four *campositos*, that the Border Patrol witnessed crossing could have been normal farmers going to farmlands in California."

The senator from Alabama asks, "So, there were no additional witnesses?"

"No, sir. That is my understanding."

"So, why were these campo…whatever you call them, not arrested?"

"Sir, I do not have the details of the crossing. I believe that the director of Homeland Security will be addressing this committee. I suggest that you ask him."

"Yes, I intend to do exactly that."

Director Calvanese remains in the witness chair for two hours, taking questions from all senators. After the two hours, the chairman dismisses him. "Thank You, Director Calvanese; you have been very accommodating."

The director of the CIA now takes a seat at the witness table. She begins with her opening remarks. "Ladies and gentlemen, my name is Margarita Scarlet Gifford. I have had the honor of directing the CIA for the last eight years."

She goes on to explain why it is likely that ISIS terrorists attacked the United States. She explains that after the FedEx attack, the CIA agents had been tracking the terrorists. "We performed raids on several ISIS terror camps. The locations of these terrorist camps are classified. I can only discuss these locations and evidence obtained in closed classified briefings. However, I can tell you that through these attacks, valuable intelligence was collected. This intelligence allowed the FBI to prevent the attacks on the nuclear power plant and the seaports." After these opening remarks, she now takes questions from the senators.

Senator Meacham asks, "Director Gifford, does ISIS still control territory in either Syria or Iraq?"

"No, ISIS does not control territory. However, let me explain. ISIS is a state of mind. There are thousands, if not millions, of jihadists throughout the world. It is this undivided belief in the fundamental teachings of the Koran that drives people to ISIS. We, as a country, need to be engaged with all nations. We must not only supply weapons, but also provide humanitarian assistance. Unfortunately, our current policy of 'America First' only makes the ground more fertile to grow terrorists. Let me give you an example. You have a beautiful lawn and well-tended bushes, flowers, and trees. However, the neighborhood around you is totally unkept. The grass is now nothing but weeds, the trash is not collected, and the homes are in disrepair. Rodents and mice are taking over the entire neighborhood. Now, I ask you, how long it will be before your home is overcome with rodents?"

The senator from South Carolina asks, "Does ISIS have a location where we believe that these terrorist activities are being directed?"

"Yes, that would be along the Syrian-Iraqi border and in the uncontrolled northwestern territory of Pakistan."

"Why do we not just bomb the shit out of those areas?"

"Not that simple. The area where we have strong evidence that ISIS has a command center is in Peshawar, Pakistan. Through the State Department, we have attempted to bring pressure on the Pakistani government. After our raid on the Osama bin laden facility in Abbottabad, our relations with the Pakistani government have been non-existent. We had been making some gains with repairing our relationships, but our policy of 'America First' has driven the Pakistanis into the Russian camp, and regarding your question 'Why not just bomb the shit out of them?' That would be a big mistake. Peshawar has a population of over two million people. The Russians have placed a major anti-missile system around the Peshawar-Rawalpindi area. In my opinion, an attack on Pakistan could be the start of World War III. Things would quickly spin out of control."

The hearing continues through the remainder of the week. The senators remain in two camps. One is of the opinion that building a 1,900-mile wall will solve all terrorist problems. The second camp wants a rational, well-balanced foreign policy that includes the building of sections of the wall. The hearings end with no resolution to the problem.

Chapter Two

PESHAWAR, PAKISTAN

Nasir Muhammed Abboud, the ranking field general, and Abd Al-Malik, the chief intelligence officer of ISIS, meet in a nondescript building conference room. Based on the encrypted e-mail from Azir Osama bin Laden (the grandson of Osama bin Laden), the attacks on the United States have been a success. Azir bin Laden considers them a success because it has again shown the vulnerabilities of the nuclear power plants. The FBI and members of the contractor company were able to prevent the destruction of the protective shield. However, the US and the world will continue to rely on Middle Eastern oil.

General Abboud is a no nonsense battlefield general on the ISIS command staff. He is a strict disciplinarian. He will not tolerate failure. Unlike General Patton who slapped his private for cowardice, General Abboud was known to summarily execute his soldiers on the battlefield for such transgressions as cowardice or disobeys orders. He has a deep hatred for Americans. During the 1991 Gulf War, Abboud was seven years old when he witnessed the murder of his parents, brother and sisters. As he was returning from his uncle's house one afternoon in the spring of 1991, an American A-10 aircraft destroyed an Iraqi tank with a hellfire missile. The pilot of the A-10 had one hellfire missile left under the left wing of the aircraft. The pilot circled around, took dead aim at the Abboud house and fired the missile. destroying his home and killing his family. The American pilot had no reason to destroy an Iraqi house, other than to not return to his base in Saudi Arabia with a missile under the wing of the A-10. From that moment in time, Abboud promised to his family that he would avenge their murder.

Abboud says to Malik, "I am not satisfied with the results; the attacks at all targets were successfully stopped by the special forces of the United States. The question is, how did they know about the attacks?"

"I can assure you," replies Malik, "that it was not from our electronic communications. Our encryption is very strong. There is no way that they could have decrypted our communications."

"The leak had to come from the drug cartel."

"I agree. The report we have from the crew on the *Ajnahh* yacht was that Juan took a tender to Mazatlán. All attempts to contact him have been unsuccessful."

"Yes, I agree. If there was a leak, it was through the goddamn cartel! We need to find Juan and torture him to extract the information—how did the infidels know about our target cities? It had to be Juan and the goddamn cartel!"

After thinking about the situation, Abboud continues. "You know that woman who was at the Tadmur, Kaghan Valley, and Chihuahua raids must be found."

"You have to give that woman some respect," says Malik. "She appears to be quite resourceful and intelligent."

"Yes, I agree. We must find that woman and kill her; otherwise, she will continue to be a thorn in our side."

"And what do you recommend?"

"I want you to design a plan to find her. We need intelligence on where she is and where she lives. We need her pattern of life."

Malik thinks about what is needed. He remembers the raid in Chihuahua City. Fayez, a dedicated jihadist, was killed by that woman. The facility there has been repaired and is still being rented by ISIS. He will personally journey to Chihuahua City and see if there are any clues.

Within a week, Malik is on a PIA plane to Dubai. From Dubai, he takes an Emirates flight to Mexico City. From Mexico City, he takes a Mexican Airlines flight to Chihuahua City.

He has the new site manager Mustafa; meets him at the airport. Mustafa has a nondescript two-door Kia. Malik says, "We need to go to our facility and inspect the building for any clues."

"What exactly are we looking for?"

"We are interested in any photos or video that Fayez may have taken that shows the infidels who ransacked the facility."

"OK, understood. Last week, when we repaired the facility, we found some small covert cameras that were hidden in different parts of the building. They were being powered by AA batteries. The batteries were dead, so I simply have them stored in a locker."

"That's great news. Let's stop by a store and buy a dozen AA batteries."

"OK, I know a store along the way."

"Excellent. This may be exactly what I am looking for!"

Malik and Mustafa stop at a hardware store and purchase a dozen AA batteries. They arrive at the ISIS building, and immediately Mustafa takes Malik to the fourth floor. Mustafa opens the drawer, and there are ten small cameras. They were used by Fayez to record in five rooms.

Malik asks, "Do we know in which rooms these cameras were installed?"

"No, sir, I did not think it was important, but I can quickly determine the room by simply watching a few minutes, and I can label them."

"Not important. I want you to view all recordings and take notes with the time when people are seen in the recordings."

"Yes, sir, that should not be a problem. Most of the recordings have no activity. I can copy and paste to a video viewer on my computer and set the detection for motion. I should be able to complete the process in a day or two."

Malik gives Mustafa an angry look. "No, I want the process completed today—ASAP."

"Yes, sir. I will have Yousef help me. We will work through the night if necessary, to get the job done."

"OK. Once you have a copy of the recording with the motion annotated, please let me know. I will begin the review immediately."

Malik tells Mustafa that he is tired and hungry after his twenty-hour trip. He will grab something to eat and take a nap. After six hours, Malik has regained his bearings and is ready to work.

He says, "Yousef, I am ready to review the recordings." He knows the approximate dates.

Yousef has done a good job of placing all recordings in a tree structure. Malik begins on the day before the raid. He quickly scans all recordings. It appears that the motion detector is working. He can see foot traffic entering and exiting the rooms. Malik's attention now turns to the Fayez laboratory. He sees Fayez and his two co-workers assembling the drones. After viewing thirty-three motion recordings, he comes to the recordings of the assault. They show two people dressed in fatigues enter the room. Fayez locks himself in the storage room. He sees the firefight and the two smoke grenades thrown into the room. Two holy brothers walk in with their gas masks. They inspect the two infidels lying on the floor. They remove the balaclavas. The infidels are placed on a gurney and carried out of the room. Malik now rewinds and loops the recording of the two infidels on the stretcher. He stops the recording where he can see the face of what appears to be the woman. It is not a frontal view, but the facial features can be seen. Malik advances the recording frame by frame. He takes pictures of the woman lying on the gurney.

"Mustafa," he says, "I have some snapshots of what I was looking for. Let me show you the pictures. I want you and Yousef to review all recordings and see if you can find any additional pictures of this woman."

Mustafa and Yousef work eighteen hours a day for the next two days. They sleep at the facility. After the two days, they do not find any new videos of the woman.

Malik is satisfied that he has some photos of the woman. He retraces his route to Peshawar. There, he meets with General Abboud.

"Sir, we now have some pictures of the woman." He shows them to General Abboud.

"Excellent," says the general. "Too bad she is not dead. If Fayez had been smart, he would have put a bullet in her head. Instead, he wants to see some X-rated rape and what happens—he is shot dead, bullet right between his eyeballs!"

"We know she is French," says Malik. "I will begin immediately. I will order our hidden fighters in France to begin the search."

Chapter Three

Paris, France

Malik travels to Paris via PIA. He has arranged with his contact to meet at the nondescript Hotel de La Tour. Directly across the street is a French restaurant with outside tables. He is dressed as a tourist, wearing a t-shirt with the Eiffel Tower on it and a hat from the French football team. They have agreed on their password: "Are you from Nice?" If the answer is "No, I am from Marseille," it is correct. If the answer is "*Nien, ich bin ein Berliner,*" they will not meet; the Paris contact has been compromised. A young man dressed in jeans, cutoff t-shirt, and flip-flops comes by and says the proper password. The youth takes a seat and joins Malik with a glass of the table wine. They talk in French about the French world champion football team and about finding work in Paris. After thirty minutes of chitchat, they agree to meet at a bench in front of the military museum. The museum has a large yard with no trees. They agree to meet at five P.M.

At the designated time, the young man is already sitting on the bench. Malik says, "This is a good start. I like people who are punctual."

"I came early to make sure we could have this bench," replies the young man.

"Are you sure that you were not followed?"

"Absolutely. We have been trained in the proper Spycraft. We all were trained by Rahal last year. By the way, how is Rahal?"

"Rahal is currently on a classified mission." (Actually, Rahal is dead, killed by the woman that they are trying to find.)

Malik gets to the meat of the conversation. "What is your name?"

"Ameer Abdullah Tassie."

"OK, I will go with Ameer."

"Yes, either Ameer or Abdullah is OK."

Malik reaches into his backpack and brings out a picture of Rose. He says, "We are looking for this woman."

Ameer rubs his chin and shakes his head. "That's not a good picture. She looks like she is dead."

"Yes, you are right. We had our artist render a sketch of what she looks like from a frontal view."

"Much better, but I have not seen this woman."

"Yes, I understand. We are certain that she works for the French Special Operations. Do we have any moles working in French intelligence?"

"No, the French Intel service is the most difficult to penetrate."

"Then we will need a different plan."

"The only thing we can do is to stake out the French Intel service building and monitor all people entering and exiting."

"Wouldn't that be difficult? I understand that they have an underground garage."

"Yes, they do, but it is actually the easiest to monitor."

Malik looks perplexed. He asks, "How is that possible?"

"Easy. The garage only requires a keycard for entry. We can hitchhike with our car and enter the garage. The actual security will be when the person enters the building. Two elevators bring the employees down to the parking garage. There are three garage floors. We can place six covert cameras pointed at the exit doors from the elevators. The cameras will record for one month. This is possible because we can set the video for two frames per second. Since you want details on the pictures, we will record as JPEG images with a high resolution. It will take thirty days, but we will have facial pictures of ALL employees."

"Ameer, you are not only punctual but damn smart. We need more people like you in the jihad."

Malik likes the plan and provides the funding to buy the equipment. He is willing to wait the thirty days to find that bitch. Malik leaves for Pakistan and will keep in touch with Ameer via WhatsApp.

Ameer and the jihadists in Paris install the cameras. The plan works to perfection. On the twenty-seventh day, Malik returns to Paris. On day thirty, Ameer and the jihadists retrieve the recordings. Four jihadist and Malik review all the recordings. It is an empty hole—there are no recordings of any woman who looks like the picture.

Malik is disappointed. He must develop a different plan before he confronts Abboud. Telling the general that the French connection was a failure will not go well. He needs to present the failure as chapter one of the plan to find the bitch.

Chapter Four

Plan to Find the State Department Mole

Peshawar, Pakistan

On the way back from Paris, Malik has ten hours to think about the next phase of the plan to find and kill that woman. He has a first-class seat on the Airbus a380. He cannot go to sleep. He keeps thinking about how, six months ago, a colonel from the Pakistan ISI told Abboud that the FBI was testing some anti-drone systems. The ISI colonel stated that he was given the information from an officer from the US State Department. Malik thinks, *I believe that the colonel said that the exchange occurred at a security conference in Abu Dhabi.* The Airbus has Wi-Fi on the plane. Malik takes out his laptop and connects to the internet. He Googles security conferences in the last year. Google finds twenty-five; however, only one was in Abu Dhabi. It was held at the Westin Hotel and Conference Center. Malik thinks, *this is a job for my computer nerds—break into the guest list of the hotel and search for the US representatives at the conference.*

Malik is the intelligence officer for ISIS. He has an undergraduate degree in computer science from a university in Lahore, Pakistan. Upon graduating from the university in Lahore, he received a full scholarship to attend the University of California Berkeley. He obtained a master's in computer security.

When he was studying for a Ph.D., he was expelled for plotting to execute the president of the university.

Malik arrives in Peshawar and feels confident that he can sweet talk Abboud and convince him that this was his plan from the beginning. He will explain that the plan to find and kill the bitch will have its disappointments, but eventually, they will find and kill her!

Malik enters the office of General Abboud and says, "General, the first phase of the operation has proven unsuccessful."

Before Malik can continue, Abboud looks at him with his sharp eyes and shouts, "WHAT THE FUCK IS GOING ON? I DEMAND A FULL EXPLANATION!"

Malik fully expected the outburst. The general is not used to failures. Malik, in his most professional voice, says, "General, like all campaigns in war, we must have options when the first attack fails. That does not mean that we lose the war. We must be resilient and move to the pre-planned second option."

"What the fuck do you know about war? I have you here for your brains. Now you tell me that that birdbrain of yours planned a total clusterfuck!"

"Sir, will you allow me to explain? I have a foolproof plan."

"Yeah, go ahead, but this better be good!"

Malik goes on to explain the State Department connection. Abboud warms up to the plan. The ISI colonel discussed the conversation with him. He now takes ownership of the plan. He keeps silent—if he likes it, he will take credit. If it has a low probability of success—then it was a Malik fuckup.

"Sounds like a great plan," Says Abboud, "assuming we find the name of the American idiot. And what's next?"

"Once we find the American diplomat, we apprehend him and torture the information from him."

Abboud does know something about torture. He says, "The best way to extract the information will be to kidnap a family member. Use live video. If the diplomat does not provide the name, torture the family member. The best family member to kidnap would be a daughter."

"OK, I will do exactly that."

"I want daily updates on the progress of the plan."

"Yes, of course, General." Malik knows that the general wants no fuckups. *He does not fully trust my plan*, he thinks. *If the plan goes south—it will be my fault. If the plan is successful, he will take credit.*

Malik goes to the computer room and says, "Brothers and sisters, we have an order directly from General Abboud. We need to hack into the Westin Hotel and Conference Center in Abu Dhabi. We need to see who stayed at the hotel during the security conference that occurred six months ago."

Bashir, who is one of Malik's best I.T. techs, says, "Sir, I have attended some of the security conferences held in the Middle East and Europe. If you join the association, they will list all of the attendees for conferences. The idea is that as a vendor, you would like to contact the attendees with your products."

"Damn good idea," says Malik. "What is the cost to join?"

"Five thousand euros per year."

"Go ahead and join."

"Yes, sir. We will join immediately. We should have the list for the Westin Conference tomorrow."

"Excellent. When you have the list, let me know ASAP."

"Yes, sir. I will let you know as soon as we have the list."

Bashir's idea does the trick. All attendees and their affiliations are listed. There are four people listed under the US State Department. The last names are Williams, Brodhead, Ramirez, and Houella. Houella's full name is Charbel Mohammad Houella, and he is the prime candidate. Prior to Bashir showing the list to Malik, Bashir Googled the US State Department and Houella was listed as the undersecretary of state for Middle Eastern affairs.

Malik goes to Abboud. "Sir, I think we found the American with the loose lips. His name is Charbel Mohammad Houella."

"Excellent, Malik. Now you are in your lane. Good work."

"I have also printed his picture from the State Department website. Is there any chance that you can confirm that this is the idiot with your ISI contact?"

Abboud thinks for a few seconds. He stands up and looks out the window. He then says, "It would be a good idea, but it is too risky. Let us do this first. Google the other names. See what rank they have at the State Department. If they are some low clerical types—then this is our person."

"Excellent idea. We will get on that immediately. As soon as we know, I will get back to you."

Malik goes back to his computer hackers. Within thirty minutes, they have the details on Williams, Brodhead, and Ramirez. Williams is listed as a security officer. Brodhead and Ramirez are only listed as employees.

Malik tells Bashir, "Good work."

He goes back to Abboud's office. "Sir, here are the results."

Abboud scans the four pages. He goes back to Williams and again reads the bio. He then says, "It has to be Houella. That is whom we need to squeeze. We need to find out everything we can about him."

"Yes, sir," says Malik. "I agree—it has to be him."

Abboud is not stupid—he knows that Malik knew but wanted Abboud to make the decision. *If it is not him—Malik can point to me. If I am right—he will give me credit. Smart guy—that is why he is the intelligence chief.*

"Develop a plan to extract the information from our pigeon," says Abboud.

"Yes, sir. I have some ideas but give me a couple of days to complete some research, and I will lay out the plan for your approval."

Malik goes back to the computer nerds and sits down with Bashir, and they start developing the plan. Bashir says, "Sir, there is only so much that we can do from here. We will need to go to America and develop a pattern of life for Houella."

"You're right, Bashir. I like you're thinking." Malik thinks for a few seconds and asks Bashir, "How would you like to go to America?"

"Yeah, but what would I be doing?"

"Same thing that you are doing here. The difference is that we will have at least two covert jihadists who will provide physical surveillance."

"Hell yeah. When do I pack?"

"We leave in one week. I need some time to fix our passports and to coordinate with our brothers in America."

Chapter Five

SURVEILLANCE AND ABDUCTION, THE HOUELLA FAMILY

VIRGINIA

Malik and Bashir leave from Peshawar to Abu Dhabi. From Abu Dhabi, they take Etihad Airlines to Detroit, Michigan. Malik has selected Detroit for two reasons; One, there is a large Middle Eastern population, and it will easier to go through US Customs. Two, he has recruited two jihadists to assist with surveillance and possible kidnapping. Malik and Bashir rent a car from Enterprise and meet with Hamza and Waleed. Malik has some business in Detroit and does not want his contacts there to know about Washington surveillance. The Hamza has a four-door stretch Denali. Hamza follows Malik to the rental, and they check in the Enterprise car. Early the fourth day, they begin their drive to Washington, DC. It is a twelve-hour drive.

On the way to Washington, DC, Malik briefs the three-man team. "Brothers, we have been tasked to survey a person by the name of Charbel Mohammad Houella. He is an officer at the US State Department. We believe that he has information that will lead us to an enemy of the Caliphate."

"What will be our specific tasks?" asks Bashir.

"At this time, we do not know what our specific tasks will be. We will first place a tail on Charbel. This will be our responsibility. Bashir, you will be doing what you do best. As soon as we know the pattern of life of the immediate family, you will hack into their social media accounts. From the combination of the information from the tail on Charbel and monitoring the social media accounts, we will make decisions on how best to proceed. Now, are there any questions?"

Hamza asks, "Will we have different cars? This Denali sticks out like a sore thumb!"

"Yes, of course. When we get to Washington, we will rent two nondescript Fords or Chevys."

"Will we have binoculars? How about cameras?"

"Yes, we will go to Best Buy and buy all of the required equipment."

Bashir says, "We need to make sure that the hotels have high-speed Wi-Fi."

"Yes, we will be staying at the Washington, DC, Embassy Suites. Before we made reservations, we ensured that the hotel had Wi-Fi throughout the premises." Malik makes sure that he always speaks with the pronoun "we." He needs to have the team buy in to the surveillance. He will allow them to make decisions with his approval.

Also, he remembers: "We shipped some GPS pucks to our hotel. They should already be there. We will retrieve them when we check in."

The team checks into the Embassy Suites. They have two rooms with double beds. After a good night's rest, they have breakfast and meet in Malik and Bashir's room. Malik begins the conversation. He hands a picture of Charbel to all team members. Hamza and Waleed will stake out the State Department building. They will ID Charbel and his car. In the next few days, they will wait until Charbel stops for some shopping. They need to have the vehicle unattended for a few minutes. They will attach a magnetic GPS puck to the undercarriage of the car. The GPS puck will be tracked from the hotel to determine Charbel's traffic pattern.

That afternoon, Hamza and Waleed park their cars one block from the State Department. When Charbel leaves, he will need to drive either left or right. From either the left or the right side, they will begin their tail. In one mile, Charbel stops at a Walgreen's drugstore. Hamza parks at the Walgreens. He has the GPS puck in his right hand. He switches a small toggle switch to "on." He fakes that he drops his cell phone next to Charbel's car. He reaches under the car and applies the puck. The GPS puck snaps to the iron bar of the undercarriage.

Hamza walks to his car and calls Bashir at the Embassy Suites. He says, "Bashir, the GPS puck is attached. Can you see it?"

"Give me a minute," replies Bashir. "I will bring up the tracking app and confirm." After about a minute, he says, "Yes, I see it." He gives Hamza the address of the location, and Hamza confirms.

"OK, you and Waleed can come back to the hotel."

Hamza and Waleed arrive at the Embassy Suites. They go to Malik and Bashir's room.

Malik says, "Great job, team. Now we track the rabbit for a few days and establish his pattern of life."

After two days of tracking, they know the address of Charbel's home. He has a very predictive driving pattern. His home address is in Fairfax, Virginia. He leaves at 5:30 A.M. and leaves work between 3 and 4 P.M. Malik tells Hamza and Waleed to stake out the Charbel house. On the morning of the third day, Hamza and Waleed park their cars a block from the Houella home. Using their binoculars and cameras, they monitor the home. They quickly establish that a son and one daughter have left for school. The wife appears to be a stay-at-home mom.

As Hamza and Waleed are conducting physical surveillance, Bashir has been busy searching the internet for any information on the Houella family. By the end of the second day, he has hacked into the Facebook, Twitter, and Instagram accounts of the daughters, Jennifer and Jessica.

As the ISIS terrorists are conducting surveillance on the Houella family, Jessica and Jennifer have been communicating via the internet. Jessica is bitching about their dad having to take a business trip to a bullshit conference in Istanbul, Turkey. She is complaining to her sister that she does not like it when she is home alone with her mom. She is too strict and monitors her time on the internet, and she also has strict rules about studying! Can you imagine two hours of homework and study. She does not know why her mom is so harsh. After all, she is a straight-A student in high school. Last semester, she got a B in algebra, and her mom went ape shit!

Jennifer says, "Calm down, sis. Dad is only going to be gone for two weeks. It's not as if he will be gone forever. By the way, when is he leaving?"

"He leaves in two weeks."

"OK, I can come down for the weekend that he is gone. We can go shopping. This will get you out of the house. Besides, Mom likes it when we have bonding time."

"Can you come down on Friday?"

"Yeah, probably. I will check my schedule and see if I can make it."

"Thanks, sis. I really appreciate how you look after your little sister."

"By the way, do not tell Mom I am coming—lets surprise her."

"OK—mum's the word. Love you."

Bashir, who is monitoring the conversations between Jennifer and Jessica, calls Malik. Malik then calls Hamza and Waleed on the hotel phone. "Hamza, please have yourself and Waleed come to my room ASAP."

"Yes, sir," says Hamza. "We will be there in ten minutes."

Soon Hamza and Waleed are knocking on Mallik's door.

"Come in," calls Malik. "It's open."

Hamza and Waleed enter and listen to the recording. Hamza asks, "OK, how do you want us to proceed?"

"Pack your bags and go to Charlottesville," says Malik. "Stake out Jennifer and find her pattern of life."

"OK. Bashir, can you provide an information package?"

"Can do," says Bashir. "I will give you a picture and the dormitory where she lives."

The next day, Hamza and Waleed are driving separate cars to the University of Virginia, in the city of Charlottesville, Virginia.

Hamza and Waleed are in their twenties. They buy some clothes that the average student would wear. They go to Target and buy some jeans, flip-flops, and University of Virginia t-shirts then they sport three-day beards and unkempt hair. They will minimize their conversations as they have an Arabic accent. The dormitory where Jennifer lives is known. Jennifer is staying at the McCormick Road Hall. Waleed goes to the university website and finds that all students have a roommate. Hamza and Waleed rotate in two-hour shifts.

They stay away from the front of the dorm. Hamza gives Waleed a small GPS puck in the shape of a lipstick tube.

Waleed asks. "Does it work?"

Hamza says, "Damn right it works. We would not have it if it did not work."

The idea is to install the GPS puck in the side pocket of the handbag. All they really need is twenty-four hours of her movements. They are interested in where she goes during the day. As Waleed is taking the first shift, he notices that some of the students are walking to a parking lot half a mile from the campus. He casually asks one of the students if he can park his car at the parking lot.

The student answers, "No reason why not. It is a long-term parking lot for students in the dorms. Generally, we only use it when we leave the campus—like when we go visit our parents."

Waleed leaves campus and drives to the hotel. He is excited. "Hamza, we have stumbled into a good situation!"

"Hold on," says Hamza. "What's the situation?"

"All dormitory students park their cars at the long-term parking lot. On Friday night, when our target is leaving to see her sister, we can snatch her!"

"OK, great work. I will let Malik know that we have a plan!"

Hamza calls Malik using the encrypted IP voice capabilities of WhatsApp. He tells Malik what they have found. The best time to abduct the target will be early evening on Friday. Charbel will be leaving the following Saturday to Istanbul. He will be there for two weeks. The kidnapping will need to occur the first full weekend that Charbel is in Istanbul. Malik now has ten days to have personnel in Istanbul to abduct Charbel.

Malik calls Abboud using an encrypted network. "General, we have half of the plan. We know when we can abduct the daughter. We will need to abduct Charbel the first Friday that he is in Istanbul."

"OK," says Abboud. "Do you have the details for Charbel's kidnapping?"

"Yes, the American jihadists will abduct the daughter. I am confident that they can do it. I now need some muscle in Istanbul."

"How many do you need?

"Four fighters."

"OK, we can move four fighters through the porous Turkish border. I will contact our fighters in Syria and get back to you within the next twenty-four hours."

"Bashir and I will leave immediately to Istanbul and start our physical surveillance of the city."

"OK, call me when you reach Istanbul."

Malik and Bashir take a Turkish airline to Istanbul. It is a ten-hour flight. They have business-class tickets. The plane has Wi-Fi. Bashir had joined the security group that was sponsoring the conference. Bashir logs in with his password, and within one hour of the flight's departure, he is reviewing the attendees. Charbel is listed as one of the main speakers. He is speaking on Wednesday and Friday of the first week. He is also speaking on Monday of the second week. The conference has a listing of four recommended hotels.

"We will be in Istanbul ten days before the arrival of Charbel," says Malik. "We need to survey the conference and the hotels' locations. After we locate the hotels, we will need to survey the possible routes from the hotels to the conference center. The four brothers from Syria need to be here on Monday—no later than Tuesday. We need to rehearse the abduction. We will not know the adduction location until we follow Charbel the first week. Bashir, you need to make a list of all the items that you will need."

"We will need a good camera, tripod, and LAN cables," says Bashir. "I will use my laptop, and I will connect it with a LAN cable to the hotel internet."

"The team from Syria will bring the items needed for the abduction. The general told me that the four jihadists are all experienced in abductions."

The following Monday, the four experienced jihadists arrive. Two are dressed in the Pakistani traditional *salwar kameez*—long cotton tunics over loose-fitting trousers and that stop above the knees. The two wearing the *salwar kameez* have long beards with no mustaches. Their beards extend to their waists.

Malik looks at the two wearing the traditional Pakistani clothes and goes ballistic.

He says in an angry voice, "What do you two clowns think you are doing? Do you think we are in Lahore? Get the fuck out of those clothes and wear some regular Turkish clothes! Also, cut your beards to some presentable length!"

One of the clowns moves over to Malik, stands in front of him, and answers angrily, "I am a true Sharia Muslim, and I will not dress in the clothes of the devil!"

"I will not have anyone disobeying my orders. I order you to remove your *salwar kameez* and dress in regular Western clothes!'

"Fuck you! I will dress as I wish. Turkey is a Muslim country. They will understand my devotion to *Allah*!"

Malik thinks, *what would General Abboud do?* He walks to the bedroom and picks up his backpack. He takes out his Russian Markova handgun. Pulls out a magazine and checks for bullets. It is loaded. He then slams the magazine in the gun handle and chambers a bullet. Then he takes out the suppressor and screws it on. He hides the gun behind his back and walks back into the main room. The jihadist who is disobeying his orders is sitting on a rug, smoking a hookah pipe. His back is toward Malik. Malik lifts the Markova handgun, places it against the back of his head, and pulls the trigger—BANG! Brain matter explodes across the room. Bashir, the team leader, and the other jihadists are totally taken by surprise.

Malik looks at the other Pakistani wearing the *salwar kameez* and says, "Clean up the mess, get rid of this piece of shit, dress in Western clothes, cut your beard, and report back to me within the hour!"

"Yes, sir." The three clean up the blood and brain tissue. They take out the body in a laundry basket and dump it in a large trash bin. They cover the body with trash and then finish the cleanup. Bashir and the two remaining members of the kidnapping team will now follow Malik's orders completely. Malik waits for the three to return. In fifty-nine minutes, they are finished and standing in front of him waiting for orders. Malik continues with his briefing as if nothing has happened.

"We have surveyed all routes, and we have a number of possibilities."

The team leader asks, "Can we go over the different possibilities? Trust me, we are experts in the area of kidnapping."

"Yes, of course, but there is one fact that we must keep in mind. Consistent with the instructions from General Abboud, we will be abducting the target's daughter on the same night. The plan is to show the target his daughter using the internet with real-time video. Using this technique will ensure that we have the highest likelihood of success."

The team leader says with some authority, "Why was I not told this? You realize that this restricts our options."

"Operational security," says Malik. "You will take the orders from me. Is that understood?"

"Sir, you are telling me that the abduction will need to occur at night!"

"Yes, that's correct."

"I was only told to come here and bag some American diplomat. I was given no conditions!"

Malik says in his best command voice, "You are a soldier of the Caliphate! If you do not complete this mission, I can always call the general and tell him to replace you."

The team leader thinks for a few seconds and says, "No, we can execute—no need to call General Abboud."

Malik smiles internally. He knows that General Abboud would see this as the team leader being a coward. General Abboud is not General Patton—a slap would not be the punishment. It's likely that the team leader would be shot!

Malik says, "Shall we proceed with the plan? We have been following Charbel for the last two days. He is very regular. That appears to be his M.O. He leaves the hotel at ten A.M., and he stays at the conference until closing at five P.M. Then he comes back to the hotel, has dinner with friends from seven to ten, and goes to the bar, and he is in his room by eleven P.M."

"So, we take him down in his room," says the team leader.

"Correct."

"So, what happens after that?"

"Bashir, do you wish to explain?"

"Yes, sir. After we capture the target, we tie him up. My computer is connected to the internet. The display will be showing a second abduction in Charlottesville, Virginia. This will be a video of the target's daughter. Malik will be the good guy, and you will play the bad guy."

"What are we after?" asks the team leader.

"Information!" says Malik.

"OK, how bad do you want me to be?"

"As bad as you need to be to get the information. However, we do not believe that the target will stonewall us—after he sees his daughter, he will spill the beans,"

"What the hell is stonewall, and who is spilling the beans?"

"Sorry—these are American expressions. Not important. I do not believe that you will need to rough him up too much."

Charlottesville Virginia

University of Virginia

Hamza and Waleed have been in Charlottesville for ten days. They have thoroughly scouted the area. They are confident that their plan will work. They will abduct the young woman on her way to her car. She will need to walk through a wooded area between her dorm and the parking lot. This is where they will abduct her. They will tie her up with flex-cuffs and throw her in the trunk of the car. They will then take her to the cabin they have rented and roll the camera. Compared to other abductions, this should be a piece of cake.

Waleed is monitoring the dorm. At 8:45, Jennifer comes out with her suitcase and a dog! Already they have a problem—they did not expect the dog! It is a German shepherd. She has the dog for protection. Waleed transmits on his radio, "Hamza, we have a problem. She has a dog!"

"What kind?"

"German shepherd."

"Shit. We need to abort."

"OK, where do we meet?"

"Come on down to the student parking lot. We can discuss our options."

Hamza and Waleed sit in Hamza's car. "We need to make a decision ASAP. We need to tell Malik to abort the abduction in Turkey. We have no bait."

"OK," says Waleed, "we have no choice—Malik will be pissed!"

Hamza sends a text to Malik: "ABORT ABDUCTION WE ARE NOT ABLE TO KIDNAP THE GIRL—SHE HAS A GERMAN SHEPHERD AS A GUARD."

Within five minutes, Malik sends a text: "WHAT THE FUCK? CALL ME ASAP ON WHATSAPP!"

"Well," says Waleed, "at least he is not here. You need to have an option when you call him. If not, he may reach right through the phone and strangle you!"

"Yes, you are right," replies Hamza. "We are going to need to break into the Houella house and hold the entire family hostage. I will tell him that's the plan and let him make the decision."

Hamza calls Malik. Before he can say anything, Malik proceeds to ream him. "What the fuck are you two idiots doing? I send you on a simple mission: abduct an eighteen-year-old girl for one night. So, what went wrong?"

Hamza proceeds to tell Malik what went wrong. When Hamza mentions the dog—Malik cuts him off.

"So, what's the recovery plan?"

"We will break into the Houella family house and hold the entire family hostage." Hamza expects Malik to praise the plan.

"That's the stupidest plan I have ever heard. You fuck up trying to abduct one teenage girl, and now you are planning on three women, one boy, and who knows how many dogs. No fucking way!

"What do you recommend?"

"Let me order everyone here to go into a stand-down. I will call you back in one hour. Let me think about it."

"Malik is pretty smart," says Waleed. "I am sure that he will come up with a solid plan."

"Sure, hope so," says Hamza. "No way do I want to go back to Peshawar and face Abboud! He may skin us alive!"

Malik calls an hour later. "Put me on speaker I want to talk to both you and Waleed. Am I on speaker?"

"Yes, sir," says Hamza. "We have you on speaker."

"OK, listen up… No fuck-ups!"

"Yes, sir…no fuck-ups."

"We have no choice but to abduct the girl on Monday. You will need to abduct her during the day—between classes. You will need to keep her in a house or cabin that is isolated. You may need to keep her for more than one day. Steal a car. Use your training and steal a car from the long-term parking lot at Dulles Airport. Make sure no one can identify you when you make the abduction. Have your plan ready by Sunday. Have your stolen the car and all items that you will need. DO NOT FUCK UP! Your lives may depend on your success."

Both Hamza and Waleed know exactly what he is talking about; General Abboud is a no-nonsense field commander. He has a reputation for shooting recruits for being cowards on the battlefield!

On Saturday, Hamza and Waleed drive to the Washington Dulles Airport. They enter the long-term parking lot. They sit in their car and wait for a vehicle with a large trunk to go in and park. They mark the vehicle. They come back in two hours and hot-wire the car. Then they drive out with the hot-wired car. They use the parking ticket from their own car to exit the parking garage. They come back the next day and drive out in their rented car. They claim that they lost the ticket and pay the maximum payment for a lost ticket.

On Saturday and Sunday, they purchase cable ties (flex-cuffs), ski masks, bike gloves, and rubbing alcohol. They also buy duct tape, thin rope, cotton balls, leg stockings, high stockings, and a can of tennis balls. On Sunday, they call Malik and discuss their plan. He approves, and on Monday, they are ready to execute. Included in the materials that they brought from Detroit are two Tasers. They made sure that the Tasers are fully charged. They will also carry .45 caliber Glocks. However, they are instructed that the abduction is to result in no person or persons being killed. The handguns are only to be used in case they get into a firefight. The ISIS high command makes it be known that they should sacrifice their lives for the jihad. If they get into a firefight, they should kill as many of the infidels and then, with their last bullets, kill themselves.

Monday morning, Jennifer is attending her classes. Her dormitory is across campus. She has a set pattern. At 2 P.M., she will take a bus shuttle from the general science building to her dormitory. Waleed is behind the bus stop protective shield that gives students shade and cover from the rain. He is sitting with his legs crossed and looks like an average student studying his textbooks. Jennifer comes down the street. She is wearing a backpack and is talking on her phone. When she reaches the bus stop, she sits down and starts looking at text messages on her phone.

A nondescript four-door white Audi comes slowly down the street. The car stops in front of the bus stop. A man quickly jumps out. He is wearing a black balaclava. He waves a handgun and tells the three women and two men there, "This is s stick-up. If everybody does as instructed, no one will get hurt. Ladies place your purses on the ground. Men, place your wallets on the ground."

One of the men suspects that something else is going on. He thinks, *Robbing college students? We do not have any money—we are usually broke.* As he is thinking about this unusual development, the gunman tells Jennifer to stand up, take her backpack off, and place it on the ground. While this is going on, Waleed is now also wearing a balaclava. He comes around, grabs Jennifer from behind, and places a small hand towel soaked with rubbing alcohol over her mouth and nose. The rubbing alcohol has a minimal effect. Jennifer is putting up a fight. She takes her elbow and slams it into Waleed's gut. Quickly things are going south for Hamza and Waleed.

The two boys, who were stunned at first, now enter the fight. They jump on Waleed and pull him from Jennifer. Hamza holsters his gun and pulls out the Taser. He shoots the biggest boys with it. The boy falls to the ground. He loses control of his muscles and convulses. The smaller of the boys is no match for Waleed. Waleed punches him in the mouth and again in the nose, and he passes out. Jennifer is hitting Waleed on the back, trying to help the smaller boy.

The two other girls are running off. They are screaming, "HELP! HELP!" Waleed turns around now that the two boys have been neutralized. He pushes Jennifer to the ground, unholsters his Taser, and shoots Jennifer, and she goes limp. Hamza and Waleed pick her up and place her in the car trunk. They quickly drive off.

Two miles from campus, Hamza stops the car. They transfer Jennifer to one of their rented cars. The two drive in their individual cars one block to Interstate 64, and then head toward Richmond. The police are looking for an Audi with two adult males. They safely pass a patrol car sitting on the side of the interstate. They exit I-64 at the second exit and drive on back roads. Waleed texts a message to Malik, "MISSION COMPLETE, BEGIN SECOND PHASE."

Malik texts a reply; "BEGINNING NOW."

In forty-five minutes, they are at the cabin they have rented near Gordonsville, Virginia. They carry Jennifer to the family room. Waleed sets up the camera and connects to a small Cisco router. The router connects to the internet. Jennifer is still out cold. They tie her to the chair and place a strip of duct tape across her mouth. Hamza sends a text to Malik: "TARGET IS NOW ON FACETIME."

It is 2 A.M. in Istanbul, and Malik and the capture team have been waiting for the "GO" message from Virginia. The capture team is staying at the same hotel as Charbel. They have stolen a card key from the maid service. They assemble in Malik's suite.

"Does everyone know their responsibilities?" asks Malik.

"Yes, we are ready," says the team leader.

"Yes," says Bashir, "I have all of the IP addresses. I will be ready to connect to the camera in Virginia."

"Do we have the lie detector equipment?" asks Malik.

"Yes, sir," says the team leader.

"What about the duct tape and a tennis ball?"

"All is in order. We are ready to go."

All of the operatives are wearing dark clothes and have balaclavas on their heads. They take the stairs to the seventh floor. They walk slowly and carefully to room number 7043. They reach back, take out the nylon gloves, and snap them on. The team leader reaches in his pocket and takes out the lock pick. He carefully opens the door. Charbel has installed the chain lock from the inside. A second member of the capture team pulls out a trim bolt cutter. He reaches in and cuts the chain. Two members of the team walk to the bedroom. Charbel is fast asleep and snoring. One member of the team gags him before he wakes up. Charbel senses his inability to breathe, and he wakes up. Team member number two has a gun to his head and places his finger to his to lips—keep quiet!

The team leader and team member three abruptly pull Charbel from his bed. He is wearing nightshirt and underpants. He is pushed onto a chair and tied to it. He is directly in front of a laptop. A Pelican case is next to his chair. One of the team members pulls out four cables with sensors. The sensors are taped to his arms and chest.

Thus far, no one has said anything. All operatives have microphones that obfuscate the voice. Malik says in a robotic voice, "We have attached a lie detector machine to your body. We expect you to tell us the truth. I want you to see the computer screen. You are going to see someone you know."

Bashir has the video viewer minimized. He takes the mouse and clicks on the viewer icon. A video of Charbel's daughter appears on the screen. He sees the video, and his eyes open until they are the size of saucers. He kicks his legs and mumbles with the duct tape across his mouth.

Malik tells Charbel, "I am going to remove the duct tape. No screaming or yelling. Nod your head if you understand."

Charbel nods. The duct tape is pulled from his mouth. Charbel opens his mouth wide and moves his jaw around.

Team member number three is the lie detector expert. He asks, "Is your name Charbel Houella?"

Charbel answers, "Yes." The lie detector needle is a smooth line.

"Do you work for the US State Department?"

"Yes." The lie detector needle is a smooth line.

The lie detector expert continues to ask a series of questions, and the answers are all yes. All have produced straight lines across the lie detector charts.

"Were you at the briefing where the FBI discussed the ability to shoot down drones?"

"No." The needle moves wildly up and down.

Malik says, "Mr. Houella, we are not playing around. If you answer one more question with a lie, we will torture your daughter."

Bashir speaks into the computer microphone. "Hamza throw some water on the girl—wake her up!"

Hamza is ready; he has three glasses of water. He throws the water directly at Jennifer's face, and she wakes up. She is confused and scared. Waleed quickly places a strip of duct tape across her mouth.

Malik says, "Again, were you at a briefing by the FBI that discussed the anti-drone program?

"Yes," says Charbel. The needle moves straight across the chart.

"Were there any French operatives at the briefing?"

"No." The needle is straight across."

"Were there any CIA operatives at the briefing?

"No." The needle moves up and down. He really does not know, but he surmises that there probably were CIA agents at the briefing.

Malik says, "You lied! Bashir, tell Waleed to strike the girl."

"Waleed, strike the girl."

Waleed takes the stocking with the tennis ball. He lifts Jennifer's right arm and strikes the funny bone with the tennis ball. Jennifer moans in pain.

The question is asked again: "Were there any CIA agents in the briefing?"

This time, Charbel answers yes—the needle forms a straight line.

Malik goes to the table, picks up the artist sketch of Rose, and asks, "Was this woman at the briefing?"

Charbel is not sure, but there was a woman at the back of the briefing room. He gives it some thought for ten or twenty seconds. He then answers, "Yes." The needle is steady.

"Do you know the name of the woman?"

Charbel quickly answers, "No." They again ask the question, and again Charbel answers no. Both times, the needle is a straight line.

Malik looks at Bashir and at the other team members and says, I think he is telling us the truth. Malik then tells Charbel, "We are going to let both you and your daughter go—but there are some conditions. You will not tell anyone that you were abducted in Istanbul. If you tell the FBI, State Department Security, CIA, NSA, DEA, INSCOM, any intel or law enforcement agency, or any family members or friends, we will kill either you or someone from your family." After the conditions, Malik shows Charbel pictures of the homes of his parents, brother, sisters, and his wife's parents. "Do you understand?"

Charbel says, "YES, I understand."

"Good." Malik tells Bashir to have Hamza and Waleed release the girl tomorrow at some public location. "And tell them to follow their training and not fuck it up!"

"Will do."

Hamza and Waleed drug Jennifer. They leave early, and in one hour, they are in Harrisonburg. They place Jennifer on a park bench and use her backpack as a pillow. They take State Route 33 to West Virginia and drive on to Detroit.

At 9 A.M., Jennifer starts to wake up. She is druggy and disoriented. She does not know where she is. She sits up on the bench, and in thirty minutes, her head is starting to clear. She sees two police officers; they are on their bikes patrolling the park. She waves her arms and gets their attention. The police officers' bike to her bench.

Jennifer says, "My name is Jennifer Houella. I think I was kidnapped. I do not know how I got here. Where am I?"

The police officers are surprised, shocked, and happy. One officer immediately pulls out his radio. "Dispatch, we have found Jennifer Houella. She appears in good health but is a little beaten up. Request an ambulance to Memorial Park."

"Ten-four, sending an ambulance immediately." The dispatcher makes a radio patch and transmits to the State Police Regional Headquarters. She says, "Be advised that Harrisonburg police have found Jennifer Houella."

"Will advise watch commander," replies headquarters.

The watch commander keys his radio button. "Attention all cars, Jennifer Houella has been found in Harrisonburg. Place roadblocks on all roads exiting Harrisonburg to fifty miles. We are looking for two white males."

There is one problem. The West Virginia state line is thirty minutes north of Harrisonburg. There is no radio interoperability between Virginia and West Virginia police departments. The watch commander must use his personal cell phone and call his friend in West Virginia. He makes the call and gets voicemail. His friend returns his call at twelve noon. By now, Hamza and Waleed are halfway to Detroit, four hundred miles from Harrisonburg.

ISTANBUL, TURKEY

Malik has given Charbel an injection with a sleeping potion. The injection is administered at 3 A.M. Charbel wakes up at 7 A.M. He is lying in his bed. He takes ten seconds to orient himself. He clears his mind and looks at his cell phone. He has four texts messages and four voicemails! He first opens the text messages. The first two read: "CALL BACK IMMEDIATELY—IMPORTANT!" The next two text messages are more alarming. They read—- "CALL BACK IMMEDIATELY—JENNIFER HAS BEEN KIDNAPPED. YOUR LIFE MAY BE IN JEOPARDY!" His voicemails are no different.

Charbel thinks for a few seconds before calling his wife. He remembers the warning: *DO NOT TELL ANYONE ABOUT YOUR KIDNAPPING!* He knows that he is dealing with professional killers. He will not tell his wife about his own kidnapping.

Charbel calls his wife. "Honey, I got your messages. Sorry, I had my phone turned off for the evening."

Before Charbel can say anything else, his wife says, "Jennifer was kidnapped yesterday, but she has been found in Harrisonburg. She is reported to be OK but shaken up a bit. She is in the hospital. I am on Route 66 on my way to Harrisonburg. The state police believe that it was a case of mistaken identity. Jennifer's roommate is Jenny Holland. She is the daughter of the Texas billionaire Jackson Holland. The police were concerned that you might also be in danger. Are you OK?"

"Yes, I am OK, but I will make arrangements to depart immediately for Washington. Call me from Jennifer's room. She is a strong girl. I am sure that she will be OK.

As Charbel is getting dressed, he turns on the TV to CNN International. Wolf Blitzer is on. He says, "A strange kidnapping occurred in Virginia. A young University of Virginia co-ed was kidnapped but released sixteen hours after her capture. Two male students were harmed when they tried to help the victims. The FBI has taken control of the investigation. They believe that the suspects have fled across state lines. I will keep you abreast of any news as the story develops."

Charbel thinks, *the kidnappers have kept their word. Thank God, that Jennifer is OK. The kidnappers are serious; I'd best keep my mouth shut.*

Chapter Six

Abboud and Malik Review the Kidnapping

Peshawar, Pakistan

Malik and Bashir are safely back in Pakistan, and Hamza and Waleed are safely back in Detroit. The capture team is back along the Syria-Iraq border. Malik and Abboud meet in the secure conference room at the ISIS facility. Abboud asks, "Malik, what information did we obtain, and what do you recommend that we do next?"

Malik responds, "First, I would like to commend you for your idea of kidnapping the daughter. It worked to perfection."

"Yes, that always works, in many of my battlefield experiences, we were always able to obtain intelligence by using the relatives of the person under interrogation."

"Yes, sir, that was a good call. The information that we obtained from Charbel indicates that the woman operative is not French. She is either with the CIA or she is NGA."

"What is NGA?"

"It stands for non-government agency."

"You mean like Blackwater Security?"

"Yes."

"So, you think it was Blackwater?"

"No, not likely. Blackwater is strictly a US Department of Defense outfit. However, we do not know."

"OK, goddamn it—so, how do we find that woman? I am getting impatient!

Malik did not expect this sudden outburst. He thinks, *Fight fire with fire.* "I have a plan. We will have our jihadist attorneys in New York investigate. We have her picture, we know that she is either CIA or NGA, and we know that she lives in Washington, DC, or Virginia."

Abboud cuts off Malik. "Now that has to be the stupidest plan that I have ever heard. Are you crazy? How are a bunch of egghead attorneys going to find that WOMAN! Goddamn it, I want action!

Malik pushes back, saying, "Sir, please allow me to complete my explanation!"

Abboud simply signals with his hand—go ahead and continue.

Malik says, "The US is crawling with private investigators. Most of these private investigators are retired law enforcement or intelligence officers. They have contacts in the CIA, NSA, DEA, FBI, and other US organizations. Money talks. Through our cutout attorneys, we contract with a private security firm to find the location and name of the woman."

Abboud likes the plan. "OK, Malik—sometimes you do amaze me. That is why you are the intelligence chief. Do we have some security firms in mind?

"Yes, I will contact our attorneys immediately and start interviewing security firms."

After one week, the attorney assigned to the task comes back with two recommendations. Malik reviews the proposals and picks one for the exact reason that the attorney did not recommend the firm: it is known to conduct its investigations on the edge of the law, and it's rumored they conduct break-ins and cell phone intercepts that are against the law.

Malik calls the attorney. "Hire the second company on the list."

"Yes, sir. They want a fifteen-thousand-dollar retainer, two hundred and fifty dollars per hour and expenses."

"Go ahead and give them a contract. Place twenty-five thousand in their contract. We need them to report to you with a written report weekly."

"Got it. They will be under contract by the end of the week."

In two weeks, the security firm is making progress. They have identified a woman who meets the physical description and who works in the Washington, DC, area. She is either CIA or NGA. They do not know her name, but it is only a question of time.

The firm stakes out the entry to the CIA and a building in Alexandria. They need to be very careful. They are performing surveillance on professional intelligence agencies. The surveillance is only to establish which location she visits the most frequently. After two weeks, she visits the building in Alexandria most frequently. Indicators are she works for an NGA.

The security firm brings in a female investigator. Her name is Mildred Anderson. She has a very good resume. She is a retired NSA employee. She is in her fifties and has a likable personality. She has worked for the security firm for five years, and she has the ability to extract information from a suspect without the suspect knowing that information is being divulged.

Mildred reviews the case folder. The objective is to find the name of the woman in the photo. She seems to work for a company by the name of White Mountain Analytics (WMA). All research on the form indicates that they are an investment and electronic surveillance company. At least, from what they have on their website, all surveillance is straight-up lawful intercepts. Mildred has friends in the NSA and CIA, and she asks them about WMA. They tell her that WMA is a very reputable company. It was founded by the former senator Jesse Montana.

Mildred is a professional, and she is good at her job. She decides that the best way to see a list of all employees at WMA is through the accounts payable department. This department will also have their salaries. Mildred asks Joe, "Who is her boss? Did we try hacking into the accounts payable?"

"Yes," he says, "that's the first thing we tried. It's not online."

"Yes, that makes sense—thought I would ask?"

Mildred must now take a different tack. The security firm is able to obtain the name of a person in accounts payable. The information is obtained from the independent auditing firm Dedoliette Audit Services. Dedoliette does have strong security; however, the hired security firm is able to hack their accounts.

Included in the accounts of WMA is the name Kathy Funicello. Mildred orders a tail on Kathy. She wants to befriend her. She will know the names of all WMA employees. The tail reveals that Kathy is very religious. She goes to a Christian church that has services on Wednesdays and Sundays. She attends Bible study on Mondays and Fridays. Mildred reads up on the church and its doctrine. Their website is very detailed. The next Wednesday, she attends the church services. The members of the church are buzzing around her. They are all delighted that she has chosen to attend. Mildred makes it known that she is in the area on a temporary assignment. She lived a few years in the Dallas area, and she tells them she is from Richardson, Texas. Mildred does not rush it—she sees Kathy and introduces herself. "Hi, my name is Mildred Anderson." From the initial introduction, they have an immediate connection. This is what Mildred is good at—it is her profession.

For the next two weeks, Mildred attends all the services and goes to Bible study. The church has a small kitchen with four tables. Kathy invites Mildred to have a chat after the Bible study. Mildred thinks, *this is perfect.* They talk about their families. They both have common areas—empty nesters. They get around to their jobs. Mildred tells Kathy that she is a retired NSA employee. This seems to please Kathy—*She is on our side. Same as we do at WMA.* One thing leads to another and Mildred says, "Your job at WMA must seem pretty boring. Same thing every week. The entry clerk inputs the hours worked and the charge number, and the computers do all the work."

Kathy says matter-of-factly, "Oh no, you would be surprised about some of the unusual methods by which employees must be paid. For example, right now, we have some weird arrangement with the CIA and MI6. We have a woman who works for WMA, but she is not WMA and is not CIA. I think she is MI6 and is on loan to the CIA, but she is paid by WMA. So, you see, we need to go in a roundabout way to pay her. Talk about the paperwork—wow. The CIA being so secret, the invoice to them is all asterisks, asterisks, and asterisks—-no name. However, our accounting system has to have a name—so I enter E.R. Mathews."

Mildred plays the dumb old blonde. "Guess you need to be on the ball and keep up with all of those requirements."

"Yeah—you get one thing wrong, you don't get paid, and management will be all over our department."

Mildred has now been visiting the church for three weeks. On her fourth week, she announces to the members that she will be returning to Richardson, Texas.

After Kathy gives Mildred the last name of Rose, Mildred tells Joe, "Her name is E.R. Mathews."

Joe is elated. He calls the attorney, and the attorney calls Malik. "Her name is E.R. Mathews. She is on loan from MI6 to the CIA. The CIA has assigned her to the WMA."

Chapter Seven

ISIS Needs an Assassin

Peshawar, Pakistan

Abboud and Malik are ecstatic. Abboud says, "We have finally found the bitch! Now we need to go for the kill. What assets do we have in the United States to go after the bitch?"

"Not so fast," replies Malik. "This will be extremely difficult. We are not dealing with some banker, politician, or even an enemy combatant. She is the cream of MI6 and the US special forces."

"So, are you saying we do nothing?"

"No, I am saying we proceed with caution. Give me a couple of days to investigate our options, and I will present to you a foolproof plan,"

"Yes—foolproof. You mean even Hamza or Waleed could execute it?"

Malik laughs. "No, not those idiots. I need to find a professional assassin who has years of experience."

"Well said. I look forward to your plan."

Malik starts his study. He first looks at a list of ISIS snipers. The list is impressive. None speak English. They would be difficult to get into the United States. He uses the terrorist network to communicate with Al Qaeda, the Taliban, and other terrorist organizations. None have an assassin who could do the job. He then has an idea. The use of the security firm in the US worked out well. He needs to find an assassin who is already in the United States! He now thinks—*how do I find an assassin in the United States?* It hits him like a ton of bricks—the answer is obvious—the darknet!

He remembers when he was a student at the University of California Berkley; some of the radical students were using the darknet to push drugs. He researches the darknet on the internet. You need an invitation from a credited user to enter. He remembers that he still has contacts with some of the radical students from the university. He was known for radical views and got kicked out for his attempt to assassinate the president of the university. Thus, he would have no problem getting his invitation. He will call his friend Ismail and simply tell him that he wants to push drugs. Malik contacts Ismail, and Ismail responds, "Good to hear from you, shithead! What the hell have you been doing?"

"Working my ass off in Pakistan. You know that I was kicked out of school!"

"Yeah, I remember, so why the sudden nostalgia?"

"I am getting into the drug trade from Pakistan, and I remembered that you were using the darknet for your contacts. I tried logging into the darknet, but I need an invitation from an established user. Can you help me?"

"Maybe. How do I know it's you?"

"Come on, shithead, you know the drill we had in college. Ask me any questions that only you and I know, and if I answer them correctly, then you know it is me."

"Yeah, that would be one way. You could also get your ass on a plane and fly here."

Malik answers, "Which airline, Pan American?

"OK, raghead, you answered the first question correctly."

Ismail provides another ten questions. Malik answers all the questions correctly.

"OK brother," says Ismail, "here is the user ID and one-time fourteen-character complex password. When you log on, it will ask you for your e-mail address. You will be sent another fourteen-character complex password. Use this new password to log on. After you log on, you have ten minutes to establish your own user ID and password. Do not fuck up any of the passwords—best to copy and paste. If you fuck up, you will be locked out!"

"Thank you, brother," says Malik. "*Allah Akbar*!"

"Forget the *Allah* bullshit. I am a capitalist pig now, two Beamers, a Porsche 911, five-million-dollar home, and fucking all the movie stars in Beverly Hills—what a life. Oh yeah, good luck on your drug trade—join me here if you wish?"

Malik would like to reach through the internet and strangle the infidel! But he's gotten what he wants, and he might need Ismail later. No need to piss him off.

Malik now logs on to the darknet—the bullshit he sees. Truly, the work of the devil. He navigates to a section of the darknet that allows for the advertisement of special jobs. Included are assassins for hire. Most are Russians, Chechens, Ukrainians, Germans, Asians, and a few Americans. He is interested in two Americans. They go by the names of "the Grey Ghost" and "Viper." Their credentials purposely do not have that much info. The assassins do not want law enforcement to be able to identify them. Malik is attracted to the Grey Ghost. He claims that he had over thirty kills in Afghanistan and Iraq and has carried out seven kills as a contractor assassin. Malik contacts both the Grey Ghost and Viper. He settles on the Grey Ghost. Neither the "seller" nor the "buyer" knows the identity of each other. All transactions are using cryptocurrency.

Chapter Eight

Adolf Wolfgang Schneider

Lexington, Kentucky

The Grey Ghost is the son of Gordon Adolf Schneider. Gordon was a tenth-generation German American. His grandfather ten times removed was in the American Revolution, fighting in the British Army as a Hessian mercenary. When the British lost the war to George Washington's Army of the Potomac, the British told the Germans, "Sorry, you are on your own."

Since the Hessians were fighting the Americans along the Atlantic Ocean, they settled in western Virginia and Kentucky. Through the years, the German Americans maintained their German roots. During the Civil War, they were in favor of the Confederate states, as they owned land and the Negroes were needed to till the fields. By the 1900s, the Schneider family were KKK members. Gordon Adolf Schneider was born in 1953. He was big for his age. By the time he was thirteen, he was six feet and one inch. He started on his middle school basketball team. He dreamed that he would play for the Kentucky Wildcats. In the 1950s and 1960s, Kentucky always had the best college basketball teams. In 1966, Kentucky was in the national finals against some small college from West Texas. The name of the college was Texas Western College. They were so small that they were not even a university. The students at Kentucky would say, "Who the hell is TWC—the Teeny-Weeny College! Gordon saved his money and rode a bus to College Station, Maryland. The final NCAA basketball game was being played at the University of Maryland Cole Field House.

The game was expected not to be close! Las Vegas had Kentucky by twenty-five points! Biggest spread ever in the finals of the NCAA basketball finals. The Kentucky coach was named Adolf Kupp! How much more German could you get? Kupp had produced some videos of his mighty Kentucky Wildcats. The players would go through some highly complex passing and shooting drills. The players would weave in and out and pass the ball at least eight times. The final player would always make the jump shot. Kupp said, "The game of basketball is very complex. Only players with high intellect and physical skills are capable of playing the game of basketball." The TWC starters were all negros. Even the sixth and seventh players off the bench were black. To add insult to injury, the eighth and ninth players were Mexicans. Cole Field House could seat thirteen thousand fans. Twelve thousand were Kentucky fans, and a thousand were TWC fans. The TWC fans all had nosebleed seats. When the game started, the Kentucky fans were holding up homemade signs: "Kentucky 100–TWC 19!" Other signs said "TWC who? Yeah, Teeny Weeny College."

The game starter, the tip was controlled by the six-foot-nine-inch TWC center. The tip went to the TWC guard. He was quick as a cat. He dribbled the ball between his legs, behind his back, and faked with his head right then left. The Kentucky players collapsed on the floor—and he threw the ball to the TWC center, who made a thunderous dunk. The twelve thousand Kentucky fans went dead silent. For the rest of the game, the thousand TWC fans were whooping it up. One of the students had a bugle, and he played "Charge" every thirty seconds. That was how often TWC was scoring. Halfway through the first half, a second student joined with a guitar, and the students were all one happy mob.

They were yelling, "Yeah, yeah, look at the score." And toward the end of the game, they were screaming, "Too dumb to play basketball but smart enough to kill stupid wildcats!"

That night in March of 1966, Gordon cried all the way home to Lexington, Kentucky. "How can a bunch of niggers possibly beat the greatest team ever assembled?" Gordon did not know it, but that night, he became a white nationalist. He hated niggers and beaners!

Gordon was a star player in high school. His school was all white, and he grew to be six foot three inches and was a power forward. His high school made it to the state finals. They played an all-black school. It was no contest: the all-black school, Martin Luther King High School from Louisville, won 75 to 59. Before the final state game, Gordon aspired to play for Kentucky. Adolf Kupp had been replaced, and Kentucky had started recruiting black players. This really pissed off Gordon. He received interest from some junior colleges, but he was not interested. He got a job driving FedEx delivery trucks. After five years, he decided to go out on his own. He bought an eighteen-wheeler and started pushing trailers across the country.

Once, when he was in El Paso, he was approached by a Texas cowboy. "You want to make some easy money?"

"Sure, what you got?"

"Deliver two trunks to Chicago."

"OK, how much will you pay?"

"Five thousand now and five thousand when you deliver."

"That's it? Show me the money."

The cowboy opened a handbag and showed Gordon fifty Benjamins.

"OK, I deliver these two trunks, and I have fifty Benjamins on the other end? How do I know you are not with the feds?"

"As far as you know, it's legit. I just need to get them there ASAP. 'Because I never told you what's in the trunks."

"OK, when do you need them in Chicago?"

"In two days."

Gordon took the money. "OK, another money bag in Chicago?"

Gordon was not stupid. He parked his truck in a Big Wheel parking lot Then he rented a van and transported the two trunks to Chicago. He had no problems. With that delivery of the two trunks, he began his movement of contraband across the country. His business driving an eighteen-wheeler across the country allowed him to see the country from New York to California and Washington State to Florida. He found that niggers were attorneys, judges, business owners, police officers, and other high-paying positions. Once, when he was in Tucson, he had to go to the hospital emergency ward. The doctors were Pakistani and Asian. The nurses were Mexican. Not a single white person in the hospital. This country was going to the dogs.

In 1985, he had a son, and he named him Adolf Wolfgang. He was called Wolf, as he grew up with an attitude. Like his dad, he was big for his age. Wolf was the school bully. He played football and basketball. He was a wrecking ball on the football field, but he played dirty: chop blocks, clothesline tackles, biting and slugging his opponents. His favorite was knocking the quarterback out of play. Often, he would hit the quarterback late. In his senior year in high school, he slammed the opposing quarterback to the ground. It was not illegal, but it was roughing the player. His team was assessed a fifteen-yard penalty. The opposing players were really pissed. During a time out, they decided to give him some of his own medicine. One player hit him high from the front, and a second player hit him low at the knees from the back. It was a dirty play, and both players were ejected, but they did not care.

They said, "Teach that son of a bitch not to play dirty."

As a result of that play, Wolfgang's knee was blown out. That ended his playing career. Wolfgang and his dad were really pissed when they saw the recording and one of the players was black!

Wolfgang was born when his dad was forty-three, and his mom died during his childbirth at the age of thirty-five. By the time Wolfgang was eighteen, his dad was sixty-one. His dad liked to hunt, but due to his age, he would sit in a blind and have the deer and turkeys come to him. Wolfgang did not enjoy hunting from a blind. He wanted to hunt his prey, use his tracking skills and find it—now, that would be exciting. For Wolfgang's graduation present, he asked his dad if they could go hunting in Montana.

"Why Montana?"

"Because I have read that in the northern mountains, there are wild goats. They are hard to track and even harder to kill."

"OK, but you know that because of my age, I cannot go climbing mountains."

"Yeah, I thought about that. Helmut, my best friend, said he would love to go. You can come also. I think the open air will do you well."

"Yeah, I would like that. Let me arrange my truck schedule to have a two-week break after you graduate from high school."

"That sounds great, Dad. I will tell Helmut that you said it was OK. We will get our guns ready and go to the firing range and calibrate the sights."

"Take my rifle, too. You never know. I just might want to go looking for some goats."

"Will do."

One week after graduation, Dad, Wolfgang, and Helmut travel to Montana. They are driving the F-150 Ford pick-up with the extended cab. The bed is covered with an aluminum cap. In two days, they are at the base of the mountains. Before leaving, Wolfgang went on the internet and paid for the hunting license. They are each allowed one wild Billy goat. The kill cannot be a nanny or a kid—it needs to be at least six years old. They can tell the age by the length of the horns. When they leave the reserve, they will be inspected. If they kill a kid or nanny (female goat), they will be fined five thousand dollars. The state is trying to increase the size of the flock.

The first day, Wolfgang and Helmut go up the mountain. They do not believe that they will bag a goat on the first day. They are simply going on a scouting trip to try and see where the goats are living. They come back jubilant. They spotted wild goats on the next mountain across a ridge. They are confident that they will meet their quota the next day. In a way, Wolfgang is sad he thought that it was going to be harder to find the goats.

The next day, they are excited. "OK, Helmut," says Wolfgang, "are you ready?"

"Damn right. Does a bear shit in the woods?"

"Glad to see you two bucks so excited and confident," says Gordon. "Make sure you don't shoot yourselves."

"Yeah, yeah, just like in *A Christmas Story*," says Wolfgang. "Don't shoot your eye out."

At the reference to *A Christmas Story*, they all laugh.

Wolfgang and Helmut go up the ridge where they saw the goats.

Helmut says, "Wolf, you go up first. View over the ridge and see if you see anything."

Wolf goes over the ridge and peeks over a boulder. "Don't see a thing."

"Makes sense. They probably move on to a greener pasture."

Wolf and Helmut move along the ridge, away from the first mountain. The walking is difficult. It takes an hour to cover a quarter mile. The terrain is very rocky.

At three in the afternoon, Helmut says, "We probably need to head back to camp."

"Yeah, you're right. Let's head back."

It takes them until five P.M. to reach where they started. They look to the ridge on the other side of their starting point.

Both take out their binoculars, and Helmut says, "There they are. It's like they know where we are."

"Yeah," replies Wolf, "when I read about the wild goats, they did say that they were very smart."

Helmut is still looking through his binoculars. "Man, those goats can climb. A group of five took a ridge in about one minute that we needed half an hour to get up."

"There is no way we can track these goats. We will need to sneak up on them!"

"Agreed. Well, as Scarlet O'Hara said in *Gone with the Wind*, tomorrow is another day."

"Goddamn it, Helmut, don't remind me of that stupid book, The North won the war!"

"It's fiction. There was no Tara or Rhett Butler."

"Yeah, but sure as shit there was a Civil War, and the niggers were freed."

Helmut drops the subject; he knows how much Wolf and his dad hate blacks, beaners, slant-eyes, ragheads, and anything that is not a WASP.

The boys make it back to the camp, and Gordon has everything set up for the celebration. He sees they have come down from the mountain empty-handed, but he says nothing. Let them yak it up at dinner tonight. The barbeque is ready with the propane tanks. The hamburger patties, onions, lettuce, tomatoes, mustard, mayo, and ketchup are on the table.

"Boy, am I starved," says Wolf. "Thanks, Dad, for fixing the burgers."

"Well, that's the least that I can do."

"I think I can eat three of those burgers!" says Helmut.

"Have at it," says Gordon. "We got plenty."

The boys and Gordon fix their burgers and devour them, along with chips and cheese sauce.

After they finish their meals, they have a post-analysis session: what went wrong, and what adjustments do they need to make?

Wolf says, "It's obvious that we cannot track them. They are extremely fast. It is their backyard. They have the advantage. We will need to scout with our binoculars and sneak up on them."

Helmut has a better idea. "Why don't we go to Best Buy and buy a drone? We can use it to scout where they are and sneak up on the goats."

"That's a great idea," says Wolf. "We will miss one day, but it improves our chances of killing at least one goat."

The nearest Best Buy is seventy-five miles away. It opens at ten A.M. They get up at seven, have breakfast, and they are on their way to Helena, Montana. They are in the parking lot at 9:30. They wait the thirty minutes and enter at 10 A.M. They are in luck: the store has a DJI-3. It costs $1,800 with accessories. They pay the $1,800 and are on their way back to the campsite. Since Gordon is a trucker, the F-150 has a small satellite dish for connection to the internet. Helmut has a laptop. He connects to the DJI site and downloads the instructions. They both have iPhone 8s. They connect to the app store and download the DJI GO app.

On the way to the camp, they decide to stop at a grass field location. They wish to practice with the drone. They stop, take out the drone, and snap in the batteries. Problem is, the batteries are not charged!

"We need to get back to the campsite," says Gordon. "I have a generator there."

In one hour, they are at the campsite. Wolf says, "Helmut, bring out the generator."

"On it."

Wolf brings out the charger, and they start charging the battery. It is now two P.M.

"Looks like you will not have a chance to go hunting today," says Gordon.

"Dad, can we stay another day?"

"Yes, I see no reason why not. I can call Charlie and ask if he can take my loads."

"Thanks, Mr. Schneider," says Helmut.

By four P.M., the batteries are charged. Wolf and Helmut turn on the drone. They read the instructions and looked at several instructional videos. They use half an hour to complete some training. Then they go up to the mountain, turn on the drone, and fly it over all the mountain passes.

After ten minutes, Wolf says, "There they are. We are in fat city. Get ready to bag at least two goats tomorrow!"

Early the next day, the two boys are in high spirits. This was their day. They fly the drone and see where the goats are located. It will be about a two-hour walk. They bring back the drone. It comes back in ten minutes. They place it in a backpack and head to the goats. In an hour and a half, they are ten feet from the ridge. They take out the drone to "peek" over the ridge. The drone goes up. They turn the camera in the direction of where the goats should be.

"What the hell?" says Wolf. "Where are they?"

Helmut brings the drone down. "Let's insert the second battery and see where they are."

They insert the second battery and send the drone back up.

"What the hell?" says Helmut. "There they are. Back where we started."

Wolf flies the drone back and places it in the backpack. They sit on the ridge.

Wolf says, "These goats have a sixth sense. They know where we are."

"Yes, it's like they can smell us."

"What did you say?"

"I said it's like they can smell us."

Wolf does the polish salute. "That's it."

"What's it?"

"That's it. They can smell us."

"Well, I'll be damned. Of course. They can smell us."

The boys do not know this, but this lesson will serve them well when they are chasing terrorists in Afghanistan and Iraq. They slowly make their way back to the camp. About one hundred yards from the camp, something is not right. Gordon is usually sitting in his chair under the tent. He is not there.

Also, the camp is in shambles, and the back lid of the truck is open. They hear voices. It is not Gordon.

They sneak around to the other side of the camp.

A white guy wearing jeans, hiking boots, a white baseball cap, and an unkempt beard is yelling at Gordon, "You goddamn white trash, tell me the user ID and password for the account!"

A second asshole has a computer connected to the internet and a cable connected to the truck satellite antenna. The asshole at the truck is a black guy.

Asshole number one is pointing a gun directly at Mr. Schneider's head and is screaming, "You better tell me the user ID and password, or you are on your way to the pearly gates!"

The second asshole yells back, "OK, I'm in! Shit, now it wants to know what the name of your first pet was!"

Wolfgang has seen enough. He tells Helmut to take out the hunting rifle. "Here's our chance to really go hunting."

"Damn right," says Helmut. "Let's kill those assholes!"

Both Wolfgang and Helmut remove their rifles from their shoulders. They slowly pull back the bolt handles and insert a bullet. Then they both lie down with their legs spread.

Wolfgang says, "I take the asshole harming my dad. You take the asshole at the computer."

"Got it."

"Fire on my command... One, two, three, FIRE!"

The two rifles bark as one shot—BANG! Both assholes are hit in the head. Their heads exploded like two watermelons.

Wolfgang and Helmut run to Gordon. He is weak and badly beaten. Helmut checked his pulse.

Wolfgang says, "Helmut, do not touch anything. The police need to see the scene as it exists. I need to drive my dad to a hospital. You stay here. As soon as I have cell coverage, I will call the ranger station and the police. They should be here within thirty minutes. Tell them we had to shoot them. They were about to kill my dad. I will be at the hospital we passed on the way back from Helena."

"Will do. Hope your dad will be OK."

Wolfgang takes his dad to the hospital. He is driving at a hundred miles per hour. Ten minutes from the camp, he has cell coverage. He dials 911 and tells the operator what is going on.

The operator replies, "OK, I will call the hospital and place them on alert. Also, I will call the state police. You will pass a regional headquarters in about two minutes. I will have a police car escorts you to the hospital. I will also send the police to the campsite."

"Thank you. I see two police cars at the police station."

"Flash your lights so that they know it is you."

Wolfgang flashes his lights, and the police cars pull out in front of him and escort him to the hospital. His dad is immediately taken into surgery. Wolfgang waits in the waiting room.

Three hours later, Helmut shows up. "The police are at the camp. I gave them a statement. They said that they would need to talk to you. They understand that your dad is seriously hurt. They will interview you later. It is most important that you stay with your dad."

Two days later, Gordon is dead. Cause of death is multiple blows to the head. His blood vessels burst. The blood could not be stopped.

Wolfgang and Helmut return to Lexington. Wolfgang has never lived without his dad. His mom died during his birth. Other than one picture that his dad kept in the living room, he's really had no real contact with any motherly love. That's one of the reasons why he's such a brute.

Soon after the funeral, Wolfgang starts collecting all his dad's belongings. As he goes through his drawers, he finds an envelope. It reads "In case of my death, please open." Wolfgang opens the sealed envelope. He is surprised. It has instructions that provide a hand-drawn map of a hidden location in his father's bedroom. He goes to the location indicated. He has to get a knife from the kitchen, and he works along a seam in the hardwood floor with it. A well-hidden panel pops up. He looks down and sees a metal trunk. The wording on the trunk reads "Fireproof Container to Save Your Valuables."

Wolfgang reaches down and, with all his strength, lifts out the trunk. He carefully opens the lid. Much to his surprise, inside are neatly stacked one-hundred-dollar bills. He pulls them out; they are wrapped in fifty-dollar bills. Each stack is worth five thousand dollars. He counts the stacks. There are one 110 stacks. One stack has been opened and only has twenty bills. The total amount is $551,000. Wolfgang is no dummy; he quickly surmises that the money was obtained through deliveries that paid with cash. His dad was hiding the money from the taxman. Included in the folder is a handwritten will. Gordon wrote that all of his earthly belongings should be transferred to his son. It's on a form that he downloaded from the internet, and it has been stamped by a notary public in Louisville. The judge signed the will and certified that it was valid. Gordon also had thirty-five thousand dollars in the bank and was free from any debt. The house and trucks all have clear titles. The two eighteen-wheelers are both worth over two hundred thousand dollars each. Wolfgang thinks he is set for life. He sells the trucks but keeps the F-150.

He decides that he will multiply his newfound wealth. He will go to Las Vegas and become a billionaire.

In two years, he's broke, and he owes over fifty thousand to a member of the Mafia. One evening, two strongarms come calling for the money. They tell him he has two weeks to make the payment or else. He knows what "or else" means! The next day, he is walking down the strip, and he sees a Marine recruiting station.

He walks in, and says, "I see where you are interested in a few good men?"

The recruiter, who is under his monthly quota, is very charming and friendly. "Absolutely, and you look like you are one of those men."

"OK, what do I need to do? I'm ready to ship out and kill my share of ragheads."

"Just fill out these forms and come back to me. I will need to ask you some questions."

"What kind of questions?"

"The standard, the standard—you know. Are you wanted for murder? Are you running from the law? Also, I will need your permission to check your medical records. I would think that would not be a problem. You look pretty healthy."

Wolfgang finishes filling out the forms and brings them to the recruiter.

"OK," says the recruiter, "everything looks OK. Just sign here and there."

"How long will it take?"

"Two, three days, no more."

"Can I ship out soon after that?"

The recruiter has seen these types before. He can tell Wolf is running away from illegal debt. He says, "If your credit checks and you have no record of felonies, I can have you on a bus to LA by the end of the week."

"That's great. I'm eager to do my part for the country!"

Three days later, Wolfgang is on his way to the LA Marine recruiting station. In one week, he is at the El Toro Marine base, taking his physical. In two weeks, he is at Camp Lejeune, North Carolina, ready for his basic training. Wolfgang completes his basic training and is assigned to a rifle platoon. He is a model marine; he could be used in a recruiting poster. Wolfgang is six foot, three inches, muscular tapered body with board shoulders, square jaw and blue eyes.

His marks are superior in all disciplines. He graduates number one in his class. The drill sergeant makes a note in his evaluation: "Great Marine, a real can-do attitude, however, he does have a quick temper."

Wolfgang's company is assigned to the Desert Warfare School in Indio, California. He knows that they are in training for their deployment to the "Sand Box." He looks forward to his deployment.

Nine months from the time that he walked into the recruiter's office in Las Vegas, Wolfgang and his company of 120 Marines are fifty miles outside of Bagdad, Iraq. Their mission is to seek and destroy insurgents. Within one month, it becomes evident to his company commander that Wolfgang is his best Marine. He has an uncanny ability to find the assholes. After he finds the assholes, his squad takes the lead, and they call for air support.

The company commander calls Wolfgang into his office tent. "Private Schneider, you have an excellent ability to find the terrorists. Can you tell me how you do it?"

"Yes, sir. You need to have a sixth sense."

"Just what the hell do you mean by that?"

Wolfgang goes ahead and tells the captain about his experience hunting wild goats in Montana. He says, "It's not where they are but where they are going. You need to study the terrain, study the map, use drones for video surveillance."

"Drones are in heavy demand. We are lucky if we can get one drone for the battalion!"

"I have two drones."

"And just how the hell did you get them?"

"On the battlefield, the enemy is using the Chinese DJI models. I have one DJI-3 and one DJI-2. They are excellent for viewing over the hill or around the next building."

"Who authorized the use of the drones?"

"I did. It was a battlefield decision! You know that bullshit about making the battlefield decisions that will benefit the mission—the mission always comes first!"

"Private Schneider, you're damn right! Your evaluation will directly reflect your command of the situation."

"Thank you, sir."

"One more thing regarding battlefield decisions. I am starting the paperwork to promote you to lance corporal."

Private Schneider has an outstanding twelve-month tour of duty. His evaluation is outstanding in all areas. He is promoted to corporal. He has found his calling. He likes the thrill of hunting people who can shoot back. He loves the idea that the smartest and most prepared person wins. The stakes are at the highest—the loser dies. Now he knows what he wanted when he went hunting for the wild goats—the goats lived because they were the most prepared and the smartest. They deserved to live, and Helmut and he deserved to lose. It was a good thing they could not shoot back—otherwise, he would have been dead meat.

After his first tour of duty, Wolfgang volunteers for sniper school. When he was in Iraq, a high number of marines were being killed by sniper fire. He wants to be assigned to the group that has the mission to find and kill enemy snipers. Wolfgang is accepted into sniper school. He is assigned to the Third Marine Regiment MCB Hawaii, Kaneohe Bay. Again, he graduates number one in his class and is decorated as the top "devil dog."

Before his assignment to Iraq, Wolfgang is assigned to the joint military base in Djibouti, Africa. For one month, the US, British, and French Special

Forces will conduct joint military exercises. Wolfgang is assigned to a company of US Marines Special Operations Command (MARSOC). Frankly, Wolfgang is bored. The snipers will go to an assigned location where targets have been set up at a hundred, five hundred, and a thousand yards. Each sniper gets one shot at each target. The motto is "One shot, one kill." Wolfgang is always the best shooter.

One day, a fellow Marine tells him, "Yeah Wolf, I hear you are no longer number one."

"Who the hell told you that?"

"Some idiot from Delta."

"Yeah, so there is a special ops guy from Delta?"

"No, I said a guy from Delta told me."

"So, is the shooter from the Seals?"

"No, the shooter is from the British SAS."

"What, some limey from the Brits? No way."

"Hate to be the one to tell you this—it is a woman!"

"I do not believe you—a woman? No way!"

"Don't be so down on yourself. She was a professional shooter. The guy from Delta said that she was an Olympic pentathlon athlete before she joined the British SAS."

"A woman, eh?"

"Yes, a woman."

"Why the hell would they have a woman in the SAS?"

"Think about it—they can hide in plain sight. You know, a burqa and chador?"

"Is she here in Djibouti?"

"No, the Brits shipped out yesterday. They have been assigned along the Turkish border. They are assisting the Kurds."

Wolfgang forgets about the incident. He thinks, *I am number one amongst the US Forces. Also, number one of all men. That English bitch cannot best me on the battlefield. Bet she is a coward when it comes to killing ragheads!*

The next eleven months, Wolfgang has more than his share of action. By the end of this tour, he has thirty-one kills, the highest number of any sniper assigned to one twelve-month tour. With two weeks left in his tour, he is assigned to the most difficult of kills. There is an ISIS sniper who has been picking off Marines. He is known amongst the terrorists as "the Equalizer."

Wolfgang thinks about his experience with the goats. He thinks smell. He studies the Equalizer's pattern of life. He has an idea. He asks that a dog handler be assigned to his team. He now has a spotter, dog handler, and a dog. The dog handler is named Phillip.

"How good is your dog?" asks Wolf.

"Best there is."

"OK, I am going to give your dog a test. If the dog does not pass, I will ask for another dog."

"OK, what's the test?"

"I am going to take some clothes from an Iraqi worker. I am then going to ask the Iraqi to hide in one of the buildings. With the wind downstream from the hiding Iraqi, I want your dog to point in the right direction and find the Iraqi. You think your dog can do that?"

"Yeah, I think so—the more the Iraqi stinks, the better he will perform."

"Good point. In other words, make the rabbit sweat."

"Yeah, you could put it that way."

Wolfgang, Phillip, the spotter, dog, and the rabbit are ready. Wolfgang tells the rabbit to get on the treadmill and work out at a slow run for half an hour. The rabbit has sweat on the back and front of his shirt. He is sweating from his brow and hair. Wolfgang takes the shirt from the rabbit. He tells him to run for twenty minutes around a track. He gives the rabbit a cell phone with a GPS. Then he tells the rabbit to hide downstream from the wind. He has twenty minutes to disappear. He wants him moving about every five minutes. He says, "Go hide yourself."

"You want me to hide so you cannot find me?" asks the rabbit.

"Yes, that's the idea."

The rabbit takes off. Wolfgang and the team give him twenty minutes.

"OK, let's go," he says.

The handler shows the sweating shirt to Tiger, the dog. He says, "He's named after the golfer. He's a real tiger on the searches."

Tiger pulls on the leash—he points north to the northwest. He continues pointing. The dog stops smells the air, and points east.

"Tiger, paw," says Philip. Tiger paws twice.

"What's that all about?" asks Wolfgang.

"The paw number indicates the strength of the odor. Four paws is the strongest. Means the scent is really strong."

Tiger pulls on the leash, going dead east. He goes half a mile, and then he stops, smells the air, and points due north. He paws three times.

"The rabbit is within a hundred meters due north," says Philip.

Wolfgang checks the GPS. "Ninety meters dead north." He pulls out his binoculars. Scans in the directions of the rabbit. He dials the rabbit.

The rabbit answers, "Bet you cannot find me, right?"

"No, we have you on top of the water tower,"

"Damn, you are right,"

"Wolfgang says to Phillip, "You're on the team. I will get the search team to visit the home of one of the Equalizer's relatives and retrieve a piece of clothing."

In two days, the search team has two *keffiyehs* that the Equalizer has worn.

"Are you sure that these haven't been washed?" asks Wolfgang.

"Smell them. What do you think?" Asks Phillip.

The next day, the Tiger team is on the hunt. There is a report that the Equalizer is in North Mosel. He is amongst the terrorist fighting a company of Marines. The Tiger team must wait for the wind to be blowing in their faces. They wait two days. There is a strong wind blowing from the northwest, perfect conditions. The Tiger team is on the prowl for half a day. Tiger indicates that the Equalizer is within a hundred meters. Wolfgang tells the team, "Stand down."

Wolf pulls out the binoculars, unstraps his rifle, and inserts the bullet. He finds an ideal location and waits. He scans for one hour. He sees a reflection at two hundred meters. It is the reflection of a scope. He has done this for two years, and he knows when it is the scope. This is it. He is ready with his rifle. His spotter signals him. "I see him at the third window, the second floor."

Wolfgang puts the crosshairs directly across the Equalizer's eyes. He slowly presses the trigger—THUD.

The spotter sees the head being blown off and blood splashing on the windows. "One shot, one kill."

"Let's get the fuck outta here!"

The team starts back to friendly lines, and ten minutes after the shooting, the team hears a woman screaming and yelling. The women are crying, and the team investigates. What the team sees is sickening. A group of Christian women is being held hostage by two armed gunmen. The armed gunmen have their backs to the door; they have their rifles pointed at the women. Wolfgang quickly thinks—battlefield decision. He has his M-16 ready. He opens up in fully automatic and kills the two terrorists. The women are now sobbing and pointing at the room next door. Wolfgang and the spotter slowly walk to the door. The spotter kicks it in. Wolfgang rushes in. The terrorists are trying to put on their underwear and pants—they are raping four young girls. The girls cannot be more than twelve years old. Wolfgang uses his M-16 barrel to motion the terrorists to march outdoors. The six terrorists snarl at Wolfgang—like, who the fuck are you? They know that the US forces are weak and will only place them in a stockade and they will be free in two weeks—then they can come back and finish fucking these infidels.

But this time it is different—when the six terrorists are all in the courtyard, Wolfgang opens up on fully automatic and kills them all. Immediately after he has murdered all the assholes, a full squad of Marines approaches in full combat gear.

Wolfgang says, "Sorry, you're late to the party!" As soon as he says that, the company commander walks over. His name is George Goodwine; he is as black as the ace of spades and is a Naval Academy graduate.

The captain says, "Corporal Schneider, you are in violation of our orders for enemy engagement. You were not in imminent danger. I will advise high headquarters and let them decide their course of action. Sergeant Gilchrist, disarm Corporal Schneider."

"Yes, sir."

Corporal Schneider receives a court-martial; however, based on his outstanding evaluations and his service to his country, the board does not find him guilty of murder. He is acquitted of all murder charges, is demoted to private, and receives a dishonorable discharge.

Chapter Nine

The Aryan Nations and Ku Klux Klan

Montana and Tennessee, USA

Wolfgang does his studies and likes what he reads about the Aryan Nations (ANS). They are using the latest state-of-the-art electronic communications applications. The ANS uses the internet to post videos, posters, e-mail, chat rooms, online bulletin boards, and video conferences. The Aryan Nations preaches white supremacy with a neo-Nazi agenda. He likes that the Aryan Nations have a commonality with several other white supremacist and neo-Nazi groups, including the Ku Klux Klan and the Silent Brotherhood. Wolfgang has read that the Aryan Nations is a well-known neo-Nazi group in the United States. He would prefer to join the KKK, but he likes the idea that the ANS is in his country, Montana.

Wolfgang reads on the internet that the Aryan Nations have suffered substantially due to the death of their leaders, ill health, and a lawsuit that cost the group its Northern Idaho camp. He learns that after the death of their leader, the ANS was split over a number of different leaders. When the ANS split into different groups, there was internal squabbling. The split created three groups, who competed for control of the Aryan Nations. The weakness of the ANS attracts Wolf; he feels that with his leadership qualities, in time, he will become one of the leaders of one of the ANS groups. As a leader, he will be able to rebuild the ANS.

Wolfgang joins one of these splinter groups. The Aryan Nations have the same beliefs as Wolfgang: white supremacy and an open admiration for Adolf Hitler. The Aryan Nations have a common ideology with several other white supremacist and neo-Nazi groups. They also have a number of camps in Idaho and Montana. These camps serve as central meeting points and rallying grounds for far-right extremists. A march that Wolfgang attends is in Charlottesville, Virginia. The march was ignited when the city council voted to remove a statue of the Southern general Robert E. Lee. The march has over a thousand Klansmen marching in plain sight, carrying tiki torches and screaming, "Jews shall not replace us!" During the march, Wolfgang goads a fellow member of the KKK into driving his car into the crowd of anti-protestors. The anti-protestors are mainly young students from the University of Virginia. The driving of the vehicle into the crowd results in the death of one female student. The driver is arrested and charged with murder.

The history of the Klan can be divided into four distinct time periods. First is the 1860s to the 1900s, during the Reconstruction after the Civil War. In 1865, six members of the Confederate Army founded the Klan in the city of Pulaski, Tennessee. The Klan was established as a fraternal social club, inspired at least in part by the then largely defunct Sons of Malta. The Klan used parts of the initiation ceremony from that group for the same purpose: ludicrous initiations, the public curiosity, and amusement for the members of the Klan. The name is derived from the Greek word "*kuklos*," which means "circle." The word *kuklos* had previously been used for other fraternal organizations in the South, such as *Kuklos Adelphon*, which means Circle of Brothers. The manual of rituals was originally printed in Pulaski, Tennessee, and was authored by F. O. McCord, one of the original founders of the KKK.

Second is the period of 1915 to 1940, with the inspiration from D. W. Griffith's 1915 silent film The *Birth of a Nation* (originally called *The Clansman)*[1] which advocated white supremacy; The film depicted the "negroes," which were played by whites in blackface, as inferior and sub-human. In 1918, the film was shown in the White House to President Woodrow Wilson. [2] Wilson is quoted as saying of the film, "It is like writing history with lightning, and my only regret is that it is all so terribly true." This general acceptance by the president and many of the politicians of the time gave the Ku Klux Klan a large boost to its doctrine of white nationalism.

Third is the 1950s and 1960s, during the civil rights movement led by black civil rights leaders such as Martin Luther King.

Fourth is the resurgence in the early 2000s after two presidential elections. The election of a black president caused a major backlash amongst the white rural middle class. After eight years of the black president's administration, a white nationalist president is elected. In his speeches, he refers to immigrants from countries with primarily black persons as "shithole countries." He also refers to immigrants from Latin America as an "infestation," reducing people of the brown races to insects or rodents. He often states, "We need more immigrants from Norway." [3] One of his radio commentators openly stated that based on the current population growth of the US, by 2050, the non-White Nordic race will be in the minority. These factors have directly contributed to the growth of the KKK. The dog whistle is "Build the wall," which is code for keeping non-whites from invading the country. The open acceptance of white supremacists by the US president has elevated the status of organizations such as the KKK and the Aryan Nations.

[1] *"Thomas Dixon Dies, Wrote Clansman". New York Times. April 4, 1946. p. 23*

[2] Attended by President Wilson and members of his family, and members of his Cabinet

[3] US. Baltimore Sun, August 23, 2019

Chapter Ten

Wolfgang Joins the Aryan Nations

Montana, USA

Since Wolfgang's days in the Marines, his appearance has changes dramatically. He is still six feet three inches, two hundred and thirty pounds, muscular and tapered body. However, he has long black stringy hair, which he wears in a pony tail. He has scruffy beard, which he keeps unkempt. His neck and arms have tattoos with swastikas, and a dagger through the heart. His blue eyes now a piercing look and his aquiline nose is more pronounced. Wolfgang's attitude and persona are "I don't give a shit." His short temper that he had in the Marines is now shorter than ever. The combination of the short temper and the don't give a shit attitude usually results in bar room fights.

Due to Wolf's appearance and general pissed-off attitude, Wolfgang has had problems finding a job. He knows something about truck driving. He contacts some of his father's friends, and as a favor to his dad, he's given work driving long-haul trucks. He holds the job for a couple of months. The job is ideal, he drives alone and has little to no interaction with people.

On a cool fall day, he has some deliveries to Montana. He remembers his days trying to hunt the wild goats. During his drive through Montana, he notices that there are a number of communities that live off the grid. One day, after a delivery outside of Montana, he rents a motorcycle. He goes to the local Harley Davidson motorcycle store and buys a jacket, boots and a Nazi type helmet. He gets dressed in his "Hell's Angel's" type outfit and drives up to the gate.

"What the hell do you want?" asks the gate attendant.

"I am interested in joining the community."

"Be at the Rocky Mountain Tavern at ten P.M. this Friday. Members will be there."

"OK, will do." Wolfgang drives off on his motorcycle.

Wolfgang needs to establish himself with the Aryan Nations, and he arrives at the Rocky Mountain Tavern at 11 P.M. It is a restaurant and bar, similar to a sports bar. Outside there are more than twenty motorcycles. The parking lot is full, with some vehicles parked in the grass. Most vehicles are pick-up trucks, although there are some late-model foreign sports cars. Wolfgang looks at the motorcycles and cars and thinks, *these assholes have money.* He walks in; the bikers all turn and give him a stare-down. He ignores them and proceeds to the bar. He orders a beer and uses the mirror to keep his eyes on the bikers.

After ten minutes, one of the bikers sits in the stool next to him. He says, "Strangers are not allowed in this bar. Recommend that you get your ass outta here after you finish your beer."

Wolfgang turns slowly and says, "Really, I did not see a sign out front saying, 'No Strangers Allowed,' shit face."

"If you're looking for trouble, asshole, you have come to the right place."

Wolfgang ignores the biker and says to the bartender, "Can I see the menu?"

The biker walks away. Within seconds, two large bikers come up to Wolfgang and say, "Hey, asshole, the boss would like to see you. Come with us to the back room."

Wolfgang is concerned. *I may see the boss, or they are going to try to beat the shit outta me.* He reaches into the pocket of his jacket and places his brass knuckles into his right hand. He is ready for any action. He walks into the backroom. There is a biker in his young thirties sitting at the table. Two women flank him, one on each side.

The Aryan Nations (ANS) biker says, "Girls, go do your makeup. Scram! Get lost!" The girls rapidly leave the room. He continues. "You know you have a lot of balls—those two dudes would have put you in your grave in no time."

"I doubt that. Perhaps you would be digging two graves?"

"OK, asshole, what the hell do you want? If you are a fed or a copper, now is the time to get your butt outta here!"

"No, I am no govie or some flatfoot."

"OK, so, who are you, and what do you want?"

Wolfgang starts to give the biker his bio. The biker says, "Hold on, cowboy. Let's start with your name. No bullshit. Your real name!"

"OK, got it. The name is Adolf Wolfgang Schneider."

"No shit, cowboy, and my name is Jesus Christ! I SAID YOUR REAL NAME!"

Wolfgang pulls out his driver's license and shows that is his name. He then goes on and gives the head biker a short statement regarding his background. This is the one time that his dishonorable discharge will be favorable. He emphasizes the number of ragheads he has killed. He then shows absolute disgust when he mentions the "nigger" that wrote him up. That was the main reason for his court-martial.

The biker then says, "My name is Gunter Helmut Spiker."

"Really? My best friend growing up was named Helmut! You can call me Wolf."

"I like Adolf better."

"Better make it Wolf—the assholes out in the fuckup world all take a major dislike to Adolf."

"Yeah, I understand. Welcome to the ANS, Wolf."

Wolf and Gunter get along like two peas in a pod. Gunter likes the strong-arm tactics of Wolf. For the next two months, Wolf acts as a personnel bodyguard to Gunter. One afternoon, Gunter and Wolf are sitting in the ANS camp, and Gunter says, "Wolf, we are low on cash. We knocked off a bank in Nebraska two months ago. The robbery produced fifty thousand dollars. We have thirty-five men and women in the camp. The money can only go so far. We need a continuous stream of money. You got any ideas?"

Wolf thinks for a minute or two. "Yeah, my dad used to run this route from El Paso. He never told me, but I suspect that he was running drugs. I guess that he was being paid five to ten thousand dollars to run drugs from El Paso to cities up north."

"Damn, that's a good idea. You need to go to El Paso and see if you can re-establish that connection."

"You think that beat-up Ford Economy van can make it to El Paso?"

"Yeah, no problem. It may look old and beat-up, but the engine and transmission have been rebuilt. We purposely make it look old —it attracts less attention."

The next day, Wolf is driving to El Paso. He remembers his dad talking about "the Cowboy." The trucking community is small. He thinks a couple of visits to truck stops and someone will know the Cowboy. He drives on I-10 between El Paso and Las Cruces. He searches on the internet and finds outgoing truck stops east and west along I-10. He visits two truck stops going west and three going east. There is a large truck stop about twenty miles east of El Paso: The Horizon Truck Stop. Over one hundred tractors and two hundred trailers are parked in the lot. The truck stop has eight pumps for passenger cars and twelve drive-in lanes for the eighteen-wheelers. There is a large food court with over ten vendors. All aisles are ten to fifteen people deep. He stands in line and orders two meat tacos with cheese dip and tortillas. As he is sitting at his table, he sees a large orange eighteen-wheeler drive up to the pumps. On the front grille is the Longhorn logo. On the doors of the tractor, written in professional letters is "Hook 'em Horns." Wolf thinks this may not be the Cowboy, but the driver may know where to find him.

Wolf goes out to the tractor. "Nice rig."

"Thanks."

Wolf starts a friendly conversation as the two-hundred-gallon diesel tanks are being filled. The truck driver is too young to be the Cowboy.

He introduces himself. "Wolf Schneider."

The Cowboy that Wolf is looking for is probably in his fifties. Wolf asks, "I am looking for a trucker called Cowboy. He was a good friend of my father. Do you know anyone by that name?"

"You are in luck. I am Cowboy Junior. Dad does not drive anymore. He is the owner of the Cowboy Trucking Company."

"Where can I find your dad?"

"His office is near here—Horizon City. Drive back west and exit at the Horizon City exit. Drive about two miles, and you will see a big sign, 'Cowboy Trucking Inc.'"

"Thanks. I will go visit him this afternoon."

"Yeah, my dad will enjoy it—he always wondered what happened to Gordon?"

Wolf drives back to the Horizon exit. He sees the Cowboy Trucking Company. You cannot miss it: big sign, tractors, and at least twenty trailers. He walks in and introduces himself.

The receptionist is a woman in her fifties. She says, "You look just like your dad. Have a seat. I will call my husband."

The Cowboy comes in, looks at Wolf, and says in loud Texas voice, "Well, I'll be damned, Gordon Junior! What drives you to Texas? I thought maybe your dad had retired from all those deliveries I gave him."

"Actually, that's why I'm here. I would like to continue being of service to you."

The Cowboy then says, "My name is Jordan Yates."

"My name is Wolf Schneider."

"Yeah, like that asshole Wolf Blitzer on the Commie Channel."

"Actually, it's Wolfgang, not Wolf."

"That's better—good name, Wolfgang, real German."

The two walks back to the office. Wolfgang then explains that his father was murdered by two vagrants. One was a "nigger," and the other was white trash.

"Did they catch the assholes?" asks Yates.

"No, I shot them—killed them both."

"Damn, did you serve time?"

"No, it was self-defense. Luckily, it was in Montana. The law in Montana is stand your ground. After that, I was really down and almost went into treatment for depression."

"Sorry to hear that—are you OK now?"

"Yeah, I joined the Marines. I had two tours of duty, killed my share of ragheads. I was given a court-martial for gunning down some assholes. I caught them raping some Christian women."

"And they gave you a court-martial for that? They should give you the Congressional Medal of Honor!"

Wolfgang went on to explain that he was willing to be a mule and continue with the loads that his dad had carried. Yates explains that he is now big time and that Wolfgang will first need to prove himself. Does he have a trucker's license? Does he know how to drive the tractor with the eighteen-wheeler? Wolfgang assures him that he does.

Yates pushes a button on the intercom. "Alicia, please have Elroy come in here."

"Will do."

In five minutes, Elroy comes in. Yates says, "Elroy, this is Wolfgang. He has applied for a job as a truck driver. Take him out to the lot, give him a rig with a fully loaded trailer, and take him through all the driving skills."

"You want me to teach him?"

No, you little urchin, he already knows how to drive. I want you to check him out, *comprende?*"

"*Si, yo entiendo.*" (Yes, I understand.)

After about a half-hour Wolfgang and Elroy come back. "This guy is an expert," says Elroy.

With the stamp of approval, Wolfgang starts his employment as a mule. He delivers contraband drugs and weapons to Chicago, Las Vegas, New York, Baltimore, Miami, Atlanta, and Washington, DC. In six months, Wolfgang brings in three hundred thousand dollars for the ANS camp.

Wolfgang is now the big man on campus, and Gunter is not happy that Wolfgang has risen to the second man at the camp. Even his women are gravitating to Wolfgang. He notes that his men and women are looking to Wolfgang for the future of the ANS encampment. One Friday evening, when both Gunter and Wolfgang are drunk, Gunter has had enough. He starts shouting at Wolfgang, "You fucking asshole—you think just because you have more than thirty ragheads pushing daises that you can come in here and push me off my throne? No fucking way—get the hell out of here. I want you outta here by sunup. Do you hear me, asshole?"

"If anyone is leaving, it is you!" shouts Wolfgang.

Gunter walks back to the bar and pulls out two Glock 45s in holsters on gun belts. He throws one of the Glocks in the holster and gun belt to Wolfgang. "OK, big shot, let's have a gunfight at the OK Corral. The last man standing runs the camp!"

Wolfgang checks the bullet clip. It has twelve bullets. He chambers a round. He walks outside and fires one round into a sand pile. He walks back in and says, "Ok, asshole, I'm ready."

Gunter is standing with his mouth open. "Now I'm really pissed. Did you really think that I would give you a malfunctioning gun?"

"I was in the Boy Scouts. Always be prepared!"

What Gunter does not know is that when Wolfgang was in the Marines, drawing and shooting a Glock was practiced every day. They would never know when they would go up against some terrorists. Gunter, on the other hand, has heard that Wolfgang made all his kills with a long rifle—what the hell does a sniper know about drawing a Glock from a holster?

Both snap the belt buckles and tighten the belts around their waists, and then they walk outside. Fifty of the bikers and ANS supporters follow them. Half are yelling, "Go, Gunter!" and the other half are yelling, "Kill him, Wolfgang!"

They walk around the bar, up the hill, and then down to a clearing in the valley. Gunter draws a line in the dirt with his boot, paces off twenty-five paces, and draws another. The two men stand on opposite sides of the lines.

Wolfgang in full-concentration mode. "Gunter, you really want to do this? Walk away now, and no one gets hurt."

"You shithead—I can tell that you're a chicken. I knew that you were fake—thirty kills, my ass. Bet that you were a cook in the Marines."

"Go ahead, asshole. You can draw first."

"Not only a cook, but also stupid."

After that last statement, Gunter reaches for his Glock. In a flash, Wolfgang draws his gun and, in one motion, pulls the trigger twice—BANG, BANG. It sounds like one shot.

Gunter falls to the ground, one bullet hole right between his eyes.

The men and women gather around Gunter. "Only one bullet hit Gunter," says one.

"No, both bullets hit right between the eyes," says another.

The ANS men lift Gunter and place him in the bed of a pick-up. The following day, he is buried in a pine box at the ANS encampment.

Wolfgang is now the undisputed ranking Aryan of the camp. He makes some major changes. The men will become more disciplined. They will receive military-type training. He installs a ranking system. He gives himself the rank of a colonel. His staff is made up of Lt. Colonels and Majors. He forms three companies. A captain heads a company. Three platoons make up a company. Sergeants head the platoons. Each platoon has three squads, and each squad has ten-foot soldiers.

Wolfgang demands discipline. He gives orders—not following them will not be tolerated, and the punishment will be hard labor. He does not believe in inflicting physical pain. He needs all of his warriors for the upcoming battles. After two winters in Montana, he decides that he needs to move his troops to a warmer climate. In the two years that he has been the commander of the Montana ANS, his unit has grown and become very prosperous. This business relationship with the Texas Cowboy has grown, and the Klan is now moving drugs, weapons, and other stolen goods. He attends the yearly ANS-KKK meeting of all leaders and wizards, which is being held at a ranch thirty miles outside of Las Vegas. The location is ideal for such a meeting: it offers physical security and is isolated from any buildings. Guards are stationed at the outer and inner fences, and video cameras with motion detection have been installed every twenty yards. The meetings are to discuss voter suppression, the burning of black churches and Jewish synagogues, and other nefarious activities. Several meetings, which are by invitation only, discuss illegal activities, such as murder for hire, prostitution, slave labor, and kidnapping.

Wolfgang is a student of history. He knows that the time to grow and harvest both men and money is during the term of the white supremacist president. His plan is to organize his ANS and KKK encampments in the model of the Italian Mafia. The Mafia has power and money. Their power comes from the barrel of a gun and having politicians and law enforcement officers on their payroll. He will venture into such illegal activities as drugs, gunrunning, prostitution, and illegal gambling.

At the meeting of illegal activities, Wolfgang meets a woman by the name of Gretchen Hannah Miller. Gretchen is married, but her husband is serving a life sentence in a New York state penitentiary. He was convicted of killing two mobsters in New York City. Gretchen is considered to be KKK royalty as she can trace her ancestry to one of the original members of the KKK, Frank O. McCord. Her husband, Klaus, obtained a kill contract on the darknet to assassinate a mobster by the name of Francisco Fenni. During the hit job, a second mobster suddenly appeared, and Klaus had to get in a gunfight. The gunfire pinned him down for ten minutes, allowing the NYPD to arrive. He surrendered when the police had him cornered, and they used tear gas to extract him from his hiding place. His arrest and subsequent trial attracted national attention. No one much cared about the two mobsters he killed, but the Manhattan district attorney was on the Mafia payroll and he was instructed to convict. It was likely that Klaus would not survive in prison.

Gretchen is in her early thirties, attractive but a hard ass. She doesn't take any bullshit from anyone. Wolfgang likes her "I do not give a shit" attitude. They quickly became friends and lovers. After leaving Las Vegas, Wolfgang visited Gretchen in Murfreesboro. She has a large encampment of over twenty square miles. It is in disarray due to her husband having been incarcerated for over three years. The camp consists of twelve buildings. Wolfgang inspects the buildings and finds the underground tunnels and bunkers. The bunkers can be entered from the interior of the buildings and are connected by the tunnels. Wolfgang continues with his inspection of the Tennessee camp. Most of the buildings are in some state of disrepair, but it's nothing that cannot be fixed. Wolfgang is interested in the tunnels and the bunkers that connect all the buildings.

"How long have the tunnels been here?" he asks.

"Since the fifties," says Gretchen, "when the country was running scared with the Russians threatening to nuke the US. We use them to hide some of the drugs and weapons that we are running to the large population centers. The US population cannot buy enough guns. We sell them at discounts to members of the NRA. You know that shooter in Las Vegas, the guy who had an arsenal in his room? All the weapons were bought from us—they were not traceable."

Chapter Eleven

Wolfgang and Gretchen Join Forces

Pulaski, Tennessee

After several trips by Wolfgang to Gretchen's camp in Tennessee and Gretchen's visit to Wolfgang's camp in Montana, they decide to combine forces and make the Pulaski-Murfreesboro camp a mega-KKK encampment. Under the direction of Wolfgang and Gretchen, the camp thrives. The drug trade connections that Wolfgang has are ten times greater than Gretchen's contacts. Wolfgang learns from Gretchen about the darknet. He likes the idea of murder contracts. He can return to his roots—hunting down humans. He's always liked the idea that humans can shoot back. However, now he is smarter and better prepared. He researches his prey; planning, preparing, and practicing. He calls it his three Ps. During the two years that he accepts contract murders, it is like taking candy from a baby. He wants more difficult jobs. His most accomplished kill was the ISIS sniper the Equalizer.

One evening, he decides to log on to the darknet and see if any contract murders have been posted. There is a post for a woman. Usually, he would not be interested; he has his rules, no women or children. However, this post piques his interest; it is a woman by the name of Isabella Rose Mathews. The post offers a hundred thousand dollars upon accepting the offer and five hundred thousand after the successful kill. The posting on the darknet states, "No amateurs need apply. The target is a seasoned special operations agent. All applicants must outline their experience in killing hard targets."

Wolf reaches back in his memory to Djibouti—*I was only the second-best shooter. Some woman from the British SAS was better*. This must be her. He excitedly answers the post. He includes in his post that he is a seasoned marine sniper with over thirty kills while in the US armed forces and that he has successfully completed four contracts from the darknet. He thinks for a few seconds and then decides to include: "I know this bitch, and we had our differences when we were both stationed in Iraq!"

Two weeks later, the individual who posted the kill contract, contacts him using a secret web browser. The browser requires an encrypted VPN to be established, and then the communications use a two-factor authentication method. Once the protocols are established, both parties agree to the requirements of the contract. Wolf accepts the conditions. The individuals who posted the killing send a picture of the target and where she is likely to be found. They further state that the target is either MI6, CIA, or NGA and provided a password and a cryptocurrency account where a hundred thousand dollars in bitcoins can be downloaded. With the acceptance of the hundred thousand, the contract is sealed.

Wolf believes in the three Ps, plan, prepare, and practice. He immediately begins planning. He still has friends in the Marine Corps. At the enlisted level, the troops do not blame him for killing those assholes who were raping the young Christian women. He contacts his friend, Sammy, who told him about the British woman.

Sammy says, "Yeah, asshole, where the hell have you been, hiding under some rocks? Ha, ha, ha."

"No," replies Wolf, "I am out in the sunshine. I own a trucking company that my dad left me. Not much but enough to earn a living."

"OK, what can I do for you? Good to know that you are doing OK. As for me, I could use a few bucks. I was injured in the fighting in Syria, and I am confined to a wheelchair."

"Sorry to hear that, bro. Tell you what, if you can do some research for me, I can offer you five thousand."

"You mean dollars?"

"Of course, dollars. What did you think, pesos?"

"OK, but can I ask why?"

"You know me, bro; finishing second best in Djibouti has always been a burr under my saddle."

"OK, so you wish to find that woman who bested you?"

"Yeah that's what I would like to know."

"Ok, I will see what I can find out."

"One more thing, bro. Keep this request from me confidential. As you know, I received a dishonorable discharge. You never know; you working with me might look unfavorably for you."

'Yeah, you are right. I will keep our discussions private."

Sammy starts working his sources, and in three weeks, he completes his investigation. He calls Wolf. "I have the information that you requested."

"Great. Can you call me on WhatsApp?"

"OK, I will download the app and call you back within the next thirty minutes."

Sammy downloads WhatsApp and calls Wolf. "OK, bro, I have the info."

"Go ahead, shoot."

Sammy starts reading his handwritten notes. "Rose Mathews is an outstanding athlete. In her last two years at USC, she was the number one athlete in the pentathlon. In her senior year, she competed at the collegiate national championships in College Station, Maryland. She scored the maximum points of any athlete. She was recognized as the athlete of the meet. USC defeated Villanova and the University of Texas for the national championship. This information was easily obtained by doing searches on the internet. Once I knew that she was a star athlete at USC, I went to the USC athletic section, and she was listed there. She is in the USC Athlete Hall of fame.

"After graduating from USC, Rose applied and was accepted into the British diplomatic corps. Her father is well known in British diplomatic circles. Rose is fluent in Arabic and Spanish. I logged onto the British diplomatic services webpage and found that she was promoted to the position of the consular liaison officer. She was assigned to Egypt, Syria, and the UAE in her four years with the British Foreign Service.

"Now the information gets a little harder to find. It appears that she resigned from the diplomatic service and enlisted in the British army. She was in British intelligence. After two years in intel, she volunteered and was accepted into the Special Air Service (SAS). As you know, the SAS is the premier special operations force in the world. The unit has existed for more than a hundred years. The SAS was the primary unit that fought behind enemy lines during WWII and is credited with significant disruptions of the German army in France, Holland, and Norway. It was the SAS forces that destroyed the German heavy-water plants in Norway, and it was the SAS that sabotaged the guns of Navarone on the Aegean Sea. As a member of the SAS, Rose had successful tours of duty in Afghanistan, Iraq, and Syria."

Wolf says, "Sammy, this is all excellent data, but I am not interested in the history of the British Special Forces!"

"Yeah, Yeah, guess you have not changed a bit, always bitching about something. Now take that burr out of your ass and listen. I have some info that I got from the Company C of the devil dogs. You do know who the devil dogs are don't you?"

"Goddamn right I know who they are. Now get on with the info."

"OK, here is what you really need to know. After Djibouti, she was stationed along the Iraqi-Turkish border. The story is she single-handedly went into enemy territory and rescued some two dozen Christian women."

"Really, how the hell did she do that?"

"Well being a woman, she wore a burqa and chador, totally concealing her identity. You know "Hidden in Plain Sight."

Wolf, "So she went into ISIS held territory and simply said, OK motherfuckers' hand over the Christian women? "

"Not quite, the story is that she left a trail of dead ISIS shitheads as she and the rescued women were escaping over the Turkish border."

"So, you think the story is true?"

"Don't know, I would need to break in the British SAS headquarters in London and find out, and I ain't that good. I am simply telling you what one of the devil dogs told me."

"So, what do you think?"

"What I think is, you better watch your rear end. This bitch you are chasing is the real deal—-a real badass!"

Wolf, "I ask you, how the hell did you get all of this info?"

"Guess you forgot. I was an intel officer with MARSOC. Remember I was the one who told you about the woman in the British Army who was a better shooter than you?"

"Yeah, I do remember."

"As an Intel officer, I had the information on personnel assignments. I also attended all joint exercise meetings."

"OK, Mr. Intel Officer, can you tell me where this Miss Rose is assigned now?"

"No can do—but I can tell you the following; Her records have been purged once she disappeared from the SAS. What this tells me is that she is either dead or assigned to the British MI5 or MI6."

"Good work, bro. Any other info you can provide?"

"No, but I can provide advice."

"Yeah, what's that?"

"She is the daughter of Ambassador Clarendon Richard Mathews and Maria Isabella Garcia. Her parents live in Bristol, England—bet they know where she is!"

Wolf says with much excitement, "DAMN, YOU'RE GOOD! If and when I have my own security firm, I will come looking for you to head my intelligence section."

"OK, I just might take you up on that."

Chapter Twelve

Wolfgang Surveys the Mathews House

Bristol, England

Wolf tells Gretchen that he has accepted a very high-paying job with his security contract work. He shows Gretchen that thirty-five thousand dollars have been transferred to their bank account. Wolf keeps sixty-five thousand dollars in his bitcoin account. The thirty-five thousand will not signal any unusual activity, as a deposit of that size is consistent with his trucking business.

Wolfgang now travels to London. He rents a car and travels to Bristol. Bristol is on the Irish Coast. The Mathews house is located in the country along a winding road. The house is an old Victorian with a front porch and two stories. Wolfgang must first survey the house. He knows that he needs intel on where Rose is. He sees that there is a hill approximately half a mile from home. He goes back to his hotel room, sits down at the desk, and connects his computer to Google Earth. He selects satellite mode, and then he zooms in on the Mathews house and notes that there is a cellar and a fenced-in back yard. He will need to know if there is a dog at home. There are tall bushes and a copse of maple and oak trees behind the house.

He now takes out a notepad and starts writing down what materials he will need. He writes down: binoculars, black pants, a light long-sleeve black pullover sweater, a black stocking cap, and light leather gloves. He will also need some black face paint. He is planning on breaking into the house, so he will need to conduct visual surveillance until he can determine when no one is home.

The next morning, Mr. Mathews is walking two Bernese mountain dogs. Wolfgang thinks, *Shit, Bernese mountain dogs have probably the best sense of smell of any dogs on the planet—better than German shepherds.*

After conducting surveillance for two days, he says to himself, "This is going to be a long surveillance." The Mathews are always home, and they have two mountain dogs. He needs to order two things from the internet: an Ozonics Odor eliminator, spray-on odor lotion, and blink surveillance cameras. He also goes to Black's Outfitters supply warehouse and buys mountain climbing boots, ropes, spikes, and other gear. The next evening, he climbs a telephone pole and installs the Blink cameras. The cameras are powered by AAA batteries and will last thirty days. They also have connectivity to the internet. Wolfgang can monitor the house from his hotel room.

After two weeks, he has not learned anything that he did not know the first two days. He plays back the recorded videos; maybe there is something he missed. The recorded video shows a telephone repair truck in the distance. He notices that the repair technician is working on a connection outside the house. BINGO—he has an idea. He can wiretap the incoming phone line and listen to the phone conversations. He logs on to the internet, goes to a website, Spies Unlimited, and orders wiretap equipment. In two days, he has it. The store is located in China. The instructions are in poorly worded English, French, Spanish, German, and Chinese. There is a warning: "Wiretapping in Your Country May Not Be Right."

Wolfgang waits until he has a favorable wind. On the third night, the wind is blowing out toward the Irish Sea. He takes a shower and scrubs his body with a strong anti-deodorant soap bar. He spreads the odor repellent lotion over his entire body. After that, he dresses in his black bugler clothes. At 2 A.M., he slowly walks toward the rear of the house. Should the dogs start barking, he will abort the mission. He reaches the telephone pole twenty yards from the house and climbs it using the gear from the REI sports store. He uses his pliers and screwdriver to open the telephone junction box. With his pen flashlight, he traces the phone line going to the Mathews house. Then he installs the wiretap box. It has two telephone lines. These lines are connected to a small cellphone with external power lines. With the cell phone connected to the power lines, the wiretap can continue indefinitely.

However, the landline which is being transferred to a cell line will need to be converted to a landline. The landline will then dial the international number at the KKK camp in Pulaski. Tennessee. Wolfgang finds an office complex in Bristol which rents office space by the hour, day, week or month. The cell which is tapping the Mathews landline in turn calls the phone number at the office which Wolfgang has rented. Wolfgang knows that it would take an expert in wiretaps to figure out exactly what is happening. He figures that there will be no one who can figure all of this obfuscation of the connections to his lair in the Tennessee mountains. The video from the Blink cameras is IP. The cameras connect to an IP router which connects to the internet at the office complex.

Wolfgang now has real time audio and the ability to monitor the video from any location that has an internet connection. He drives to London, takes a plane to Atlanta, and drives to Murfreesboro-Pulaski area of Tennessee. The entire operation has taken fifteen days. He has converted a cabin in the camp into an operations center. From the operations center, they can monitor the video and hear all telephone conversations. It is manned twenty-four-seven by eight Klansman.

Chapter Thirteen

Rose Receives a Tip

Alexandria, Virginia

On a lazy day in Alexandria, Virginia, Rose, and Claude are having a hoagie at the company cafeteria. Kathy Funicello from accounting comes in with a bag from Kentucky Fried Chicken. She sees Rose and Claude and asks, "Do you mind if I sit here with you?"

Rose says, "Not at all. Have a seat. My name is Liz Walker. This is Coby Robertson."

"Thank you. My name is Kathy Funicello. I work in accounts payable. I am the clerk who inputs all the hours from your timecards. You know, the clerk no one knows who ensures that all employees get paid."

Rose, Kathy, and Claude continue through their lunch hour, talking about family and the weather. To Kathy, it's evident that Rose is British—her accent is a dead giveaway.

As they are departing, Kathy whispers to Rose, "May I see you in private later today."

"Of course. How about at 3 P.M. in the main conference room on the first floor.

At 3 P.M., Kathy and Rose meet in the conference room.

"Ms. Liz, something has been bothering me for the last month."

"Yes, and you think I can help you?"

"No, it's not something anyone can help with. It is only that I need to confess to you."

Now Rose is thinking that she needs to act like a priest and take confession. "Of course, you can confide in me—kinda like woman to woman."

"First, I should tell you that I know your real name."

"Oh, and what is my real name?"

"Rose Mathews."

"And what makes you think that it is Rose Mathews?"

"Ms. Rose, in accounting, we know everything. For example, I know that you are MI6 on loan from the CIA."

"Kathy, why are you telling me this?"

"Last month, I met a woman by the name of Mildred Anderson. At least, that is what she told me. I met her at my church. She was from Richardson, Texas, and was very nice and friendly. During the month she was here on business, she joined the church and accepted Jesus Christ as her savior."

Rose is a good listener—she knows that this is going somewhere. She imagines that Kathy needs help in her marriage and maybe with co-workers. For some reason, women always gravitate to her to tell her their troubles. She thinks that perhaps Kathy sees her as a stranger from England and can confide in her.

"Yes, go ahead. Continue."

"During our conversation, I told her had we had an Englishwoman working for us by the name of Rose Mathews. I never really thought much of it—after all, we hire foreigners all the time with green cards."

"Did she ask anything else?"

"No, that's all. I have been thinking about why she would be asking those questions. This morning, when I sat with you and heard your accent, it occurred to me that the lady asking those questions was probably immigration. Being in accounting, I pretty well now everything, and I have never seen any information from you regarding immigration. I hope I did not get you in trouble."

Rose gives Kathy a million-dollar smile and says, "No, I am not in trouble with immigration. I do thank you for your concerns."

"Thank you very much; this takes a big weight off my shoulders!"

Immediately following the discussions with Kathy, Rose calls Claude and Alex on the secure line. "Please meet me in the SCIF. I need to discuss an item that has come up."

Claude says, "Be there in ten minutes."

Alex says, "Give me fifteen to wrap up some paperwork due today."

Claude and Alex walk into the SCIF at 4:30. Alex says, "What's up? Sounds important."

"Maybe," says Rose. "Need you're your opinion on an item that has come up."

Both Alex and Claude say, "OK, all ears."

Rose gives Claude and Alex the details of the conversation she had with Kathy. "Looks like my location has been compromised. Any ideas why this Mildred Anderson would be interested in me?"

Claude says, "I think we can assume that your life is in danger."

"Who besides ISIS has a bone to pick with you and the entire WMA team?" asks Alex.

"It has to be ISIS," replies Rose. "Any individuals I may have problems with in England know that I have been assigned to the CIA."

"We need to bring Senator Montana into the mix," says Claude.

"Agreed."

Claude picks up the intercom phone and calls Senator Montana. The senator joins the group thirty minutes later. Rose briefs the senator.

He says, "This sounds serious. I need to inform Directors Margaret Gifford and Hector Calvanese from the CIA and FBI. As soon as we leave this meeting, I will let them know that your location has been compromised. OK, team, any ideas?"

Claude says, "We can conduct our own investigations and see if we can locate this Mildred Anderson."

"Agreed," says the senator, "but let's have the FBI contact the homeland investigations. If I get pushback or if the FBI cannot get on this ASAP, then we jump in and pick up the ball."

"If I were to place a bet on who is interested in finding out my location," says Rose, "it would be ISIS. The ISIS headquarters in Peshawar is still in existence."

"Yes, I agree. As we all know, the Senate Intelligence Committee came to the correct conclusion that the attacks on the nuclear power plant and the roads, tunnels, and bridges were directed by ISIS. The proof that we had was discussed with the Pakistani government. However, the evidence was circumstantial. The Pakistanis would not even admit that there was a training camp in the Swat valley of the Hindu-Kush Mountains. The Pakistanis did conduct an inspection of the ISIS Peshawar facility. They claim that it is a legitimate drug processing and weapons factory. The Pakistani government let it be known that they will not tolerate another bin Laden-type raid. This exchange was carried on all Pakistani news broadcasts, in all newspapers, and on social media. Our satellite surveillance indicates that the Peshawar area has been heavily fortified. Pakistan has notified the US ambassador that a missile or massive bomb raid on the ISIS facility will be seen as an act of war. The US has little to no influence on Pakistan. They are heavily encamped in the Russia circle of influence."

"So, the most likely threat is coming from ISIS," says Alex. "If that is the case, ISIS will attempt an assassination using either a hit team from the Middle East or from the US."

"Yes, I agree," says the senator. "The CIA and the FBI should contact DHS and see if any suspicions actors have entered through legal ports of entry. Do we have any suggestions on assassins from the US?"

"Assassins may be found on the darknet," says Rose. "We need Louie and his IT team to do some digging to see what they can find."

"Excellent idea," says Claude. "I will brief Louie on the problem and see what they can find."

Louie and his team are the absolute best when it comes to the internet. Louis Norman Gilbert is twenty-eight years old. He has a master's in computer science from the University of Arizona. After graduation, he did freelance work in Silicon Valley. After an extensive search by the senator, Louie was hired to head WMA's IT division. Once aboard, he hired the best software programmers/hackers that money could buy. His team of programmers provided the software for the signals, surveillance, and skunkworks divisions. Some of the advanced surveillance products that the skunkworks division designed were the drone surveillance systems with the different payloads. The drones were designed with solar cells to charge the batteries, allowing an extended flight time. The payloads are video and audio. The video packages include cameras from X10 to X50 magnification and audio packages that allow ten independent pencil beams to intercept and record audio conversations.

The next day, after everyone has had time to think about the problem, they call a meeting to do some brainstorming. They invite Jeff and Vinny to participate in the discussions. Neither are special operations, nor are they egg-heads like Louie and his IT team. However, what they lack in brainpower, they make up for with street smarts. They have participated in several missions where their solution to the problem was "out of the box." The team will need some ideas that are not written in "Counter-Surveillance 101."

Claude opens the discussion and gives a quick overview of the problem. He says, "The problem is simple, but the solution is unknown. We need to think out of the box. It can be assumed that there is an assassin or a hit team that has been given the mission to assassinate Rose. The likely assassin has been sent by ISIS. The problem we have is how to find him before he finds Rose.

"We need to set up counter-surveillance around the WMA building," says Alex.

"Make sure that Rose drives around in a bulletproof car," offers Mateo.

"Perhaps Rose and I should take an extended trip to some far-off island," suggests Claude.

As the special operators discuss all of the options, Jeff and Vinny have an offline conversation.

Jeff finally speaks out in his loud voice: "We think we got it. You know Vinny and I read all the Mission Impossible and Jason Bourne books. In a Jason Bourne book, when they wanted info on the target, they could get it by some really ingenious shit. The fucking rabbit was very smart, and he would always be one step ahead of his pursuers." Jeff keeps telling them the sci-fi story in the Jason Bourne book. After ten minutes of "blah, blah, blah…"

Vinny says, "Hey, bro, get to the point!"

"Oh, yeah—the good guys hacked into the social media of the daughters of the rabbit. Man, those girls spilled the beans. They would always tell their friends, 'Guess what my old man is doing,' and on and on. Well, the rabbit did not say a damn thing. He followed strict operational security, but the daughters would get on their smartphones and text all day on Messenger, Twitter, and Facebook. This bullshit about security—no one ever turns it on."

Claude, Alex, Mateo, and Rose look dumbfounded—*Just what exactly does this have to do with the assassin?*

Vinny sees their confused faces. "We guess that your assassin friend reads the same books as us. Bet they have a tap on your friend's phones." Vinny stops, walks to the far wall, rubs his two-day-old beard, and says, "Bet they have wire-tapped your parents' home, that is how they are going to find where you are."

After a pause, Vinny continues: "When we search Rose's parents' home and find the tap—we cannot let them know that we know, and we set up a trap!"

Claude says, "Now, that's really some sci-fi shit! Jeff and Vinny get your feet on the ground. You need to think out of the box—not out of this world."

Jeff and Vinny are disappointed that the team does not think much about their idea—they shuffle their feet and look at Rose like puppy dogs that have been scolded.

Mateo starts to say something, but Rose interrupts. "Wait for one minute, guys. Jeff and Vinny might be onto something. The hit team found me, right? Well, once they know who I am, it will not take a genius to figure out who and where my parents live. My mom has a landline phone—she never wanted it taken out. Plus, if the assassins are state-sponsored, they can intercept the cell phones."

"Damn right it makes sense," says Alex. "Let's get a team to England and inspect the phone lines at your parent's home."

"OK, I can call some friends in Bristol, and they can drive over to Mom and Dad. Explain to Dad that I want to talk to him out of Mom's earshot… Some surprise I have for her. I will then call Herbert's house, my dad's friend, and then he can tell Dad what is going on. I will tell him not to discuss this subject at home—the assassin may have room bugs."

"Good idea," says Claude. "Who do we send?" In unison, they all look at Jeff and Vinny.

"Why not?" he says. "We are on our way."

Jeff and Vinny need to have a reason why they will be at the house. They then converse for ten to fifteen minutes, and then Jeff asks Rose, "Do your parents have solar panels?"

"No, pretty sure they do not have any."

"OK, then we go there for an inspection for solar panel installation."

"Do you guys even know anything about solar panels or electricity?" asks Alex.

"Yeah, man!" says Jeff. "Was a roofer, electrician, plumber, and candlestick maker before my employment with WMA."

Rose asks Jeff, "Is there anything you have not done?"

"I also was a headstone recaller."

"What the hell is a headstone recaller?"

"My father-in-law sold headstones—you know, for dead people. Well, some of those assholes—sorry, I mean relatives—did not pay. I had to jump the fence at night and repo the headstone."

"So, you're a jack of all trades," says Mateo.

"Pretty much. Just never been an astronaut—so don't tell me to jump on a rocket and go to the moon?"

"We should be OK on the moon," says Rose. "No assholes on the moon—at least not yet!"

Jeff and Vinny now have some work to do. They order a magnetic sign that reads "Sun Power Inc." and, in smaller letters, "Power is the Future." They log on to the internet and find a sizeable three-bedroom home in Bristol, England. It has a garage and is set back from the main road. They arrange for a two-week rental. They will buy or rent all of their supplies in England. They do take wiretap detectors and telephone pole climbing boots. They will also take the drone. They decide that it would be best to ship the solar panels. The amount of equipment needed becomes too large to ship via FedEx or UPS. They will need to ship via a commercial shipper.

Vinny looks at Jeff and says, "We should ask for one of the WMA Gulfstream 650 aircraft. Claude and Alex are pilots. We can ask—if it's a no, then everything is delayed two weeks."

Vinny goes to Rose and Claude. "Our shopping list is growing, and we will need to ship via commercial carrier. The paperwork and customs bullshit will require a two-week delay."

Claude looks at Rose and says, "You take the WMA aircraft. Best that none of the operators who were involved in the Buchanan mission participate—you never know, these assholes may also have our names and photos."

Vinny thinks, *that was easy.*

He tells Jeff, "OK, we are all set. We take the Gulfstream. Real royalty, bro!"

In one week, Vinny and Jeff are flying directly to Bristol. The two things that cannot fit on the plane are a stretch van and a cherry picker. These have both been ordered via the internet. They land at the commercial terminal at the Bristol Airport and rent a two-door nondescript English car. Jeff jumps in the driver's side, and Vinny in the passenger-side. They look at each other, and Jeff says, "Guess you're driving."

Vinny has some problems getting used to shifting gears with his left hand and driving on the left side of the road. They leave the airport, and he says with some concern, "Do I really drive on the left side? Hope these English drivers know that." After driving for ten minutes, he gets the hang of it.

They arrive at the Airbnb house; it is ideal, with a big two-car garage, three large bedrooms, kitchen, family room with a sixty-inch TV screen, dining room, and two full baths. They see a note on the kitchen cabinet: "Wi-Fi password, Bristol5282."

Jeff says, "Great, they have Wi-Fi and cable TV." They see a note on the TV: "Any movies downloaded; the price will be added to your bill. Have a nice visit to Bristol. If there are any problems, a list of phone numbers is on the fridge door. The McKinley family."

Vinny says, "Nice family. We need to leave this place clean, just like we found it."

"Should not be a problem," says Jeff. "We will be using the garage the whole time we are here."

Jeff and Vinny decide to do a drive-by. The Mathews house is set back with a view of the Irish Sea from the back window. They arrive at the house at 6 P.M. with the sun setting toward the back yard. They really do not to expect anything—if the hit squad is truly professional, any listening devices or cameras will be well hidden.

The next day, they pick up the rental van. They come back to the rental home and load up the van with the solar panels, electrical equipment, and other items. Most importantly, they load the telephone wiretap and room bug detectors. They also have the drone, which they will use to view all of the areas around the house. When using the drone, it needs to appear like they are inspecting the roof.

Jeff and Vinny have work uniforms with the names "Ralph" and "James" stitched on the front left sides of the work shirts, and the backs have the emblem for Sun Power Inc. The van has a magnetic sign with "Sun Power" written in big orange letters. Vinny added a sun with rays emanating from it. They look very professional.

The house has a circular driveway. Jeff and Vinny park the van in front of the house. As they park the van, the two Bernese dogs start barking. Vinny says, "There goes the automatic doorbell." They make a mental note of the barking dogs and continue up the walkway to the front door. They ring the doorbell.

Mrs. Mathews comes to the front door and greets them warmly. "Hello, you must be from the solar panel company."

"Yes, ma'am," says Jeff. "We will first be doing some inspection of the outside and the roof. We will need access to the power panel breaker box."

Mrs. Mathews says, "Of course. Just drive around to the back. I will have my husband come around and show you the power box in the garage."

"Thank you very much," says Vinny. "We will complete our inspection today and try not to bother you."

"Oh, it is really not a problem; perhaps I can fix some tea for an early-morning break."

"Yes, that would be very nice. Thank you."

Jeff and Vinny want to look like a normal work team. They do not know if there is a video camera or a bug in the house. This will be the first thing they check. As they drive around the house, Jeff says, "Wow, for a lady in her fifties, she sure has aged well. Now we know where Liz gets her beauty." Both Jeff and Vinny have agreed that no mention of Rose will be made. Only in the van. If mention of Rose is needed, they will refer to her as Liz—unless either Mr. or Mrs. Mathews mentions her name. The Mathews have also been instructed through their friend Herbert to keep the conversations professional.

Jeff and Vinny step out the van and view Mr. Mathews. He is a healthy six feet tall and is in his sixties. His shoulders and arms are well toned with muscles. He keeps himself in good shape. They can see that he works out with the weights. The dogs are now in the back yard. They are growling and barking at Jeff and Vinny.

Mr. Mathews extends his hand and says, "Welcome to the Mathews house. I heard you say that you wanted to see the power panel box. Follow me, and I will show you."

"Thank you," says Jeff. "The inspection will be completed today. We will not install any of the solar panels until we take all dimensions and order the proper materials."

"Yes, that sounds like a reasonable thing."

"Can we inspect the electrical outlets inside the house?"

"Yes, of course."

The plan is to check for audio bugs in the house. Should there be any, the American accent will give Jeff and Vinny away. Vinny goes to the van and breaks out a Pelican case on wheels. He extends the case handle and rolls it through the garage door and into the house. Both Vinny and Jeff raise their trigger fingers to their lips and give the "silent" sign. Mr. and Mrs. Mathews understand. Vinny and Jeff check all the rooms and find no bugs. They also make a thorough inspection and find nothing. They take a piece of paper and write NOTHING FOUND. Mrs., Mathews brings them some tea and biscuits. They take them outside and take a ten-minute break. As they are sitting outside on some beer barrels, they do visual surveillance of the property. After they finish their tea and biscuits, Jeff says, "I'll take down the ladder and start the roof inspection."

Vinny then says, "You know those cookies were pretty good!"

"These cookies are called biscuits by the Brits, dummy."

"Biscuits, they look like cookies to me."

"Vinny we are in England, the Brits eat cookies when they have digestive problems, are you having problems doing number two?"

"OK, OK I get it, these are biscuits."

"Good, I don't want you to be embarrassed in front of Mrs. Mathews."

"Thanks, let's get on with the job, I will now prepare the drone," replies Vinny. "When you are on the roof, you can direct that you want a video recording of the roof. Make this look real. While the drone is up, I will slowly record all the trees, homes, telephone poles, power poles, sheds—everything will be in the highest resolution. I will record as MPEG4…thirty frames per second. We can review the recordings tonight."

"Good plan, OK, here goes."

"Do not fall off the roof, bro. I got no time to take you to the hospital!"

"Yeah, fuckhead—remember, I worked as a roofer for a couple of years. I'm like a monkey when I am on the roof my element."

Vinny laughs. "Just get your ass up there, and I will have the drone up before you crawl your fat ass up."

Jeff and Vinny are the best of friends; they have been in life-threatening situations fighting terrorists in New York and Mazatlán. They have a bond that only brothers in war have.

They complete their work for the day and drive back to the rented home.

Chapter Fourteen

COMMAND CENTERS

TENNESSEE AND ENGLAND

Wolf has two Klansmen monitoring the wiretap on the Mathews landline.

Joey is in position number one. "I have some action at the target house."

Emmitt is in position two. "Yes, I see it. Are we recording?

"Yes, we are always recording."

"Better make sure. If not, Wolfgang will eat us for lunch."

"Check, we are recording."

"Better get Wolfgang. He needs to see this!"

Wolfgang comes in. "What do you two shitheads have?"

They explain the situation to Wolfgang. He asks, "You guys think this is legit?"

"Yeah, it's legit. Those aristocrats made the low-level workers drink their tea and cookies outside. They did not even offer them lawn chairs. Made them sit on beer barrels. Yeah, I would say they are legit."

"Any indication that they found or are looking for the cameras or the wiretap?"

"None."

Joey says, "I did a scan of the phone recording. No call was made to a solar panel company. That's not right."

"No, I do not think that is unusual," says Emmitt. "Only the old lady uses the landline. If I had to guess, it was the old man who made the call to the solar panel company."

Wolfgang says, "Good thinking. I agree it would be the old man who would make the call. Did any of you two shitheads check out the solar company?"

"Yeah, it checks out. There is a solar company by that name in Bristol."

"OK, continue to monitor and let me know of any unusual developments."

Airbnb House

Bristol, England

Jeff and Vinny are back in their rental home. They discuss their first day of inspection. Vinny starts the conversation, saying, "We now know that there are no bugs in the house."

"Makes sense," replies Jeff. "With those two Bernese dogs, there is no way anyone could enter that house without them raising a ruckus. Maybe one dog, but not two."

"Yes, I agree."

"Let's now look at the video. We need to look carefully at all of the frames using high resolution and see if we can detect any cameras or unusual equipment indicating a wiretap."

Vinny copies the video recordings to the laptops and they start their inspection of the recordings. Within ten minutes of viewing the video, Jeff says, "Vinny, take a look at the section with the time stamp 00.08.15."

Vinny fast-forwards to the time stamp. They both view each recorded frame. Jeff says, "Take a look at the power pole. Looks like a Blink camera."

Vinny also looks at the still frames surrounding the time stamp 00.08.15. The still frames are all recorded in very high resolution. This allows for recordings to be analyzed by zooming into the different sections of each frame. They both view the camera attached to a power pole.

"No question that's a Blink camera," says Jeff. "We can now assume that we have been recorded. The assassin now knows that we are here. We should be OK—our disguise should work. We need to put on our best acting. The assholes need to be convinced that we are legit. The next thing we need is to inspect any taps on the phones."

"Agreed. Let's take a look at the phone line leaving the house."

"OK, I recorded that section of the house both at the beginning and at the end of the recording."

"You look at the first five minutes, and I will look at the last five minutes."

Since Vinny was the recorder, he finds the pertinent recording section first. He says, "OK, I have the area where the phone line leaves the house and the connection to the telephone pole. The phone line enters a junction-type box. From that point, we lose the connection. The exit from the junction box is a thick cable connected to the next telephone pole."

"OK," says Jeff, "time to bring out the cell phone intercept package. Tomorrow we can fly the drone and intercept cell phone traffic. We can then detect the connection of the tap to a cell number, and we can have Louie and his IT team determine the location of the intercept phone."

"OK, let's do it."

"Hold on a minute. We will need to have Mrs. Mathews make a phone call. Only then can we determine that the landline is wiretapped."

Jeff now connects the laptop to the Wi-Fi of the rented house. He starts the encrypted VPN and connects to the WMA facility in Alexandria. He types up a report on the camera findings and types the following to Rose:

LIZ, WE NEED TO HAVE MRS. MATHEWS MAKE A PHONE CALL ON THE LANDLINE. MAKE THE CALL IN THE AM. HAVE MR. MATHEWS MAKE A CALL ON HIS CELL PHONE IN THE AFTERNOON.

Rose, aka Liz, knows why they are requesting the phone calls. She has Claude call Herbert using WhatsApp. He tells Herbert to contact Mr. Mathews. He tells Herbert to speak to Mr. Mathews to call using a burner phone. "Do not use your own cell phone."

Herbert understands and tells Claude, "Will do."

Claude calls Mr. Mathews—both are using burner phones.

"Have Mrs. Mathews make a call tomorrow to her friend Matilda," says Claude. "Have her talk about a new recipe on how to make stuffed cabbage.

Have her make the call at 10 A.M. Then, using your regular cell phone, call the golf course and make a tee time reservation for the coming weekend. Your call will be at 2 P.M."

"OK, I already have a reservation; I will call and ask for a different tee time."

"OK, that will work."

Claude uses the encrypted VPN to send a message to Jeff and Vinny. The message reads: "Mrs. Mathews will make the call tomorrow to her friend Matilda about a stuffed cabbage recipe. The call will be at 10 A.M. Mr. Mathews will make a call at 2 P.M. The call will be to the golf course. Do you copy?"

"Copy."

Jeff and Vinny park the van about half a mile from the Mathews house. Vinny prepares the drone with the cell phone intercept system. All calls being made in the area will be intercepted by the drone system. The phone calls are all pass-through. Jeff can connect to the cell intercept system (CIS) and can monitor the calls. Jeff launches a recording application that will record all calls being made from the Mathews landline number. Vinny starts flying the drone with the CIS at 9:45 A.M. At five minutes after 10, Vinny sees that Mrs. Mathews is dialing.

Matilda answers the phone. "Hi, Maria, good to hear from you." They go on and talk about their garden, clothes, weather, vacations, and Mrs. Mathew's talks about her cabbage recipe. Vinny and Jeff have heard enough. The only way that the conversation could be intercepted by the CIS was if the landline was being tapped and transferred to a cell number. Within the junction box on the telephone pole is a physical connection from the landline to a cell phone number. The cell phone number is recorded in the CIS application. It is a number from the Southeast British Telephone Company.

Jeff says, "OK, we have proof positive that the landline is tapped. Now we get Louie and his boys to trace the cell number that is being used to transfer the call. They should be able to trace it and find the asshole."

Vinny says, "One down and one to go. We need to use the CIS to monitor the call to be made from Mr. Mathew's cell phone."

At 1:45, Vinny and Jeff again fly the CIS. They intercept the call made by Mr. Mathews to the golf course. However, the call is not transferred to a second number. Now Jeff and Vinny know that Mr. Mathew's cell phone is not tapped.

Jeff needs to talk to the Virginia team. He, Vinny, Claude, Alex, and Rose are soon participating in an encrypted talk group using the WMA comms server. Jeff begins the discussions. "The landline is definitely wiretapped. There are four Blink cameras installed around the property. I am ninety-nine percent sure that the cell phones are not being intercepted."

Vinny adds, "We swept all the rooms in the house—no bugs. We are sure that no bugs could have been installed. Those two Bernese mountain dogs have a very keen sense of smell and pick up the smallest odor. Hell, they know when we are coming as we are turning into the driveway. When we are working outside, the dogs look at us, and they are growling and showing their teeth. They are protecting their territory."

"What is the phone number that is connected to the tapped device?" asks Alex.

"Yeah, we got the number." Jeff gives him the number.

"Can you do a GPS on the number?"

"Yes, we did that. The GPS indicates a cell tower in the business district of Bristol."

"You need to take the drone CIS and intercept any outgoing calls."

"OK, we can do that, but Mrs. Mathews will need to make at least one call."

"We can have Mrs. Mathews make a call to the bakery and order biscuits. You know the Brits are always eating biscuits."

"Good idea. Set up the call tomorrow. Rose can call Herbert, and he can tell Mr. Mathews to make the call."

"No problem," says Claude. "Mr. Mathews and Herbert go back a long time. I think they went to college together, and they both served in the British Diplomatic Corps. They play golf every Saturday and Wednesday."

"OK," says Vinny. "We will set up in the business area and see where the tapped phone calls."

The next day, Mrs. Mathews makes the call. They see the incoming call but not the outgoing call.

"OK, Jeff," says Vinny, "you're the surveillance guru—what the hell does that mean?"

"Easy Vinny, the tapping phone line terminates in one of those office buildings. We find the answering phone, and we find the asshole!"

Woah, dude! Finding the office or home where that phone line terminates is out of my lane. This is a job for our trigger pullers—Claude, Alex, or Mateo!"

Jeff smirks and says, "What are you, some candy ass?"

Vinny looks at Jeff and shakes his head. "You are going to get us killed!"

"I was just kidding, man—just kidding."

"OK, we need to have a conference call with the team in Alexandria. Let's see what they want to do."

That evening, Bristol time, and afternoon in Virginia, the team has a conference call. They use the encrypted VPN connection to the WMA server.

Jeff gives the team a detailed briefing, He says, "The main items are: one, no bugs in the house, two, video cameras connected to the cellular service, three, the landline is tapped, and four, the tapped video and audio are connected to a cell phone in the business district. Also, the connected phone is making a connection to a landline.

"How do you know that it's a landline?" asks Claude.

"The phone does not have GPS. We could verify that it is a landline by sending a text—you will get a message that the phone number cannot accept text messages."

"Good point."

Rose says, "You guys have done a great job. Go ahead and complete your inspection of my parents' house. When you finish, stand outside and, using your clipboard, give my dad an estimate of the job. Make it look very formal—you and Vinny do your acting. Maybe have Vinny show him the video of the roof. If the hit squad are real pros—which we now believe they are, they will look at every motion to assure them that the solar inspection is the real deal."

"No problem," says Jeff. "Showtime, the Academy Award—it's in the bag."

Chapter Fifteen

Assassin Comms Connection

Virginia and Bristol

The team assembles in the WMA Sensitive Compartmented Information Facility (SCIF). Jeff and Vinny are connected using the encrypted WMA server connection. The server is used to configure an intercom channel, which allows for full-duplex high-fidelity voice communications. Claude asks Jeff and Vinny to provide an overview of their findings in Bristol.

Jeff says, "We arrived on Sunday. Immediately after that, we conducted a drive through." He then presents the findings. It is as if Jack Webb on *Dragnet* told him, "The facts, Jeff, only the facts." Jeff, with some input from Vinny, does just that—only the facts.

Alex then adds the following, "We need to investigate where the tapped line terminates. This will lead us to the location of the assassins. Jeff, can you describe the sector where the cell tower is pointing?"

"Yes, it is pointing to a two-story office building. It has an advertisement that office cubicles are available. These cubicles may be rented hourly, daily, weekly, or monthly."

Rose adds, "Sounds ideal. We need to try to find which office has the connecting phone number. The only way we can do that is by breaking into each of the cubicles. We will need to send Jeff and Vinny assistance."

Mateo now enters the discussion. "Needs to be me and Alex. We cannot risk that Rose be exposed. This would be too dangerous."

The team members all agree. "Yes, that is the next logical step," says Claude.

In two days, Mateo and Alex are on a British Airways plane to London Heathrow Airport. The WMA plane is waiting at the commercial terminal. That evening, Mateo and Alex are at the Airbnb house rented by Jeff and Vinny. Sending Mateo and Alex is ideal. They will present themselves as Spanish businessmen. They will be in Bristol for one week and need office space.

The next day, at 10 A.M., they enter the business center building. The office is located on the first floor, two doors to the left. They enter the office, and the receptionist greets them with a heavy English accent, "Good morning, gentlemen. May I be of assistance?"

Both Mateo and Alex have professional three-piece business suits, white shirts, and polished shoes. They both have dark, neatly trimmed beards. Mateo responds to the receptionist with a slight Spanish accent, "*Buenos Dias, señorita.* We are interested in renting an office room for one week. We assume from your advertisement that you have a room to rent?"

"Yes, we do have two rooms available that might fit your requirement."

Alex says, "*Muy bien.* May we see the rooms?"

"Certainly. Allow me to find the keys, and we can walk up to the available rooms." As they are walking down the hallway and to the elevator, she explains, "When a customer requires more than one week, we try and rent the upstairs rooms. The hourly and daily customers usually are in and out for their time period; thus, the downstairs rooms and cubicles rent better."

The receptionist opens the door with a key and shows them the room. It has two desks; two cheap office chairs, and a bookcase. The receptionist then says with a certain amount of pride, "We have a 100Mbit Wi-Fi and unlimited phone service. Of course, if you make international phone calls, we will charge you for them. When we get the phone bill, we will bill you the difference. We will require a two-hundred-pound deposit for any international calls."

Mateo and Alex both look at each other and are thinking, *PERFECT.*

Alex then says, "This is exactly what we need. We will take it."

"Glad you like it. Let's go back to the office, and we can complete the paperwork."

As they are walking back to the office, Mateo asks, "Is it common for your rooms to be rented for a week or more? We may be extending our stay here in Bristol for a few more days or perhaps another week."

As they enter the building office, the receptionist takes out some forms, clips them to a clipboard, and says, "My name is Maggie, and yes, we do have customers who rent for more than one week. For example, a room two doors from you has been rented for a month. Do not know what business they are in, but I know they come to make international calls."

Mateo and Alex simply nod. Alex completes the paperwork and says, "Will a check be OK?"

"Only if it's from a British bank."

"OK, we understand. We will be paying in pounds."

Maggie gives Alex two keys and a swipe card, she says, "The swipe card will get you into the facility after hours. The building is closed from 6 P.M. to 6 A.M. Should you need to enter the building after these hours, you can use the swipe card. This building is very safe. We will ask you not to give the card to anyone not authorized. Should you lose the card, please let me know immediately. All the cards have an ID. We can easily disable the card from our computer."

Alex then has a question. "Maggie, we are an international consulting company. We have customers around the world, which may require that we work during the evenings from our office. Is there any added security during the evening hours?"

"No, not really. However, we have security cameras in our parking lots. We have our parking lots well lighted and we have security cameras in the hallways. The cameras are always recording. They all have about one week of recording—the security firm that installed them told us that. If anything happens, let us know ASAP. The recording over one week will be overwritten."

"Looks like you have done an outstanding job on security," says Mateo.

"Yes, our owner, Mr. Pummernickel, is big on security. He told me that the security cameras are in a closed loop. Something about hackers will not be able to connect to the camera system through the internet. He is a security freak. Does not even use e-mail. Says that the government reads and listens to all our communications. Personally, I do not care. If the government listens to my conversations, they will die of boredom!"

Mateo and Alex make themselves the best conversationalists—they listen. Maggie is a source of information. She's told them everything they need to know except who rented the two rooms on a monthly basis. Alex and Mateo know how to break into the two rooms; they have the lockpick tools. The problem will be the hallway cameras. They will need to contact Louie and ask for his advice.

They get back to the rental and give Jeff and Vinny a briefing on what they found. They then call Claude and Rose and provide them with a briefing. They all agree that they need to bring Louie and his IT team into the equation.

Rose says, "Give us one hour. I will call back. We need to have Louie, Brad, and senator Montana on the conference call." Brad is Bradley McKinnon; he is a retired FBI agent. His last assignment with the FBI was as the head of the Hostage Rescue Team. He is currently the head of the WMA skunkworks division. They need to have WMA management in the discussion, as the next few steps will require a break-in and entry.

In one hour, the complete team is assembled in the SCIF. Alex provides a detailed briefing of the findings. He says, "When we break into the two suspected rooms, the hallway cameras will record us. They are not connected to the internet."

"Louie, what is your recommendation?" asks Mateo.

"OK, you need to buy a router; the router needs to be a CISCO model 1345SP. After you buy the router or order it from the internet, you will connect it to the closed video network. Before you connect the router, I will install a software application on it that will counter any security software that may alert that a new device has been added—in other words 'blacklisted.' Call us after you have the router. Connect it to the internet and call me."

"Roger that," says Alex.

"Can you explain what you will do once we have the router configured and connected to the security system?" asks Mateo.

"Yes, of course," says Louie. "We can monitor the video as the break-in is occurring and disable the recordings. We will patch the recordings so that only a professional forensics laboratory would know. The issue will be the time stamp. The shorter the deleted recordings, the better. In other words, you guys need to get your ass in gear and do a Speedy Gonzales."

"OK, got it."

Alex says, "We will get started on buying the router immediately. We will probably need to order from Amazon. Most likely, that specific router is not available at a local store."

The team looks at Brad and the senator. The senator says, "Let's do it." He reminds them, "If we fuck up and get caught, you guys are just common, every day, garden-variety burglars breaking and entering."

Alex and Mateo nod. Alex says, "Yes, sir. Been doing this for over ten years and never been caught. Don't intend to make this any different."

"I have complete faith in your abilities. Compared to all the other incidents, this should be a piece of cake. *Buena suerte!*"

After the FONCON, Alex logs on to the internet, goes to Amazon Prime, and orders the router. It will arrive in two days. In the meantime, the Bristol team starts their planning.

Mateo says, "We first need to enter the office. There are cameras on the first and second floors. Louie will need to doctor the video after the recordings have been completed. No going around that. After we enter the office, we can have Jeff be ready to replace the router in the security room. We will need comms to coordinate. The key will be timing. After that, we can go upstairs and use the lockpick to open the two suspected rooms."

"We should have Claude or Rose ship the pick gun," says Vinny. "It will be much faster."

"Good idea," says Alex. He thinks for a few seconds and says, "Vinny, we will need a lookout."

"Will do, I can let you know if we have someone approaching the front door."

"Jeff, you will need to have Mrs. Mathews make a call to Matilda. They often talk after 9 P.M., but not after 10."

In two days, both the CISCO router and the pick gun arrive. Jeff connects the router to the internet. He calls Louie on the encrypted voice phone and gives him the IP address. In two minutes, the lights on the router are blinking red and blue lights. Louie is in the router.

In five minutes, he tells Jeff, "OK, restart the router."

Jeff restarts it. "OK, done."

"That's it. Now we wait until tomorrow night."

Alex then comes on the line. "Rose, we need to have your mom call Matilda at 9:45 GMT."

"Got it, will do. I will have Claude contact Herbert and use the normal roundabout comms circuit."

"OK, we are ready to start tomorrow night at 9 P.M. We will be on channel one, the operational channel. Everyone from Alexandria will be monitoring only. We need to minimize the chatter. We need to be at the two rooms no later than 9:40. Mrs. Mathews will be on the phone from 9:45 to 10:10."

The next night, they all dress in dark clothes, black or brown. They are tenants in the building; thus, there's no need to wear covert clothing. They have rented a black sedan and gone to an auto parts store and bought the dark silk screens to place on the windows. Vinny will sit in the car as the lookout. They agree on radio protocol. If Vinny says, "Smooth," it will mean stand down; person or persons are entering the building." If Vinny says, "Buster," abort the mission. They agree that if they need to abort, they will all go to their legally rented room. All operators are wearing earbuds with a push-to-talk button.

At 9 P.M., Jeff, Mateo, and Vinny enter the building with their legal scan card. They go to the second floor and enter their office suite. Alex exits the office and goes to the first-floor men's room. He checks to make sure that the hallway is clear. Then he goes back in the men's room and keys his radio. "Jeff, all clear. Come on down."

Jeff carries a briefcase with the router and cables. As he is coming down the stairs, Alex takes out the pick gun. He inserts the master key in the key slot and turns on the pick gun, and in ten seconds, the door opens. Jeff exits the stairwell and enters the office. He quickly pulls out the router and plugs in the cable and power cord. He pushes the PTT button and says, "Louie, ready to plug in the router."

Louie answers, "Ready."

Jeff inserts the RJ-45 plug into the security router and holds his breath—nothing.

Louie says, "That's good. I'm in—go ahead with the search. I can see the video from all cameras."

Jeff will remain at the server location. Alex goes upstairs to the second floor. Mateo has been listening. He waits by the door, hears Alex coming up the stairs, and exits. He joins Alex at the door of the first suspected office. They snap on tight gloves. Alex applies the lockpick gun. The door opens—they are in. It is now 9:44. They start their inspection. Mateo motions with his hand: over there, the phone. They inspect the phone and the phone line—nothing. This is not the assassin's office.

They leave the first office and go to the second office. As soon as they enter, they see a small equipment rack. The phone jack on the wall has two prone jacks: one cable to the phone and one to the equipment rack. Leaving the equipment rack is a second cable connected to a wall jack. Quietly Alex and Mateo know what to do. Mateo unscrews the back panel. He takes two alligator clips and connects them to the phone line. It is now 10 P.M. The cables from the alligator clips are connected to a small box the size of a cigarette pack. The readout on the box displays a ten-digit number. The number starts with +1-615—and the seven-digit number. The number is to the US, with an area code in the Nashville-Murfreesboro-Pulaski area of Tennessee. Alex pushes the "store" button. The number will be recorded to memory. He disconnects the alligator clips, and Mrs. Mathews hangs up her phone. Mateo says, "That was close."

Alex keys the radio. "Louie, we are done—go ahead and do your magic."

"OK, this will take about thirty minutes. Jeff, leave the server connected."

"Roger, will do."

Alex says, "We will return to our office and wait there."

Jeff has located the router behind the server rack. It is on the floor.

After fifteen minutes, Vinny comes on the radio. "Woman entering the office building."

"Jeff," says Alex, "try and hide the router—make yourself small."

"Should have listened to my wife," says Jeff. "Need to lose weight. OK, I will set the router on the equipment tray and dress up the cable. Do we know if the lady is coming into the office?"

Vinny replies, "Cannot tell, but it's best to assume that working this late, she may be an office clerk."

Two minutes later, the office door opens. The woman sits at the desk and turns on her computer. She starts typing on the keyboard. After ten minutes of typing, she picks up the phone. She starts talking to a man who appears to be her boyfriend. She says how much she misses him and that, hopefully, he will be back in the next week. She says, "Edger, I don't know how much longer I can go without sex. I am really horny. I am even looking at some of the old geezers who are renting offices in this building." She goes on for one hour. Finally, she finishes and says, "Ah, shit, I almost forgot why I came in tonight. I need to check the mail server. I am supposed to restart the server after the updates." She goes to the backroom, turns off the mail server, and then turns it back on. As she is leaving, she notices the router sitting in the equipment tray. She shakes her head and mumbles, "Damn maintenance crew, never cleans up. I need to tell Mr. Pummernickel to fire those two idiots." She leaves the office and locks the door.

Jeff, who has been listening, says to himself, "Just my luck. Here I sit with a boner and can't get no satisfaction!" He keys the radio. "Alex needs to check on the hallway. I am coming out."

After the check, Alex and Mateo reassemble in the rented office. They key the radio channel and ask Louie, "Are we clear?"

"Yes, all clear. However, on your way out, when you disconnect the router, you need to be out in less than ten seconds. If you are not out in ten seconds, the cameras will record you leaving the building, I can only erase the recording with a ten-second advance window."

Jeff who has been listening says, "OK, can do."

Vinny has also been listening on the radio channel. He says, "All clear on the outside."

The crew goes down to the first floor. They open the office door. Mateo enters the office and joins Jeff. They go back to the server room. Mateo goes around the equipment rack. Jeff picks up the router. Mateo is ready to disconnect.

Mateo says, "On three, ready?" Jeff signals thumbs up. "One, two, three, go!"

They quickly disconnect and carry the CISCO router and reconnect the normal router. Alex, Mateo, and Jeff scamper out the door and exit the building. They look at their watches, and Mateo says, "Eight seconds—not bad."

Chapter Sixteen

Using a Hologram

Virginia and Hollywood

The Bristol team takes the WMA Gulfstream 650 back to Alexandria, Virginia. The entire team meets in the WMA SCIF. They review all the data. Of major interest is the phone with the US international code +1 and the Tennessee area code 615, which includes the area of Nashville, Murfreesboro, and Pulaski.

Claude says, "Louie, can we hack the service provider billing records and determine the subscriber for the 615-phone number?"

"This may be a problem," replies Louie. "The number 615 is a landline number. Most service providers do not have these landline numbers with subscribers on the internet. These numbers have been around for one hundred years. The billings are computerized but not on the internet. However, I will give it a try, but there's no guarantee."

Senator Montana says, "OK, give it a try and let us know."

"Will do."

Rose says, "So the problem is that we do not know who owns the phone number in Tennessee right?"

Claude says, "Yeah that's the problem."

Rose then says, "We need to lure the assassin from his lair."

"And just how do we do that?"

"I can have my mother make a phone call to Matilda. She will be very excited that her daughter and boyfriend will be joining them for their traditional golf vacation. We can have a location in a remote area like Scotland. The assassin will see this as the opportunity he is looking for. The place will be in an area where there is a thin population. We will be able to identify the asshole before he gets off a shot."

"Are you shitting me?" says Alex. "You want to put yourself out as a trophy kill and have this asshole take a shot at you? I don't like it. I say no way, Jose!"

Jeff and Vinny, who have a crush on Rose, also do not like it. Jeff says, "If we have Rose as a lure, then I will volunteer to dress up like her. Let the asshole take a shot at me!"

Vinny says, "Jeff, you're too fat. No way will you double for Rose. I can do a better job!"

"Thanks, guys," says Rose, "but no one is acting as my double. If we do it, I will be the lure."

Senator Montana listens to the back and forth. He then says, "I like the idea. Let me—"

Jeff interrupts. "Have you gone nuts?"

The senator holds up his hands. The group goes quiet. He says, "Give me five minutes to explain. First, we will NOT expose Rose to any assassin! I have a good friend with whom I grew up in New Mexico. His name is Juan Ramos—I have known him as Johnny. Johnny lives in Hollywood. He has a movie company that produces sci-fi films such as *Star Wars*. Last month, I had dinner with him in Phoenix, and he was telling me that he had a hologram machine that would produce the exact images of any items. In particular, people. Do you remember the *Star Wars* movies, where the character Obi-Wan Kenobi appears as a hologram? Well, Johnny's team has a hologram machine that can be programmed to replicate a human, and the software can be programmed to have the hologram make movements. He told me that someone looking from a distance could not tell the difference between the real person and the hologram."

The group now understands the recommendation from the senator. Rose says with excitement. "I like it, how do we get the hologram machine?"

"Let me make some calls and see if Johnny will let us borrow the machine. Besides, Rose, I will need some volunteers to journey to California and learn how to operate the machine."

In unison, they all raise their arms; it is like in first grade when the teacher asks, "Who wants ice cream?"

The senator calls Johnny. "Yeah, Johnny, how are you doing?" They talk for several minutes about their golf game, getting older, and their grandkids. After the preamble, Senator Jesse Montana gets around to the subject. "Johnny, when we had dinner last month in Phoenix, you mentioned that you had designed and built a life-size hologram machine."

"Hey, sure did, Jesse. Not only do we have one, but we built two—need one as a backup."

"Johnny, as you know, my company deals in the security business. Something has come up where we could use one of your machines. I could either buy one or rent it for a few weeks."

"I would not think of charging you for its use. We have been friends since childbirth. Turns out, we have completed all of our shots using the holograms. You are welcome to use one, or two if you prefer."

"OK, great. My team and I will be out there the day after tomorrow."

"Great, see you then."

Following the phone conversation, Jesse calls the team and lets them know. "We are good to go on the holograms—meet in the SCIF in one hour."

The team meets in one hour. They are all excited about the new technology.

The senator opens the meeting. "Johnny gave us the green light on the hologram machines. We need a team to go with me for training. The core team needs to be Rose and Louie. Rose will be the person to be hologramed, and we need a programmer. Also, we need two technicians to receive training." He looks at Jeff and Vinny. "OK, you guys are in," They both raise their thumbs up.

Alex and Claude look at each other. Claude says, "You need pilots for the plane."

"OK, you guys win. The entire team goes. Also, Jeff, have Matt Gorman from your division join the team. When we are all in Los Angeles, we can plan the 'sting' for our assassin asshole."

Jeff and Vinny like the reference to *The Sting*. It is as though they are going to Hollywood to film a movie. Of course, they are doing the real thing, but they never think about it as "the real thing."

They arrive at the airport in Los Angeles and deplane at the commercial aviation terminal. They drive to the Hollywood Ritz-Carlton and check into their rooms. That afternoon, they drive to the movie set where they have the hologram machines. Jesse greets Johnny, and introductions are made. Three technicians from Johnny's movie company bring out the hologram machines. The items that make up the machine are small laser devices and a laptop computer.

The lead technician says, "Let's all have a seat over here. I have arranged the folding chairs in the back corner of the movie set. I would first like to explain how the hologram machine works. I assume that some of you guys are familiar with lasers and software?"

"No problem," says the senator. "Be as technical as you think necessary."

"OK, great. Just needed to know the audience." The hologram technician now provides a detailed explanation of how the hologram machines work. "A hologram is a photographic recording of a light field rather than an image using a lens. It is an encoding of the light field as an interference pattern of variations in the opacity, density, or surface profile of the photographic medium. I am sure that all of you are familiar with how a TV paints an image on the screen. In TV technology, a cathode ray tube sends a beam across the screen and paints a picture. Holograms are created in a similar way. The difference is we use a laser light. We need a minimum of four lasers, which 'scan' the hologram object. The inference produced by the laser beams scanning the items is recorded and transmitted to the receiving lasers using the fiber optic cables. The receiving lasers, which are positioned at the four corners of the receiving location then reproduce the exact image scanned.

The laser technician continues: "I have set up a demonstration." He points to four lasers guns set up as a rectangle, one laser at each corner. He then points to the opposite side of the movie set. It is approximately fifty meters from the recording set where he points out the receiving lasers, which will project the hologramed image. He places a six-foot chess piece in the center of the recording devices. Then he turns on the lasers. He looks at the screen and makes some adjustments. He flips a switch, and the identical chess piece image appears in the new location on the opposite side of the movie set.

Vinny says, "Hot dog! Amazing! Just like beam me up Scottie in Star Trek, this is really cool."

Louie, who has been listening very intently, says, "How will it work if the object is moving?"

"We can handle some movement," says the technician, but we need to restrict it to slow-motion type movements."

"Where is the restriction, laser scan, transmission, processing, or software?"

The technician now knows this crowd is not the average one; they are way above his head. He looks at Mr. Ramos.

"Louie—I think that's your name, right?" asks Johnny.

"Yes, sir."

"The hologram was designed and built under a contract to my company. Their chief engineer is a man by the name of Ismail Mankowitz. He has a PhD from Stanford. I will call him this afternoon and have him come by and discuss these items with you."

"Thank you, sir."

The demo continues. Rose raises her hand and asks, "Will the hologram transport the image of a human?

"Of course," says the technician. "Would you like to volunteer?"

"Will it cause any harm?"

"No harm. It is actually safer than placing your cell phone to your ear."

"OK, where do I stand?'

Just place your feet on the footprints, similar to a full-body scan at the airport,"

"Got it." Rose steps on the platform. The tech flips the switch, and like magic, Rose is transported fifty yards to the other side of the movie set.

"Can I move my arms?" asks Rose.

"Yes, go ahead." The image maintains synchronization as long as Rose moves in slow motion. She makes a movement like 'safe at home plate.' The image shows the beginning of the movement and the end of the safe sign.

Louie and Ismail pull an all-nighter. They quickly determine that the areas that need improvement are the processing power and the software. Louie has brought the ten-board, four-processors-per-board parallel processor with the Linux operating system. Louie and Ismail port the software from the Windows 10 operating system in a Dell computer to the custom-built forty parallel processors. Immediately they see an improvement in performance. They spend six hours streamlining the code. By 10 A.M. on the second day, they are finished. Louie and Ismail replace the Dell computer with the Linux. They first use it on an old fashion clock to see the second hand move across the face of the clock. The image is excellent, with no notable lag time, and the motion is continuous.

Louie calls the team. "Rose, I think we got the hologram where you want it. Can you gather up the team and come check it out?

Rose is very excited. "Great work, Louie. We will be right over."

The team arrives in half an hour. Immediately Rose duplicates the safe motion. The image is precise. An observer looking at the real image and the duplicate would not be able to detect the difference. The only thing that would be a giveaway is that the real image has the laser guns in the four corners. After Rose gives the hologram her blessing, all of the team members want to see themselves duplicated. Jeff and Vinny make sudden moves: quickdraw, fall down, jumping jacks, and moonwalking. The image is the exact replica of the real McCoy.

After Vinny make every imaginable quick move he can think of, he goes into one of his patented think modes. After rubbing his chin and pushing his hands through his hair he says, "So let me get this hologram gizmo correct. It is a Virtual Information Transport and Restoration system?"

Jeff, "Are you stating the obvious or asking a question? Is what you said, is it a Virtual Information Transport and Restoration system, or in short, VITR?"

"That's it," say Vinny, "We call our gizmo VICTOR!"

Once the team is convinced that the "VICTOR" will work. The planning starts. Rose takes the lead.

She says, "My parents have been taking golf vacations to Scotland for years, even when I was a little girl. We have my mom call Matilda and say with excitement that this year, her daughter Rose and her boyfriend will join them for their traditional two-week vacation in Scotland. We select a location where we are in control of the environment. We select a ranch or farmhouse that is remote from cities. The assassin will likely feel that he has the advantage. However, being in a remote location will allow us to identify the assassin through surveillance of the likely airport, car rentals, and hotels. In addition, we can fly the drone for twenty-four-seven surveillance. Unless someone sees a show-stopper, we proceed with the details."

Claude says, "OK, we have the high-level plan. I recommend that someone other than Rose or myself fly to Bristol and brief Mr. and Mrs. Mathews on the details. The ideal person would be either Jeff or Vinny. They make a return visit as the solar experts. Perfectly natural. We first need to have them select the vacation spot. We will give them the required parameters."

Rose thinks for a few seconds. *Yes, we need to talk to my parents directly. If Herbert tells my dad, who tells my mom that I will be a lure, she may have a heart attack. Especially after what happened to Karrie.* Karrie, Rose's younger sister, was murdered by a terrorist wearing a suicide vest. Karrie was riding a bus when the terrorist exploded the Semtex-10 that was strapped to his vest.

The solar panel items were left at the Mathews property storage shed. At the time, it was not known if Jeff and Vinny would need to return to the Mathews house—it was the right call.

That evening, Jesse has dinner with his friend Johnny. He says, "I would really like to thank you for the use of the hologram equipment."

"No, no, it should be me thanking you," replies Johnny. "Do you know how much the upgrades your software expert completed will benefit me? With the ability to create holograms showing all action, I will take the lead in producing sci-fi films."

"It's been a real pleasure working with you—thanks for the help."

"By the way, that English gal you got working for you, she is s real head turner. If she ever wanted a career in the movies, she could easily be like a Jennifer Garner in *Peppermint*."

Jesse smiles and says, "She is the real deal—a real badass."

"Really! Well, my offer is doubled; tell her that if she gets tired of killing assholes, she has a job in Hollywood.

Chapter Seventeen

Mathews Vacation

Bristol and Scotland

Jeff, Vinny, and Alex fly from Los Angeles to Alexandria, Virginia. The WMA team still has an office at the building in Bristol. After Jeff and Vinny talk to the Mathews, Alex will use the lockpick gun to enter the suspect's office. Since they know the office number, the lockpick guns are smaller than the one they used initially. It will look like he is a customer. No one will note it if they play back the recording.

The three stay two nights in Alexandria and fly to Bristol. Alex will remain at the rental until the night that Mrs. Mathews makes the call to Matilda. Jeff and Vinny again rent a white panel van, apply the solar panel magnetic sign, and head to the Mathews house. They now know that all of their actions outside of the home are being recorded. They are satisfied that no bugs exist in the house. Mr. Mathews makes arrangements for him and Mrs. Mathews to have dinner at the country club Saturday night. Mr. Mathews, who is well known, requests a corner table away from any eavesdroppers. The dinner is at 7 P.M. Mr. and Mrs. Mathews arrive first. Ten minutes later, Jeff and Vinny arrive. Both are dressed in suits, ties, and polished shoes and have combed their hair. They look like sales representatives pushing cemetery plots.

The greeter at the door welcomes them to the club. Jeff tells her their names, and she says, "Yes, Mr. and Mrs. Mathews are waiting at the bar. I will show you the way."

Mrs. Mathews sees the two and waves. "My, you look so different."

"Thank you, ma'am," says Vinny.

After some small talk, Mr. Mathews opens the conversation. "I heard from Herbert. He told us that it would be best if we had a face-to-face conversation."

"Yes, sir," says Jeff. He gives the Mathews the complete story of why he and Vinny were disguised as solar panel professionals. He tells the Mathews about their house, that it is under video surveillance and the landline was wiretapped. He then goes on to tell them about the hologram machine. Vinny interjects throughout the discussion. As the evening progresses, Mrs. Mathews takes a liking to Vinny. Jeff detects this, and he slowly lets Vinny take over the explanation of the hologram. Mrs. Mathews wants assurance that her daughter will not be in danger. As Vinny is explaining the hologram, it is obvious that neither Mr. nor Mrs. Mathews know that their daughter is a trained killing machine. "A real badass!"

Finally, Mrs. Mathews is convinced that Rose will not be in harm's way. Jeff, who is a golfer, turns the conversation to golf. Immediately Mr. Mathews jumps in: "We take a summer vacation to Scotland every year."

"Great," says Jeff. "I have played the Old Course, Carnoustie, and Gleneagles. I liked Gleneagles the best. It reminded me of the American courses." Jeff then uses the opportunity to tell the Mathews that Rose and Claude want to join them for their next summer vacation. Both find it odd that Rose is asking in a roundabout way.

Mrs. Mathews says, "Why doesn't Rose just call me and ask to join us?"

Now the entire plot has to be explained to the Mathews. After Jeff, with help from Vinny, explains the reasoning—Rose's parents understand and agree to do their part.

Jeff is prepared for the conversation. He reaches down to his briefcase and pulls out a map of Scotland. There is a circle on it between Saint Andrews and Carnoustie. Under the circle is a note from Rose: THIS WOULD BE IDEAL, MAMACITA AND PAPI. LOVE YOU. As Mrs. Mathews reads the letter, she starts to tear up. She sniffles and says, "This had to come from Rosita. Only my children call me Mamacita."

Vinny says, "OK, Mamacita—ah, Mrs. Mathews. You will call Matilda tomorrow and ask her if she can take care of the dogs. Can you do that? Tell her you will be gone for two weeks from this Saturday. You and your husband will be departing on a two-week golfing vacation. You will be very excited because Rosita and her boyfriend will be joining you."

"Oh, no, we always take our dogs with us."

"OK, mention that the dogs will be with you and ask her if she can please keep an eye on the property."

"That's not a problem; she does that whenever we are away."

Alexandria, Virginia

As the Bristol team members are in discussions with the Mathews, the remaining team has been busy in Alexandria. WMA has a contract with the Alexandria Police Department. The company takes the cars as they are delivered from the factory and configures them with radios, laptop computers, IP-encrypted internet, sirens, klaxon lights, heavy-duty dumpers, and the grille partition between the driver and passengers in the back seat. To complete this work, the company has rented a garage with twenty-foot ceilings and three garage doors. The vehicle garage has twenty thousand square feet of space with the three garages separated by high walls. The garages are connected using double doors to move equipment or workbenches between them.

In one of the garages, "VICTOR "has been set up. Rose has been sitting in the "primary movie set" and practicing falling off her chair to the right and to the left. She needs to simulate a bullet striking her in the head. All of the WMA operators are familiar with what a sniper bullet does when hitting the head.

Mateo says, "Everything looks good except the head is not exploding as it would if a sniper bullet hit it?"

Rose agrees. "We are going to need Louie and his team to modify my body as I am falling."

Claude makes a call to Louie. "Louie, we are going to need you or your team to make some modifications to the hologram software."

"OK, Chris and I will be there. Where are you?

"We are at the vehicle facility on Eisenhower Avenue. Near the FedEx office."

"OK, I know where it is—I was there with Jeff a couple of months ago. Give me two hours; I am working on high-priority items on our security software program."

"OK, we will take a break and have an early lunch hour. See you in a couple of hours."

In two hours, Louie and Chris, who is one of his senior programmers, arrive at the vehicle facility. Claude and Rose explain the problem to them.

Louie looks around and sees the forty-processor Linux hardware. Chris and Louie walk over to the processor. They both connect their laptops to it and start typing on the keyboard.

Louie asks, "Is there any way that you can show me what the head will look like when the sniper bullet hits it."

Rose opens her laptop and searches Google for "Rifle shots to targets." She says, "Louie and Chris, take a look at this." The video shows what happens to watermelons, melons, turnips, cabbage heads, and other fruits. The video narrator goes on to explain that these items are simulating the head of a person. He explains that the bullets from sniper rifles are longer than the average bullet. He explains that the cartridge is packed with extra-high explosive.

"Wow," says Chris, "pretty gruesome. Louie. What do you think?"

"With software, we can do anything."

Louie and Chris talk amongst themselves. Louie then asks that two recordings be made, one with her head tilting left and one tilting right before she falls from her chair.

"No problem," she says. "Let's roll."

Matt has remained quiet during the exchange of what is needed. Finally, he says, "Since I will be the technician who will handle the 'movie scene,' let me and Mateo set up the primary and playback scenes. It will be vital that we have as much training as possible before we set up at the actual location."

They all agree. The two sets are made ready.

Matt says, "I will find a sound that simulates a shot being fired. Rose, when you hear the shot, do your thing and make the fall."

"Great idea," says Louie. "This will give us the point where we integrate the software that has the exploding watermelon."

They all know that it will be a simulated Rose head, but no one wants to mention that it is her head. Louie and Chris complete the integrated software in less than three hours. If you did not know that it was fake, you would swear that Rose was killed by a sniper bullet. Every time the hologram is played, they all look at Rose. *Is she still alive?*

Bristol, England

Jeff, Vinny, and Alex are back at the Airbnb rented house. The day after Jeff and Vinny have dinner with the Mathews, Alex goes to the cubicle rental building. He arrives at 9 A.M. and goes to the office they have rented. He takes out the small portal lockpick gun and a pair of headsets with alligator clips. He exits the office, walks at an average pace, and stops at the assassin's office. He takes the lockpick gun and inserts the key, and in ten seconds, he enters the office. Alex has been here before, so he knows what he wants to do. He clips the alligator clips to the outgoing landline and connects the 3.5-millimeter plug to a small electrical box, which acts as an analog phone. He connects the headsets to the electrical phone box, and he waits. In fifteen minutes, the earphones come alive—there is an incoming call. He sees in the display of the electrical box the +1 615-phone number being dialed.

Mrs. Mathews is on the line with Matilda. Matilda answers the phone. "Hi, Maria, it's a beautiful day. Would you like to go for a walk? You know your dogs could use the exercise."

"Yes," says Maria, "that would be very nice. I can meet you at the park at two this afternoon." Matilda starts talking about gardening, but Maria interrupts her.

She says with much excitement, "Mattie, Mattie, I need to tell you something!"

"Yes, of course. You sound so excited. What is it?"

"My husband had a call from Rosita on his cell phone. Guess what?" Before Mattie can answer, Maria says, "My daughter and her boyfriend will be joining us for our summer vacation! I am really excited to see her and her boyfriend."

"That's great. Will I hear wedding bells soon?"

"Perhaps, maybe a surprise when we are at our rental in Scotland."

"Remember, let me know when you leave. I will check on your house while you are away. By the way, where are you staying?"

"We will be staying at a cottage just north of Dundee, near the village of Forfar. As soon as I have the address, I will let you know. Richard is taking care of the rental property. However, I am fairly certain that we will be staying at my nephew's villa, The Sea Serpent, near Forfar."

"I think that's great that you will be seeing your daughter. Is she still working in the intelligence field?"

"Yes, I think so; you know, she never tells me anything. Richard says that it is super-secret and she cannot talk about it."

"Yeah, we are all so proud of her."

Matilda laughs. "Your daughter may be the woman James Bond."

Murfreesboro, Tennessee

It is 3 A.M. in Tennessee. In the evening hours, two Klansmen are assigned to monitor the calls. The frequency of the calls is on average one or two per night. With the light load, one Klansman dozes off on the couch. The second Klansman monitors the calls. The alert starts blinking on the display—incoming call! The Klansman puts on his headsets and gets ready to monitor the call. As he is listening, he kicks the Klansman sleeping on the couch. With much excitement, he barks, "Joey, wake up! We got something really hot!"

Joey wakes up and rubs his eyes. "Yes, asshole, what's up?"

"Shut up and put on the headsets."

"OK, OK, hope this is not a recipe for stuffed cabbage."

Joey puts on the headsets and starts listening. He says, "Holy shit, this is it! Should we wake up Wolf and let him know?"

"No, we have the recording. Last time we woke him at 3 A.M., he reamed us. It can wait."

"OK, hope you're right."

Bristol England

Cubicle Office Complex

Alex has been listening to the two Klansmen. He disconnects the alligator clips, packs the analog phone, stuffs them in his backpack, and leaves the office complex. He joins Jeff and Vinny at the Airbnb.

"How did it go, Alex?" asks Jeff.

"Outstanding. You coached Mrs. Mathews very well. She said all the right things. I was able to listen to the assholes monitoring the call. One of the monitors was named Joey. They referred a major player by the name of 'Wolf.' He is either the assassin or the chief asshole. We need to make a call to the team in Alexandria and brief them on our findings."

"So, you think that the fish took the bait?" says Vinny.

"Absolutely, hook, line, and sinker!"

"Yippee-Ya-Kio," says Jeff, "the 'sting' is set. The hunted now becomes the hunter. I am gonna like this hunting party. Better than when my brother and I hunted squirrels in the Virginia forest!"

Soon Alex, Jeff, and Vinny are on an encrypted conference call with the Alexandria team. They provide the status of each of the teams.

Rose says, "Claude, we need to find the ideal rental to set up VICTOR."

"Agreed,' says Claude. "After we find the ideal rental, we provide the info to your parents through our back channels. We will need one more phone call with the address of the vacation home."

"Agreed," says Rose. The conference call ends, and Claude and Rose start searching for the ideal rental.

Rose finds what she thinks is the ideal vacation property. Before she makes the reservation, she contacts Herbert. "Uncle Herb, I have found the ideal location for our vacation with my parents." She gives the address of the property and the link on the internet where they can view it. She tells Uncle Herb to please pass the information to her parents to get their approval. Two days later, he and Rose talk about the rental property.

"Rose," says Herb, "your dad says that they already have a property that they have been using every year. It belongs to your cousin Robert. He has done very well as an attorney. He had a small villa built near Forfar, Scotland. I am sending you a link through the encrypted file transfer service that we have been using. The name of the villa is The Sea Serpent."

Rose is obligated to download the file. She does and is amazed. It is perfect. She contacts Uncle Herb and tells him, "Uncle Herb, tell Mom and Dad that we will be honored to use cousin Robert's vacation home."

Jeff and Vinny must complete their actions regarding the solar panel installation. The Alexandria crew needs to start packing the hologram equipment and a complete package that includes weapons, drone, cameras, clothes, and other ancillary gear. The WMA 650 Gulfstream returns to Alexandria ready to fly the team to Scotland. The vacation will begin two weeks from the coming Saturday. They have seventeen days to complete all planning.

Assassin Prepares the Plan

Murfreesboro, Tennessee

Joey and Emmitt are excited to tell Wolfgang about last night's recording. Wolfgang walks into the monitor room at 7:30. Before he can say anything, Joey and Emmitt are talking over each other.

Wolfgang screams, "Yeah, assholes, cut it out! One at a time." He points to Joey and says, "OK, so what's going on?"

"We had some major activity last night. The old lady was yacking with her friend about a vacation to Scotland."

Before Joey can continue, Wolfgang interrupts. "So, what's the big fucking deal about a vacation? This only means that we are going to have a dead hole for two or three more weeks!"

Emmitt quickly says, "We know where your prey will be!"

"What the hell are you talking about? Come on, get with it."

"Yes, sir. The bitch Rose and her boyfriend will be going to Scotland with the old lady and the old man."

"So, you heard this last night?"

"Yes, sir." Emmitt thinks that Wolfgang will praise him for giving him the information on the bitch.

Wolfgang's face grows angry, and he shouts, "WHAT THE HELL IS GOING ON?! I TOLD BOTH OF YOU ASSHOLES THAT IF THERE

WERE ANY CALLS THAT HAD TO DO WITH THE WHEREABOUTS OF THE BITCH, I WAS TO BE INFORMED IMMEDIATELY! Now, what do you not understand?"

Joey then says, "Last time we gave you a message at 2 A.M. you were—"

Wolfgang interrupts, saying, "You stupid idiots, now queue up the recording, I would like to listen."

"Yes, sir."

The recording is queued up and Wolfgang listens intently. "OK, good job. We still do not know the address."

Emmitt says, "Yes, but the old lady said that as soon as she knew the address, she would let her friend know."

Wolfgang gives Emmitt a disgusted look, "Brilliant, Einstein. You think I'm stupid? I heard the old woman. Stay on the monitor stations and let me know when we have the address."

"Yes, sir," Joey and Emmitt answer in unison.

Wolfgang leaves the monitor room and begins the three P's—planning, preparation, and practice. He knows that this will be the most difficult of all the assassinations that he has successfully completed. The prey in this case is an expert special operations agent. He needs to think this through.

He quickly determines that he must have a spotter. He decides that he will have Wilhelm Strassman assist him in this contract kill. Wilhelm can be trusted entirely. He has been a member of the camp for two years. He is the first cousin to Wolf's girlfriend, Gretchen Miller. Wilhelm is known in the camp as Will. Will was born in Montana and raised in a trailer camp in rural Mississippi. Will's mom is Gretchen's sister. Will has always been big for his age. As a young boy, he was always getting into fights. He never was a good student and always said, "Who the hell needs an education? I can always pick some pocket, knock off a convenience store, or carjack a car." His fault was that he could easily be influenced by the gangs and hoodlums in his neighborhood. At the age of eighteen, he joined a gang that was dealing in drugs. It was easy money. He was given the task of transporting drugs from the Mexican border to Jackson, Mississippi. One night, while driving through East Texas, he was spotted by the Texas Highway Patrol for speeding. He thought that he could outrun the cop. He was right—but he could not outrun the radio. After more than five minutes into the chase, he lost his tail. He thought he was in the clear. Up ahead, he saw the blue police lights. He quickly made a U-turn and headed back in the opposite direction. Again, blue lights. He made a stupid decision to blast through the roadblock. As he drove through the roadblock at ninety miles an hour—BANG, BANG, BANG, BANG! Four tires blew.

The car flipped over four times, and he was thrown from the vehicle. The next day, he woke up in the hospital handcuffed to the bed. He was found guilty of possession of drugs, resisting arrest, and endangering the lives of police officers. He served two years in the Texas penitentiary. After being released from jail, he again found the dark side of humanity. He joined a gang called "the Sons of the Confederacy." They wanted to return life to the way it was before the Civil War. They became fans of President Trout. They liked his mantra, "Make America Great Again." To them, it meant "Back to the Future."

The gangs were influenced by all the Trout crowds yelling and screaming, "We will not be replaced." To the gangs, this meant that they had to take action. They decided to burn black churches. The gang members convinced Will to torch three of them. The FBI took over the case and were close to arresting Will. He traveled to Tennessee and sought his cousin Gretchen.

Gretchen took him in, but she told him, "You screw up, and we kick you out—maybe we turn you over to the FBI and receive the reward."

"Don't worry, you will get no problems from me."

Will has been in the camp for two years. Over time, he's become close to the camp leader, Wolfgang. He likes Wolfgang, who is a natural leader and does not take shit from anyone. He loves the military discipline that Wolfgang introduced to the camp. Over the past two years, Wolfgang has successfully carried out four contract murders. Two were mafia crime bosses, one was a crooked politician, and one was an organized crime stool. None received any headlines. The killings were relegated to the back pages of all of the newspapers. Having selected Wilhelm as his assistant, Wolfgang needs to plan the assassination carefully. He writes down a list of the many items that need to be planned.

- One: Use the satellite viewing from Google Earth to understand the terrain around Forfar.
- Two: Dogs will be at the vacation home. Order an Ozonics machine.
- Three: Order the best human odor elimination money can buy.
- Four: Buy insect repellant.
- Five: Buy two rugged backpacks.
- Six: Order four Pelican cases.
- Seven: Order a DJI-4 drone with a high-definition camera.
- Eight: Camo clothes from the hunting store.
- Nine: Two night vision goggles and infrared monocle.
- Ten: Black face paint, tight-fitting gloves.
- Eleven: Sharpen the hunting knife
- Twelve: Check out the sightings on the long rifle
- Thirteen: Pack my own bullets with high-explosive power.
- Fourteen: Practice with Wilhelm on the firing range.

After the completion of phase one, Wolf and Will travel to Scotland. The long rifle and ammunition will be shipped via DHL. The shipping forms will address the need for the long rifle for hunting purposes. All other items can be shipped via regular DHL packaging. The preparation phase will need to be completed on site. He will wait until they have a specific address.

The address of the vacation home is intercepted by Joey and Emmitt two days later. The intercept occurs at 3 A.M. Tennessee time. Joey calls Wolfgang immediately after the call ends. Wolfgang takes the call and says, "OK, good work. I will be in at 8 A.M."

Joey looks at Emmitt and says, "Fucking asshole!"

Wolfgang and Wilhelm will need a cover story when they journey to Scotland. They research on the internet and find that there are wildcats and feral mountain goats. Their cover story will be that they are photographers interested in still shots and videos of these two animals. According to the article on the internet, wildcats are extremely hard to view. They are very cunning and will avoid contact with humans. This will explain the cameras, drone, Ozonics odor suppressor, body lotions, and their clothing.

They make their arrangements to rent rooms at the Malmaison Hotel in Dundee, Scotland. Dundee is a town of over 150,000 inhabitants. Wolfgang believes that it is better to hide in the big city. They will take a flight to London. There, they will rent a four-wheel Land Rover. This will be in concert with the cover story of driving to the countryside to photograph wild animals.

One week before the Mathews are driving to their vacation spot in Forfar, Wolfgang and Wilhelm arrive in Dundee. The following day, they dress in their "hunting" gear and drive to the address of the house to be rented by the Mathews family. They first do a drive-by and note any unusual features that may cause a problem. The rental property turns out to be a secluded villa. There is an entry gate to the property with a sign that reads "The Sea Serpent." The terrain around the property is rugged, with small hills. The brushes are very heavy and will be difficult to traverse. Wolfgang is licking his chops. He says to Wilhelm, "This situation is ideal. My guess is that they have selected the property for privacy. This is to our benefit."

"The dense bush will require that we be close to the house," says Wilhelm. "This is good and bad. The good is that the shot will be easier. The bad is that we may be spotted. Also, remember they are bringing their dogs. We will need to have the wind blowing toward us."

"Tomorrow we return. Be ready for a long hike. We will park our Land Rover a good two miles from the property and recon the site on foot."

"I noted a clearing about two miles up the road. We can park there and continue on foot."

"Agreed. We will need our heavy clothing. Looks like the bushes have thorns."

The following day, Wolfgang and Wilhelm dress in their heavy hunting clothes. They also take the DJI-Phantom-4 drone. They have outfitted it with an expensive ten-thousand-dollar camera. They park the Land Rover two miles from The Sea Serpent. They start on their way to the house. The going is very tough. Wolfgang says, "Reminds me of my training in the Marine Corps, jungle warfare in Panama." He sees that Wilhelm is having a problem keeping up. He tells him, "Come on, suck it up."

Wilhelm says, "Don't worry about me. I am a little slow, but I am like steady Eddie. I will get there."

What looked like a one-hour hike takes three hours. They are finally two hundred meters from the house. Wolfgang takes off his backpack and pulls out the drone. He tells Wilhelm, "When I was in Iraq, the ragheads used these drones. They could get them from a Chinese website for one thousand bucks. We in the US Marines had shit. I had to shoot up a bunch of shitheads to get a couple of these drones. They really work well; I could see over the buildings or the mountain. I saved hundreds of lives. After my commander found out that I was using equipment that was not listed in the table of equipment, he reamed my ass. Can you imagine—these fucking ring knockers don't know a damn thing about fighting to win a war."

Wilhelm is confused. "What the hell does a table of equipment and knocking a ring have to do with flying drones?"

"Exactly," says Wolfgang. "Not a damn thing!" He thinks, *best to leave this military jargon to myself—Wilhelm will never understand. He is here because of his eyesight and his loyalty to the KKK.*

Wolfgang cannot find a clear area to launch the drone. He snaps on the propellers and installs the camera. He has Wilhelm hold the drone over his head, and then he starts it. All four propellers turn on. Wilhelm almost loses his grip, but he somehow manages to hold on tight.

Wolfgang yells, "OK, let go!"

Wilhelm let's go, and the drone takes off like a jackrabbit, straight up through a clearing in the trees. Wolfgang sends the drone to three hundred feet. He clearly sees the house.

Wilhelm is looking over his shoulder at the display. He says, "Holy shit, that's not a house. It's a mansion."

"More like a villa."

"Who the hell owns a villa like that?"

"Brits. They have a lot of money. Probably some lawyer, doctor, or company CEO. The old man, he is a retired ambassador. Probably has a lot of rich connections. He likely arranged with one of his rich friends to use the villa. He thinks that the remote location will protect his daughter,"

“He’s dead wrong. You outsmarted those idiots. We know exactly where she is. I am really looking forward to next week when we knock the head off that bitch.”

Wolfgang flies the drone around the villa. He does not want to get any closer than the three hundred meters. The video is all recorded; he will analyze the video tomorrow. They still have five days before the Mathews party arrives.

Chapter Eighteen

Wolfgang Prepares Plan B and C

Dundee, Scotland

Wolf is confident that that the plan will work; however, in the Marines, they always had a plan B and plan C. The main plan is simple: Wilhelm and he will lie in wait at the chosen sniper nest for a clear shot at the target. There is some chance that the target may never provide a clean shot; thus, Wolf needs to have contingency plans. He knows that the Mathews play golf. He assumes that they will likely play the courses in the Forfar area, In Scotland, all golf courses are public, unlike in America. Wolf studies the Forfar area using Google and finds two golf courses within three miles of the villa, plus the Saint Andrews course. He has a couple of days to kill, so he and Will go golfing three of the four days. He calls the Forfar and Kirriemuir Golf Clubs and makes a tee time. The Saint Andrews Old Course does not have any tee times available until Friday.

Wolf tells Will, "We are going golfing the next two days."

"I didn't bring my clubs."

"That's not a problem. I didn't bring them either. We can rent sets at the golf course. Will, when we are there, we need to be aware of possible sniper sites. The site needs to be behind some bushes or trees, and it needs to have a clear line of sight to the golf course and an easy exit, preferably near a road."

"I thought we were going to kill the bitch at the villa?"

"This is a contingency plan."

"What the hell is a con-tin-e-gee."

"Contingency, you idiot! It is a backup plan in case the bitch never sticks out her head."

"Oh, I get it, kind of a second plan. This should work out well. I am not a very good golfer. I spend most of my time in the woods and bushes trying to find all my lost balls. This is perfect. I will bring a small notebook and take notes. You know those professional golfers are always taking notes. I will look like a real pro!"

For two days, Wolf and Will play the local golf courses. In Scotland, there are no golf carts. All green fees come with a caddy. The two caddies are very polite and professional. After Wolf and Will finish their rounds, the two caddies wash the clubs and expect a tip. The tip is only one pound. After the caddies are back in line for the next golfers, they give Wolf and Will the finger and shake their heads. "Ugly Americans."

Will's caddy says, "That bloke had to be the worse golfer I have ever seen. If I didn't know better, I would think that he purposely was playing from the rough—what an idiot!"

On the way back to their hotel, Wolf asks Will, "Well, did you find any good sniper nests?"

"Boy, did I, more than one. The trees and bushes on fairway number fifteen were parallel to a country road, a nice getaway spot."

"Good work Will; hopefully, we will not need to set up a sniper nest at one of these golf courses. Tomorrow we will play at Saint Andrews, the Old Course. I have only read about the Old Course, and it is not suitable for a sniper nest. The course does not have any tall bushes or trees. It was built along the North Sea, and it is known as a links course. The only hole that is next to a road is the Road Hole. However, the road is the main road into Saint Andrews, where hundreds of tourists are shopping in the gift shops. It would be impossible to set up a sniper nest and have a realistic getaway plan."

"So, boss, if we cannot use the geezer course to shoot the bitch, why are we playing the course?"

"Will, if you are a golfer, you need to at least once play at the birthplace of golf. Every golfer dream of playing the Old Course in Saint Andrews. It is on their bucket list."

"OK, I understand, kind of like visiting Montgomery, Alabama, the capital of the Confederacy. That's on my bucket list."

"Yeah, something like that."

Chapter Nineteen

The WMA Team Prepares the Plan

Farm on the Rappahannock River

Jean Claude St. Pier was an outstanding high school football player in Louisiana. He was heavily recruited by every major university in the US that had a football program. He chose the University of Southern California, where he was an all-American middle linebacker. He was drafted by the Oakland Raiders and made the fifty-two-man roster after his first year in the pros. After his first year as a professional football player, a close friend of his, Pat Tillman, who played for the Arizona team, was killed in Afghanistan. Jean Claude soon joined the Rangers and served several years in both Afghanistan and Iraq. He preferred his middle name, "Claude." It sounded more masculine. Throughout Claude's career in football and the military, he lived by the seven P's: plan, prepare, practice, prevent, piss, poor, and performance." He had first heard of the seven P's from his Pee-Wee coaches when he was six years old. He liked the motto, and as he went through his life, the seven P's took on more and more significance. The planning for the fake death of Rose make it absolutely necessary that the seven P's be followed—failure is not an option!

Claude will design and implement a plan that will be near foolproof. He has been around for a number of years; he knows that a plan is only good until the first shot is fired on the battlefield. He will use a one-hundred-acre farm along the Rappahannock River in north-central Virginia. The farm is the property of the Montana family. The senator's aunt Betty lives on the farm. The farm is ideal for planning and acting out all of the parts for the simulated attack on Rose.

The team meets in a building used to maintain the farm equipment. Two folding tables with folding chairs are used to gather the team and discuss the strawman design. The simulated attack will need workers to address the different action characters. Claude has been provided additional personnel, all WMA employees.

Claude begins the discussion: "Matt, you and Kyle will set up and configure the hologram scenes. We have the floor plans and video of the rooms of the rented home." He shows them a video from the inside and outside of the rented home. It is actually a small villa. It consists of three levels and a basement floor. Most importantly, the second level has a wraparound balcony. The corner balcony has a high roof with a three-foot decorated wall protecting the occupants from falling. The corner of the terrace is ideal for the simulation of the shot. The terrace is viewable from two sides, the east and north. Claude now shows a hand-drawn sketch of the corner balcony. It shows Rose sitting inside the building.

He says, "Matt, you will need to build a scene that resembles this configuration. The inside scene must closely resemble the surrounding items from the outside scene."

"I do not think that this will be a problem," says Matt. "We will make sure that the scene is pristine and has as few items as possible. The major problem will be the seamless integration of the people seated with Rose."

Claude turns to Louie. "What do you think? Will this be a problem?"

"Not likely," says Louie. "The hologram processor and software have now been upgraded to handle any items painted by the lasers."

Rose asks, "Is there any restriction to the size of the hologram field?"

"Good question," replies Louie. "I do not know the answer, but we can run some tests and quickly find out."

"Matt and Kyle will work with Louie to determine the outer limits of the hologram," says Claude.

"Will do," replies Matt. "One request. Can we have Rick from the comms division join us? He is a good carpenter. We need expertise in this area."

"Consider it done. I will have Rick here first thing in the morning."

Claude now turns his attention to Mateo. "Mateo, you will simulate the sniper. This will be your assignment."

"OK, will do," says Mateo. "I did bring my M24 sniper rifle. In preparation for this simulation, I also made my own bullets with high-power gunpowder. The rifle has the scope mounting brackets, so I am ready for daytime and nighttime shooting. I do have a question. Will I need a spotter for the simulation?"

"Yes, let's try and simulate to the last detail. We may find some problems that we will need to overcome. I will assign Kyle to act as your spotter."

"From what distance shall I fire the shot?"

"Good question. Let's fire from one, two, and five hundred meters. This will be important for the travel of the shot."

"Yes, and don't forget the shot detector. It will be different based on the distance to the shot location."

"Good point. Do we have any experts in this area?"

"As a matter of fact, yes, we do. Did I hear that you are having Rick help out with the building of the simulated porch?"

"Yes. Matt said he was going to see that Rick would be here tomorrow."

"OK, have Rick give us some advice on the shot-detection system."

"Will do."

Rose has been listening to the simulation of her death. She says, "Excuse me; I have an idea for the death scene. We need to have a situation where there is as little motion as possible but looks realistic. I would recommend that I be playing bridge, especially where I am the dummy."

The entire party sitting at the table starts laughing when Rose makes reference to the dummy. Mateo thinks, *she is going to be shot at and she still has a sense of humor.*

"Great idea," says Claude. "Now we just need to find three people who know how to play bridge."

The attention turns back to the shooting scene. "Mateo," says Claude, "have you used the shot-detection hardware?"

"Yes, but it does have limitations. The further the shot, the less accurate it is. Inside of two hundred meters, it will detect the location to approximately two meters. Outside of two hundred meters, it's anywhere from five to ten meters.

"For those of us who are not familiar with shot-detection technology, can you provide a quick tutorial?"

"Sure. It's actually pretty simple. You need at least three shot-detection stations. Each station has a small microphone antenna array that receives the sound waves. We call them sound antennas for just antennas for convenience. Each station has a small processor that determines the angle of arrival. This is referred to as the line of bearing, or LOB. The three stations are connected by some communications media. A process like a laptop receives all three LOBs, and the location of the shot is where the three LOBs intersect. This is how we will find shithead."

"Sounds pretty simple," says Rose. "Will it work?"

"We will soon find out."

Mateo, Claude, and Rose walk out of the conference. Mateo walks to the equipment van and pulls out four Pelican cases. Each case has a small microphone antenna. They walk out to the field and place stakes in a triangle. The legs of the triangle are approximately five hundred meters apart. They walk back to the conference area and place the antennas and the processes on the table. Mateo connects an RS-232 cable to the base of the antenna and connects the other side to a battery-powered processor. The antenna is carried outside the equipment building.

Mateo then calls Rick to come into the equipment building. He says, "Rick, take this starter gun and walk toward the big oak tree. Also carry this handheld radio. Start walking till I call you on the radio to stop."

Rick looks at the microphone antenna and the RF cable and says, "Yes, I can do that, but with the small antenna, you will not get more than twenty yards of accuracy."

"We need at least five yards."

"Never happen unless you have the sound of a bazooka that you are pinpointing."

"So, what do you recommend?"

"You need a good pre-amp with a good noise figure. Something with better than a three-to-one ratio."

"What the hell is a noise figure?"

"An amplifier that amplifies the signal and reduces the noise. Also, I would install a programmable filter after the pre-amp. This way, we can tune a notch filter. The notch filter will allow only the sound from the gun. Using the pre-amp and the notch filter will increase the range to better than one thousand meters and give you an accuracy of five meters!"

"OK, let's do it."

"Give me a half-hour, and I can order the items from the internet. We should have the items by tomorrow."

The next day, the pre-amps and the programmable notch filters arrive. Rick unboxes the items. He takes one dipole antenna and connects the pre-amp and the notch filter. The output from the notch filter is connected to the processor. A laptop computer is connected to the process. Rick launches the Firefox web browser. He enters the URL, and the laptop connects to the gun-detection application.

Rick then tells Mateo, "OK, we are ready to test. Have Matt take the antenna and pre-amp outside. Bring the CAT-5 cable inside and connect to the laptop. After that, have Matt take a radio and select channel 5, the maintenance channel."

Matt completes the instructions and picks up the starter gun. He straps on the belt and holsters the gun. He then inserts one cartridge into the gun and slips the additional five cartridges into his belt web pockets. He says, "Ready," and then he keys his radio and says, "Do you copy?" Nothing. Again, he says, "Do you copy?" Nothing! He looks at his radio—it is on channel one. He does the Polish salute and whispers, "Stupid ass—he said channel five." He turns the radio knob to channel five and repeats, "Matt here. Do you copy?"

"Yeah, I copy," says Rick. "Where the hell are you?

"Sorry, had a brain fart. I'm OK now."

"OK, go one hundred paces and stop."

Matt stops at one hundred paces and keys his radio. "I am at one hundred paces."

"Go ahead and shoot the starter gun."

"OK, here goes." BANG!

Rick looks at the audio spectrum and programs the notch filter to the frequency spectrum. He then says, "OK, fire again."

"OK. One, two, three—" BANG!

"OK, I think we got it. Go to two hundred paces and repeat." The exercise is repeated at three, four, and five hundred paces.

Rick says, "OK we have the first detector calibrated to five hundred paces." He and Matt calibrate detectors two and three. They are ready for a location test. Rick, Matt, and Claude set up the detectors in a half-moon. The center detector is about twenty paces behind a straight line from detectors one and three.

Matt takes the starter gun to about three hundred paces from detector number two. Over the radio, Rick says, "OK, Matt, fire the gun." Two seconds later—BANG!

The display on the laptop shows three LOBs. They bisect at a point 320 meters from detector number two. Rick takes the mouse on the computer and inserts a pushpin on the Google map. The pushpin displays the latitude and longitude.

Rick keys his radio. "Matt, using your cellphone, what is your location?"

Matt takes his cellphone and determines his location. He tells Rick, "My position is X and Y."

"OK, they match. Great job. Come on back to the equipment building."

Rose and Claude have been observing the testing. Rose asks, "Do we need to calibrate using a sniper rifle?"

"Absolutely," says Rick. "You are ahead of me."

"I ordered pizza," says Claude. "Let's take a break and get back to our testing this afternoon."

Mateo goes outside and yells, "Pizza! Everybody take a break!"

The ten workers head to the equipment building like horses coming back to the barn. After the pizza break, Rick goes back to the supervision of the porch simulation. It is essential that the dimensions be within one inch of the actual villa wraparound porch. The porch needs to have the exact views from the north and east sides. The remainder of the day is used to finish the porch and set up the hologram and the bridge table in the equipment building.

The next day, the simulated porch, bridge table, and hologram sensors are in place. The gun detectors are placed in the half-moon configuration. The previous day, LAN cables were connected to the three gun detectors. The detectors now are connected using wireless mobile ad-hoc network routers. These routers are known as MANETs and allow the LAN cables to be replaced. This configuration will be required in actual operational conditions. After the "movie set" has been completed, testing will be needed with a sniper rifle.

Claude asks Rick, "Are the gun detectors in place?

"They are good to go," answers Rick. "I am at the computer terminal and will adjust the notch filter using the actual sniper gunshot."

"Mateo, do we have the sand barrel for the target?"

"All set," says Mateo. "I have my M-24 sniper rifle and bullet belt. Ready with twenty-four bullets."

"OK, all team members check your radios, channel five. Mateo, how copy?"

"Mateo here, I copy loud and clear."

"Rick?"

"Ten-four."

"OK, Mateo, move to location one. Transmit when there,"

"Roger." After a moment, Mateo says, "I am at location one."

"OK, go ahead and shoot on three—one, two, three—fire."

BANG!

"Rick, did you detect the shot?"

"Weak. I need to adjust the notch filter."

"OK, tell us when to shoot again."

"Go ahead," says Rick a few seconds later. "Fire at will."

BANG!

"Got it. That's it."

"Mateo," says Claude, "move to any location and fire at will."

Thirty seconds later—BANG!

"Rick, what's your reading?" asks Claude. Rick gives his location.

Mateo says, "Correct." They complete ten different places on the east side and ten positions on the north side. Claude is satisfied that they have good locations.

"OK," he says, "now we need to integrate the sound of the shot with the hologram."

Louie is aware that his turn will be when the shot detector has been properly calibrated. Integrating the sound of the gunshot will be reasonably easy. In thirty minutes, he has integrated the software. The hologram sensors are turned on. The bridge table is seen at the simulated hologram set.

Louie brings up a simulated cartoon character of Yosemite Sam. Yosemite Sam is moonwalking.

Claude tells Mateo, "Walk to any of the locations where you took a shot. When you get there, call us on the radio."

"Will do." Two minutes later, Mateo looks through the sniper scope and fires at Yosemite Sam. Yosemite Sam falls to the floor, simulating his death.

Louie says, "Ask the players to take their seats at the bridge table."

The four players are Matt, Kyle, Rick, and Rose. The hologram has an exact replica of each.

Louie sees the four players replicated on the hologram. "Rose, take the deck of cards and start shuffling. Now deal the cards." Louie is intently looking at the replica; he wants to make sure that all actions are smooth.

Mateo comes on the radio: "Claude, before you ask me to shoot, I need to make sure that it is really a replica and not Rose!"

"It is a replica," says Claude. "Stand by."

Louie is intently looking at the hologram replica. He is rubbing his three-day growth of beard and nodding—he is thinking. He says to Rose, "As soon as you hear the shot, tilt your head slightly to your right. This will allow me to integrate the killing sequence with your live actions."

"Like this?"

"Yeah, but a little quicker."

She tilts her head again, and he says, "Perfect—yeah, that will do it."

Claude asks, "Are we ready?"

"Ready," says Rose.

"OK, Mateo, you can fire at will."

Thirty seconds, one minute, two minutes pass...nothing. At a little over two minutes, Mateo walks in. He says, "Guys, I have to look at the setup—it seems too real. When I look through the scope, I swear it is Rose. I gotta be sure that I am not shooting at a live person!" He walks through the two sets. He sees where the "real" Rose is behind the building wall. He sees where the fiber optic cables run between the two sets and carefully inspects the three-dimensional characters being replicated by the hologram.

Rose is still seated at the table. She says, "Mateo, thank you very much. Do not worry; there is no way in hell that I will be anywhere close to the outside shelter. Watch this." She gets up and walks off the inside set. Her image disappears on the outdoor set.

Mateo shakes his head and says, "Wish Alex was here; maybe he could take this shot."

Again, Rose says, "Come on, man up. I am OK!"

Mateo picks up his M-24 sniper rifle and heads back up the hill. He reaches his sniper nest, goes down to one knee, and aims at the image. He finds Rose in his scope and then he puts down the rifle and picks up the radio. "Ready to fire. Please assure me that I am aiming at the image."

"I can assure you that it is the image. Fire at will," says Claude.

"Roger." Mateo raises his M-24 and finds the image of Rose. He puts the crosshairs on her head and slowly pulls the trigger—BANG —WOOSH! He hears the bang of the bullet and the compression of air as it flies to its target. Within milliseconds, he sees the head of Rose explode into a million pieces! He starts trembling and sweat starts pouring down his face and onto his chest. His hands are shaking. He starts to stand up and his legs are wobbly. He walks back to camp. He is nervous and keeps telling himself, "It was fake—it was fake."

He walks to the holograms sets. The team is viewing the recording. He sees Rose and he lets out a big sigh of relief. "Man, I really thought I had killed you—it really looks realistic!"

Rose says, "Thanks, Mateo, you are a doll."

With the enactment of the death of Rose, the team is ready for their flight to Scotland. The plan is to meet up with Jeff, Vinny, and Alex. They will be staying in Edinburgh the week before their stay at The Sea Serpent. The Mathews will travel by car and meet up with the team on the Friday before their arrival at the rental on Saturday.

Chapter Twenty

Team Meets in Scotland

Edinburgh, Scotland

Rose, Claude, and Mateo fly the G650 Gulfstream to Edinburgh. The hologram equipment shot detection gear, all of the required weapons and other items are on board the aircraft. As is typical, the weapons are stored in hidden compartments. Claude and Rose also ship their golf clubs. Alex and Jeff have requested that they pick up theirs. Claude and Alex are single-digit handicappers. Rose is also a good player. She grew up in a golfing family. Her father, brother, and uncles all play golf. She has a good swing, hits excellent drives, and is a good putter. They plan to play some golf after they have all items in place and their primary mission thoroughly planned and completed in tabletop practice sessions. Jeff, Vinny, and Alex drive down from Bristol. They have booked rooms at the Waldorf Caledonian in downtown Edinburgh.

The first order of business is to review the preparation for the fake assassination. Claude asks Jeff to review the status of the solar panel installation at the Mathews house. Jeff says, "Everything went well. We completed the installation of three panels and wiring the electrical output to the battery bank. The battery bank is connected to a DC-to-AC converter, and this output is connected to the power panel. We had a licensed electrician complete the inspection, and everything looks normal. I am sure that the assassin will review the recorded videos and be convinced that everything is legit,"

Vinny then says, "When I told the inspector that we had a drone, he asked that we fly it and use that for the inspection of the roof installation. I gladly complied. When I flew the drone, we recorded with the video cameras. After inspection, we should be OK. Also, after I completed the drone flight, I made sure that the inspector was reviewing the recorded video. The review took place outside. I made sure that the inspector was in clear view of the cameras. Everything is legit and it should convince the assholes that we were really there to install a solar cell electrical system."

Alex adds, "I broke into the assassin's office at the rental cubicles. I wiretapped the outgoing +1-615 number. Mrs. Mathews made the call and clearly told her friend Matilda the address of the rental property. As we suspected, I was able to hear the assholes on the open line. They were excited. They said that a person by the name of 'Wolf' would be pleased to hear that they now had the address."

Rose asked, "Did you hear Wolf talk?"

"No, my guess is that Wolf was not at the monitor site."

"OK guys, good work," says Claude. "Let me give you a recap of the Virginia activities. Mateo, can you provide the summary?"

"Will do," Mateo replies. "The hologram sets were completed. Rick, Matt, and Kyle did a great job of building a replica of the outside veranda. Rick, with the help of Matt and myself, set up and calibrated the shot detection system. Rick added a pre-amp and notch filter. MANETs were used to connect the detection points. Rick gave us strict instructions regarding the installation of the gun-detection equipment. Try to install the antennas at a high position such as a tree. Also, camouflage all of them as best as possible. The pre-amp must be installed as close as possible to the antenna. The notch filters are installed at the inside computer terminal."

Alex says, "May I ask a question?"

"Certainly—go ahead."

"Do each of the antenna feeds need to have a notch filter?"

"Good question. I also asked that question. The short answer is yes. According to Rick, we could have combined the antenna feeds and used one notch filter, but this would add workload for Louie. He would then need to identify the three antenna feeds with software. We decided that it was best to keep the antenna feeds separate."

Mateo now continues with the simulation of the assassination of Rose. "Claude, if you don't mind, can you provide this summary? I would rather not talk about it. The video is still in my head, and it looks too real."

Claude begins to tell him that he will take it from here. Rose interrupts, saying, "Let me provide the summary."

Claude looks surprised. "OK, Rose, as you wish."

Rose says, "We set up two scenes, one inside and the outside set that would display the replica of the images. The action for the players was a game of bridge. The four actors were displayed on the outside hologram set. The shooter, from three hundred meters, put a bullet in the head of my image. The software, written by Louie, simulates my head being blown into a thousand pieces. I must admit, after seeing the video, I had to pinch myself—am I still alive?"

Alex asks, "How were your images and the…ah, head being blown off integrated at the precise moment?"

"I will take that question," says Claude. "Louie used the sound of the gunshot. It is essential that the sound of the gunshot be clear, as the gunshot detection system will trigger on its sound."

"We cannot have the image react to bird chirps, dogs barking, or any other sound," says Mateo. "According to Louie, he also wrote the system with special gun shot-recognition features. He said that he used frequency cells. Some high-tech stuff—but if Louie wrote it, you can take it to the bank. His stuff always works."

"Yes, I agree," says Alex. "Thanks for the explanation."

"OK, tomorrow we drive by the rental property," says Claude. "It is about a one-hour drive from here. We leave at 7 A.M. Any further questions?"

"Yes, I have one," says Jeff. "Did you lug all of our golf clubs for dead weight, or are we going to hit the links? I looked at the map. Saint Andrews is southeast of the rental property, about a thirty-mile drive. I suggest that after the drive-by, we see if we can play golf at the Old Course in Saint Andrews."

"Great idea," says Alex. "if we cannot play on the Old Course, we can play the New Course or the Jubilee."

"My father is a member at the Saint Andrews Golf Club," says Rose. "I can probably use his name to get a tee time on the Old Course."

"That will be great if we play the Old Course," says Jeff. "I can mark off the number one item on my bucket list!"

Vinny then looks at Mateo and says, "Are you game for scuba diving? I hear that there are some great reefs off the coast of Scotland."

"Hell yeah," replies Mateo. "We can go scuba diving while they ruin a perfect day by hitting some little round ball."

The following day, Rose, Claude, Alex, and Jeff drive to the rental property. It takes them one hour and fifteen minutes to arrive at the main gate. The property has a gate with a keypad. They have been given the combination but decide that it would be best not to enter it. Their rental starts tomorrow, on Saturday. They drive down the winding road and find a small parking area with an emergency phone booth. They fake a need for a call while Jeff takes out the drone. In two minutes, the drone is flying. Jeff flies it at five hundred feet and records the property. The drone flight is for seventeen minutes. Tonight, they will review the video recording.

Jeff brings the drone to a landing. Alex catches it, and Jeff quickly unscrews the propellers, removes the camera, and places everything in a Pelican case.

Claude then drives to Saint Andrews. As they are entering the town, Jeff notes that there are dozens of souvenir and clothing shops. Claude drives to the golf course with Rose, and they walk in to try to see if they can obtain a tee time. They enter the pro shop, and Rose says, "Good morning. We are here on business. Would it be possible to get a tee time?"

The attendant says, "Of course. Let me see. The first tee time would be a week from this Wednesday. You will also need a letter from either a member or from your golf pro."

"Is there any way we can get one today?"

"Impossible. This is the Old Course at Saint Andrews. We are booked year-round."

"OK, is the golf pro in today?"

"Yes, but he is giving an early lesson. He can be found on the practice green."

"Thank you."

Rose tells Claude to wait for her in the pro shop. Claude asks, "In other words, get lost?"

"Well, if you want to put it that way—YES!"

Rose goes to the SUV and pulls out her putter and four golf balls. She walks to the putting green and starts putting. After hitting the four balls to the second practice hole, the golf pro comes running to Rose and says with much joy, "Well I'll be damned, Isabella Rose Mathews! Boy, is it great to see you? Your dad talks about you all the time. After you left for USC, I read about your great career in America. Your dad told me about your two years in the diplomatic service. I am truly sorry for the death of your sister. My condolences to you and your family."

"Thank you, Ian," says Rose. "Yes, I really do miss her."

The golf pro's name is Ian Campbell. He has been the golf pro at the club for over fifteen years. He knows Rose from when she was a star athlete as a cross-country runner in high school. Her dad is a member of the club and plays golf there at least three or four times a year with his friend Herbert. Rose took golf lessons from Ian when she was in her teens.

Ian says. "Have you kept up with your golf? You had a good game as a teenager, so I would imagine that you still get a decent score."

"It's not bad, but as always, it could be better."

"Are you playing today?"

"I would like to, but according to the pro shop attendant, there is no opening till next week."

"OK, let's go to the pro shop and get this fixed."

They walk into the pro shop, and Ian tells the attendant, "Edward, see that Miss Rose gets a tee time today!"

"Yes, sir." Edward looks at his computer and tells Rose, "Your tee time is at 2:15 this afternoon."

"Thank you," says Rose. She turns to Ian, and they continue talking about old times for the next half hour.

Rose leaves the pro shop and finds Claude. "We have a tee time at 2:15."

"It's good to know that you have pull in Scotland."

"Yes, the golf pro knows me from my teenage years. He knows my dad and Herbert. Now we need to tell Jeff and Alex that we have a tee time."

Rose and Claude go back to the souvenir shops and clothing stores. They finally find Jeff and Alex trying on some golf outfits. Apparently, Jeff has convinced Alex that they should go native. They are trying on knickers, tall socks, Ben Hogan golf caps, plaid shirts, and colorful shoes.

Rose looks them up and down says, "You guys sure look cute."

"You have to dress like true Scotchmen," says Jeff. "The golf gods will be good to us."

"By the way, our tee time is at 2:15."

Jeff looks at Alex and says, "Great, just enough time for Scottish stuffed cabbage with a couple of beers and the practice range."

At 2 P.M., the Mathews foursome is on deck. Rose looks like a golf pro on the LPGA circuit. She has on a bright pink miniskirt, matching golf shirt, and earrings. Her shoes match her outfit. Her hair is in a ponytail, with the hair pushed through the cap hole. Claude is also well dressed in blue designer pants, Old Course golf shirt, black shoes, and a golf hat. Jeff and Alex have matching knickers, plaid shirts, bright orange shoes, and Ben Hogan golf hats. They both look a young Rodney Dangerfield.

They tee off on the first tee; Claude and Alex hit 260-yard drives. They are ten yards in front of the water burn. Jeff hits a banana slice 230 yards. It ends up in the tall rough. He uses his foot wedge, and the ball is thirty yards in front of the water burn. Rose tees off on the women's tee. Her drive goes over the water burn and is on the edge of the first green. Claude and Alex have a par. Rose has a birdie, and Jeff has a double bogey.

The Old Course at Saint Andrews was laid out the 1800s. It is a links course, which means that it forms a link from the land that was used for farming and cattle grazing to the sea. The original founders of the golf course basically used the land to build a recreational area. To preserve land for "farming" or needed use, the golf course was laid out along the North Sea. The course has eighteen holes. Nine holes out, and you make the turn, and then nine holes back to the clubhouse. To preserve land, a number of the greens are shared by the outgoing nine holes and the incoming nine holes.

The Mathews foursome completes the first nine, and they make their way back on the incoming holes. The fifteen incoming green is shared with the fourth outgoing fourth green. The foursome on the outgoing green is made up of four men. Two are older men in their sixties, and two are younger men in their early thirties. The younger of the two men is rough and has an uncombed beard. He is yelling at his caddie, "Goddamn it, you pointed to the wrong flagstick. Now I have a sixty-foot double breaker to the left and then to the right. I will be damned if you are going to get a tip!"

The caddie is an old Scottish man wearing a tie and appropriately dressed. If you did not know any better, you would think that he was the golfer and the loudmouth American was a caddie.

The caddie replies, "I am most sorry, sir. I thought I had pointed out the red outgoing flag."

"Well, you sure as hell did not do that—you told me the wrong flag. I will report your bad caddie behavior to the caddie master. Hope you get your ass fired!"

The golf ball that belongs to the loudmouth is two feet from Rose's ball. The proper etiquette is to have the loudmouth mark his ball and have Rose finish her putt. The loudmouth American knows nothing about etiquette.

Loudmouth walks to his ball, looks at Rose, and says, "Well, lassie, are you going to mark? Your ball is in the way." Rose says nothing and marks her ball. The loudmouth putts his ball, picks it up, and claims that his ten-foot putt is a "gimme."

Rose, Claude, Alex, and Jeff finish their putts. They are walking to the sixteenth tee. Jeff says, "What an asshole. I should wait at the eighteenth green and punch that son of a bitch in the mouth."

Alex says, "You are going to have to wait in line—I'll get to that loudmouth before you do."

"Now you know why we Europeans call you 'ugly Americans,'" says Rose.

"Yeah, I can see that," says Claude.

The loudmouth, his friend, and the two older men move on to the fifth hole. Loudmouth continues to slam his caddie. He blames him for giving him the improper yardage. He blames him for not reading the putt correctly. Even when he hits a good shot and the caddie says, "Good shot," loudmouth says, "What the hell did you expect? Of course, it was a good shot!"

By the seventeenth tee, something is bothering loudmouth. He says, "Wilhelm, did you notice that good-looking lady on the fourth green."

"Yeah," says Wilhelm, "I sure did. She was quite a looker."

"No, no, you idiot. Did you notice anything else?"

"Yeah, I sure did. She had a nice ass and a set of jugs to make a cow envious."

"Wilhelm, you're a stupid shit! It was our target—that was her!"

"No shit, really?" Wilhelm rubs his chin and rakes his hand across his hair. "Yeah, that was her! Maybe we can find her in the clubhouse drinking some expensive French wine. We can knock her off there."

Wolfgang says, "Wilhelm, you will never learn. Remember the three Ps: plan, prepare, and practice. Have we met any of those three requirements to knock her off in the clubhouse?"

"No, none."

"Exactly, dumbass!"

Chapter Twenty-One

Arriving at The Sea Serpent

Forfar, Scotland

The plan is to arrive early on Saturday. The assassin will likely be surveying the rental early on the first day. He will probably want to confirm that Rose is on the property. This surveillance can be done from a location farther from the shooting location.

Jeff, Vinny, Alex, and Mateo will arrive on Saturday afternoon. Jeff will be the cook, and Vinny will be a houseboy. When they arrive, they will be off-loading groceries and household items such as cleaning supplies, mops, detergent, brooms, etc. Alex and Mateo will arrive sixty minutes after Jeff and Vinny in a Land Rover with a magnetic sign that says, "Abbott Security." It will be natural to have two security guards assigned to Rose and Claude. After arrival at the property, they will conduct a thorough inspection of the property. Rose, Claude, and the Mathews' will be arriving later that afternoon.

The property has a servant house detached from the main building. This is where Alex and Mateo will bunk. Jeff and Vinny will stay at the main house. The property has six bedrooms, two on each floor. Jeff and Alex will bunk in the basement. Rose, Claude, and Rose's parents will also arrive late on Saturday. Claude and Rose will have the bedroom on the top floor. Rose's parents will have a bedroom on the main floor. The kitchen, dining room, family room, and veranda are on the main floor. Once Rose and Claude get situated, they will set up the inside and outside hologram equipment.

Before leaving Virginia, Rick had voiced some additional concerns. His concern was: "What happens if the assassin sees such inviting targets that he starts shooting at the images? The images will be Claude and the Mathews."

Rose then said, "You have a point. Do you have any suggestions?"

"Yes, as you know, I am a hunter and very familiar with guns. I have a motorized gun turret. I can mount a rifle to the turret and work with Louie to have the turret point the gun to the intersection of the shot detection LOBs. The assassin will have bullets fly around this head, and he will not have time to aim and shoot at any other person."

"Excellent idea," said Claude. "How long will it take to implement?

"Not long. The gun turret is motorized and controlled by a small processor. My guess is that Louie can implement the integration in less than a couple of hours."

"OK, let's do it."

Now, within thirty minutes, Louie has the shot-detection system integrated with the gun turret. It has been offset one meter high. They want to make sure that they do not kill the assassin. They want him captured alive. The gun selected is a special one used to destroy the drones that attacked the nuclear power plant in Buchanan, New York. The special rifle fires three rounds with one pull of the trigger. This is the primary reason that Abboud and Malik want Rose killed. She was the main reason for the success of the prevention of the destruction of the Indian Point nuclear power plant.

Rose and Claude will also be responsible for the setup of the gun turret. The turret will need to be moved daily depending on the direction of the wind. During the conversations between Rose's mother and her friend Matilda, it is important that they mention the dogs. Rose, Claude, Alex, and Mateo are all experienced special operation agents. If the assassin is a professional, and all indications are that he is, he will set up his sniper nest down-wind from the Sea Serpent, so that the wind is blowing in his face. He will not risk the dogs smelling his body odor.

On Saturday, the preparation begins. Jeff and Vinny have rented an enclosed white van.

Vinny says, "Jeff, should we buy the household items or the groceries first?"

"We buy the household items first. We will need to buy the groceries later since they will need to be placed in the refrigerator." Jeff and Vinny arrive at The Sea Serpent at 2 P.M.

Mateo and Alex depart in a Land Rover. It has a magnetic sign that reads "Abbott Security." They are armed with Glock .45 handguns and have knives sheathed on their belts. They are wearing cargo pants, brown golf shirts with the Abbott Security logo, and black baseball caps with white letter A's. They leave at 1 P.M. and arrive at The Sea Serpent at 3 P.M.

The Mathews arrive in Edinburgh on Friday night and check into a small hotel which allows pets. They have their two dogs, Winston and Monty, who are sizeable Bernese mountain dogs. Bernese mountain dogs were initially used in the Swiss Alps in the canton of Bern, Switzerland. The dogs, which have a keen sense of smell, will play a significant role in the fake death of Rose. Claude and Rose move to the same hotel where Rose's parents are staying. When Rose's parents arrive, Rose and Claude are waiting in the lobby. The Mathews' SUV drives up, and Rose runs outside to meet her parents.

"Mamacita and Papi, great to see you!"

They hug each other. Rose and her mom kiss on the cheeks. Claude hugs Rose's mom and shakes hands with Mr. Mathews. Then he politely asks the three to go inside and check in. He will carry their luggage.

Maria turns and tells Claude, "You can leave the dogs in the boot. We will pick them up after we check in."

Mr. Mathews says, "It's been a long drive, and I'm starving. How about we have some dinner?"

"Yes," says Rose, "We have not eaten. We were waiting for you."

Rose and Claude help the Mathews to their room. Rose is chatting with her mom, and Claude is talking with Richard, Rose's dad. Maria says, "Give us fifteen minutes to freshen up, and we will meet you in the dining room."

"OK, Mom. See you in fifteen."

While Maria is freshening up, Richard goes out to SUV, takes out Winston and Monty, and takes them for a walk. He comes back in fifteen minutes, and Maria is ready. The dogs are fed, and they are wagging their tails. They go down for dinner to where Rose and Claude are seated and drinking iced tea. They have selected a table far from the tall windows and in a corner. They want maximum security, where no one can eavesdrop. The server brings the menu and asks the Mathews, "Would you like something to drink while you look at the menu?"

"Yes," says Maria, "iced tea, please."

"Hot tea, please," says Richard.

The group looks at the menu. The server returns with the drinks, and they order their food.

After some small talk about life in Bristol and life in Virginia, Richard asks the question: "Is everything in order at The Sea Serpent?"

"Yes, Dad, but let me fill you in on the details."

"Yes, we would like that," says Maria.

Rose gives them the background on how they found out that there was a contract on her life." We explored all possibilities, and one of the best methods of obtaining information on a subject was to hack the phones of the target's relatives or friends. For example, if we wanted to find out something about Aunt Betty, you might hack into the phones of cousins Becky or Kathy."

"Oh, I see. So, the bad guys tapped my phone and just waited until I said something about you."

"Yes, but you were told not to discuss either myself or Richard Jr. It was only because we found the taps, and through Herbert, you were told what to say."

"So, it worked. By the way, the two young men who installed the solar panels were real gentlemen."

"Also," adds Richard, "they were real pros; they really knew about solar panels and did a real professional job. When the inspector came by, he said that it was the best job that he had ever seen."

The conversation now turns to the plans at The Sea Serpent.

Rose says, "Claude, can you give Mom and Dad the plans using the hologram?"

"Certainly." First, Claude needs to explain the hologram technology. He says, "The owner of WMA has a childhood friend who is a Hollywood movie producer. The producer, John Ramos, allowed us to borrow a hologram set. The hologram will allow us to project an image of Rose to the outside veranda. We tested the system at a test facility in Virginia. After some modifications to the software, we have the system working to perfection. Someone a hundred or more meters away will not be able to tell that they were looking at images."

"Have you decided on the scene that will be projected?" asks Richard. "Before either Claude or Rose can respond, Mrs. Mathews interjects.

"Oh my God, whatever you do, it must be totally safe. I have already lost one daughter to terrorism; I cannot have Rosita killed by those terrorists!"

"Mom, it is totally safe. When we are at the villa, we will demonstrate."

"OK, but it better be safe; otherwise, I will not allow my daughter to be put in any danger!"

Claude thinks, *if she only knew what Rose really does*. He changes the subject and says, "By the way, the villa is an excellent property. How did we get so lucky to have a small mansion?"

"Oh, you did not know?" says Richard. "The villa belongs to my nephew Darrin Walker. He is the son of my sister Patricia."

Claude looks at Rose. "Rose, you never told me that."

"The Sea Serpent is new," continues Richard. "It was built five years ago, after Rose left the nest. She was in the British Army when the villa was built. She would not have known about The Sea Serpent."

Claude says, "We can continue our discussions on the roles we will be playing when we arrive at the villa."

"It's early today," says Richard. "We have sunlight until 11 P.M. in Scotland. How about we hit the links and play nine holes?"

"We played eighteen at Saint Andrews today, but I'm game for nine more."

Claude looks at Rose, and she says, "Go ahead, boys. My mom and I have a lot of catching up to do. We will stay here at the hotel and rest up."

"Richard, says Maria, "don't forget your sweater. It will get cold in the evening."

Claude and Richard leave. They pick up their golf clubs, grab their sweaters, and head to the links at 7 P.M.

The next day, the Mathews, Rose, and Claude sleep late and depart for The Sea Serpent at 3 P.M.

Chapter Twenty-Two

First Day at The Sea Serpent

Forfar, Scotland

On Saturday, Wolfgang and Wilhelm are at the parking lot of their hotel in Dundee. It is 6 A.M.

Wolf asks, "Will, did you pack some box lunches for today? It will be a long day."

"Sure did, boss. I also packed toilet paper and napkins."

"Good job. Let's go through a checklist before we depart. Do we have the binoculars?"

"Check."

"Black face paint, goggles?"

"Check,"

"Handguns?"

"They are in the hidden compartment of the equipment case. Also have ammo in the compartment."

"OK, good work. Do we have the infrared monocle?"

"Check."

"OK. We have a full tank of petrol and water bottles?"

"Check."

"Did you go to the bathroom? It will be a long day."

"I'm OK."

"OK, let's roll!"

Wolf and Will are wearing thick brown cargo pants and long-sleeve shirts. They learned from their initial recon that there are bushes with thorns. They arrive at the chosen parking spot at 7:30. They park the SUV and silently pack their backpacks. They follow the procedures that they practiced in the last two days. They blacken their faces, place the black woolen stocking caps on their heads, and place the goggles on their heads above their eyes. They slip on their backpacks and start walking to the observation point. As expected, there is dense brush, trees, and tall grass. At 8 A.M., they reach the observation point. They take off their backpacks and lay their binoculars and monocle on a rock next to the chosen location. They pull off their stocking caps and place green baseball caps on their heads. They take out a blanket, lay it on the tall grass, and sit on some rocks. After a short rest, they lie prone, looking toward the villa.

Wolf says, "OK, now we wait."

"OK, boss, I'm ready with my binoculars."

They wait and wait. At 10:30, Will starts to get up, "Gotta take a piss." As he walks away from the observation point, a light-blue four-door Audi drives up the driveway to the villa.

Wolf says, "Goddamn it, Will, get your ass back down here and help with the observation."

"Sorry, boss, but when you gotta go, you gotta go."

"Shut up and start your surveillance!"

"I'm on it!"

Wolf and Will, looking through their binoculars, see a middle-aged woman open the driver's door and start walking toward the house. She is well dressed and is carrying a briefcase. She uses a house key and goes inside the villa.

"What the hell is she doing boss?" asks Will.

"Normal rental procedures. She's probably from the rental company. She's probably checking to make sure everything is in order."

"Like what?"

"Will, just shut up and do your assignment."

"Sure thing, boss, just tell me what to do."

"Just keep looking."

At 2 P.M., a white van pulls up. Will says, "Hey, boss, we got some action. I see two men climbing out of the van. They are opening the doors, and they are taking groceries into the house."

"Yes, I see them," says Wolf.

"I think one is a cook. The other must be a gofer."

The two men make four trips to the van. The gofer closes the back doors and parks the van. He walks to the equipment shed and takes out a weed whacker and brush clippers. He starts trimming the sidewalk.

Will says, "Hey, boss, the gofer is the gardener."

"Good, he and the cook will offer no threat. We can forget about them."

At 3 P.M., a white SUV drives up to the house. The SUV parks, and two well-built men step out. They are wearing brown cargo pants, camo shirts, and brown baseball caps with an A on the front. The SUV has a sign on each door with the name "Abbott Security." The two men are armed with holstered handguns. They move to the back of the SUV and pull out two gun carrying cases. The cases are long and are used to carry AK-47s. The two men walk up the driveway and check the sides of the driveway for a hundred meters. They return and stand guard at the driveway.

At 4 P.M., a Volvo XC40 SUV pulls up the driveway. As it stops, the cook and the gardener come running up to it. The cook and the older man take the luggage in the house. The gardener takes the two dogs for a walk.

An Aston Martin pulls up the driveway. As the car drives up, the two guards run alongside, similar to Secret Service agents guarding the presidential limousine. The Aston Martin stops in front of the garage door, and the door opens. The car drives into the garage.

Will says, "That must be our target. Did you look at that car? Who the hell do they think they are—James Bond and Wonder Woman?"

Wolf says nothing. He is thinking, *this is not going to be easy. They are taking maximum-security precautions. We will just need to monitor the scene. Eventually, they will lower their defenses, and when they do, we attack.*

It is now 7 P.M. It has been a long day. Wolf tells Will, "OK, let's wrap it up. We'll come back tomorrow and establish a pattern of life."

Will does not know what is meant by a "pattern of life." He says, "Roger, the pattern of life will be very important!"

On the way back to the hotel, Wolf is thinking about an incident in Iraq. The US special forces were using infrared cameras on the Rover drones. The cameras could not detect any of the ragheads. However, they knew that they were there. A unit of Marines was dispatched to find the ragheads and report their co-ordinates. Using his high-powered scope on his sniper rifle, he was able to find the terrorist location. He asked himself, *how did I see them, but not the one-million-dollar Rover drone?* Much to his amazement, the stupid ragheads were covering themselves with ten-dollar thermal blankets. The blankets were standard issue for the US military in cold climates. He remembers how he felt—a ten-dollar blanket defeated a one-million-dollar machine—so much for the enemy being dumb. He then does a Polish salute, slaps his forehead, and tells Will, "Tomorrow we go to the outdoor sports store and buy some thermal blankets."

Second Day Actions by the WMA Team

On the second day, Alex and Mateo come out from the servant quarters. They are planning on installing the gun-detection system. They stand in the drive-way and point to locations surrounding the villa. They need to have the items not be seen when conducting physical surveillance. They carefully pack bin-oculars, ropes, which they tie to their belts, and a radio to remain in contact with the team. The radios are all encrypted; thus, should the assassin have a radio intercept system, he will only know that RF transmissions are occurring. The audio is all scrambled using encryption algorithms.

Alex says, "We need to make sure that if the assassin is monitoring us, he believes that we will be conducting perimeter security."

"OK," says Mateo, "I will move to the northeast and southeast corners. The gun-detection system is in our backpacks and is not viewable by an observer. After we are well hidden by the forest, we will install the shot detection system."

"Got it," says Alex. "I will install the northwest and southwest systems."

"Remember the instructions from Rick. Install the antenna as high as pos-sible but not above the tree line. If we install above the tree line, the assassin will be able to see it."

"Got it. Also, snake the power cable around the tree trunk. Make it look like a vine. The battery pack must be totally hidden."

"Yes, if there is a part of the system that can be found, it is the battery. We need to make sure that it is totally hidden."

As discussed, Alex and Mateo move to the back of the SUV. They talk for a few minutes and point to the perimeter of the property. They open the hatchback and pull out two backpacks. They loop the backpacks on their backs and start walking to the outer edge of the property. They disappear under the dense foliage.

Five minutes after Alex and Mateo disappear; Jeff comes out of the villa. It is approximately 4:15 P.M. He jumps in the van and heads to the grocery store. He returns at 5:30 P.M. with the van full of groceries. Vinny comes out and helps with carrying the groceries into the villa.

After all the groceries are in the refrigerator and cupboards, Jeff and Vinny sit on a bench and rest

Jeff says, "OK, Vinny, showtime. We need to play our roles."

"Damn right. I can see us receiving an Oscar—best supporting role!"

Jeff is dressed in all white. He has an apron around his waist and is wearing white shoes. Vinny is wearing old jeans and a sweatshirt with the emblem of the Manchester football team. He is wearing Adidas black high-tops and a light-brown baseball cap. He has work gloves stuffed in his back pocket. The van, which is backed up to the kitchen door, is parked by Jeff. Vinny then walks to the equipment shed and takes out a gasoline-powered lawnmower, weed whacker, and hedge clippers. Vinny checks out the weed whacker. He walks back into the shed and comes out with a petrol can. He pours petrol into the weed whacker and checks the lawnmower. He also pours petrol into the lawnmower. Vinny then continues with the yard work. He starts the weed whacker and starts trimming the driveway and sidewalks. For the remainder of the day, he tends to the grass and hedgerows. He also skims the pool, removes the cover from the whirlpool hot tub, and sprays the bushes with an insect repellant.

As Vinny is busy doing yard work. Alex and Mateo are installing the gunshot-detector system. The biggest problem is walking through the foliage. After they find the approximate spot they have marked on their maps, they search for the proper tree. It needs to be strong enough to hold their weight, but not too tall to extend over the other trees. The antenna cannot be exposed. Neither Alex nor Mateo are electrical engineers, but they know that leaves are not suitable for radio waves. You do not need to be a rocket scientist to know that radio waves are absorbed by the leaves. Fortunately, the shooter will be on high ground; thus, the sound will easily travel to the antenna. The MANET routers, which are being used to communicate with the house computer system, operate in the L-band, which is minimally attenuated by tree leaves. After about 6 P.M., Alex and Mateo come down from their perimeter surveillance. They again stop behind their SUV and discuss their actions. After a short five minutes, they open the hatchback, place their backpacks in the SUV, pull out two Pelican cases, and walk inside the villa. For the remainder of the evening, they remain inside.

Now the activity switches to the inside of the villa. Two major items must be completed: the hologram and the gun turret. Mateo takes the lead on the hologram, and Claude takes the lead on the gun turret. Mateo needs help with the hologram; he goes to the door and yells, "YEAH, VINNY, COME INSIDE! YOU NEED TO DO SOME DUSTING!" There is no dusting to be done, but the assassins may have some high-gain parabolic dishes to pick up sound.

Mateo now has Vinny help him with the hologram. He says, "Vinny, take out all of the equipment on the cases marked 'movie set' and place them on the family room floor."

"OK, got it. Let me wash up, and I'll be right back." Vinny proceeds to carefully take out all the equipment and place it in a logical sequence on the floor.

Mateo places the computer equipment on the worktable. Then he directs Vinny to place the laser sensors on the four corners at the bottom and at the top. The total is eight sensors per scene. The inside sensors on the top are not a problem. They are installed on ceiling struts. The external sensors will need to be installed on the ceiling of the veranda. Mateo looks at Claude and Rose and asks, "What would you advise for the outside sensor?"

Richard has been listening. He says, "Let's give Maria a birthday party. We can hang balloons and streamers from the inside wall of the veranda posts. She does have a birthday next week. We can install a streamer with her birthday date next week—we are just posting the banners early to have a two-week celebration."

"That is a great idea," says Rose. "One more week—what's the difference. After all, we did say in the phone calls that we would be here for two weeks."

"OK," says Alex, "let's Google party stores near here, and I can go and buy the birthday supplies." Alex finds a store in Forfar. It is a twenty-minute drive away. The store closes at 8 P.M. It is 7:15.

Vinny and Jeff volunteer as gofers. They both say in unison, "We can drive to the party store and pick up the items. Just give us a list."

Alex gives Jeff a list of items. Vinny tells Jeff, "Let's roll. We only have thirty minutes."

Jeff and Vinny dash out the door and head to the party store. Sixty minutes later, they are back at the villa. They not only have the party items, but also two pizzas, all meat and a sausage pepperoni.

Claude says, "Alright, pizza. Let's take a break and eat the pizza while it is hot."

They all take a break and have pizza for dinner.

After the pizza Richard says, "My advice is that Vinny and Jeff take the step ladder from the equipment shed and start hanging the party balloons and streamers. As they are installing the balloons and streamers, they can install the ceiling sensors. Vinny and Jeff will be the natural choice to install the banners. It doesn't make sense to have the guards, Maria, Rose, or myself installing the banner. Perhaps we can have Claude supervising."

Mateo says, "We will need to make sure that the inside scene is low enough so that the projected hologram fits under the streamers."

That evening, Vinny and Jeff, supervised by Claude, make the party preparations. During this time, they install the hologram sensors.

After the completion of the two sets, the gun turret is set up and completed. The problem will be that it cannot be tested. They will need to rely on the testing conducted at the farm in Virginia.

Rose says, "Is there any way that we can test the gun detection program?"

"Actually," replies Vinny, "there is. It is called a Doppler test."

"OK, Vinny," says Claude, "what is the Doppler test?"

"It uses an internal test program. A test signal is injected at the antenna connection using a multi-coupler. The test program interjects sound waves at different times and calculates the location of the simulated sound origin."

"Great. Can we test the system?"

"Absolutely." Vinny goes to the computer terminal and selects the test icon. A Google map appears. He moves the mouse over the map and left clicks. A pushpin is displayed on the screen.

"OK, now I will hit 'start test.' On the second screen, the LOBs will appear, and the intersection of the lines will show the origin of the sound. It should be close to the pushpin on the original screen." Vinny moves the mouse over the start test. He left-clicks on the "radio" button.

Jeff says, "Yeah, the LOBs are right on, directly over the location of the pushpin."

Claude then says, "What do you think, Rose? Are we ready for showtime?"

"Yes, but we need to go over the responsibilities of all team members once we hear the shot."

All team members agree. Claude says, "OK, it's been a long day. Let's convene tomorrow for breakfast at 9 A.M. and go over all responsibilities."

Chapter Twenty-Three

Third Day at The Sea Serpent

Forfar, Scotland

Wolfgang and Will need to wait until 9 A.M. They leave their hotel in Dundee, drive to the outdoor sports store, and buy four thermal blankets. They drive to the location of The Sea Serpent and park their Land Rover two miles from the villa. They drive their Land Rover deeper into the woods and leave a note that they are bird watching in case a forest ranger comes by. They find the path to the observation point and repeat the walk of the previous day. Today they will try and establish patterns of life: What time do they get up? Where do they eat? Do they use the pool? What time? They have golf clubs, so when and where do they play? Who plays golf?

Wolf tells Will, "On your pad, take notes. Write down what they are doing with their time. We need to know what the guards are doing. The most important items are what the target is doing. You think you can do that?"

"No problem. Remember, I am here because of my eagle eye—I will not miss anything!"

Wolf thinks, *He is here because he is loyal and will run through a brick wall if I ask him!*

Will lies down in a prone position. He has his binoculars with a strap around his neck. The thermal blanket is next to him. He brings up the binoculars and starts scanning the property. He says, "Hey, boss, they were busy last night after we left. Looks like they had a birthday party or are going to have one."

Wolf takes his binoculars and brings them up to his eyes. "Hey, I see what you mean. That is good because the birthday party will be outside. Good catch, Will."

Will puffs out his chest. He likes it when the boss compliments him. "Thanks, boss."

"Keep on looking. This is the type of info that we need."

For the rest of the day, there is no action outside. The guards seem to come out every two or three hours. They only walk around the driveway and circle the house.

Will thinks, *guess they learned their lesson. No more adventures into the bushes full of thorns.*

Because of the activity from last night. Wolf makes a decision that they will stay at their posts for the evening. It looks like the target, her boyfriend, and her parents are night owls. He tells Will, "We will remain at our posts until mid-day. If there's no action, we leave and return at 6 P.M."

Other than the guards coming out every two or three hours, there is no action. Wolf and Will leave and will return at 6 P.M.

WMA Team Plans Their Actions

The WMA team meets for breakfast at 9 A.M. Jeff, who is a jack of all trades, prepares scrambled, over-hard, and boiled eggs. He cooks French toast, bacon, and English muffins. To drink, they have coffee and orange juice. Dessert is a mixed fruit salad. The breakfast is at the dining room table, which is open to the family room. Alex and Mateo have completed their morning surveillance. In accordance with the plan, they will always have a guard outside the house. Alex is at the table. Vinny takes a breakfast plate with drinks to Mateo.

After breakfast, they begin their walk through the actions of all players, starting with the hologram deception this afternoon. The afternoon session will not involve Rose. A table tennis match between Jeff and Vinny will take place. There is no concern that anyone will be shot, as the table tennis will occur inside. There would be no reason for the assassin to shoot at either Jeff or Vinny. Even if he did, it would be the images on the second set. Nevertheless, all individuals must be ready to act.

Claude, as the team leader, begins the discussion. "The first thing we do this afternoon is send our drone up to five hundred feet. Using the X20 and X50 lens, Vinny and Jeff will record and scan the video to see if we can pinpoint the shooter or shooters."

Vinny asks, "Do we bring down the drone and offload the video to analyze?"

"If we bring it down, adds Jeff, "we stand the chance of the assassin seeing it."

"Leave it up," says Claude, "and view the video in real time."

"OK, we should be able to detect any humans with the infrared camera."

"By all indications," says Rose, "this assassin is a real pro. The chances of detecting him by video are slim."

"Why would you say that he is pro?" asks Jeff.

"The way he has gone about finding me, wiretapping my parents' phone, was thinking out of the box. This is what special operations personnel are taught. I think he is an American. The reason is the Nashville, Tennessee, area code. I think that this goes back to ISIS in Pakistan. They used a cutout to find me at WMA, an American security firm. ISIS's thinking was that with the success of the American security firm, they have contracted out the job to a professional hitman. When we started this investigation, we were all of the opinion to find and kill the hitman. We can still do that, but it would be better to track him back to his lair."

"OK," says Claude, "here are the options. One, we track him back to his home base. As of now, it appears to be the Nashville, Tennessee, area. Two, we capture him alive and see if we can extract information from him. We doubt this will work—it is possible that the contract job was through the darknet, in which case he would not know the identity of the person or organization contracting the job."

"If this is a contract job through the darknet," says Alex, "then we stand a good chance of learning the identity of the assassin and the contracting organization."

"Why do you think that we would be in good shape to find the identities of both parties?"

"Because of the hologram. The assassin will want to film the killing. This is the only way that he can prove that he has successfully completed the job."

"Excellent point," says Rose. The assassination has to occur in the daylight hours. This will produce the best video." They all agree that a daylight hologram would be best.

Jeff now throws in his thoughts, "The surveillance division has been working with law enforcement against pedophiles using the darknet to show sex acts using underaged children. The IT division has had some success in breaking through the onion servers."

"Was the onion server investigation carried out by Louie?" asks Claude.

"Yes, who else?" With that, the group has high confidence that Louie will be able to peel the TOR servers and find the recipient of the monies related to the kill and the sources of the funding. "However," says Jeff, "it will be imperative that the assassin believe that the kill was successful."

Mateo says, "Now I know why Louie told me that the software that he and Dr. Ismail Mankowitz had written had some hooks to be able to find the video on the internet should it be posted on one of the secure chat rooms on the darknet."

Vinny then says, "If anyone would like a tutorial on the TOR servers, I can do that later today."

"Thanks, Vinny," says Claude. "Not now, but I will take a rain check on your tutorial when we are back in Virginia." Claude continues. "We need to test the hologram projection. Jeff and Vinny, bring up the table tennis from the basement arcade room."

Jeff and Vinny go down to the arcade room and bring up the table tennis. Claude tells Alex to have him and Mateo conduct a security run. They will be able to see the hologram from fifty meters without having to battle the thorns.

Vinny and Jeff set up the table. Claude turns on the inside set, and Rose turns on the outside set. The holograms immediately come to life. It can clearly be seen that Jeff and Vinny are playing table tennis. Claude sees a problem: when the ball leaves the real set, it disappears on the projection set. Claude says, "Cut—that's not a good idea. We need a static set."

"Let's hope that the assassin was not viewing the hologram," says Rose.

They are lucky—-Wolfgang and Will have taken a break from 12 to 6 P.M.

Alex and Mateo come in from watching the hologram video. Alex speaks first: "It was a great video. It would fool anyone."

"Looked real to me," adds Mateo. "I could also most hear Jeff smashing the ball toward Vinny. Also, both are pretty good players. I agree with Alex. Looked real to me."

Claude asks, "Did you see anything out of the ordinary?"

"No, nothing," says Alex.

"How about you, Mateo?

"No, everything looks perfectly natural—like I said, like the real thing."

"Why, was there something wrong?"

"No, everything went without a hitch."

"OK, tonight after dinner, we will have the bridge table set up. Richard and Maria, will you be ready for the challenge? Rose and I are pretty good."

Maria answers, "We will be ready, but I hate to embarrass you, little girl."

"Don't hold back," says Rose.

After some friendly ribbing, the Mathews go to their room and get ready for dinner.

Claude, Rose, Alex, Mateo, Jeff, and Vinny will all have a responsibility once the shooting starts.

"Vinny," says Claude, "you will be on the drone. Once the shooting starts, the gun turret will shoot three rounds above the assassin's head. It will take him at least one minute to gather his belongings and start his escape. He will likely leave some items behind. The return fire will not be expected. What he must retrieve will be the video camera. Without proof of a successful hit, he will not leave without the camera. We can assume that he has been using some type of heat shield. When he escapes, he will not have the heat shield. Vinny, you need to track him and tell us the coordinates."

"Roger that. I will be ready."

Claude turns to Jeff. "You will be manning the comm subsystem. First, make sure that we have the encrypted SONIM integrated IP phone and a 'talk around' radio. Configure channel one as the operational channel. Have channel two for the field operators. That will be Rose, Alex, Mateo, and me. Channel three is the logistics channel for you and Vinny. Prepare a radio for Richard and Maria. Place all members on channel five. If anyone transmits on channels five, it will take priority. Use only if you have an emergency."

"Got it."

"Jeff, you will also need to man the cell phone intercept system. The assassin will likely have a cell phone. If he is in trouble, he will want to use it."

"Understand, will do."

"OK, now we come to the field operators. Plan A is to track the assassin. Vinny and Jeff, you will be playing a significant role in directing the team to tail the assassin. He will be on foot for the first one or two miles. After that, he will need some type of transportation. Since there is no water, the escape will be by some vehicle. We need to identify the car before he arrives and place a GPS puck. With the GPS puck, we can track the assassin."

As the team is discussing the assassin's escape routes. Richard has been listening. He says, "By the way, there is a large garage next to the servants' quarters. The last time we were here, I noted that there were two ATVs in the garage. There is also a flatbed trailer. Should you need to transport the ATVs, you can use my Volvo. It has a trailer hitch."

"Thank you," says Claude. "That's good to know. OK, I think that we are set for this evening, dinner, and bridge. When we start playing bridge, man your battle stations. Be ready to roll when you hear the shot.

Sniper's Nest

Wolfgang and Will take a break from twelve noon to 6 P.M. They arrive at the observation point at 5:45. They pack up and walk half a mile to the shooting location, known as the sniper's nest. They have been careful to wear thermal blankets like they are Mexican ponchos. They bring all their supplies. They have added the M-24 long rifle, Nikon camera with a telephoto lens, and a tripod.

Wolfgang does not think that he will make the shot tonight. He still thinks that he does not have a good feel for all of the people in the target's group. He is not worried about the cook or the gardener. They are non-factors. They will offer little to no resistance. The old woman and the old man will also be non-factors. He worries about the target's boyfriend and the two guards. The best scenario will be to have the target and one of the three in his field of view when he takes the shot. His experience has been that when he hits the mark, anyone surrounding the target will freeze for two or three seconds. He will take advantage of this and kill as many people as he can that are in this field of view. Hopefully, whatever they are doing tonight will be repeated the next night. Should this be the case, it will be to his advantage.

The next thing he needs to do is to carefully plan their escape. The thick foliage is not good. He will find a parking space closer to the sniper nest. He and Will need to escape from the sniper nest and be in their Land Rover within twenty minutes of the kill. The guards will likely know the area where the shot came from. They will do one of two things or a combination of both: run up to the area of the shot or jump in their SUV and drive around to the access road. The access road presents a potential problem. If the guards react fast enough, they could cut him off from the straight road back to Dundee. He would then need to drive the long way around toward Forfar and Carnoustie. He decides that he will not take the shot tonight. He will continue with the intel collection. Perhaps starting tomorrow, he will take the shot. There are still too many variables that need to be decided.

Wolfgang and Will get settled in at the sniper's nest. They have their binoculars and the infrared monocle next to their bodies. Wolf decides not to set up the camera with a tripod. Still too early; they need more intel. They have been looking through their binoculars when Will says with much excitement, "Boss, boss, take a look at this. The target, boyfriend, old woman, and old man are sitting ducks. They are playing cards."

Wolf takes a look. "Too good to be true."

"Boss, let's take the shot now!"

"No, not yet. We could take the shot, but we do not have our escape route carefully planned."

"What do you mean? We take the shots, blast all four of the idiots, and there is no one to follow us. We get away clean."

"Did you forget about the guards?"

"Oh yeah—we can stay here and pop them off when they run up the hill."

"Yeah, and what if they do not run up the hill. They jump in their SUV and drive around to the access road and cut us off. Did you ever think of that?"

Will rubs his chin and thinks. "Oh yeah, but when they are running to their vehicle, we shoot them down. I can bring my rifle and help. Hell, it will be fun. Better than shooting ducks at the county fair."

Wolf thinks, *He has a point. Maybe that's plan A. I need a plan B and maybe a plan C.*

The Sea Serpent Villa, WMA team

As Jeff is preparing dinner, Maria walks into the kitchen. She sits at a bar with high stools overlooking the kitchen and asks, "Jeff, is there anything I can do? I would like to be of some help around here."

"Certainly, I am preparing a Spanish paella."

"Wonderful, I cook paellas all the time. I can certainly help you with the preparations."

"OK, I cooked the chicken, pork, and Italian sausage last night. I am getting ready to cook the rice with saffron. I could use some help in dicing the peppers, tomatoes, onions, and cucumbers."

"OK, just tell me where they are, and I can prepare the *soffirta.*"

"What's the *soffirta?*"

"Oh, you don't know? The vegetables and chili peppers that I will dice are known as the *soffirta* in Spanish. Maybe you did not know that I was born in Monterrey, Mexico. I have dual citizenship, Mexican and British. I met Richard when my parents attended a party at the Peruvian embassy. It's a long story, and perhaps I can tell you the story later this week when we have some downtime."

"OK, it's a deal—Rose's life story later this week." Maria senses that Jeff has a crush on her daughter. *Who would not? She is so beautiful, charming and intelligent.*

Maria walks down to the lower level and brings up the vegetables and chili peppers. Jeff is now preparing the rice with the saffron. Maria dices all of the vegetables. She takes out a large pan and pours a small amount of olive oil into it. She takes the diced tomatoes, onions, cucumbers, green bell peppers, and hot peppers and drops them into the pan. She stirs the *saffirta*. The *soffirta* will cook for fifteen minutes, until the tips of the onions start turning brown.

Jeff looks at the *soffirta* and says, "OK, we can now drop the meats into the pan." The meats are added to the *soffirta*, and the pan is covered. It will be ready in ten minutes. They want the meats, which were cooked last night, to mix with the vegetables. They all need to be at the same temperature. In parallel to the main dish being prepared, Jeff has shrimp and clams in boiling water. The shrimp are all unshelled, and the clams are cooked until they open. This only takes five to ten minutes. Twenty minutes after Maria started cooking the *soffirta*, everything is ready.

Jeff says, "OK, place the rice in the two large serving bowls."

Maria does exactly that. "OK, done. Ready for the meats and *soffirta*." Jeff carefully spoons the main ingredients over the rice. Maria nicely mixes the ingredients with the rice. "OK, Mr. Jeff, you can add the shrimp and clams."

Jeff adds the shrimp and clams. He also sprinkles green peas over the dish to give it an excellent colorful presentation. He covers the two plates with kitchen towels to keep them warm. Maria has prepared a mixed salad and has cut the watermelon into one-inch cubes. The drinks will be red *sangrias*. In thirty minutes, dinner will be ready.

At 6:30, Jeff announces, "Ladies and gentlemen, dinner is served." The paella dishes are uncovered, and the team starts serving themselves.

Claude says, "If the taste is anything close to this beautiful presentation, it should be really good."

After they have all served themselves paella and salad, Vinny comes around with a pitcher of red sangria. The pitcher has cut oranges and slices of watermelon. Each glass has a slice of an orange with a cherry attached to a toothpick.

Rose says, "Jeff, this is delicious. Perhaps you should be a professional cook."

"Thank you, but major credit goes to your mama. I think that after she started helping me, she directed all the timing. She is a damn good cook. She told me that she is Mexican. So, guess what we will have tomorrow?"

"That's great," says Alex, "but I need first to enjoy the paella. Great job, Maria and Jeff."

Richard proposes a toast, "To the two greatest cooks in the world." They raise their glasses, and in unison, they all say, "To Maria and Jeff,"

For the remainder of the evening, they enjoy their meals and restrict themselves to only two glasses of the sangria. They have some preparations to do for the "bridge party."

At 7:30, their dinner is completed. The entire crew helps with the cleanup.

By 8 P.M., the bridge table is ready.

Claude is directing. "Mateo, go ahead and turn on the inside and outside holograms."

"Turning on now. Holograms are operational."

"Vinny, set up the bridge table."

The inside set now has Vinny setting up the bridge table on the simulated veranda. Vinny moves in and out as he carries the fold-out chairs to the set. He needs two trips and one additional trip for the deck of cards. It is important that when the hologram is turned off that the inside set match the outside set.

Claude says, "Richard, go ahead and move to the first chair and sit down."

"Ten-four, moving now." Richard is seen sitting on the first bridge chair.

"OK, team, get ready. Rose and Maria will enter now." Maria and Rose enter and take their seats. The image of Rose is the most exposed.

Claude now enters and sits opposite Rose. They start playing a game of bridge. Bridge games usually last thirty to sixty minutes. This no exception. They continue to play bridge for two hours. No shootings take place. The game ends, and the bridge players leave the table. Vinny takes down the inside set. He brings in the chairs and bridge table. Mateo then turns off the holograms. Now both the inside and outside sets are identical, there is no table or chairs, the verandas are free of any items.

After the bridge game, they all meet for their daily debrief. The fact that no shooting took place was expected. If the shooting is to take place, it will be on the third or fourth day. They are all experienced special operatives. The assassin will need to have all of his actions preplanned. The first sighting of the target will be intelligence for the assassin. By the third day, he will have sufficient intel to carry out the shooting.

SNIPER NEST:

Wolfgang and Will have been watching with much anticipation. Will says, "You were right, boss, the assholes are night owls. They played bridge in the veranda until 11 P.M. From the type of glasses, it looks like they were drinking hard liquor. They were probably drunk by ten. I noticed that the lights did not go off until after 1 A.M."

"In the evening, where were the dogs?"

"They were outside in the fenced yard."

"As I suspected, the dogs are being used as the first line of defense. Our current shooting location is too far, over two thousand meters, and the wind is too strong. The wind will affect the fight of the bullet. We are going to need to go down to a thousand meters."

"At a thousand meters, won't the dogs detect us?"

"Yes, you're learning, Will. We will need to check the wind direction. It needs to be blowing away from us. Also, we will apply the odor eliminator lotion and bring the Ozonics machine."

"Yeah, boss, you think of everything. Where did you learn all of these things?"

"Years of experience in Afghanistan and Iraq—chasing down ragheads and killing every one of those motherfuckers!"

Wolfgang and Will pack up their gear and plan to shoot the target tomorrow night. Wolf will check the wind direction and decide the location of the sniper nest. He still has some apprehension about the escape plan. He needs to think this through and put into place contingencies. He will sleep on it and decide what, if any, backup plans need to be put in place.

Chapter Twenty-Four

Fourth Day, the Attack

The Sea Serpent Villa, Scotland

Wolf cannot sleep and wakes up at 4:30. Something is bothering him. He's concerned about the guards. He does not know if they will be able to escape to the truck before the guards come around and block their exit. Early in the morning, he has the solution. They will rent some ATVs. He will move the ATVs to within half a mile of the sniper nest. They can be on them within fifteen minutes after the kill. He will use trails and back roads to escape. They will rent another four-wheel vehicle and park at Forfar. It will be about a half-hour ride on the ATVs, but they will have a clean escape.

Wolf calls Will at 5 A.M. "Will, wake up—we have a long day today."

"This early? I thought we said that the assholes were night owls. What's the rush?"

"Get your ass in gear and meet me in the lobby in fifteen minutes!"

"Yes, sir."

Will comes down from his room. "What's up?"

"Got a new plan for the escape. I will tell you on the way to the rental." The only car rentals are at the airport. Dundee is too small, so they drive to Edinburgh. It is a two-hour drive. On the way to the airport, Wolf tells Will the plan. They arrive at Edinburgh Airport at 7 A.M. and depart at 7:30. Will drives the new rental, and Wolf drives the Land Rover. They drive to Forfar and park the new rental in what appears to be a commuter lot. Both are now back in the Land Rover. At 8 A.M., Wolf calls several ATV rentals. They are closed. He waits until nine and calls again; the second rental has two ATVs available. He asks if they have a flatbed trailer. They do.

"Thank you very much. Can we pick up the ATVs and trailer today?"

"Absolutely, just come by and ask for Harry—I will have them ready. Will this be cash or credit card?"

"It will be cash."

"Very well, you will need to leave your passport with us. Will that be a problem?"

"No, I will have my passport with me."

Wolfgang has been around long enough to know that these types of situations will occur. Back at the Tennessee camp, he has two specialists making fake documents. He has counterfeit passports from South Africa, Poland, Russia, and Australia.

Wolf and Will need to go back to the car rental place in Dundee and exchange the Land Rover for one with a trailer hitch. By 1 P.M., their Plan B getaway plan is now in place. They go back to their hotel.

Wolf says, "OK, let's take a nap—it's going to be a long day. We may be on the run all night."

"All night! No way, boss! You are going to plug the bitch, her boyfriend, and the two guards all in ten seconds. Hell, when the cook, gardener, old man, and old woman come out crying, you can mow them down as well."

"Yeah, if I can get the bitch and her boyfriend—I will be thrilled."

"By the way, should I take my rifle? I can help with the guards."

"OK, but no ammo until I give you the OK to load. I do not want you shooting me in my ass."

Wolfgang and Will take a nap and hang around the pool. They drink a couple of piña coladas and mai tais. At 4 P.M., they get ready for the main event. Wolf checks the wind direction.

He says, "Shit, the wind direction will require us to move the ATVs. We guessed wrong. The wind has shifted."

They wanted to be at the sniper's nest by 5 P.M., but the shift in the wind direction has caused the first of many decisions that will be made that were not anticipated. They arrive at the Land Rover parking spot and quickly apply the odor eliminator lotion. Wolf packs the Ozonics odor eliminator machine, and they slip on their backpacks, strap on their knives, and holster their Glocks. They check each other to make sure that everything is in order.

Wolf says, "Better take the walkie-talkies; you never know, we may need them if we get separated."

"I have my binoculars and monocle in my backpack. Should I take the infrared monocle as well?"

"Absolutely."

It is now 8 P.M., and they are three hours behind schedule. They settle in at the sniper's nest. In their rush to stay on schedule, Will has not covered himself at all times with the thermal blanket. He is always lagging behind, so Wolf has not noticed the security breach. They arrive at the designated sniper nest. Wolf quickly takes out the M-24 sniper rifle. He attaches the scope. Will has the monocle and is using the range finder and checking the wind direction. As Wolf predicted, their target is again playing bridge.

Wolf thinks about his days in the Marines. When he participated in the joint warfare exercises, the flyboys from the Air "Farce" had all of the cushy jobs. They ran into their Quonset huts and directed the air drones. Some fucking warriors—they were playing video games. They never encountered the enemy face to face like the Marines. During the exercises, they had even less battle time. The flyboys were always playing bridge. You would think that they would play poker. Once, when he jokily said, "Why don't you fly girls play a man's game like Texas hold 'em?"

They said, "Mind your own fucking business, blockhead. You do not have the brainpower to play this game." Ever since then, he hated all people who played that chickenshit card game—bridge.

He looks through the scope. "Will, give me the distance."

"One hundred thirteen meters."

"Wind."

"Wind is at eight knots north to northeast—blowing in our face."

"Location of the guards?"

"See only one."

"OK, let's do a calibration to the possible guard locations. SUV?"

"One hundred and twenty meters."

"Next to the garage?"

"Ninety-eight meters."

Wolf goes on and asks for a total of ten possible guard locations. He agrees with Will: *If I can take out the guards—I will do it.* He thinks of his time on the battlefield. More than once, he took out the prime target and two or three ragheads. Now he waits until there is a guard change; they will be together at that time—that will be "D" time.

They wait fifteen minutes; it is now 9:30.

The guard in the house comes out. He is talking with the second guard.

"OK, Will, here we go. Roll the camera."

"Camera rolling."

"Recheck it. We only get one take."

"Check...camera rolling."

Wolf looks through the scope. Target on crosshairs, he makes the adjustments for distance, height, and wind. He slowly starts squeezing the trip.

The Sea Serpent, Hologram Sets

The fourth day begins. They will again repeat the bridge game. However, the daytime activities must continue like there was no threat. They have the usual breakfast. Maria has taken over the cooking duties from Jeff, who is now the busboy. For breakfast, they have *huevos rancheros* with coffee, orange juice, and Mexican *dulces* (candy). After their breakfast, they meet in the family room and plan their day.

Claude, as the team leader, begins the discussion. "Let's first have last night's debrief. Vinny, did we see anything with the drone video?"

"No, I did not see any unusual activities. I did see a possible incident with the infrared camera. The infrared at night shows all objects that emit heat. Unfortunately, this is summer in Scotland. In the twilight hours, the leaves are radiating heat. Thus, it is difficult to detect small objects. Large objects such as a cow or horse are easy to differentiate. I had several objects that could have been portions of a person, like an arm or leg, but these objects occurred in the entire 360 degrees of view. It is possible that one of these heat signatures was a person's arm or leg, especially if the person had a thermal blanket over their body."

Rose responds, "Yes, in Iraq, we did witness the terrorists using thermal blankets to defeat our infrared cameras."

"Does that mean that our assassin is an ISIS raghead?" asks Jeff.

"No, not likely. I think it is a person with special ops experience. We've had several instances where a special operations soldier from Delta or one of the Seal teams went gone off the reservation and joined such organizations as the KKK or the white nationalists. I attend a classified briefing where several former special operations agents were caught on CNN and MSNC marching with the white nationalists in Charlottesville."

Alex says, "When I made my initial recon of the property, I could feel that someone was watching. It is the sixth sense that you develop from years of experience. I was in Fallujah with the Seals, and we could always tell when the natives were watching. We could not see them, but they were there. It was the same when we conducted the property recons."

Mateo adds, "I went up to the mountain on the north side, about fifty meters. The simulated scene looks real. If the jackass is out there, he will bite—no doubt!"

"OK," says Claude, "let's have a typical day until this evening. Rose, we will not expose you until the hologram tonight. Your call What would you like to do outside the property?'

"Let me ask my mother. Perhaps we can go sight-seeing—ah, don't worry, it will be in an enclosed area, like a museum."

Rose and Maria go off to the couch and start looking at some brochures.

Maria says, "How about the castle in Perth?"

"Perfect."

Alex and Mateo will be detailed to act as security guards. This will be natural. They will make it a point to show that they are accompanying the two ladies—perfectly normal.

The day is completed with no incidents. At dinnertime, Maria prepares a typical English dish: dumplings and stuffed cabbage. The book on the Brits is that they do not know how to cook, but not Maria; the meal is absolutely delicious.

Jeff says, "Mr. Mathews, how do you stay so slim with a great cook like your wife?"

"Yes, it is a problem. I have to run and burn off at least a thousand calories a day."

They finish their dinner and prepare for the bridge game. All actors know their parts. Vinny arranges the card table and chairs. Mateo checks out the hologram equipment. Claude checks out the gun turret. Vinny is on the drone, and Jeff has the comms.

Maria, Richard, and Claude first take their seats. Rose then follows and sits at the most exposed position.

A half-hour passes, and Mateo goes outside to relieve Alex. Mateo and Alex are conversing; Rose and Claude have the playing hand. Rose is the dummy.

The evening is tranquil and serene. It is 9:37 in the evening. The sun is still on the horizon with scattered clouds. The hills around the villa are hiding the sun, so the property is totally in the shade. The house is surrounded by a lovely garden. There are two water fountains, which were designed with three drinking levels for birds. Outside, the crickets and birds can be heard chirping. Bees, hummingbirds, and butterflies are pollinating and dancing on the flowers. The garden has Scotch thistle, bog myrtle, gorse, heather, bluebells, honeysuckle, and crepe myrtle. In the background, the TV is on at a low volume. The CNN international announcer is discussing the latest issues with Brexit. Parliament is in full disagreement.

Suddenly there is a suppressed BANG; the hologram image of Rose's head explodes. Three loud BANGs immediately follow. All hell breaks loose.

Sniper Nest

Wolfgang takes a deep breath and slowly squeezes the trigger—THUD. The bullet leaves the chamber at supersonic speed. Wolfgang keeps the scope on the target—crush, the explosion of the head. Direct hit. He starts to scan for the boyfriend when he hears three rounds and simultaneously feels the compression of the supersonic bullets directly above his head. He immediately reacts to the incoming fire. He pushes himself back to seek cover. As he is in a reverse crawl, he hears the gunshots from the guards. The bullets are hitting below the sniper nest and are creating a dust bowl. Will is following suit. He also is crawling back to seek cover.

Wolfgang screams, "Get the hell outta here! The hell with the other targets. The prime target is dead. Will, pick up the camera, get your ass in gear, and let's get the hell outta here!

"What-what happened?"

"No time to talk. I said get the camera, and let's shag ass!"

"What about my rifle?"

"Forget it. I have mine. How many times do I need to tell you we need to get out of here? They know where we are. We are headed for the ATVs."

As they are running through the brush, Will says, "Good thinking, boss. Good thing we have the ATVs."

"Shut up, Will. I need to think. We got some serious pros after us!"

The Sea Serpent Villa

Immediately following the shots, the team goes into action.

Vinny is viewing the video from the drone. Jeff is in charge of the comms. Alex and Mateo take the point and run to their SUV and drive to the location being vectored by Vinny. Claude and Rose are at the makeshift command post. They will spring into action once the assassin shows his intentions.

Richard and Maria stand back, behind Claude and Rose. They now allow Rose's team to do their work. Both Richard and Maria are proud of their daughter and her professional team. They are confident that they will apprehend the person or persons who attempted to murder their daughter.

Chapter Twenty-Five

Fourth and Fifth Day, the Chase

Southern Scotland

Wolf and Will are in full retreat. Both are having an adrenaline rush; their heartbeats are racing at 130 to 140 beats per minute. Wolf is at the head of the two-man run to the ATVs. To combat against the thick foliage and the bushes with the thorns, they are wearing thick cargo pants and long sleeve shirts. The thick clothes protect them from the spines and the sharp leaf edges. But the thorns, broken branches, and thick leaves are sticking to their clothes. Wolf is using his arms to thrash at the bushes. He loses his sense of direction as he seeks openings in the bushes.

Will shouts to Wolf, "We are headed in the wrong direction!"

"Shut up and follow. I know what I am doing."

They are moving in an easterly direction. The ATVs are due north. After walking quickly for fifteen minutes, Wolf stops to catch his breath.

He says, "The ATVs should be right around the corner!"

Will knows that they are nowhere near the ATVs. He says in an apologetic voice, "Sir, I think they are due north."

"Why would you say that?"

"Sir, when we left the shooting location, the sun was setting to the west.

The ATVs were due north from there. We have been moving directly in the opposite direction of the setting sun."

Wolf thinks for a few seconds. "Yeah, you may be right—so, why the hell did you not open your trap and tell me that we were going in the wrong direction?"

For the first time in his relationship with Wolf, Will does not say anything, but he does think, *FUCKING ASSHOLE!*

Wolf knows Will is right. The best thing would be to retrace their steps and go back to where he turned right. He should have gone straight. Instead, his pride affected his decision. He turns left and heads north. His thought process is that he will move north for five minutes and then turn left again. They walk and run for another ten minutes.

Will says, "Wolf, I recognize this spot. We are close. Let's make a left turn, and the ATVs should be there."

"OK, lead the way, smartass." As they reach the ATVs, it is 11:15. As they are mounting the ATVs, they hear three rounds in the distance: Bang—Bang—Bang. The leaves above them are being hit. Small branches and leaves start falling on their heads. They turn the keys on the ATVs and rumble off to the east. "Let's get the hell out here," says Wolf. "They are mad as hell—like hornets after you poke their nest."

The sun has set, and there is no sunlight for this leg of the journey. Wolf has mapped out the path to Forfar. There is a hiking trail two hundred meters east. After they reach the trail, they will turn left and follow the path to Forfar. The bad part is that it will soon be dark. They will need to use their lights. They reach the hiking path and turn left. After only ten minutes, it is dark. He makes a decision: they will travel at a slower pace and not use the lights. The hiking path has a number of forks in the road. They stop at each one, and he takes out the hand-drawn map and uses the cellphone flashlight. At every fork, Wolf signals either to the left or right. He calculates that they should reach Forfar at twelve midnight. Midnight comes, and they are not at the Forfar parking lot.

He mumbles to Will, "Fuck this shit." He takes out his cellphone and tries the GPS. His phone has been on all day—no battery, the phone is dead. "Will, check your cell phone."

"Sorry, boss, my cell phone is dead."

Wolf looks at his map and then looks up at the stars. The sky is overcast. He again says, "I'm fucked."

"Boss, I think we are near. See the light on the water tower. That's the water tower for Forfar!"

Wolf thinks, *Guess Will is not an idiot*. "OK, lead the way—let's head for the water tower."

They drive to the water tower, but they still do not know where the parking lot is located. Will is very observant. He sees the water tower and scans the town, left to right. He says in a matter-of-fact way, "The parking lot is right around that corner. It is behind the hardware store." It is now forty-five minutes past midnight.

"Good memory, Will, let's go." They drive around the corner. Then they go to the area where the rental should be parked. It is not there! Wolf says, "Goddamn it, someone stole our truck."

Will looks around and points to a sign. "NO OVERNIGHT PARKING." Below this, the sign says, "Unauthorized vehicles will be removed at 12 midnight."

"Shit." Wolf remembers what they always said in the Marines: "Your plan is only good until the first shot is taken."

"Now what, boss?"

"Shut up, Will, I'm thinking." After a couple of minutes, Wolf looks at a tourist map. "OK, we ride ATVs north. We need to find a secluded farm and hotwire a car."

Neither Wolf nor Will notes that they both have only a quarter tank of gas.

WMA Team

The Sea Serpent

The shot fired by the assassin hit Rose's image and exploded at the base of the veranda retainer wall. There will be a need to have a carpenter come out and make some repairs. Claude goes over and takes his Gerber knife and digs out the slug.

Rose says, "Nice trophy. Bet no one has the bullet that killed them."

"Rose," says Maria, "how you can be so cool about the attempt on your life?"

"Sweetheart," says Richard, "they know what they are doing—she's going to be just fine."

Immediately following the shot from the assassin and the three shots from the gun turret, Alex and Mateo pulled out their Glocks and started firing in the direction of the assassin. After they emptied their twelve-bullet cartridges, they reach down and pull out a magazine from their ammunition belts. They quickly eject the empty magazine and insert a fully loaded one into the handle of the handgun. They run to their SUV and start driving on the road adjacent to the assassin's nest.

"OK Alex," says Mateo, "let's stay on the road and receive instructions from the command post."

"We are on the road headed in the direction of the gunshots," Alex says over the radio. "Request a vector?"

"OK, I can see your truck," says Vinny. "Continue on the road toward Kirriemuir."

Vinny, Jeff, Claude, and Rose are at the makeshift command post. Richard and Maria are staying back and out of the way. They have been instrumental in helping to carry out the fake assassination scene and have a stake in the outcome.

Jeff is in charge of communications. "I have reconfigured the radio comms. All members are now on channel one. I will conduct a roll call. Alex, do you copy?"

"Copy."

"Mateo, do you copy?"

"Copy."

Vinny, Claude, and Rose give thumbs up.

Vinny says, "We have two tangos on foot headed in a northeasterly direction. They are traveling at about four to five miles per hour."

"Alex and Mateo," says Claude, "hold your position. The tangos are moving in your direction."

"Copy that," replies Alex. "We will hold, waiting for your directions."

"I have a change in direction," says Vinny. "Tangos moving east. Looks like they are headed toward Forfar."

"Alex," says Claude, "Move your vehicle one-mile east."

"Roger, will do."

Fifteen minutes later, Vinny comes back on the comms. "Tangos now moving north."

"Copy," says Alex.

Five minutes later, Vinny keys the radio. "Tangos moving westerly. They are headed back toward Blairgowrie."

"They are using some tradecraft," says Mateo, "probably checking to see if they are being followed."

"Maybe," says Rose. "They may also be lost. We will keep tracking and keep you advised of tango location."

"Roger that. We are on standby."

"Rose may be right," says Claude. "The tangos think they have a kill. They have to believe that we are pissed. Kind like our queen bee has been killed."

"Why not have either Alex or Mateo fire some rounds in their direction?" asks Jeff. "Make them think that we are on the chase?"

"Good idea," says Rose. "What do you think, Claude?"

Claude thinks about it for a few seconds and says to Vinny, "Give me the most probable location of the tangos in ten minutes."

"Can do—they will be one mile south of the Forfar road." Vinny gives Alex and Mateo the coordinates.

"Got it," says Alex.

"I will position myself to intercept the tangos and fire a few rounds above their heads," says Mateo.

"I have the tangos moving north toward you," says Vinny. "They will be one hundred meters south-southwest in two minutes." Vinny waits two minutes. "Mateo, fire at eight o'clock from your position."

Mateo fires three rounds from his Glock—BANG, BANG, BANG.

Vinny says, "Holy shit, they are traveling on wheels. I can see the heat from the engines. They have turned off their lights."

"Yes, I can hear the engines," says Alex. "My guess is they have mounted some all-terrain vehicles."

"Yes," says Mateo, "I caught a glimpse of the ATVs. Headed east toward Forfar."

Claude says, "Rose, we will need your dad's Volvo with the trailer hitch."

Richard has been listening and viewing the twin displays. He walks over to the side door and takes the car keys that are hanging from the key hooks. He says, "Try not to wreck it. I only bought it last year."

"Don't you worry about the car," says Maria. "Just make sure that my little Rosita is going to be OK."

Claude takes the keys. "Thank you. Let's go, Rose. I will get the ATVs ready. We may need them tonight." Claude and Rose run outside to the garage. They enter the combo on the keypad, and the garage door opens. They rush to the ATVs and push them outside. Rose runs to the Volvo and backs it up to the flatbed trailer. She expertly backs up the Volvo to the hitch, and Claude pushes down on the holding cap. He takes the safety pin and inserts it in the hitching gear. Rose drives the Volvo to the ATVs. Claude fuels both. Rose walks to one, turns the key, and—GURUMMM, GURUMMM—it starts, she drives the ATV up the ramp and onto the flatbed. Claude finishes fueling the second ATV. Rose comes around, mounts the ATV, turns the key, and GURUMMM. She drives the second ATV onto the flatbed trailer. Claude secures the two ATVs and the two five-gallon gasoline tanks with thick bungee cords. The entire operation has taken them a little under ten minutes. They rush back in the house.

Vinny says, "Don't know what those two idiots are doing. They seem to be driving in a circle."

"Fuckers are lost," adds Jeff.

"The shots fired by Mateo have them concerned," says Richard. "They now know that they are being followed. That's why they turned off their lights."

"Hey, Dad," says Rose, "you would have made a good intel officer."

"Yeah, all those years at the embassies—I learned something from those eggheads."

"Eggheads, what the hell does that mean?" asks Vinny.

"That was their name before they became nerds," says Richard.

"Yeah, I kinda like it. Guess I'm an egghead?"

"Vinny," says Jeff, "get back on focus."

"Yeah, right. The tangos have been spinning their wheels inside a fifteen-mile area. If we are lucky, they are gonna run out of gas. By the way, why are they called tangos?"

"Tangos for targets, also bogies for bad guys—I think," says Jeff.

"I don't really give a shit—tangos and bogies sound like I am in a movie with James Bond!"

As Vinny and Jeff have some good-natured ribbing, Claude and Rose have been watching intently. After slow progress riding their ATVs for more than ninety minutes, the tangos finally make it to Forfar. They drive around the town very slowly, keeping the noise from the ATVs to a low rumble. They stop at what appears to be a parking lot. As the tangos are walking across the lot, they seem to be arguing. After five minutes, they mount back on their ATVs and head north.

Chapter Twenty-Six

Fifth Day, Storage Shed

Somewhere in Scotland

Using the infrared camera on the WMA drone, Vinny has been able to track the two tangos continuously. The display at the command post displayed them mounting their ATVs and heading north.

When it was determined that the two assassins were using ATVs, Claude and Rose departed from The Sea Serpent. They drove toward the town of Forfar to meet up with Alex and Mateo.

Claude says, "Vinny, vector me to the location of Alex and Mateo."

"OK, continue on your road toward Forfar. Location is five miles north."

"Provide status of the two tangos," says rose.

"Tangos are circling the woods two miles south of Forfar."

"We are currently parked off the road in the rest stop," says Alex. "Rest stop is named Little Loch."

"Are you on the right or left?" asks Rose. "Is there room to park the ATV and the trailer?"

"Negative, no room. We will drive on to Forfar and check for the area to offload the ATVs," says Alex.

"Roger. Thank you."

Vinny says, "Hold on, guys, the tangos are approaching Forfar."

"Alex and Mateo," says Claude, "how far are you from Forfar?"

"Around the corner. Five minutes out," says Mateo.

"Hold on," says Rose. "Do not approach the tangos. They are armed and dangerous. Wait for us for support."

"Roger. Will wait immediately outside the city."

Vinny, with much excitement, says, "The tangos have mounted the ATVs and are headed north. They are using hiking paths. Lights are on. They are moving much faster. Estimate ten to fifteen miles per hour."

"Vinny," says Claude, "give Alex and Mateo the nearest town north of Forfar."

"Will do. Stand by. The area north of Forfar is open rugged hills. The nearest town is Balmoral."

"OK," says Alex. "I see it on my map. Will need to drive around toward Blairgowrie and to Balmoral. GPS says fifty-five minutes."

"We are driving to Forfar," says Claude. "Off load the ATVs, and we will track using them."

Jeff, who has been silent throughout the chase, says, "I have googled the area north of Forfar. The satellite view indicates rugged mountains. It does have several hiking and horse trails."

Claude and Rose follow the tangos on their ATVs at a safe distance. The idea is to track them. The tangos have been on their ATVs for over three hours. Claude and Rose calculate that they will soon run out of gas. Then they will be easier to track. It is now 2 A.M. The tangos will also need to stop and get some rest. Daylight is early in the summer season in Scotland. The sun is scheduled to rise at 3:49.

Wolfgang and Will

Wolfgang and Will leave the Forfar parking lot at 1 A.M. The going has been rough. They do not know the area. It is rugged and hilly. Wolf knows that they cannot push the ATVs past their limits. They cannot risk having a broken ATV. He signals Will to stop; the ATVs are getting hot. They need to cool down. As they stop for ten minutes, Wolf can hear the ATVs that are tracking them. He thinks these guards and the target's boyfriend appear to be real pros.

How in the hell were they able to return his fire after he killed the target is really puzzling? The incoming fire when they first mounted the ATVs is also puzzling. Now he has some ATVs tracking them in the middle of Scotland. He takes some time to think. As he is resting on the ATV, he asks Will, "Do you have the infrared monocle?"

Will looks puzzled. He goes to his backpack and searches. Then he pulls out the infrared monocle and says, "Is this it?"

"Well, don't just stand there. Bring it to me!"

Will is tired, and he shuffles over to Wolf and throws it to him. Wolf is not expecting the throw. The monocle hits Wolf in the forehead and drops down on some rocks and cascades down a natural set of stone steps. Wolf is really pissed. He says, "Goddamn it, Will, I am trying to get us out of this clusterfuck. You think you can help?"

"Sorry, boss, I am really tired."

"Yeah, I told you to get some rest this afternoon. I told you it was going to be a long night—-but no, you went to the bar and had piña coladas and mai tais. OK, pick up the monocle and let's forget it."

Wolf knows what he is doing—he takes the monocle and scans the sky. After six minutes, he stops. *Yeah, just as I thought, a goddamn drone!*

The moonlight is reflecting off the propellers. Will says, "Do you see something, boss?"

"Yeah, hand me my rifle." Will chambers a bullet and gives the rifle to Wolf.

Wolf gets on his knees and places his elbow on a boulder. He uses the rifle strap for added stability and views through the scope. The drone is only at five hundred feet, and it is a sitting duck. He places the crosshairs on the drone and fires. He sees the drone explode into a thousand pieces. He mumbles, "Assholes. Now let's see how good you are at tracking."

The Sea Serpent Villa

Vinny and Jeff have been the eyes of the chase team. From the drone, which has been following every move of the tangos, Vinny has been directing Claude, Rose, Alex, and Mateo: Claude and Rose on the ATVs and Alex and Mateo on their SUV.

Vinny calls on the radio, "Tangos have stopped. The ATV has been turned off. Looks like they are resting their bodies and possibly letting the ATVs cool down. I see some unusual activity. Looks like they are having some discussion. Probably planning their next move."

Jeff says, "Hold on. One tango is holding his rifle. Looks like he's getting ready to shoot. Repeat, Rose and Claude, take cover. He may be trying to take a long shot."

"Copy," says Rose. "We have taken cover."

Vinny sees a yellow-reddish ball explode, and his screen goes black. "Shit, those fuckers have hit the drone!"

"The drone has been hit," says Jeff.

"OK, understood," says Rose. "We can hear the ATVs. We will track on sound. They have been running for over four hours. They will soon run out of gas."

Jeff has an idea. He turns to Richard and asks, "Mr. Mathews, you told me in our discussions in Bristol that Winston and Monty can track game. Is that right?"

"Yes, that's correct. When they were pups, I took them through a training program. If you can give them the scent to track, I believe they can track anything."

"OK, I'm on my way to the sniper nest," says Vinny. "I bet that in their haste to get out and start running for cover, they left some clothing items."

Jeff, Richard, and Maria wake up the dogs. Maria feeds them, and then she lets them out into the fenced back yard to do their business. Jeff takes the keys for the Aston Martin and runs to the garage. He opens the garage door, walks around to the driver's side, and pulls out the car. He drives it around to the kitchen door of the villa.

Vinny is coming down from the sniper nest. "We are in luck. I found two baseball caps. The sweatbands are exactly that, sweatbands." They place the baseball caps in two Ziploc bags.

Jeff is driving, and Mr. Mathews is riding shotgun. Winston and Monty occupy the entire back seat. Jeff waves at Vinny and Maria. "Let's roll. He keys his radio and will drive to the nearest location where either Rose or Claude can meet them to pick up the dogs.

Vinny goes back to the command post. It is now only Vinny and Maria directing the action. Vinny will be using the GPS from the team members to direct their movement. However, they have now lost the ability to track the tangos—they will need to rely on Winston and Monty.

Rose agrees to drive back to the major road to Blairgowrie. This the last known location of the tangos. The ATVs from the villa have supply carts attached over the back wheels. Winston and Monty will ride in them. Rose volunteered to pick up the dogs since she has known them since they were puppies.

Rose meets Jeff and her dad at the designated location. Her dad gives her some commands to use on the dogs. He says, "Take the caps, let them both smell them and give the command 'Find'—that's it. They will immediately start sniffing the ground to try and find the owner of the smell."

"Will they be able to track them if they are on their ATVs?" asks Rose.

"I doubt it, but once they are on foot, no problem. They will track as well as the best bloodhound money can buy!"

"OK, I got it."

Jeff sure wishes he could go with Rose. He needs to protect her just as he did in the Chihuahua raid. He looks at her and says, "Stay safe, keep your head down, and good luck—break a leg!"

Rose goes back to join Claude. The dogs seem to enjoy the ride. They stick their noses into the sky and enjoy the wind blowing around their ears and snoots.

Rose asks Claude, "Any change in status?"

"Yes, the tangos rode the ATV for only five minutes. I think they are now on foot. I was waiting for you to pick up their tracks."

"OK, let's ride to the last known location of the ATVs and begin to track using the dogs."

Rose keys her radio. "We are headed to the last known ATV location. We will need to approach with caution. We know that they are armed and will use their weapons."

Rose and Claude reach the location of the abandoned ATVs. Rose keys her radio. Alex and Mateo, what is your twenty?" (Note: twenty is radio talk asking for their location.)

"We are approximately five miles from your location," replies Alex. "Move yourselves between our location and Blairgowrie."

"Copy, moving now."

Wolfgang and Will

Wolfgang and Will are now on foot. They rode their ATVs for five minutes after shooting down the drone. Then the ATVs sputtered to a stop—out of gas. Will says, "We are out of gas."

"OK, we now go on foot. Take only what we need. It will be daybreak in an hour. We need to seek shelter and get some rest."

"I have seen some sheds that appear to be storing hay for the cattle."

"Good point. We'll keep our eyes open and see what we can find." He thinks for a few seconds and then says, "Let's walk for an hour and get some distance from our pursuers."

"Do you think they can track us now that we have shot down their drone?"

"No, I do not think so. The security contractors are nothing more than mall cops. Probably have no tracking experience. With the drone out of commission, we now hold all the cards."

"Yeah, we are the pros, and they are amateurs."

"OK, Will, let's move it. We need distance between us and our pursuers."

They walk for one hour, and it is now 4 A.M. The sun is behind the mountains on the east side.

Will says, "Look at the building at ten o'clock. Looks like a storage shed."

Yes, that may be ideal. We will investigate and see if we can hunker down."

They cautiously approach the storage shed. Wolf tells Will, "You stay here, pull out your walkie-talkie, and keep in comm. Tell me if you see anyone approach."

Wolf approaches the shed in a cat-like fashion, running from bush to tree to bush, and reaches the shed double doors. He peeks through a crack in the wall and then pushes one of the doors open. He carefully steps inside. As he suspected, there is no one in the shed. It is strictly a storage shed. He keys the walkie-talkie. "Will, come on in, but keep your ass low. You need to make yourself small, just like we practiced at our camp in Tennessee."

"Roger, on my way." Will reaches the storage shed and carefully opens the door. Wolf has taken off his backpack and is resting on a bale of hay.

Wolf says, "We need some rest. Go ahead and get some sleep. Four hours should be OK. I will wake you up at 8 A.M. Then I will then get some rest. We will stay here till nightfall. Eat one of the energy bars."

Will eats one of the energy bars, and in five minutes, he is asleep. Wolf sits next to a crack in the wall and tries to stay awake. He is still not sure that they have lost the tail.

WMA Team:

Rose and Claude have added two new team members, Winston and Monty. They drive to the location where the tangos abandoned their ATVs. Rose reaches into a Ziploc bag and pulls out the one baseball cap. She holds the cap up to the nose of Winston. She goes to the second Ziploc and pulls out the second baseball cap and puts it at the nose of Monty.

Rose then issues the command, "FIND."

Both dogs wag their tails and start sniffing the ground. The dogs circle around the ATVs. Winston goes out to the tall grass. He sniffs the grass, looks back at Rose, and gives a low, "Woof."

Monty runs over to Winston. He also sniffs the tall grass, looks at Rose, and gives a low, "Woof."

Rose says, "OK, we have the trail. Dad told me to let them loose—let them roam free. They will not stray further than ten or thirty yards. They will find the trail and always look back for an attaboy. He also gave me a bag of treats. He said to reward them as they continue to track."

Claude keys his radio, "Don't know whose idea it was to use the dogs—but good work. That's thinking out of the box."

Jeff says, "Roger, we have you on GPS. By the way, the dog collars also have GPS, so we also have the location of Winston and Monty. The strict instructions from Maria are, 'Don't lose the dogs!'"

"Yeah, not sure who she wants to protect more, Rose or the dogs."

Maria grabs the radio from Jeff and says, "All three."

"Roger, we all understand. Alex and Mateo, park your SUV and start walking toward us."

"Vinny, give me a vector," says Alex.

"Your vector is 195 degrees from north. Rose and her three companions are ten miles from your location. Tangos are somewhere in between."

"Roger, on our way. We should have them in a pincher sometime today."

The movement of Rose, Claude, and the dogs is slower than expected. The tangos have some professional experience. The dogs lose the trail, only to pick it up several hundred yards later. It appears that the trail they are leaving is zigzagging. Perhaps the tangos are moving and looking back to cover their six? It is now 6 A.M., and they have covered two miles from the abandoned ATV. Both Rose and Claude are walking. The ATV makes too much noise—it would be a dead giveaway.

They continue their slow but methodical search for the trail. Winston and Monty are doing a good job. They come to a hill about two hundred meters in height. Ninety percent of it is rock, and the trail leads straight up. It is evident that the tangos are purposely making it difficult to track them. An average person would simply try to move from X to Y location and would go around the hill.

Claude says, "If they went up, they will need to come down." Claude carefully sneaks up the hill to ensure that they are not using it as an observation point. After thirty minutes, he comes down from the hill—they are not there. Next, they take the dogs around the hill to pick up the scent. After another forty-five minutes, they again pick it up.

Vinny comes on the radio. "Alex and Mateo, you are within five hundred meters of Rose's location."

"OK," says Alex, "Vector me in."

"It is dead south; you are now one hundred meters from Rose and Claude."

"Yes, I see them. Thank you."

Upon reaching Rose and Claude, Alex says, "I brought some charged batteries for the radios. You are probably running low. How can we help?"

Rose thinks for a few seconds. "Have Vinny vector you to our ATVs. We have some blankets and sleeping bags. At some time, we will need some sleep. We have now been up over thirty-six hours."

"OK, Mateo, let's go. Vinny, vector me to the ATVs."

"Roger." Vinny gives Alex and Mateo the directions to the ATVs. An hour later, Alex and Mateo return with them.

Claude says, "We will leave the ATVs at least a half-mile behind us. I am fairly certain that we are close."

Wolfgang and Will at the Storage Shed

At 8 A.M., Wolf wakes up Will, who has had four hours of sleep. He tells Will, "I only need three hours of sleep. Wake me up at 11 A.M. Sit here and look through this crack in the wall. If they are tracking us, it will be from this side."

"If I see them," says Will, "do I wake you up?"

Wolf looks exasperated. He says, "Of course, shithead—wake me up." He lies down on the straw, and within two minutes, he is asleep.

WMA Team

The dogs have picked up the scent on the other side of the hill. The tracking is getting easier. The tangos are now traveling in a straight line.

Rose says, "The tangos traveling in a straight line indicates that they have lowered their security protocols. They think that they have lost us. They are probably overconfident now that they took out the drone."

It is now 10 A.M. They come over a hill and see the storage shed. The dogs are twenty yards in front and making a beeline to the shed. Rose remembers what her father told her: "They will not venture more than twenty yards in front of you. They will always look back to get reassurance that they are doing a good job. If you want them to come back—reach in your dog treats bag and hold the treat out. They will come back."

The dogs are excited. They look back at Rose, she holds out a treat, and they both come back to her. As she is giving them a treat, she says, "Claude, put the leashes on Winston and Monty."

Claude opens the clip and attaches the leash to the dog collars. He says, "OK, let's confirm that the tangos are in the storage shed. You take Winston and circle counter-clockwise, and I will take Monty and circle clockwise. If they have not exited the shed, then the dogs will find nothing. If they do find a trail—well, then we keep going. Make sure we stay out of sight from the shed. They will likely have a lookout."

Rose and Claude take forty-five minutes to complete the circle. The dogs do not find an exit path. They now have confirmation that the tangos are in the shed. They confer amongst themselves. It has been a long day and night. No one has slept for thirty-six hours. Alex and Mateo have sleeping bags in their backpacks. They both go back and drive the ATVs to a half a mile from the gathering point. They've brought more sleeping bags. Claude volunteers to take the first watch. Rose, Alex, and Mateo cocoon themselves in their sleeping bags, and they are all asleep within two minutes. They all sleep until 2 P.M. Alex wakes up first. He tells Claude to get some sleep. Claude inserts himself in his sleeping bag, and he falls asleep in one minute. By 6 P.M., they have all had six hours of sleep. They are all fresh and ready for the capture of the two tangos.

Storage Shed Tangos

Wolf left instructions for Will to wake him at 11 A.M. That would only be a two-hour nap. At the designated time, everything is quiet. Wolf has been edgy the last six hours because of a lack of sleep. Will makes what Wolf calls a battlefield decision and lets Wolf sleep through the designated time. Will is confident that no one is following. He is sure that Wolf will be happy with his four hours of sleep.

Wolf wakes up at 2:15 P.M. He's had five hours of sleep. He looks around, gets his bearings, and says, "Will, what time is it?"

"It's 2:15 in the afternoon."

"What the fuck? I told you to wake me up at eleven this morning! When the hell are you going to learn to follow orders? If we were in the Marines in Iraq, I would have you shot!"

Yeah, boss, but I was being cautious about looking out the cracks on all sides. You have said that I have eagle eyes. We are clear of the assholes following us. The shooting down of the drone has left them with no eyes. There is no fucking way that they can find us. Besides, you need your sleep. We cannot go around some country that we know nothing about with you not having a clear head."

Wolf thinks for a few seconds. "Yeah, you're right. Better that I have some sleep. We can use this afternoon to plan our actions tonight."

"Why the hell do we need any planning? We just walk out, find some car we can hotwire, and we're outta here."

"Hope so, but we need to plan for the worst and hope for the best."

"OK, so, what should I do?"

"Give me a minute or two to think." Wolf walks around inside the shed. He was too tired in the morning, and he was concerned about the security guards that were guarding the villa. Now he is sharp-minded and thinking. He climbs the bales of hay and sees an old tractor inside the shed. Probably hasn't been used in years. He carefully examines the tractor, and it seems to be in fair condition. The tractor does not need a key. It is an old-fashioned type. The starter is on the floorboard. He thinks, *this is not gonna help.* He climbs down and walks to the front of the shed. He looks at the tractor's front. It has a crank that collapses at the elbow. He snaps the crank out. It is now ready to crank. He looks around and sees a five-gallon gas can. He walks over and twists the cap. He opens it, and there is about half an inch of gas. He takes the gas can, and using a funnel, he pours the gasoline into the tractor's gas tank.

"Will, come on over to the tractor. Sit on the driver's seat, I'm going to crank it, you put it in neutral, with the brake on, then turn on the spark/ignition, set the choke and throttle to one-half open and I will crank. After it starts give it some gas.

"OK, ready." Wolf, who is six foot three inches and 230 pounds, cranks the engine. After three tries, the engine comes to life.

"OK, cut it off. Press the off switch!"

"OK, got it." Will is bewildered. He says, "Are we going to plow the land?"

"No, we ain't plowing. I got an idea; it's called a DIVERSION." Wolf goes to the back of the shed and says, "Will, I got a job for you."

"Sure, boss, just tell me what it is, and I will get right to it."

'See the farmer's clothes on the ground?"

Will looks at the clothes and says, "Yeah, I see them."

"Take the clothes, use some of the wood in the shed, and make a strawman to sit on the tractor. When you place the strawman on the tractor, tie it down."

"Yes, sir, I'm on it."

An hour later, the strawman is on the tractor.

"OK, Will, here's the plan. We still do not know if those shitheads are out there waiting for us. We are gonna open the double doors and tie the gas pedal all the way down. We will also tie the steering wheel to go straight. The tractor is going to blast out of here like we are trying to escape. If the guards are out there, they are gonna come out shooting. When that happens, you will run to the small hill on the south side. Lie down and start shooting. Just shoot even if you do not see anything. When the shitheads stick out their heads, I will shoot them with my sniper rifle."

"That's a brilliant plan. Too bad I'm not the one doing the shooting!"

That's the plan he tells Will—the real plan is that he is banking on the double diversion. One, the tractor, and two, Will running to the hill. This will allow him to escape. Will is just a soldier and sometimes pawns need to be sacrificed.

WMA Team

Rose, Claude, Alex, and Mateo are now confident that the two tangos are in the shed. The team has an advantage. They have supplies, food, drinks, and sleeping bags. They are all experienced special operations agents. All have been in worse situations. The two tangos have the disadvantage of running low on supplies, primarily food and water. It is not likely that they planned for an extended escape plan. When the team discusses their options, they all agree: "Wait them out."

Rose says, "I think that we can expect them to try and escape tonight."

"I agree," says Alex. I recommend that we all take one of the four sides. I will take the west side."

"I will take the east side," says Rose. "I need to stay with the dogs. I will take the dogs back about a mile and tie them to an ATV."

Claude and Mateo will take the south and north sides.

Claude says, "Remember, they are armed. When we had the drone, we were going to track them to their point of departure. That is no longer possible. They know that we are in hot pursuit. The plan now is to capture one or both alive. We need to know who paid for the kill."

"Rose," says Mateo, "if at all possible, you need to stay in the background. Remember, you are not upstairs sitting on the stairs of the pearly gates." None of the team members can say the word "killed."

"Roger," replies Rose, "I got it—but sure would like to put a bullet in the head of the shooter."

"Which brings us to an important point," says Claude. "One is the shooter, and one is the spotter. We must treat both as the shooter. The shooter still has the long rifle—he shot the drone out of the sky. They are both very dangerous."

The evening there is a full moon. Tall, fluffy clouds fill the horizon. As the sun starts to set at 10 P.M., the horizon to the west lights up with the sun's rays. They streak through the clouds like reddish-yellow searchlights crossing the sky. As the sun continues to set and darkness consumes the light, the birds can be heard chirping, wolves can be heard howling in the distance, and lightning bugs are flashing their lights in the low-lying grass. Rabbits can be seen dashing amongst the heather, and squirrels can be seen gathering acorns and climbing the trees. It is a quiet and scintillating evening, as it always seems to be before an all-out shooting scene erupts.

Wolfgang goes over the plan with Will. Precisely one hour after the sun has set, the double doors will be open, and the tractor will exit, rumbling to south. At maximum speed, the tractor will travel at ten miles per hour. The moonlight will clearly show the strawman. The bouncing of the strawman will make the tractor look like there is a driver at the controls. When the tractor is thirty yards from the shed, Wilhelm will sprint to the small hill on the north side of the equipment shed. Wolf hopes that his pursuers will take the bait of one of the two diversions. When he sees the pursuers rush the tractor and Will running to the north hill, Wolf will quickly exit to the east.

It is now 11:36, one hour after sunset. If this were a movie set, the director would state, "Action." Wolf cranks the tractor, and the engine coughs to a start. Will ties down the steering wheel and jams the gas pedal to the floor. The tractor blasts out of the shed like a racehorse leaving the starting gate. The strawman is silhouetted against the moon. The tractor is headed south across the level field of three-foot wild grass.

Mateo says over the radio, "Tango is escaping on the tractor. I am taking action to push the tango off the tractor." Mateo waits until the tractor has passed his hiding point, and then he comes up behind it. He needs to run at an all-out dash to keep up with it. The tractor is a diesel and makes a loud, rumbling noise that masks Mateo's steps. He thinks, *Good thing the tango is driving at an all-out speed.* He needs to concentrate on the front of the tractor and overcome the driver within the next five minutes, he cannot continue running at an all-out sprint.

When the tractor is thirty yards outside the gates, Will comes running out at full speed. He pumps his hands like a hundred-meter runner. When he is ten feet from the forest line, he dives behind the bushes. He sees that one of the guards has spotted him, and he pulls out his Glock, which has a fifteen-bullet extended magazine, and starts firing in rapid succession at him.

Alex sees the tango unholster his handgun and dives for cover. He hears the bullets hit the tree limbs above his head. He takes out his radio and transmits, "The second tango at the north end."

Claude replies, "I will circle around and come from behind. Keep him pinned down."

"Roger, will do." Alex fires his handgun above the tango hiding at the north end.

Wolfgang is watching the action. His plan is working. The diversion has flushed the three guards. Wolfgang thinks, *I was right. There are two guards and the boyfriend. No sign of any other asshole.* He waits ten minutes and senses that now is the time to head east. All of the pursuers are tied up with Will and the strawman. He carefully exits toward the east, running with his waist bent to lower his profile. He seeks the highest point. He needs to make sure that Will is killed. He cannot afford him being taken alive. Will talks too much. He has his binoculars and the infrared monocle he used to shot down the drone.

Mateo has overcome the tractor; he grabs the driver and pulls him down. He looks at the strawman and keys his radio. "Team we have been snookered. The driver on the tractor is a dummy." Alex and Claude hear the transmission, but they are occupied with the second tango, who is hiding behind the north hill and is putting up a fight. He continues firing his handgun like he has a bucket of ammo. Will mumbles, "When the hell is Wolf going to kill these fuckers, I cannot keep shooting forever!"

Claude says, "I am thirty yards from the tango. Alex, make some noise. Fire your handgun. I need a fix on the son of a bitch."

"Roger."

From Alex's location, a barrage of bullets is fired at the hiding tango. Claude now has a clear view of the tango. He is pulling the trigger, but the handgun is not firing. He is out of ammunition.

Claude walks toward the assassin and yells, "It's all over! Drop the gun and come out with your hands up."

Will reaches down for his knife and attacks Claude. He lets out the rebel yell: "Ya-Ya-Hwa-Ya-Ya!" Claude wants to take him alive. Wilhelm "Will" Strassman a seventh-generation Confederate rebel who will follow Wolfgang's orders: "Do not let them take you alive." Claude deftly moves to the right. As the knife hand comes across Claude's body, he comes down hard on the right arm. Will loses his knife. In the same motion, Claude grabs the back of Will's neck, slams his right foot behind Will's left leg, and pulls back on his neck, and Will falls like a sack of potatoes. Will is a big man and will not go down easily. As he is falling to the ground, he kicks his feet, much like a five-year-old who is not getting his way. For a big man, he springs up to his feet with surprising speed. He grinds his teeth and says, "Come on, asshole. I'm going to kick your ass."

As he circles Claude, Alex comes from behind and grabs Will in a bear hug. Claude punches Will once, twice in the stomach. Alex takes a pair of flex cuffs and ties his hands behind his back. Will is soon lying on his stomach, with Claude, Alex, and Mateo looking at him like he is a ten-foot tiger shark. Claude grabs Will by the hair and tells him, "Get up, asshole. You've got a lot of talking to do." Claude, Alex, and Mateo look very imposing.

Will is grabbed by the hair and arms. Mateo and Alex pull Will's arms back and secure the flex cuffs. Mateo has a full beard and long hair. His black t-shirt and cargo pants are drenched with sweat and covered in grass stains from chasing the strawman on the tractor. He looks at Will and says, "Asshole, you are in a shitload of trouble."

"I didn't do a damn thing," replies Will. "Wolf shot the bitch. I am only a gofer."

"You know that means you are an accessory to murder."

"Maybe, but my aunt has some pretty highfalutin lawyers."

"Wilhelm, we know that you are connected with the terrorist camp in Tennessee."

Will looks surprised and says, "How the hell do you know that?"

Alex, who has been watching, moves in to play the bad cop. He slaps Will across the face and yells, "Look, motherfucker, you are a lowlife gofer! Your boss doesn't give a shit about you. Did he come back and help you when you were shooting at us?"

Will thinks about this. *He's right. Wolf said that I would draw the fire and he would shoot the assholes. Where is he? Probably running off to London. He used me as a sacrificial lamb.*

Mateo jumps back at him: "Look asshole, we can help you. If you answer our questions, we can tell the prosecuting attorney that you were very helpful and provided valuable evidence. Right now, you are looking at the death penalty."

"If I cooperate, what will that mean?"

"Definitely no death penalty, maybe five or ten years. On good behavior, probably no more than two years,"

Will thinks, *Shit, I spent two years in the pen already. It wasn't that bad. Based on what I know now, I can probably be the top dog there.* "OK, what do you want to know?

"What's the name of your partner?"

Will without thinking says, "Wolfgang, but we call him Wolf."

"Does this Wolf have a last name?"

Now, Will has his senses, he says, "Yeah, Schmitt, eh, eh, Schmitt."

The team now know the name of the assassin, the asshole told them that his name was Wolf.

"Where is Wolf's camp?" asks Mateo.

Will, "Though you said it was in Tennessee?"

OK, asshole, don't play games with me," says Mateo.

"OK. OK, it's between Murfreesboro and Pulaski, Tennessee."

"Has Wolf killed others for hire?"

"Probably. Wolf always talks about his kills in Iraq and Afghanistan from when he was in the Marines."

"OK, but what about kills in the US?"

"Yeah, probably. I overheard him and my aunt Gretchen talking about the money they got from him being a sniper."

"How many people live in the camp?"

"About a hundred."

"Does the money that Wolf earns from his hire for murder support the camp?"

"Yeah, that and what they bring in from the so-called dinner theater the Red Rooster."

"Why do you say so-called?" asks Alex.

"Because it is also a whorehouse. They buy girls from the coyotes and force them into slave-sex."

"Are the girls being held as prisoners?"

"Yeah, they also beat them and have them chained in what they call the slave quarters. I once complained and Aunt Gretchen told me to shut the fuck up. She said that they were sub-human. That the president called them an infestation of roaches. If we can profit from roaches, then it's OK."

Claude says, "OK, when we get back to the villa, we will put everything in writing and help you with the district attorney."

Will does not know that a murder did not occur. He thinks that is has talked the lawmen into giving him a good deal. He has come to the realization that Wolf has hung him out to dry.

The four start walking to the south. Will has his hands tied. The team is not concerned that he will try and run away. He is in good spirits. He believes that he has talked himself into a good deal.

Wolfgang has been watching the capture of Will. After the group subdued Will, the two guards and the boyfriend could not be seen. They were behind some large bushes and a copse of trees. Forty-five minutes later, Will and three men were walking south. Wolf cannot allow Will to be interrogated. He unsheathes his sniper rifle, attaches the scope, and rests his elbow on a tree limb. He thinks for a few seconds about killing Will, reloading, and shooting one of the guards. He remembers his shot that killed the bitch. He doesn't know what happened, but those guards are not the garden-variety mall guards. Wolf takes the sniper rifle off his back; he pulls back the bolt and inserts the bullet. Wolf screws on the suppressor and thinks, *no I don't need the suppressor.* He unscrews the suppressor. He needs to be careful; these fuckers know what they are doing. He makes his decision to shoot Will and get the fuck outta there. He waits to get a clear shot. He has Will in his crosshairs and squeezes the trigger—Alex, Claude, and Mateo hear the THUD. Will's head explodes. Al three immediately hit the ground.

Unknown to both Wolfgang and Rose, the two are only fifty yards from each other. Rose hears the shot. She can tell from the sound that it is an M-24 sniper rifle. It can only be from the sniper. Rose has been listening to the radio traffic. She knows that one of the assassins was captured. Based on the shot she just heard, she surmises that it is the spotter who was captured and that the sniper is uncaptured. Rose quickly seeks cover. She is with the dogs; she gives them the command to be quiet. The dogs lie down at her feet. She pulls out her Glock and if the asshole comes around the bend—it will be curtains.

She also has her backpack. The assassin does not see her, but Wolf does see the second ATV. He runs to the ATV. Rose only has her Glock. At two hundred meters, she cannot hit the assassin. As he is running to the ATV, Rose pulls out a camera with a telephoto lens and starts snapping pictures. She gets perfect snapshots of Wolfgang, frontal and right profile.

Wolfgang revs up the ATV and heads for Forfar. As soon as he finds a car, he will hotwire it and get out of Dodge ASAP. Wolf will later do a self-assessment. Aside from killing the bitch, he was lucky to escape with his life. Back at the camp, he will say that Will was killed in action by some contractor assholes. After he is back in camp, he will make sure that Will be given recognition for sacrificing his life for the cause. He will make up some story that he single- handed held the enemy at bay and he killed three of the enemy. While Wilhelm was fighting the enemy, he was allowed to escape. Which is pretty much true, except the story will be that the enemy killed Wilhelm.

Chapter Twenty-Seven

The Darknet

Alexandria Virginia

Before leaving the fields of southern Scotland, the WMA team needs to clean up the site where Will was murdered by Wolfgang. Before removing the body and all evidence of the killing, Alex lifts Will's fingerprints from all fingers. The body is taken to one of the many lochs in Scotland, weighed down with heavy rocks, and sunk in the middle of the loch. All team members are exhausted from their four days of chasing the assassins. They all get a good night's rest, and after a hearty breakfast from Maria, they assemble in the villa family room and debrief on the activities of the simulated assassination.

There are several good points: the hologram worked to perfection, the gun turret likely saved the lives of Alex and Mateo, the use of Winston and Monty was a good idea, and several other minor wins. There were also some areas for improvement: the destruction of the drone, the killing of the assassin's spotter, and the failure to capture the assassin. The group then discusses what is needed going forward.

Rose says, "The photos taken of the assassin should be extremely helpful in identifying his name."

Jeff immediately jumps in and says, "We need to have Louie's team start monitoring all the airport cameras in Europe and find what flight the assassin takes to the US. The photos taken by Rose will be a big help." All team members agree.

Rose says, "Good idea. Jeff, contact Louie immediately and have him start searching."

"Roger, will do." Jeff excuses himself from the conversations and sends an encrypted e-mail to Louie. Included in the e-mail are the photo attachments. Within minutes, Louie replies. He will start immediately.

Mateo says, "Rose, you need to contact the CIA. Send the fingerprints from the spotter, and let's get an ID."

"OK, will do." Rose is technically employed by MI6. She is on permanent loan to the CIA. The CIA has assigned her to work with the WMA team. The official title on her assignment to WMA is the CIA's "Contract Technical Representative (COTR)" The CIA has in place a black contract with WMA.

The discussion now turns to the assassin. Rose asks, "Who contracted the assassin?"

From the one person who would not be expected to answer the question comes a comment: Vinny. He says, "Don't know who contracted the shithead, but I know how Louie will find the asshole."

"How?" asks Claude.

"Well, you remember back a couple of days when we were discussing the internet and the subject of the darknet came up?"

"Yes, I do remember. You were going to give us a tutorial on the darknet, right?"

"Yeah, that's right."

"OK, now is the time."

Vinny says, "The darknet working with the TOR network is very complicated, but I will reduce it to a simple example. The darknet websites are accessible only through networks such as TOR, or 'The Onion Router project.' The TOR browser and TOR-accessible sites are widely used by darknet users and can only be identified by the domain 'onion.'"

Claude says, "Hold on a second. What is a domain?"

"A domain is a distinct group of computers under a central administration or authority. For example, the computers at WMA would be classified as a domain."

"OK, got it. Thanks. Go ahead and continue. Remember, we are a bunch of blockheads. Keep it simple."

Vinny continues. "The TOR network provides anonymous access to the internet. Using the TOR network allows a sender and recipient to send and receive messages with the other not knowing where the message originated. Let me give you an example of how it works. Let's say you enter the subway station at the National Airport terminal. You take the subway to the exchange substation at Federal Triangle, and you take the orange line to Dupont Circle. You exit the subway and take a train to the Rockville station. Now, how does the person at the Rockville station know that the journey started at National Airport? The answer is he does not know."

"Oh," says Rose, I see. The party waiting for the person who departed from National Airport really does not care. All he really wants is the person who arrived—who cares where it originated, right?"

"You got it. Now imagine that there are ten thousand train stations. This would make it even more challenging to determine the beginning of the journey. Now let's substitute network servers for the train stations, and let's replace an encrypted message for the person. Now you see how the TOR works. There are so many servers, or train stations, that it is challenging to know who originated the message.

"So far so good," says Alex. "So, if it is so difficult, how will Louie determine who contracted the assassin?"

"Ah, that's the beauty of what Louie and that scientist from the movie company did. They embedded a 1,024 scrambled bitstream in the hologram software. When the assassin's camera videotaped the killing scene, the scrambled bitstream was also recorded. Think of the video as a picture of the Mona Lisa. The picture is a fake, and the painter, Louie, has embedded 1,024 dots in the picture. When the photo is taken, voila—the 1,024 dots are part of the picture taken by the camera."

The team members are looking at Vinny with perplexed faces; he knows that they almost understand. "Now, remember the subway example. Let's say that the person who entered the subway at the airport terminal is wearing a red cap from the Washington baseball team. He keeps that cap on throughout his journey through the different stations. Now all I need is to have some video from each station, and I can determine where he first entered the subway station. The actual code that Louie will need to write will be a lot more complicated than my presentation. He will still need to decrypt the messages, but he's done that before, so it should not be a problem."

Rose looks at Vinny. "You're getting good at this tech stuff. Congratulations on the explanation of the darknet and the TOR network, but I will stick to my lane."

Vinny feels pretty good at the attaboy coming from Rose. He simply says, "Thank you. Hope you liked it."

Three days after the gunfight at the storage shed, the hologram, gun turret, and drone pieces that can be salvaged are shipped via DHL. As Alex. Mateo, Jeff, and Vinny are getting ready to drive to Glasgow and board the WMA G650 aircraft and are saying their goodbyes, Claude comes from the makeshift command center and says, "Sit down, team, I have some information from the CIA."

They all take a seat and are expecting bad news. Claude sees the worried looks on their faces and says, "Not to worry, we now have the identity of the two assassins."

"That is good news," says Alex. "Should make it easier for Louie to find the endpoints of the TOR network."

Claude reads from one of the printed papers in his hand. "First, the shooter. His name is Wolfgang Adolf Schneider. He is from Lexington, Kentucky. Star athlete in high school. He worked as a truck driver for two years. When his father was killed on a hunting trip, he inherited some money. He gave up his job driving an eighteen-wheel. The rumor was he was transporting drugs for the cartel, but this was never proven. In Las Vegas, he joined the Marines. The enlisting sergeant wrote in his application that he was probably running from the Vegas Mafia. Likely he had gambling debts. In the Marines, he received a battlefield promotion from private to corporal. His record shows that he had a knack for finding the ragheads. After his first tour, he was recommended for sniper school. After sniper school, he served his second tour in Iraq. His record shows that he currently has the record for the most kills of any sniper serving there. He was credited for finding and killing the most feared ISIS sniper. Then he was court-martialed. No record of why he was court-martialed, but he was reduced to private and booted out of the Marines.

Rose asks, "Does the record indicate if he was ever in Djibouti?"

"No, but you know that if you are stationed in Iraq, you will be assigned to Djibouti for joint exercises. Why do you ask?"

"I think I know the guy. We crossed paths when I was in the SAS. The rumor was that he was really pissed when I replaced him as the best shooter ever to have undergone training in Djibouti. When he was told that it was a woman in the British SAS, he went ballistic. He wanted a contest—man to woman. By then, my unit had left, and we were stationed near the Kurdish border. After my tour of duty, I was recruited by MI6."

"What about the idiot who had his head shot off?" asks Jeff.

Claude shuffles some papers and reads, "The spotter's name was Wilhelm X. Strassman. He was born in Helena, Montana. Had only a grammar school education. From the age of sixteen, he was a drifter and had some minor scuffles with the law. At the age of twenty, he was arrested by the Texas Highway Patrol. He was speeding and evaded a roadblock. They found fourteen ounces of marijuana, and he was booked for speeding, endangering law enforcement officers, and marijuana possession. He was sentenced to three years in jail and served two years. After he was released, he found the wrong crowd and set fire to three black churches in Mississippi. He is currently wanted by the FBI for hate crimes. Apparently, he has been on the run for the last two years. It is believed that he is hiding in the hills along the North Carolina-Tennessee border."

"Boy, we sure know how to pick them," says Alex.

"Yeah," adds Vinny, "they ain't no choir boys."

"When we are in Virginia, we will work with Louie to trace the origin of the murder contract," says Claude. "We need to know who has a contract on Rose. Any ideas, Rose?"

"Yes, I sure do—I have been involved in five attacks by ISIS. First, there was the successful rescue of the hostages in Tadmur, Syria. Second, all the terrorists we killed in the Kaghan Valley of Pakistan. Third, the Chihuahua raid, where I nearly lost my life. Fourth, the nuclear power plant in Buchanan, New York. Fifth, the Mazatlán incident." Rose thinks for a few seconds and says, "It has to be ISIS!"

Chapter Twenty-Eight

Wolfgang Meets Malik

Islamabad, Pakistan

Wolfgang leaves the killing field of Scotland. He escapes on the ATV and immediately finds a car in Forfar. He hotwires the vehicle. It is early morning, and the only airport that has a rental car office open is in Glasgow. He drives to Glasgow and parks the car in a rundown section of the city. He rents a nondescript car and uses one of his many passports. By 6 A.M., he is on the motorway to London. He drives for three hours and stops at a roadside hotel. He needs time to think. First, he gets a few hours of sleep.

He wakes up at 3 P.M. and sits on the lounge chair and thinks, *what happened? These guys chasing me, they are pros*. He laughs to himself and thinks of the discussions he had with his dad. He told his dad hunting animals was not a sport—they did not fight back! He enjoyed Iraq because there was always the chance of the hunted becoming the hunter. He always felt that he would prevail because he was smarter and better prepared. This time, he more than met his match. He sits there for over an hour. No TV, no one to blab in his ear. Just him and the four walls. He closes his eyes and replays every event since the shot that he took at the target. He has his first thought: how did the target team know where he was, and how were they able to shoot within less than a second after he took the shot?

He has the camera with the recording of the kill. He connects the camera USB to the ethernet connection on his computer. He downloads the complete video of the day. Will and he decided to change the sniper location due to the different wind conditions. The recording was from 8:15 to the shooting at 9:35. In twenty minutes, the video is downloaded, and he plays it from 8:15 to 9:40. Then he plays and replays the thirty seconds when the target was killed. There is no question that it was the target. His concern is the three shots that were taken 1.2 seconds after he pulled the trigger. They are equally spaced. He plays the video in slow motion. Bang, one second, Bang, one second, and Bang. He concludes that the shots were not fired by a human. They were fired by an automatic gun turret. He has seen videos of a Russian gun turret that can be triggered by an external action. This is precisely what the target team did. Now things are starting to get clearer. *I am sure that I hit the target—but did I?*

He plays the video in slow motion, over and over, and he sees that he definitely hit the target. He thinks—*I am missing something, but what?* He again takes ten minutes to think. Then he has an idea. He rewinds the recording to 9:30, five minutes before the shot. He then views the video one frame at a time. There are thirty frames per second. In one minute, there are thirty times sixty frames, which equals 1,800 frames. In two minutes, there are 3,600 frames. Wolfgang is determined to look at each one. He reaches the frame where he can see the bullet inches from the target's head. The bullet enters the head, and there is an explosion. He stops it and replays; he rewinds and replays. He does this at least ten times. He determines that after the bullet enters the brain, the head exploding is two frames late. He does not know how they did it —but he shakes his head—game on. He has met his match. *I shot a hologram of the Brit! I have to give it to that British woman soldier; she is good. She has my respect. But I have a contract, and I need to honor it. Be careful what you wish for, you might just get it—the hunter is now the hunted.*

However, he needs to give it some thought. *The five hundred thousand dollars for the hit still looks' good. I need to use photoshop and doctor the video. The assholes paying me will never know the difference.* He again needs to think and look at all angles. *How will I do this?* He decides to doctor the video. Take out the three shots and synchronize the bullet to the explosion of the head. If he found it, the customer may also find it. He decides to communicate directly with the customer using the TOR network, but he will not send the video. He will tell them that he has video evidence of the kill. He is concerned that once he sends the video, they will not pay. Can they meet at a neutral site in Europe? He will show only photos.

Wolfgang starts his laptop and inserts the LAN cable into the RJ-45 plug provided by the hotel. He signs onto the darknet. Using several ID and complex passwords, Wolfgang navigates to a chat room. He then sends an encrypted message using WhatsApp. The text message goes to a predetermined cell phone number, which was prearranged with the customer. Both the customer and Wolf follow well-established protocols. When establishing contact passwords, it is best to use phrases. Using complete sentences makes it impossible for any eavesdroppers to guess the proper response. The message reads: "The rain in Spain falls mainly on the plain." He will wait for the proper response. Two hours later, the answer comes back: "Yes, but it is also raining in N'Djamena." Communication has now been established. Wolf begins the text exchange. Malik, the ISIS intelligence chief is on the other end.

Wolf: "THE JOURNEY IS COMPLETE."

Malik: "WHAT GOODS HAVE BEEN FOUND?"

"AS PLANNED, THE JOURNEY FOUND THE DIAMOND."

"MAY I SEE THE DIAMONDS?"

"I WOULD LIKE TO MEET FOR THE EXCHANGE."

"THAT WAS NOT THE AGREEMENT."

"UNDERSTOOD. I HAVE NO GUARANTEE OF COMPENSATION."

"WHAT DO YOU RECOMMEND?"

"THAT WE MEET AT NEUTRAL SITE."

"I WILL NEED TO DISCUSS WITH MY SUPERIORS."

"I WILL CONTACT YOU WITHIN THE NEXT HOUR."

"OK, I WAIT FOR YOUR RESPONSE"

Wolfgang thinks, what happens if they do not agree? He decides to play hardball. If they do not agree to the meeting, he will refuse to show the photos.

Malik seeks the advice of General Abboud. The General is directing all activities from their safe haven in Peshawar, Pakistan.

Malik says, "I have been in contact with the contract assassin."

"Did he complete the mission?"

"He claims he did."

"After he shows proof, thank him and tell him that the bitcoins will be transferred within the next day. But as we discussed, do not transfer the bitcoins. Serves him right for providing proof of the murder and no method to force us to complete the exchange—fuck him."

"Sir, it is not that simple. He wants to meet at a neutral site to guarantee the transfer of the agreed-upon five hundred thousand dollars."

"Goddamn it, does no one ever honor their contract?"

"Sir, I have an idea."

"Yes, go ahead."

"We meet at a neutral site that we control. I will make sure he understands that if he is trying to scam us, he will be as good as dead."

"Where do you recommend that we meet?"

"We will meet in Islamabad. It is the power of our country. We will give him the impression that he is dealing with the Pakistani ISI."

"Yes, that's a good idea. Make sure when you meet that you have some muscle with you. Dress your assistants in Pakistani special forces uniforms."

"Yes, sir. I will contact the infidel and set our conditions."

After three hours, Wolfgang's cell phone using WhatsApp sounds an alert for a message. The message reads: "LOG ON TO THE FOLLOWING URL..." The URL is the ISIS website in Peshawar. Wolfgang types the website URL in his browser, and he is connected. From the website, he downloads an encrypted VPN tunnel. Wolfgang's cell phone alerts him that he has a second message. The text message has the password to log on to the ISIS server. The text reads: "PASSWORD ONLY GOOD FOR ONE SESSION. PASSWORD MUST BE ENTERED CORRECTLY—YOU ONLY HAVE ONE TRY."

Wolfgang enters the password, and he can now send and receive a text. Malik comes online.

Malik: "We are prepared for a meeting in Islamabad. Meet at the Hotel Serena in Islamabad. The room has been reserved under the name: John David Williams for one night. Reservation is for this coming Tuesday night. Check into the room, and we will contact you at your hotel. Please confirm."

Wolfgang types: "I would prefer a hotel in Paris or Berlin."

"The location is not negotiable; we will be in grave danger if we travel outside of Pakistan."

"OK, I understand—I will be at the Serena Hotel on Tuesday evening for a Wednesday meeting."

"One more thing, you will need photos and/or video as proof that you have the diamond."

"Understood. I will have the requested proof."

Wolfgang is outside of London. It is Friday; he gets on the internet and books a flight leaving Sunday for Islamabad. Wolfgang will arrive early and check out the hotel. He needs a new wardrobe: suit, shirt, tie, shoes, underpants, and socks. He also buys regular tourist clothes: Bermuda shorts, plaid shirts, a baseball cap, and tennis shoes. He needs a haircut and his beard trimmed. On Sunday, he is on a flight to Islamabad on Pakistani Air Lines (PIA) flying the Airbus a380. He arrives on Sunday afternoon dressed in his tourist clothes. He takes a taxi to a second-rate hotel, which he found on the internet. He has two days to survey the Hotel Serena and be prepared with any contingency plans.

The evening of the Monday before he checks into the Serena Hotel, he takes the typical three-wheel taxi to the seedy part of town. Before he hires the taxi, he asks the driver, "Do you speak English?

"Ya, a little."

"I need you to take me to a gun shop."

"Guns are not allowed in Pakistan." Wolfgang slips the driver a fifty-dollar bill. The driver puts the fifty in his pocket and drives on to a brothel. Wolfgang is dressed in the traditional *salwar kameez*; it is a long cotton tunic over loose-fitting trousers. The trousers are held up by a string that acts like a belt. Wolf is wearing open-toed sandals held by a strap around the heel. He is also wearing the *Chitrali* cap. Wolf has used black face paint to hide his white skin and is sporting a beard and semi-long hair. The driver tells him, "Ask for Muhammad Abdullah Ali. He will be able to help you.

"After Wolf dismounts from the three-wheeled taxi, the wheel of the taxi spins on the dirt road and it dashes off. Wolfgang walks into the bar. Some hardened men look at him with suspicion. They are sitting on rugs with their legs crossed Indian style. Most of the men are smoking from a hookah pipe. The women are all prostitutes and mark him as a possible client with money. The bar looks like the cantina in *Star Wars*; it only lacks R2-D2 and Chewbacca. A tough-looking man with the face of Genghis Khan walks up and greets him, "*As-salamu alaykum,*" and Wolfgang answers, "*Alaykum As-salamu.*"

Wolfgang asks, "Speak to Muhammad Abdullah Ali?" The Genghis Khan lookalike points to a door in the back. He walks over and opens the door, and then he signals with his hand by wagging his fingers below his hand. Wolfgang steps into the room and stands in front of a big, fat man who looks like Atilla the Hun. He is seated behind his desk.

Muhammad does not offer him a seat. He says in broken English, "What you want?"

Wolfgang answers, "Handgun."

"Be expensive."

"I have money."

"Rupees, euros, or dollars?"

"Dollars."

"I have 9mm, made here in Pakistan."

"How much?"

"Thousand dollars."

"I give you five hundred."

"Seven fifty."

"Six hundred."

Finally, Muhammad says, "Seven hundred, no lower."

"Deal."

Mohammad places the gun in a paper sack.

Wolfgang asks, "How about magazine and bullets?"

"Magazine two hundred dollars, and twelve bullets one hundred dollars."

"Deal." Wolfgang gives Muhammad a thousand dollars. He loads the magazine and slams it into the handle of the handgun. He walks out of the brothel.

Wolfgang walks outside and looks left and right. Thugs are hanging around the bar. He decides to pull the gun out of the paper bag. Fortunately, he loaded the magazine in the presence of Atilla the Hun. He makes it a point to eject the magazine, and then he slams it back into the handgun. He inserts the gun under his *salwar* trousers. He walks two blocks with his head on a swivel. On the third block, he flags down a three-wheeled taxi, and he is headed back to his hotel.

On Tuesday morning, he takes a taxi to the Serena Hotel. He walks around the hotel and then goes inside and checks out the lobby, restaurant, bar, exercise room, and pool. He needs to check out the elevators and top floors. He pretends to do some window shopping and waits for a crowd to assemble to take the elevator up. A group gathers, the elevator doors open with the signal up. He casually walks to the group and takes the elevator up. The hotel has twelve floors. The last floor for the elevator is floor ten. He exits with an elderly couple. He is very polite and allows them to exit first. They go right, and he goes left. From the tenth floor, he will survey all floors using the stairs. He checks all the floors. He makes mental notes of the ice and beverage machines. On the third and second floors are the business suites. He notices that there is a VIP suite/business room with the title "The Masood Khan Room." On the first floor, he checks out the kitchen and laundry rooms.

After thoroughly surveying the Serena Hotel, he goes back to his hotel and checks out the doctored video and still frames that he has extracted as pho tos. He has decided to leave the three shots from the gun turret in the video. He inserted several duplicate frames to have the gunshots be random; the shots will appear to have been taken by the guards. On Tuesday afternoon, at 4 P.M., he checks into the Serena Hotel. As instructed, he as a room under John David Williams. He checks into room 4010. It is on the fourth floor. The business center and meeting rooms are one floor down. He relaxes in his room until 6 P.M. He decides to go to the restaurant across the street and sit there and drink tea. Before he leaves the room, he takes the extra blankets from the closet, rolls up the sheets, and tucks them under the bed blanket. It looks like a body sleeping under the covers. As he leaves his room, he places a hair strand across the door jamb. He predicts that an advance party from the paying customer (ISIS) will likely come by and determine if he has checked in. They will probably pay the front office for his room number, and they may want to search his room. All of the photos and videos are in his backpack.

At 8 P.M., after the front desk has a shift change, he walks in and checks in under the name Manfred Edelman. After his customer told him that they had a room for him under John David Williams, he called and reserved a room under Manfred Edelman. When he made the reservation, he asked for a room next to John David Williams. Wolf leaves a message with the front desk that he is expecting a critical phone call. Should they receive a call, he instructs them to call him on his burner phone. Wolf leaves strict instructions not to transfer any calls to his room. He will take a message, and he will call back. He purchased a burner phone at one of the many kiosks in Islamabad.

At 9 P.M., he has checked in as Manfred Edelman. Manfred has room 4011, which is across from 4010. At 10 P.M., his burner phone rings. It is at the front desk. They have a number for him to call back.

The person on the phone says, "Hello, Mr. Williams. I trust that your flight was pleasant and that you are comfortable at the Serena Hotel?"

"Yes. I had no problems; my flight was uneventful."

"And how is your room at the hotel?"

"Very good. Thank you for making the accommodations."

"Do you have proof of the diamond?"

"Yes, I have the diamond. I have it well protected. I am looking forward to our meeting tomorrow."

"Yes, we are also looking forward to our meeting at 10 A.M. in the Masood Khan Room."

"OK, I will see you there."

Wolfgang thinks, *fucking ragheads, they must think I am really stupid. I now know that they will have a wet team in John David William's room sometime tonight. They will be stunned when they have feathers flying when they shoot the pillows.*

Wolfgang installs a laser on the inside of the door. He uses Velcro to install the laser at the lower end of the door. When the door to room 4010 opens, the alarm on his phone will sound. He will know that someone has entered the room arranged by the Pakistani customer. At 2 A.M., the alarm sounds. He is dressed in his cargo pants and a black t-shirt. He slips on the hotel sandals and grabs the 9mm pistol. He screws on the suppressor. He chambers a bullet. As he is walking to the door of his room, he hears two suppressed gunshots. This really pisses him off. "Goddamn assholes," he whispers. He carefully opens his door, walks across the hall, and uses the hotel key card to open the door to room 4010. The wet team assassins are busy searching through the chest drawers and his suitcase. He aims at one of the killers and fires. The assassin falls to the floor. As the second assassin starts to reach for his gun, Wolfgang takes the handle of his gun and knocks the killer out. He pulls off the balaclavas being worn by the assassins; they are obviously Pakistani. They look like ISIS fighters. He ties the assassin who is unconscious to a chair, stuffs a small face towel in his mouth, and wraps a regular towel around his mouth. He will wait until the asshole regains conscious and use him to lure his boss to the room.

Thirty minutes later, the assassin is awake. Wolfgang takes his own phone and searches for the translation app. He finds it and enters in English: "COME UP TO THE ROOM." The translation shows the Urdu text. He finds a text string on the phone of the assassin. It is obvious that the other end is his boss. He enters the Urdu text on the assassin's phone. The answer comes back: "COMING UP." He waits for two minutes, and there is a knock on the door. He opens the door and points his 9mm pistol at the head of Malik. He waves his gun to have Malik come in, and then he points to the chair at the hotel desk. He tells Malik, "Transfer the money, asshole."

"May I see the evidence?"

"Fuck you. You are in no position to set demands! Now, transfer the money."

Malik does not move. He says, "The contract was you kill the bitch, and we transfer five hundred thousand dollars to your bitcoin account."

"You are right; the contract WAS five hundred thousand. It is now one million. After you tried to kill me, the contract is void. Now, transfer the one mil."

"I need proof."

"OK, you want proof; I will give you some evidence. Wolf takes the cloth belt from the hotel robe, wraps it around the neck of the second assassin, and starts choking him. The assassin's eyes grow large, and he tries screaming. He wiggles in his chair. He goes unconscious.

Malik says, "Stop, OK, OK, I will do it." He logs onto the internet and enters the ID and password for the ISIS bitcoin account. "OK, what is your bitcoin account number?"

Wolfgang gives him the number, and Malik transfers the funds. Wolfgang makes the calculation of the value of the bitcoins to dollars—it is only five hundred thousand dollars.

"I said one mil."

"We don't have one mil in the account."

"I am losing my patience with you, asshole. You think I just fell off the turnip cart? Transfer the money, asshole."

Malik looks at the unconscious assassin and knows that Wolf means business. He logs into the ISIS working bank account. Malik is glad that they only keep the amount under five hundred thousand in the account. He shows Wolf that the account, it has $255,000.

"Transfer it all," says Wolfgang.

Malik completes the transfer. Wolfgang now ties Malik to the chair. He stuffs a face towel into his mouth, takes the cloth belt from around the neck of the assassin, and wraps it around Malik's face.

Wolfgang packs his bags. As he is leaving, he throws down a picture of the shot that killed Rose.

He says, "I am a man of my word. The bitch is dead." He closes the door and flips the sign to "Do Not Disturb."

Wolfgang drives to Peshawar and crosses into Afghanistan through the Khyber Pass. He drives to Kabul Airport and boards a plane to Abu Dhabi with a connection to Dulles Airport. From Dulles, he takes a flight to Nashville. At the airport in Nashville, his girlfriend, Gretchen, picks him up at the curb.

Malik, who is tied in room 4010, bounces his chair to the edge of the desk. He works on the cloth that has him tied. After three hours of rubbing the cloth against the side of the desk, it is loose enough to where he can untie his wrists.

He unties the belt around his face and pulls the towel from his mouth. His immediate concern is what to tell General Abboud. He has decided to make up a lie; after all, he has the most essential item—proof of the death of the bitch. He needs to make sure that no one can give a different story. He takes the cloth belt that was initially used to strangle the second assassin, and he finishes the job. As he is choking the ISIS fighter, he tells him that he is dying for the jihad. Soon he will have his seventy-two virgins. He needs to have the room cleaned. He calls a select group that ISIS has that specializes in the clean-up of killings. They have a lot of experience. Second, he needs to rehearse the lie to Abboud. The less he tells him, the better. He is thankful that he is in Islamabad and Abboud is in Peshawar. It will be a two-hour drive to Peshawar. He will tell the driver to go slowly; he does not want to be stopped by the police.

He arrives at the ISIS headquarters and enters the General's office. The receptionist looks at Malik and says, "Please take a seat. I will tell the General that you are here."

"Thank you." Malik sits for fifteen minutes. He hopes that this is an indication that the General is very busy.

Finally, the receptionist says, "You can go in now."

The general and Malik greet each other. Malik immediately shows the General the picture and says, "The bitch is dead."

"Good, and did your plan of killing the infidel work?"

"No, sir, he was too experienced. It's obvious that he's had some type of special operations training—probably the seals or Delta."

"Yes, I thought that it would probably not work."

"Yes, sir. You were right." Malik now knows he is in the clear. As long as the General thinks that he was right it will pass with time.

"And did you need to make the payment?"

"Yes, sir." The General does not ask, and Malik will not tell how much he actually paid.

"Very well, I need to get back to my business. The US is pulling its forces out of Syria, and we need to take advantage of the pullout."

"Yes, sir. As you predicted, it's happening sooner than expected."

"Yes, Trout is a gift from *Allah*!"

Chapter Twenty-Nine

Video Conference Call

Virginia and Scotland

Senator Montana, Alex, Mateo, Louie, Jeff, Vinny, and Rick are in the WMA conference room. Rose and Claude are at The Sea Serpent Command Post. They are preparing for a video teleconference between the two sites. The WMA Virginia site has a ninety-two-inch, high-definition flat-screen TV. The Sea Serpent has a sixty-two-inch, high-definition flat-screen TV. Both monitors have two cameras. One displays the entire group, and the second camera will always display the speaker in a picture in picture.

Rose begins the discussion. "Have we heard or seen anything on the darknet?"

"No," says Louie, "nothing on the darknet. I am one hundred percent sure that if the assassination video was being transferred across the darknet, we would get an alarm."

"Would we detect it even if they were using the TOR?" asks Vinny.

"Absolutely. This would be one instance where using the TOR would actually help to detect the video."

"How would that help?" asks Claude.

Louie looks perplexed because it is apparent to him why the TOR would help to detect the video. He says, "The TOR is made up of thousands of servers. The obfuscation using the TOR is because files being transferred bounce around these thousands of servers; thus, it is easier to detect. Does that make sense?"

The group still does not understand. Vinny then helps out Louie. "Remember my example of the subway stations?"

They all nod their heads. "Yes."

"Well, the video that is changing stations is actually a person. If you know who the person is at each station there is an alarm, then—voila, you have an alarm at each station."

Rose then says, "Yeah, I get it." They all give Vinny a thumbs up.

"Sorry, Louie," says Vinny. "I thought you could use my help. But don't worry, I will never be a programmer."

"No apology needed," replies Louie. "But I do have the info we were after."

"What, did you do wave your magic wand?" asks Jeff.

"Almost. The magic video facial recognition. As recommended, we hacked into all of the airport cameras in Europe. We got a hit from Heathrow Airport in London. The 'Wolf' boarded a PIA a380 airbus plane to Islamabad. Four days later, he boarded an Emirates plane from Kabul to Dulles. From Dulles, he flew to Nashville on American Airlines."

Everyone knows what that means.

Rose puts it into words: "The 'Wolf' has bamboozled ISIS. He convinced them that Rose was killed, and he has the reward money."

"I don't get it," says Jeff. "Why not get the money transferred through the darknet?"

"Here is Wolf's problem. He sends the video. ISIS sees the video. What incentive does ISIS have to make the payment? The answer is none! Wolf went to Pakistan to get paid!"

"Based on what we have seen," says Alex, "I bet Wolf left a bunch of dead bodies in Pakistan."

"Yeah, he made it out—he's our problem now," says Rose.

Chapter Thirty

Ethan and Reuben Join the Team

Video Conference, Virginia and Scotland

Claude says, "We need to debrief the Virginia team on the confession by Wilhelm." He provides a detailed summary of the confession made before Wilhelm was shot by Wolf. He explains that there is no written confession. However, Alex, Mateo, and he believe that what Wilhelm had told them was likely the truth.

Senator Montana has been seated in the video teleconference room. He wants to get a firsthand report of the performance of the hologram. He owes his friend Johnny Ramos an explanation of how the hologram performed in a real-life environment. He says, "Hold on. We need to get Brad McKinnon. He needs to hear the Wilhelm confession. Jeff, can you have Brad paged and request that he attend the meeting."

"Yes, sir." Jeff calls the front desk, and immediately there is a page for Brad McKinnon.

"Mr. Brad McKinnon, please come to the main conference room." Five minutes later, Brad walks in. "What's up, guys?"

"Brad," says the senator, "as the director of the skunkworks division and as a retired FBI agent, we need your advice on a killing that occurred in Scotland."

Claude now begins a summary. "Before our captive was killed by his partner, he gave an alarming picture of what is going on at a white nationalist camp in Tennessee." He goes on to explain the murder for hire, drugs, gunrunning, prostitution, and girls being held as slaves.

Brad says, "Let me get this straight. The confession was verbal by your captive, and your captive is now dead. Is that right?"

"That's right."

"Also, you had a firefight with the captive and roughed him up?"

"Correct."

"We have multiple problems. One, you were in a foreign country. I won't even ask you—where is the body? Second, the confession that you heard was verbal. Any attorney fresh out of law school will say the confession was under duress. Three, it was verbal, and you have nothing in writing. That fresh attorney will say you made it up. And last, if you take this story to any law enforcement officer, he will likely arrest you!"

"That's why we called you in," says the senator.

"OK, now, let's look to see what we can do. I recommend that we have the director of the FBI, Mr. Hector Calvanese, come over for a follow-up of the ISIS nuclear power plant attack. I believe that there is a connection. After all, it was the ISIS branch in Pakistan that contracted for the murder of Rose. We do not lie but only tell him that an attempt was made to kill Rose. It was not successful. We tell him the truth; we captured the spotter. While he was confessing, the sniper shot him—again the truth."

Rose says, "This is Tadmur act two. We need surveillance of Wolf's camp. Remember the Tadmur, Syria, operation where five hostages were successfully rescued? They were being held by ISIS. A combined British and French team led the rescue operation. Alex, you were at the Tadmur raid—is there some resemblance?"

"Yeah, we need surveillance, but it cannot be Mateo, Claude, or yourself. And certainly not me. Wolf saw all of us in Scotland. He has even seen Jeff and Vinny. We are going to need some operators who have not been burned. Brad, what do you think?"

"Yes, you are correct. I have two operators with years of experience who completed a rescue operation in Latin America. WMA was hired by a Texas oilman to extract two workers from the turmoil in Venezuela. The WMA operators' names are Ethan Jones and Reuben Tellez. Both have years of experience in special operations and have been employed by WMA for over three years.

"Yes, we know Ethan and Reuben," says Claude.

"Yes, Ethan and Reuben are excellent," says the senator. The WMA has a total of twelve special operators in the skunkworks division. All are American citizens with top-secret clearances and contracts currently held with the CIA and the FBI. In addition to the government contracts, the WMA will accept a contract with a private company. Generally, these contracts are for protection in a foreign country or the rescue of kidnap victims. Successful rescues have been completed both domestically and in foreign countries.

The senator continues. "Ethan and Reuben have successfully completed missions in North Korea, Iran, and recently the extraction of the oil workers in Venezuela. I also believe that we need to bring in the FBI. I have known FBI Director Calvanese since his days as the head of the NYPD counter-terrorism unit. Hector and I go back fifteen years. He can issue a type-one surveillance task, only physical surveillance. We can have the FBI assist in the surveillance."

"Hold on," says Mateo. "Won't the FBI want to take the case?"

"Normally, they would," says Brad. "However, the surveillance would be an extension of the ISIS nuclear power plant and seaport attacks. Is it possible that ISIS is now recruiting domestic terrorists? The working agreement that ISIS in Pakistan has established with the Juarez drug cartel has brought millions of dollars to their ISIS bank accounts. Money can buy anything."

"OK," says the senator, "I will contact Hector and arrange for the meeting."

"Ethan and Reuben will conduct the up-front surveillance," says Claude. "They will be assisted by Rose, Alex, and Mateo."

"How about using Jeff or Vinny to fly the surveillance drone?" asks Mateo.

"Remember," says Alex, "Wolf shot down the drone in Scotland. He will likely have some full-time spotters viewing the sky. Having the FBI join us will allow the tasking of satellites using national assets."

"Good point," says the senator. "I will also contact Dr. Gifford from the CIA. She will have a priority to task the national assets."

"I will first use Google Maps to provide accurate coordinates," says Alex. "Also, I will ask Dr. Gifford to task the National Reconnaissance Office."

"We will need to conduct thorough research of the area of Murfreesboro and Pulaski, Tennessee," says Claude. "We will need a cover story."

"Ethan is from Huntsville, Alabama," says the senator, "which is across the border from Pulaski. If my memory serves me right, he can easily fall into the Tennessee-Alabama accent. He is also a graduate of the University of Alabama and is a die-hard 'Roll Tide' fan. I would recommend that you talk to Ethan about a cover story."

"Yes, sir. We will do exactly that."

The next day, Claude, Alex, Mateo, and Rose meet with Ethan and Rueben. Claude and Rose give Ethan and Reuben the background story of ISIS, the murder contract on Rose, and the activities in Scotland. Claude then details what Will told them before Wolf murdered him.

Ethan says, "Sounds like we have some problems in Tennessee. If I understand correctly, we need to conduct physical surveillance of the KKK camp. Is that correct?"

"Yes, that's correct," replies Claude. "You will likely have some assistance from the FBI covert activities team."

"OK, I have some experience with the FBI covert HRT teams stationed at Quantico. Hopefully, they will assign a member of the team I know and with whom I have had previous experience."

"We are contacting the FBI Director. Hopefully, he will be here tomorrow. I will have you at the meeting."

"OK, sounds good."

"Ethan, I understand that you grew up in the Huntsville, Alabama, area. We will need a cover story when you conduct the surveillance. Any ideas?"

Ethan thinks for a few seconds, rubs his chin, and then says, "The city of Huntsville is Rocket City, USA. It seems like every citizen is either a government employee or a contractor working on some rocket program. We could have a cover story of two employees of an FBI cut-out company researching some new rocket engine."

"Yeah, but do you know anything about rockets?"

"Some, enough to bullshit most people. I have a bachelor's in electrical engineering with a secondary in aeronautical engineering from the University of Alabama. I worked a couple of years with a Beltway bandit. After a few years in private industry, I felt that I needed to do my fair share of fighting ragheads. Joined the Army, and one thing led to another and found me in Delta Force chasing the Boko Haram in Africa. I was with the group of special forces who rescued some of the girls who had been kidnapped by the shitheads."

"How much experience in physical surveillance?"

"Plenty. In surveillance operations, you need to become part of the scenery. I have imitated bushes, trees, grass, water lilies, and even some large animals. Better to have a partner. Usually, these types of operation will go on for days, if not weeks."

"Agreed. That's why we have Rueben Tellez attending the meeting."

Rueben has been listening to Ethan. He says, "Great to work with you again, Ethan."

"Yes," says Claude, "I understand that you recently completed a rescue operation in Venezuela."

Reuben says, "Yes, that's correct. Before I tell you about the Venezuela operation, let me throw in my two cents on the cover story. I think the cover story regarding rocket engineering in Huntsville is good. However, we will likely need to stay in the Pulaski-Murfreesboro area for some time. A better cover story for the area would be mountain climbing. Let's face it; we do not look like a couple of nerds. No offense, Ethan, but you look like the middle linebacker for the Tennessee Titans."

"No offense taken," replies Ethan. "Frankly, looking like a middle linebacker is not all that bad."

Reuben continues. "Now, mountain climbers, yep, that's us. Besides, our training in Delta had us climbing mountains all the time. If my memory serves me correctly, the Smoky Mountains are in that area."

"Good point, Reuben," says Ethan. "I think that your idea of the cover story being mountain climbers is much better. I agree. Several fairly high mountains align from east to west along the Smoky Mountains' spine. These mountains start at the Pigeon River Gorge. They are the Thunder, Silers

Bald, and Clingmans Mountains. All have peaks from five thousand to six thousand feet."

"We need to make our mountain climbing legit. I have some of my climbing gear in storage. We can go by Ganger's and complement our gear with anything that we are lacking."

Rose has been listening to the conversation amongst the three. She throws in her thoughts: "Gentlemen, I think we have an excellent start for a plan. However, I need to warn you. You are not dealing with an average bad guy. Wolf is very clever and will be a formidable opponent. I know him by reputation. The rumor in Iraq was that he had a sixth sense. He enjoys the thrill of the hunt. He prefers humans to animals. I was told that he always chose to go after the best snipers that ISIS had. I would not doubt that he has figured out that he did not kill me. Maybe I also have a sixth sense. I can almost get into his brain, and I can sense what he is thinking. So, I warn you: DO NOT TREAT this tango as a regular Joe Blow—he will have some defenses set up against any surveillance of his camp."

Ethan says, "Rose, can you give us a background of the 'Wolf?'

"Yes, I will tell you what I know from my days in Iraq. I heard that he always wants to be the best in anything he does. When I scored a higher score in the sniper contest, he was really pissed. He ranted that he wanted to have a mano-y-mano competition with me. By the time he found out that he was only second best, I had shipped out and was no longer in Joint Base Djibouti. I believe that when he saw the post on the darknet for my assassination, he determined that this was his solution to him finishing second best in Djibouti.

"He was given very high marks for killing the best sniper that ISIS had. I understand that he outsmarted him by using bloodhounds and drones to track him down. When he determined that ISIS was using drones for surveillance, he requested drones through military channels. When he was refused, he appropriated the drones from ISIS and used them against them."

"Why did he receive a dishonorable discharge?" asks Reuben.

"He lined up half a dozen of the ISIS terrorists and shot them with his M-16."

"Why did he do that?"

"The ISIS shitheads had captured some Christians and were raping all of the women. Wolf caught them in the act, and he proceeded to act as judge, jury, and executioner. Frankly, I can see why he did it. The captain who wrote him up was black, and this was the straw that broke the camel's back. He converted at that time to a white nationalist. After the court-martial, I lost track of him until his contract to have me assassinated."

"Thanks, Rose. The more we know about our opponent, the better."

Reuben and Ethan then finish up the discussions by providing a summary of their Venezuela rescue.

Ethan says, "We conducted two-day surveillance on the house where the oil workers were being held captive. The area around the house had heavy foliage, which consisted of tall grass and brush. We were able to disguise ourselves with the natural habitat. Using a combination of high-powered binoculars and an infrared monocle, we were able to determine the number of guards and the location of the hostages."

Reuben then says, "We broke into the house at 2 A.M. and overtook the two guards. They offered little resistance. We tied the guards to the chairs and escaped from Venezuela through the Colombia border near the city of Cucuta."

Chapter Thirty-One

Discussions with Directors Calvanese (FBI) and Gifford (CIA)

Alexandria, Virginia

Senator Montana calls on the secure phone line and requests a conference with FBI Hector Director Calvanese and CIA Director Margarita Gifford.

The conference is set up for 5:30 P.M. Both directors have full days, and the conference call can only be arranged after duty hours.

Senator Montana says, "Recently a kill contract was advertised on the darknet for our MI6 agent Isabella Rose Mathews. Making a long story short, I will get to the point. The assassin was hired by ISIS, the same branch that attempted to destroy the Indian Point nuclear power plant.

"I take it that Rose is OK," says Gifford.

"Yes, she's fine."

"So why the conference call?" asks Calvanese.

"In conducting the investigation of the assassin, we have uncovered some major nefarious activities in the United States."

"Do we have any physical evidence or confessions of these activities?"

"No, that's the problem. The confession was made by the assassin's spotter. We were able to capture the spotter, and he confessed to major illegal activities in the Pulaski-Murfreesboro area of Tennessee."

"Great. Where is the spotter?"

"Dead. The assassin, whose name is Wolfgang Adolf Schneider, killed the spotter when we were transporting him to our safe house."

"Where did this killing take place?" asks Gifford.

"Forfar, Scotland, close to Saint Andrews."

"So, you are telling me that the intelligence that we have is from a dead person?" asks Calvanese.

"That's correct. The information is solid. I would stake my reputation on the info that was collected by my team."

"That's not the problem. I am sure that we could not obtain a search warrant without some information that we have some illegal activities occurring. Let me task my office in Nashville to do some investigating and see what they can find."

"Hector, before you do that, I would like for you to talk about this KKK camp with my team."

"Why—is there a problem?"

"Yes, again we have solid info that the KKK camp has some informants inside law enforcement. We need to proceed cautiously and keep this info to a very few people we can trust."

"So, what are you recommending?"

"I would suggest we meet at a safe house in Northern Virginia or Maryland and that we discuss the details of the issues."

"It looks like this is strictly a domestic issue," says Gifford. "I agree that we need to investigate. Keep me in the loop. At this time, you do not need any CIA assets. Frankly, you already have our best asset—take care of her. By the way, do the Brits know of the spotter being killed?"

"Yes, the Mathews were on vacation in Scotland when the assassination attempt occurred. Mr. Mathews, Rose's father, contacted Scotland Yard. They have been informed."

"Thank you."

"Jesse," says Calvanese, "my calendar is full this week. We will need to meet in the evening. I recommend that we meet at our location in Vint Hills Farm, Virginia."

"You mean the building that was formerly occupied by Army Intel Research and Development."

"Yes, we have a safe house in building number 49. Send me the names of the WMA employees who will attend, and I will have the names at the guard shack."

"Brad McKinnon, my director of the skunkworks division, has asked that Tony Vega, chief of the hostage rescue team be present. Would that be possible?"

"Yes, I think that's a good idea. I will see that Tony is at the meeting."

"Thanks. see you Thursday night at 9 P.M.

Vint Hill Farms is an old Army outpost located about fifty miles to the northwest of Washington, DC. It was an HF intercept station in the 1930s and throughout WWII. This was the radio station that intercepted the Japanese communications to their ambassador detailing the attack on Pearl Harbor. Due to bureaucratic paperwork, regulations, and the lack of priority, the decrypted message did not reach Pearl Harbor before the attack began. After WWII, the station was referred to as "the Farm" and was used extensively by the intelligence community. In the eighties and nineties, the intelligence activities were transferred to the Department of Defense (DoD) installations in New Jersey. The Farm is currently being used by the Federal Aviation Authority. It houses over a thousand air traffic controllers, who manage the entire Eastern United States. The Farm is isolated in the Virginia countryside, and the surrounding buildings are ideal safehouses for the CIA, FBI, DEA, ATF, NSA, DIA and any of the other eighteen alphabet US intel agencies.

On Thursday at 9 P.M., the team members from WMA and the FBI meet in building 49. Attending from WMA are the special operators Claude St. Pier, Rose Mathews, Ethan Jones, and Rueben Tellez. From WMA management is Senator Montana and Brad McKinnon. The FBI is represented by Director Hector Calvanese and the HRT team leader Antonio "Tony" Vega. Hector and Tony know Senator Montana, Claude, and Rose. All five were directly involved in defending against the ISIS attack on the nuclear power plant.

Tony, who is in his thirties, athletic, and who presents himself very well, immediately sees Rose and smiles broadly. "Good to see you, Rose. I understand that ISIS advertised on the darknet for an assassin to murder you. Obviously, the attack failed—boy, is that good to hear!"

"Yes, that's correct; fortunately, we detected the surveillance, and we were able to prevent my demise."

Senator Montana says, "We are all glad that we have some pretty good people, and we faked her death using holograms."

"Let me guess," says Tony. "Louie did his fancy programming and created a double—and the assassin shot the double!"

"Pretty close," says Rose.

"Man, that Louie can do anything—he is worth his weight in gold."

"OK guys, enough of the attaboys. Where does the FBI fit into his investigation?" asks Hector.

Jesse, Rose, and Claude can detect that Hector is under stress from working with President Trout.

Claude gets down to the facts. He tells the FBI director and Tony what Wilhelm said. "We are hundred percent certain that what he told us was the truth."

"Did the spotter tell you this under duress?" asks Tony.

No. However, Wilhelm believed that he had been an accessory to the murder of Rose. Using the murder as leverage, we got the spotter to confess that major illegal activities were occurring at the KKK camp. The spotter, whose name was Wilhelm X. Strassman, confessed when we explained that Wolf was using him. After several hours of interrogation, Wilhelm gave us some shocking news." Claude lists out for Hector and Tony all the illegal activities.

Hector says, "Based on our phone call earlier this week, I pulled the reports from our Nashville office. The KKK camp is running a legit business. They own a trucking company with over one hundred tractors and four hundred trailers. They move goods from the Mexican border to all major cities in the US. A second legit business is a dinner theater by the name of the Red Rooster. As things stand now, there is no way we could have a judge issue a surveillance warrant."

"Yes, I had the same thoughts," says the senator. "The angle that we could use is that the attack on Rose was a contract by ISIS. In fact, by ISIS advertising on the darknet for the murder of the special agent who was most responsible for our success in the prevention of the attacks on America, ISIS is continuing the fight. Second, we know that the assassin, Wolfgang Adolf Schneider, traveled to Pakistan and met with ISIS intelligence officer Malik!"

Tony says, "Chief, the senator has a good argument. If we don't at least survey the KKK camp, we could be guilty of dereliction of duty. We are required to follow and investigate every possible terrorist lead. I would say that this is a BIG lead."

"Agree," replies Hector. "I will contact the Nashville office and have them work with WMA on the surveillance."

"Not a good idea," says Claude.

Hector is taken aback. "Why not?"

"The intel we have is that the KKK has informants inside of law enforcement. I know that you think that your agents are all squeaky clean, but remember Snowden; he had every security clearance that NSA offers, and he bolted! We need to handle this using the HRT assets in Quantico. They will be clean."

Hector thinks for a few seconds, rolls his lips, nods, and then says, "Yes, it is the prudent thing to do."

"Great, then," says the senator. "We are in agreement."

"I need to tell you the rules of engagement," says Hector. "This is only a surveillance task. Deadly force can only be used to protect oneself—I am authorizing surveillance only." He looks at Tony and the WMA operators and says, "Understood?"

They all say in unison, "Understood."

Ethan, who has kept quiet, says, "Mr. Vega, you should know that our cover is going to be mountain climbers. Make sure the FBI agents you assign are not afraid of heights. Also, it would be good if they had some experience in the use of pitons, screws, carabiners, ropes, webbing, harnesses, rappelling devices, and other climbing gear. We intend to stay true to our cover—we will be mountain climbing."

"Ethan and Reuben," says Tony, "you can drop Mr. Vega. Tony will do just fine. OK on the mountain climbing. I got a couple of agents who mountain climb as a hobby. I understand that they went to El Captain last year, and they both completed solo climbs."

"WOW," says Reuben, "solo on El Captain. I think that's good enough! By the way, what are their names?"

"Travis Coolidge and Gersian 'Gerri' Copal. Both Travis and Gerri are experts in concealment, and they will be a valued pair to your four-man team. I will see that they are at your planning meeting next week."

Chapter Thirty-Two

Surveillance Plan

Vint Hill Farms, Virginia

For the sake of security, the combined WMA-FBI team decides that building 49 at Vint Hill Farms, Virginia, is the best location. The Farm also has quarters that have been left over from when it was a military base. Claude and Rose have one house, Ethan and Reuben have a second house, and Travis and Gerri have a third house. All homes have three bedrooms and are well equipped with a kitchen, living room, dining room, family room, and two full baths. The dining room in Ethan and Reuben's house is larger; thus, they will meet there and plan the surveillance. The team decides that Ethan, who is the most experienced, will be the team leader.

Ethan opens the meeting and says, "Guys and lady, I want these meetings to be structured but unstructured. What I mean is we will stick to the subject or items until we have a consensus. But if there are conflicts in the planning, I will make the final decision. We will be true in our plan and in our execution." They all understand—somebody has to be in charge.

As the team leader, Ethan starts the planning meeting. He says, "Travis, can you have the FBI task the National Geospatial-Intelligence Agency to obtain satellite images of the Murfreesboro-Pulaski area."

"Will do."

"If you have any delays," says Rose, "I can use my connections with the CIA to give the request some higher priority."

"Thanks, Rose."

Travis and Gerri are quickly introduced to Rose, Claude, Ethan, and Rueben. The FBI agents are most impressed with Rose. They are especially impressed with her war record and her lead part in the recent ISIS attack on the nuclear power plant and seaports. The FBI agents who were involved in the prevention of destruction of the nuclear plant, bridges, and tunnels had very high respect for the MI6 agent. Now they know that the MI6 agent was Rose.

Travis and Gerri give a quick summary of their experience. Both served in Afghanistan and Iraq and joined the FBI HRT team in the last five years. They successfully participated in the surveillance of several white nationalist camps in Montana and Idaho and also in the rescue of kidnapped victims. They then give an overview of their recent mountain climbing of the six-hundred-foot El Capitan cliff.

"Your climbing of the El Capitan south cliff is most impressive," says Ethan.

"Thank you," says Travis. "We are looking forward to the surveillance of the KKK camp; hopefully, our mountain climbing will be of some benefit."

The first day is used to make an outline of all equipment that will be required. The surveillance equipment of cameras, lens, infrared monocle, and odor elimination lotions and machines is discussed. A list is made of the mountain climbing equipment; most items are available from their personal stock. However, some are missing and/or need replacement. They decide to have members of the team go to different outdoor stores and purchase the required equipment. For the sake of security, team members will go to different stores from Richmond to Baltimore and buy the items. WMA provides the petty cash for the purchases. The main things that are lacking are camping equipment. The equipment they have looks like it is government-issued. They need to purchase equipment that a non-government climber would be using. However, it does need to have a camouflage pattern.

The second day, they have the downloads from the Geospatial Reconnaissance Agency. The pictures are incredibly detailed. Items of three feet are distinguishable. The images have a very high digital resolution. This allows for the selection of a portion of the picture to be zoomed without losing resolution. The team then starts the inspection of the KKK camp. It is located on the spine of the Smoky Mountains. The KKK camp is approximately twenty miles by twenty miles. The camp is located in the mountains. Real estate records indicate that the owner of the property is Gretchen Hannah Miller. Title records show that the property has been passed from generation to generation since the mid-1800s. The Confederates used the property like a fort to protect themselves against the Union forces. The Civil War ended before there was a need to fight. Since it was not considered as a Civil War memorial, the property continued to be owned by private individuals. The property was immediately on the edge of the Smoky Mountains National Park. It was in very rugged mountain territory. However, in the middle of the camp was a five-mile-by-five-mile area that was suitable for farming. No doubt the inhabitants used the camp for growing the food to sustain the settlement. The camp also indicated an area for cattle grazing.

Having studied the picture from the Geospatial Agency, the team decides that the physical surveillance will occur from the east and south sides. Both sides have two-hundred-foot cliffs that protect the camp. It is unlikely that the leaders of the camp will expect anyone to be capable of scaling the cliffs.

Rose contacts her point of contact (POC) at the CIA and asks, "We need reconnaissance photos from forty-five degrees of the following coordinates." She sends an encrypted text to her CIA POC with the coordinates. Twenty-four hours later, they have pictures. The four mountain climbers carefully review the photos. It is decided that Gerri Copal will climb the cliff as a solo (no ropes). After he does the climb, Gerri will drop a rope to the three members who remain at the base. The three members will scale the cliff using the rope. The supplies and equipment will be lifted using a specially designed bucket used by mountain climbers. The four team members will need to have tents and meals ready to eat for at least two weeks. It is decided that climbing the cliff daily will only offer an opportunity to have the team discovered. The team will need to approach the cliffs from thirty miles out. The approach will need to be on foot.

Gerri has been on the internet. The Smoky Mountain area has over eight hundred miles of trails. He says, "There is one hiking trail that will come to within twenty miles of the KKK camp. To climb the cliff and take the equipment and supplies needed for the two-week stay, each backpack will need to weigh eighty to ninety pounds. The weight is not a problem. The problem is that normal mountain climbers would not be carrying such a large backpack."

Rose has a recommendation: "When we were surveying the neighborhoods of Washington, DC, we had an employee from WMA by the name of Matt Gorman help with the surveillance. He did an excellent job. He is black and is read into the program. I recommend that Matt drive a van to one of the many camping sights and that he transports the items needed for the two-week sustainment."

"Did you say Matt was black?" asks Travis.

"Yes, I did."

"Perfect. No one would ever suspect a black person of spying on a KKK camp."

"I like it," says Ethan. "Who can talk to Matt and have him join us for the final day of planning?"

"I can take care of having Matt assigned to the team," says Claude.

The next day, Matt is at the Vint Hill Farms safe house, and he is read into the program.

Chapter Thirty-Three

Smoky Mountains, Tennessee

Placement of Surveillance Team

The final day of planning and preparation has the team loading two extended twelve-foot vans. Rick, who had the idea for the gun turret, is assigned to drive the van with the four special ops operators. It will be a two-day trip. They will stop at the Virginia-Tennessee border near Bristol, Tennessee, and check into a hotel. The second day will be to the Smoky Mountain trails. Rick will drop off Travis and Gerri fifty miles out from the base of the cliffs. Then he will drive ten miles and drop off Ethan and Rueben. At each drop-off, the team will walk the thirty and twenty miles to the campsite where Matt will be with the rest of the gear. Matt will depart two days later and stop at Base Camp One. From there, the four special ops agents will walk the twenty miles to the base of the cliff. The last twenty miles will be without a trail. The twenty miles will involve steep ridges, dense foliage, and low-hanging trees. and the area is known to have scorpions, poisonous spiders, and snakes. They all have high hiking boots with ankle leggings to prevent bites on their feet and ankles.

As the four-man team departs Vint Hill Farms and is taking the entry ramp to Interstate 66, Rick announces, "By the way, I am a smoker. I won't smoke in the van, but if you don't mind, I'd like to stop at every rest stop and take a smoke. Is that OK?"

Reuben says, "I think it's a good idea. Keep your mind fresh—the last thing we want is an accident."

The rest of the team says, "Fine with us. It is a two-day trip. If we get to Bristol too early, we may not be able to check in—take your time. We will be sleeping in the back seat."

Ethan, who is riding shotgun, is busy looking at maps. He says, "Have you been to the Smoky Mountains area before?"

"Many times," says Rick. "You may not know, but I am an outdoorsman. I fish and hunt. Last year, my nephew and I drove to Chattanooga and visited Clingmans Dome. The dome is the highest point in the Smoky Mountains. We camped for four days and fished the Tennessee River. Had a great time as the fish were really biting. We would reach our daily quota by mid-morning, so we had time to go hiking and sightseeing."

"That's great. What did you think of the area?"

"Felt like I was Daniel Boone. You know, Daniel Boone was a native of Tennessee. Legend has it that he fought a fourteen-foot grizzly bear. I think as the years rolled by; the grizzly would grow one foot every time the tale was told. Assuming that the story is true, grizzlies would grow more than eight feet when standing on their hind legs."

For the rest of the drive to Bristol, Rick and Ethan are like two peas in a pod. They talk back and forth, and they trade stories of their adventures. Rick has stories of his hunting, fishing, and drone flying. Ethan has stories of his firefights with shitheads and his narrow escapes with his life. Rick stops at every rest stop and smokes his cigarette. At 4 P.M., they pull into a Hampton Inn seventy-five miles inside the Tennessee border.

The second day, they leave at 9 A.M. Three hours later, they are outside the city of Nashville. They drive on to Murfreesboro, and by 2 P.M., they are driving through Pigeon Forge on State Highway 441. They drive to Athens, Tennessee, with stops alongside a hiking trail. Travis and Gerri open the back hatch and pull out their backpacks. They are dressed like typical hikers, and they start on their thirty-mile journey to Base Camp One.

Rick drives the van on State Highway 441 and stops at a roadside park ten miles from where Tavis and Gerri dismounted. Ethan and Rueben open the back hatch and place their backpacks on their backs. Both have walking sticks and start their twenty-mile journey to Base Camp One.

Matt started his journey with a fully loaded van. He has a large tent that will easily conceal all of the equipment that will be needed for the one- or two-week surveillance. Matt leaves early, at 5 A.M. He will drive all day to Athens and pick up State Highway 441. He has made reservations at a camping site that is twenty miles from the KKK camp. Matt arrives on schedule at 7 P.M. He checks in at the entry shed and selects an area far removed from the rest of the campsites. He expects the first team to arrive between 8 and 9 P.M. The second team should be there by 10 P.M. Included in the materials are five fold-out beds to allow a good night's sleep before the trek to the base of the cliffs.

At 9:15 P.M., the first team, arrives. At 10:30 P.M., the second team, arrives. They greet each other and know what they need to do—get a good night's sleep. It may be the last one for the next two weeks. Matt will remain at the base station to provide any supplies that they may need. They have brought the WMA drone, not for surveillance but for communications. The drone has been outfitted with some mobile ad hoc network routes (MANETs). The router will act as a relay point to allow communications from the survey teams to the base station. From the base station, a wireless router is available for connection to the internet. Comms will be available to the base station and to the WMA facility in Alexandria. The preferred method of communications will be text. Voice is not to be used unless absolutely necessary; they are concerned that the voice may be intercepted by human ears or parabolic antennas. Matt has received training from Vinny, and they do not expect any problems. Vinny will be on standby should any problems develop with the comms drone. As a backup, the team will have two Iridium satellite phones.

At 7 A.M., the four-man team has its last hot breakfast. Matt prepares eggs, pre-fried bacon, grits, OJ, and coffee. At 8 A.M., they are ready with their eighty-pound backpacks. Ethan leads the way. He keeps checking his compass and continues on the predetermined path that was chosen using the digital geospatial maps. The going is tough. Adding to the difficulty, it starts to rain.

The team is used to the rain, as special ops training involved hours of exercises in Panama, where it was always raining. The rain comes down in buckets, which is typical in the Smoky Mountains. The creeks all start to overflow, and the walking becomes more difficult. Ethan decides that it would be best to wait out the storm. They find some high ground, settle under a tree, and pull their pouches over their heads.

Two hours later, the rain stops, and the sun comes out. The creeks are still full of water, so the danger regarding snakes is at the maximum. Sure enough, several water moccasins are spotted, but they are just like people. They do not want any confrontation, and unless you step on them, they will leave you alone.

What should have been a one-day trip takes the team two days to reach the base of the cliff. They are at the base station at 4 P.M. They have enough sunlight to make the climb, drop the rope, and establish the camp on top of the mountain cliff. Travis and Gerri pull out the photos taken from the satellites. They check the hand-drawn climbing path that they prepared at Vint Hill Farms and make some adjustments. The climb will be a combination of solo and freestyle.

Gerri and Travis layout the equipment that will be required to climb the cliff: harness, rope, carabiners, pin hammer, protection equipment (pitons/screws), runners, sling, ax (piolet), crampons, hard helmet, two 125-foot ropes, and backpack. The cliffs are two hundred feet; thus, the lines need to be a combination of 250 feet.

"OK, I'm ready," says Gerri.

"I will be on the binoculars and provide any advice you may need," says Travis.

"Before you start," says Ethan, "let's check the comms. The radios are encrypted, and they will transmit on low power. They are on a 'talk around' channel. The range is limited to about five hundred yards. No chance of an intercept."

Gerri has the radio in his holster tied to his belt. He has a half headset on his left ear. The transmit is voice-activated; thus, he does not need to push a button to talk. He says into the mic, "Comms check. Copy?"

"Copy," says Ethan.

"Copy," says Reuben.

"Copy," says Travis.

"OK, here I go." Gerri is like a fly. He quickly goes from crevice to crevice and climbs the first thirty feet in two minutes. Then Gerri takes out his pin hammer and pounds in two pitons and screws. He carefully places his hands and feet on the pitons and climbs to the next level. Gerri climbs another fifty feet and again uses the hammer to pound in three pitons with screws. He is now at eighty feet.

He communicates with Travis using his voice-activated radio. "Travis, take a look at the mountain above me. Which way is best?"

"OK, give me a second to take a look." After about thirty seconds, Travis transmits on the radio, "Left will be better. You have more crevices; however, it is a bit longer. You may need to pound in a few more pitons and screws."

"OK, going left." Gerri climbs another ten feet left and five feet up. He stops and hammers in three pitons and screws. Gerri is now at 120 feet. The last eighty feet, he pounds in pitons and screws at two locations.

At one 195 feet, he pounds in the last set of pitons and screws. He uses the pitons to pull himself up and grabs the top of the cliff.

One hour and thirty minutes from the start of the climb, Gerri is looking down and throwing the rope down to the base of the cliff. He ties the line to the trunk of a tree.

"I have secured the rope to the base of a tree. Check it out. Bring up the rest of the equipment so that we can use the basket for the surveillance items."

"OK," says Travis, "I am coming up." He checks the rope. Then, with sixty pounds of items in his backpack, he quickly climbs to the top of the hill. Ethan and Rueben start tying the basket to the rope. Travis and Gerri have constructed a pole using a fallen tree trunk to place a pulley at the end. This will allow for the surveillance equipment to not be damaged when pulling it up to the top of the cliff.

Ethan and Rueben stay at the bottom and place the surveillance equipment in the basket. After four basket trips, all surveillance equipment is at the top. Ethan and Rueben straddle the rope and pull themselves up to the top of the cliff.

The pulley system is taken down and hidden in the bushes. They will need it when they exfiltrate.

Chapter Thirty-Four

Wolfgang Debriefs Gretchen

Drive from Nashville Airport to KKK Camp

Wolfgang arrives from Pakistan. Waiting for him in the cell phone lot at Nashville Airport is Gretchen. Wolfgang texts her: "Landed. Picking up luggage now. Pick me up at the American Airlines gate."

Gretchen replies: "Driving the blue Nissan four-door. See u soon."

Wolfgang picks up his two suitcases and walks out the American Airlines arriving gate. Gretchen drives the Nissan to the curb, opens the trunk, hops out of the car, and comes around to help with the luggage. Wolfgang picks up the large, heavy bag and places it in the trunk. Gretchen says, "Hope everything went well."

Wolf picks up the second suitcase and places it in the trunk. "Good to be home."

"Do you want to drive, or should I?"

"No, you can drive."

"OK. You are probably pretty tired?"

"No, actually, I had a business-class ticket from Dubai and was able to get ten hours of sleep."

"Wow, that's not like you. You must have been really tired."

"Yeah, I can tell you about my adventures as you drive to the camp. Let me begin with the most important thing."

"Yeah what's that? You killed the bitch?"

"I had to go to Pakistan to collect the posted reward. Those fucking ragheads were not going to pay. I had to kill one camel shithead and almost killed a second."

"Did you collect the five hundred thousand?"

"Yes, since the shitheads did not want to pay. They tried to kill me. I told them that the amount was double, one mil."

"So, they paid the one mil?"

"No, I first got the $500, 000, then I demand the extra $500,000. I had the fucker tied to the chair, and I started choking his assassin. After that, he showed me his account. It had only $255,000. I told him to transfer it all. So, we got a total of $755,000.

"That's fantastic. Good job."

"Maybe."

"What do you mean, maybe?"

"As Paul Harvey would say, let me tell you the rest of the story. Will and I did shoot what we thought was the bitch. It was a lure. The best I can figure is that she knew that there was a reward for her death. Somehow, they lured us to a villa in Scotland. I had her in my crosshairs and hit her square in the head. A second after I took the shot, we had incoming rounds. The shots were so close that I felt the air compression of the bullets passing within inches of my head. We were lucky that we were not killed. Fortunately, Will and I had rented some ATVs, and we were able to escape. The target had some professional guards. They tracked us using a drone. I was able to shoot down the drone, but somehow, they continued tracking us. We hid in farm equipment shed, and we made our escape. Unfortunately, Will was captured, and he was killed in the gunfight."

"So, you're telling me that my nephew Wilhelm was killed?"

Wolfgang has decided that he will not tell anyone the truth about Will's death. Will died a hero to the KKK Klan. Wolf has made up a story that Will fought three of the guards and that it was only because of his bravery that Wolf was able to escape. He thinks, *actually that is not far from the truth.*

"Yes, Will put up a valiant fight. He was surrounded by the three guards and fought like a wolverine. As the battle raged, he attacked the guards with the 'Rebel Yell.' The Yell was heard throughout the valley. He killed two of the guards. With his last bullet, he killed himself. He did not want to be taken alive. I am sure that he did not want to give up any of the activities that are ongoing at the camp."

"He died a true hero to the cause!"

"I agree. Without Will's sacrifice, I would not be here. He acted as a diversion to allow me to escape."

"Wow, I never knew that my nephew would act in such an unselfish manner."

"Yes, I am thinking of naming his company the Wilhelm Strassman Company."

"Yes, he would like that."

"Now, back to my concern that the bitch is still alive. After I escaped with the help from Will, I hotwired a car and made it halfway to London. I had the recording of the kill. After carefully analyzing the recording, it was obvious to me that the timing was slightly off. I came to the conclusion that it was a hologram and not the actual target."

"Then how did you convince the Pakistani customer that it was a kill?"

"After viewing the recording frame by frame, I converted two of the frames to photos. I used these to receive the reward."

"They must have been thrilled; they gave you the additional $255,000?"

"Let's just say that I am very convincing."

"OK, I get it, from the barrel of a gun! I won't even ask how you got out of that shithole country; hopefully, you didn't piss off too many people."

"Not to worry, they got other things to worry about like the U.S. Navy placing a couple of cruise missiles up their assholes!" Wolf thinks, *the defenses I set up need to keep in mind that ISIS may send a kill squad to Tennessee. They will not be interested in the Grand Ole Opry.*

After their discussions regarding Pakistan and Scotland, the conversation turns to the Homefront. Wolfgang asks. "How's everything with the camp?"

"The normal, nothing I cannot handle. We had to use some strongarm tactics in Santa Fe and Galveston. The loadmasters at two of the companies with whom we have contracts were giving our loads to our competitors. I had

Klaus and Manfred pay them a visit. After a few busted heads, everything is back on track."

"Yeah, we need to use muscle every once in a while; otherwise, some of these startups will try and take our business. I assume that we are still paying the loadmaster under the table to get prime rates to move the loads?

"Yes, we need to keep the loads moving."

"Any diamond loads from the Mexican border?" By "diamond," Wolf means drugs.

"Yes, we have had a good month. I will show you the ledger when we get to our office."

"OK, good to hear that all is in order."

"One more thing," adds Gretchen. "The Red Rooster is doing well, with clean money and the money from prostitutes. We have found a new coyote; his name is John Little. He claims that he also goes by the name of Juan De la Toro. He looks like a mean motherfucker. Says he has contacts with the Juarez drug cartel and members of MS-13. He can get us some good-looking pussy that doubles our profit margin."

"You know how I feel about anyone new. Where did this Juan come from? Who knows him? Are you sure he's not an undercover agent?"

"No fucking way. He came to us through the Juarez Drug Cartel. Seems like he knows Fernandez, the Juarez drug lord. I hear he is on personal terms with him. Ain't no way that a personal friend of the most powerful man in Mexico would be an undercover agent."

"Who checked him out?"

"Our El Paso loadmaster, Alfredo Alvarado, knows the Juarez cartel chief of staff, Garcia. Garcia told Alvarado that Little was the real thing—a top-notch coyote, knows all the police chiefs. He can get anything through Mexico and, most important, through the US-Mexico border."

"OK, I would like to meet the wetback."

"OK, but don't call him a wetback to his face. When you meet him, he will look like John Wayne with a beard. Very presentable and a smooth talker. That's how he gets the best-looking prostitutes to sign up for the work in the United States."

"OK, I get it. I will be on my best behavior."

After a two-hour drive, they are nearing the front gates of the KKK camp. There is a steel gate with a keypad and speaker. They approach the entrance and look straight up at the camera. The guard viewing the video from the camp guard shed says, "Welcome home, Colonel." The guard gate opens, and Gretchen drives into the camp.

Wolfgang Makes Defensive Preparations

At 7 A.M. the following morning, Wolfgang calls a staff meeting. Present is one Lt. colonel, two majors, and three captains. Wolfgang has organized the camp with a strict military chain of command.

Lieutenant Colonel Klaus Sondermann is a thirty-two-year-old former truck driver. Wolf befriended him while they were both moving drugs and weapons from the Mexican border to U.S. cities. Wolf likes Klaus for several reasons, one, he is punctual, two, he always dresses well, three, he is a student of the confederate south and four, he has a strong dislike of any non-whites. This includes Negroes, beaners, slant eyes, and ragheads. Soon after Wolf established the KKK compound in Tennessee, he recruited Klaus as his second in command.

He begins the meeting. "Colonel Sondermann, provide a status of the camp perimeter protection."

"We have a twenty-four by seven watch. Two guards per watch. One guard drives the four-wheel ATV around the fence perimeter every two hours. Video from the thirty-six cameras is viewed at the guard shack. All cameras have motion detection with alarms."

"Colonel double the guards. Drive the outer perimeter with two guards every hour."

"Sir, I will need more men. I only have eight men assigned to guard detail. I will need eight more."

"Major Jacobson," says Wolf, "detail eight men from the three companies to guard duty."

"Yes, sir."

"Colonel Sondermann, provide a status of the guard dogs."

"The two dogs are healthy and do well in their weekly training."

"Buy two more dogs. Make sure they are trained and that they are German shepherds. Also, modify the dog runs for two sections. Partition at zero and 180 degrees, with zero being north."

"Yes, sir. I will get started tomorrow."

"Some new items," says Wolf. "I have ordered two eagles to patrol the property. The trainer will be here tomorrow at 1 P.M. Major Salkowski, query the men and find two soldiers who will volunteer to handle the eagles. If no one volunteers assign two men from B Company."

"Yes, sir."

Colonel Sondermann says, "Sir, may I ask why the eagles?"

"I have a lot of experience using drones for surveillance. Both sides, good guys and bad guys. We need to protect ourselves against drone video surveillance."

"Sir," says Major Jacobson, "we are doubling and adding more protection. Would you mind telling us who the enemy is?"

Wolf thinks for a few seconds. He could tell the major to take a seat and say, "Top secret, just do your job." However, when he was in the Marines, the troops did better when they knew why they were killing ragheads, protecting the locals, or patrolling a given area. Wolf says, "Good question. As you know, I was away on a foreign mission. The mission netted the camp a little under one million; that is a one with six zeros. The successful mission pissed off several shitheads. It would be prudent to prepare for any retaliation."

"Yes, sir. We know your motto: plan, prepare, and practice—the three Ps. You have taught us well."

Colonel Sondermann says, "Perhaps it would be good to have some camel cocksuckers try and invade our camp. We will give them a lesson that they will never forget. I will order the men to double their training, run twenty miles instead of ten, one full hour of shooting, martial arts, and knife throwing. Also, I recommend that we place a guard on the south cliffs. Never know; some of those ragheads may have some goat experience. I understand that they take their liberties with goats!"

At this, all staff members laugh.

"Yeah," says Major Jacobson, "they may think that those Deltas or Seals are some mean motherfuckers. Wait till they get a taste of our firepower. They will quickly be on a trip to visit their seventy-two virgins."

Wolfgang thinks *this will not be a walk in the park. If we are attacked, it will be the guards and the MI6 special ops woman. Then again, if it is the bitch, maybe I can regain my honor.*

Chapter Thirty-Five

Physical Surveillance

KKK Camp, Tennessee

The four-man team has climbed the northern cliffs leading to the KKK camp. It is the most unlikely approach to be taken by any surveillance team. However, just as it is difficult for any surveillance team, it is equally difficult for any counter-surveillance. The four-man team has researched the area using the high-definition photos taken by the Geospatial Satellite Agency. They are incredibly detailed; however, there is nothing like being on-site. The area has steep hills, deep valleys, and dense foliage. They cross a couple of paths that appear to have had ATV traffic. They must avoid these paths, as they expect the guards from the KKK camp to use the paths to perform any anti-surveillance activities. The selected surveillance location is approximately five miles from the top of the cliffs. They will need to follow a zig-zag path to reach the spot. The real walking distance will be closer to ten miles through rough terrain. Carrying eighty pounds on their backpacks, it will take nine to eleven hours. Two hours from the cliffs, they hear the engine from the ATV.

Ethan cups his hands to his ears and points to ten o'clock. He signals the others to lie low and places his gloved hand across his mouth: *Stay quiet.* All four operators immediately fall to the ground. They all have X30 binoculars in holsters strapped to their waist-belts. From a prone position, they point the binoculars in the direction of the engine noise. The ATV has one rider, and it is moving slowly across ruts and small boulders on a path that has been made by rainwater. The ATV is bouncing up and down. After about five minutes, it stops.

Ethan whispers, "Looks like he is having problems."

"The back wheels of ATV are spinning," says Travis. "It is stuck on a boulder."

They see the driver get off and attempt to dislodge the ATV. He has no luck. He then jams small logs under the ATV and builds a fulcrum with rocks and a tree branch. It does lift the ATV, but he needs help to push it forward. He gives up and takes the radio from the dash of the ATV and tries to communicate with the KKK camp. It appears he has no luck. After about ten minutes, he gives up. He takes some water bottles from an ice chest mounted on the back of the ATV and starts walking back to the KKK camp. After about ten minutes, he is out of sight.

Ethan says, "OK, we are clear. Let's resume our hike to our spot." They all signal thumbs up and resume their walk to the observation point. The team has some difficulty traversing the landscape. It is a lot more rugged than they could have determined from the satellite photos. The plan was to make it to the observation post on the first day. At 7 P.M., with only one hour left for sunlight, they decide to call it a day. They only have two miles left, but it will be rough hills and thick foliage, and scorpions have been noted under every other rock. They find a suitable area to pull out their sleeping bags. They sit on some boulders, open some MREs, and have a meal.

Ethan says, "Better get used to these MREs. This will be our breakfast, lunch, and dinner."

"Good thing we got these from our FBI friends," says Reuben. "Their MREs have a touch of the French cuisine."

"Yeah, you wish," says Travis.

"Well, it's better than having to eat roots."

"Yeah, you're damn right."

After some good-natured ribbing, the four try to get some sleep. It's been a long day. They still have four or five hours tomorrow.

The following morning, they are up as the sun is rising.

"What's for breakfast?" asks Gerri.

"I saw some cinnamon cream breakfast bars," says Ethan. "Take two of them."

"OK, these bars are from the weight-loss outfit. See the label, Nutrisystem. My wife buys these to lose weight. Frankly, they are pretty good."

"OK but eat two or three. We are burning two or three thousand calories a day, and we need to replenish."

After eating breakfast, they are on their way to the observation post. From half a mile, they see the eight-hundred-foot hill. Like all settlements, the KKK camp is in the valley, where there is a river and fertile ground to allow farming. Surrounding the settlement are more than ten hills of varying heights. The chosen hill has deep foliage and steep grades on all sides. They have selected a spot that is halfway up the mountain. The top of the hill would be a better spot, but an observer from the camp could more easily find them.

Ethan points to the spot and motions for the team to follow him. They are approaching it from the direction opposite from their approach to the camp. A hundred yards from the area chosen, they set down their backpacks. They know the drill. They must totally camouflage their clothes, cap, gloves, and all outward apparel. They undress to their skivvies. They first use some hand wipes and thoroughly wipe their body of all sweat. They then apply anti-body odor from a spray can. They then take out clean skivvies, pants, socks, shirt, cap, and gloves and paint their faces black.

Ethan says, "Reuben, take out the two Ozonics machines."

"Roger." Reuben takes out the two machines and turns them on. "Gerri," he says, "take one of the machines and follow me." Reuben and Gerri carry two Ozonics odor eliminators to the ridge and place them toward the camp.

Gerri says, "OK, that should take care of any dogs."

"Reuben has the Bengay ready in case the dogs get to close," says Ethan.

"Roger that." Reuben looks at Travis and Gerri and says, "This Bengay has saved our asses more than once!"

"Never seen that before," says Travis. "Good idea."

They will run the Ozonics machine continuously. They have three battery packs and a solar blank to enable charging the batteries. Ethan and Reuben will take the first watch, Travis and Gerri will rest for eight hours, and the teams will switch for the duration of the surveillance. They believe that they will have all the required intel in three days, but they are prepared to stay up to two weeks. After settling in, they try establishing comms with Matt at the base camp.

Ethan transmits on the radio, "Matt, do you copy?" No response. "Matt, do you copy?" No response. "OK, let's go to the backup comms."

Rueben pulls out the Iridium satellite phone and sends an encrypted text message to Matt and the Vint Hills command post.

"Team Alligator is on location. Do you read?"

Base Camp: "Copy, 5 by 5."

Base VHF: "Copy, 5 by 5."

"OK, Alligator will send updates daily."

Base camp: "Standing by. Shout if required."

Base VHF: "Standing by. Break a leg."

"Roger. Out."

The team has established encrypted text with Matt Gorman at the base station and at the command post in Vint Hill Farms (VHF) Virginia. The Iridium phone also has voice, but they will only use it if their location has been compromised and all hell is breaking loose. They do not want any unneeded sounds.

Ethan and Reuben lie on their stomachs. They both have half headsets and will only whisper and use hand signals to communicate. They are using the 30X60 binoculars and a 30X60 infrared tube binocular. Adjacent to their prone position is a camera on a remote turret. The turret is automatically controlled; it will follow the pointing angle of Ethan's binoculars. The camera has a 30X60 lens. The picture can be taken by either Ethan or Reuben by pushing a button.

It is 4 P.M., and Ethan and Ruben see men and women walking within the camp. They both have a writing pad, and they are taking notes to describe the people they are surveying. It will be vital that they know how many men, women, dogs, and cattle are in the camp.

Around 6 P.M., they see four men come out with two eagles. The eagles are on the arms of the trainers. The trainers have leather sleeves on their arms where the eagles are perched. The four men are talking, and they point to a distant location. From there, a fifth person launches a drone. The drone goes up to about five hundred feet and comes across the KKK camp. At five hundred feet, the drone is barely visible. As the drone flies over the camp, the trainers move their arms forward, and the eagles take off. They are a pretty sight. They soar into the air and reach an altitude of one to two hundred feet above the drone. The drone operator is purposely controlling the drone in a random flight pattern. The drone flies in a circular route, changes altitude, and stops and starts. The eagles fly closer and closer to the drone. In a flash, they strike. The drone operator sees the attack and flies the drone at maximum speed to the left and dives at a forty-five-degree angle. The eagles adjust their flight paths in an instant and come ever closer to the drone. As the drone is changing its flight pattern, the first eagle strikes. The eagle talons, which are three to four inches in length, grab the drone from the center. The drone disintegrates and falls in hundreds of pieces to the earth. The eagle trainers and the two other men are high-fiving.

Ethan says, "That was impressive."

"Good thing Vinny, Jeff, or Louie did not see that," says Reuben. "They would not like having their baby being killed like that."

"Yeah, but leave it up to those three eggheads. They will probably come up with a defensive method."

"They will likely be performing more training. I guess that the KKK members are undergoing training. There will be more training flights. We will need to record the eagles and see what our eggheads can cook up."

"Yeah, we did bring a video recorder. It was one of those things where it was better to have it and not need it than not have it and need it. I will make sure that the camera is available tomorrow.'

The rest of the evening is pretty slow. The teams continue taking notes on the people they see. At ten P.M., they are ready for the shift change. They have agreed that the observing team will come back to the exchange area and have a debriefing. Then the teams will switch.

Ethan says, "It was a good move not having Vinny fly his drone. We saw quite a display; the eagles destroyed a flying drone. The drone operator tried his best using defensive measures. It was no match. We will need to record the eagles attacking the drone—I am sure that the whiz kids can come up with some defense against them."

"I have collected a lot of notes on the different people," says Reuben. "By my count, there are eleven men and three women. I did not see the dogs, but I heard them. I guess that the dogs will be running tonight. Keep an eye out for the types of dogs and how many."

"OK," says Travis, "will do. How did the camera and Ozonics work out?"

"No problem. Should be OK."

With that, Travis and Gerri duckwalk in their full camos over to the same spot that Ethan and Rueben were using. They check out the two-infrared single-tube binoculars, and within seconds, they can see the dogs running inside the perimeter fence.

Travis says, "Let's concentrate on the dogs, guard towers, cameras, and when the lights go out on the buildings. Let's see if we can detect body heat from inside the buildings,"

"OK," says Gerri, "got it. I can take the buildings, and you take the dogs and cameras on the perimeter fence."

"OK, got it."

For the next two hours, Travis and Gerri are busy surveying their areas of responsibility. By 1 A.M., all the building lights are out. Travis notes that at times, there are four dogs in his scope. However, they never run together.

At 2 A.M., Travis says to Gerri, "Take a look at the dogs as they come together. They are together for shorts periods, and then two dogs start running to the right, and the other two are no longer in view. What do you think?"

"Yes, I see what you mean." Gerri thinks about the disappearing dogs and then says, "I think I got it!"

"Yeah, are you going to tell me?"

"Let me look at the next time they come together, and I will then be certain."

For the rest of the evening, things are slow. Finally, the four dogs can be seen. They appear to be growling at each other, but they never circle each other.

Gerri says, "OK, I got it. The dogs are separated into two sections. Each section is roughly one half of the property. This way, they always have dogs on each side of the property. My guess is they have dog gates at the fences that separate the sections."

"Yes, I think you are right. Make sure that we write that down."

At 6 a.m., Travis and Gerri walk back to the exchange point and provide a debriefing to Ethan and Reuben. Travis explains that there are four dogs.

"There are two fences. They are separated by approximately ten yards."

Ethan says, "You mean like two perimeter fences, one inside the other?"

"Yes, that's correct. Also, the two perimeter fences are divided into two sections. Each pair of dogs' guards one of the sections. This gives them continuous protection around the entire camp."

"You mean, kinda like a horse track?"

"You got it."

Reuben asks, "Any unusual activity in the buildings?"

"I don't know about unusual," says Gerri, "but they do gather in one of the buildings, kind of like they are having a committee meeting. I could only see the people going in and out. I counted over thirty persons. With the infrared, it was difficult to tell the men from the women. But if I had to guess, probably a ratio of six to one—favor of the men.

"OK," says Ethan, "that's a good summary. Rest up. Reuben and I will take the first-day shift. I will provide an overview of the findings after the end of the second day. I know that Vinny and Jeff will be interested in the eagle attacks."

Chapter Thirty-Six

Physical Surveillance, Second Day

KKK Camp, Tennessee

After a one hour of debriefing, Ethan and Reuben take the second day shift. They are rested, and they duckwalk wearing their full camouflage dress. They are hoping that they can again witness the training of the eagles. They now have a video camera to record the eagles attacking the drones.

As they lie down, they hear reveille being played. Fifteen minutes later, there are three companies of three squads. Each squad has eleven men, and each company has thirty men and some women. Each company is headed by a captain. At the head of the battalion is the lt. Colonel. Standing with the Lt Colonel is three Klansmen with flags attached to their belt holsters. The flags are a swastika, the Confederate stars and bars, and the 1865 United States flag. All of the Klansmen and several women wear the Confederate uniform. After the full battalions are in formation, four officers march to the head. Behind the four officers steps an eight-person band.

The Lt. Colonel, shouts, "MARCH IN REVIEW!"

The flag bearer and band march straight out, make a left turn, and start playing "I Wish I Were in Dixie." Following the band are the three companies. The band and three companies march using the German army goosestep.

They march in a circle in front of the senior staff. As they pass, the captain barks, "PRESENT ARMS!" The Klansmen take their AR-15s off their shoulders and place the barrels directly in front of their faces with the gun handles in front of their belt buckles. They turn their faces toward the senior staff. All three companies march in front of the senior staff. After they present arms, they return to their original formation. The senior staff marches in front of the formation.

Colonel Schneider takes a bullhorn and says, "Klansmen, we are here to posthumously honor Private Wilhelm X. Strassman. Private Strassman gave his life to protect this camp. He single-handedly killed three communists who wish to defeat our cause. May white nationalism return to this land. Make America Great Again—return to white supremacy."

Lt. Colonel Sondermann then reads an announcement: "By the power vested in the KKK, from now on, Company C will be known as the Wilhelm X. Strassman Company."

Colonel Schneider calls out, "Parade rest."

All of the ninety-nine Klansmen give the Rebel Yell: "AWW-EEE-OH, AWW-EEE-OH."

After the Rebel Yell, the Klansmen return to their barracks. An hour later, they, are marching in their battle fatigues to the training area. The three companies start running at a fast jog with fifty-pound backpacks. From the satellite photos, there is a ten to twelve-mile track inside the camp. The three companies start their exercise runs at 8 A.M. and runs around the track two times. They complete their runs and classroom training at 12 P.M. After a one-hour lunch break, they all march to their respective training areas. One company is taking shooting practice, one company is training in martial arts, and one company is training in what appears to be a schoolroom.

At 2 P.M., Ethan and Reuben retreat to the exchange area. Travis and Gerri are ready in their full camo outfits. Ethan decides to have only a ten-minute debriefing; there are too many activities going on in the camp.

He says, "This morning was a major find. There, are three companies of thirty-three Klansmen each and staff. The count is 110 men and women. They are organized as a battalion. This morning, they had a formal march in a review parade. After their lunch break, they marched off to their respective training areas. It appears that the afternoon is used for specialized training."

"OK," says Travis, "we will take it from here."

Travis and Gerri are in their camos and in the prone position by 2:15 P.M. and they start scanning the camp with their binoculars. The still-frame camera and video cameras are ready to be used as required. The still-frame camera takes high-definition snapshots throughout the afternoon. These snapshots will be analyzed back at the VHF post command. The plan was to use the MANET to send photos back in real-time for analysis. However, this link could not be established. At 4:30 P.M., six Klansmen, and two trainers walk to a clearing area with the eagles. Today two drones are flying across the camp. The eagles are now perched on what appears to be a simulated tree stump. They hear the hum of the drones and take to the air.

Upon seeing the six-man team and the eagles, Gerri starts filming with the video recorder. The two eagles fly upward in the direction of the drones. It is apparent that they do have "eagle eyes," as they immediately spot the two drones. Both eagles fly to drone number one. The drone operator turns the drone away from the camp, and as fast as the drone can fly, it is sent away from the camp in an attempt to escape. The eagles are too fast. Within minutes, they overtake the drone and attack. The eagles are like WWII Japanese kamikaze pilots, diving at a sixty-degree angle. The talons of the first Eagle strike the drone, and it disintegrates, its pieces falling to the ground in a scatter pattern.

Upon seeing the successful hit, the second Eagle aborts the attack to drone number one and turns back to the second drone. The drone operator of the second drone has reduced the altitude of the drone to ten feet above the treetops. He is attempting to hide the drone amongst the foliage. The second Eagle sees the drone, and it follows the fight pattern of the drone. The drone has collision avoidance software, thus, the operator takes the drone below the level of the treetops. The drone is flying through the valleys of the trees. It smoothly maneuvers around all the trunks and branches, much like a cruise missile flying on a "nap of the earth" attack. One eagle is flying directly behind the drone, advancing at a fast rate. Within seconds, it will overtake the drone. The second Eagle is flying above the drone. It is keeping an "eagle eye" on the drone. It is as if the eagles have their own form of communication. The trailing Eagle did not attack the first drone. The Eagle with altitude has communicated to the trailing Eagle: "Your turn." The trailing Eagle overtakes the drone and smoothly reaches down and captures it. The propellers on the target keep turning and are winding in a high pitch. It is trying to escape from the Eagle. The fighting is to no avail. The Eagle grips and squeezes with its talons and destroys the main housing of the drone, which is the drone microprocessor. The propellers stop turning. The Eagle keeps the drone in its grip and returns to the trainer.

When the two eagles return to the trainers, they are rewarded with live rabbits. The rabbits are torn apart by the eagles with the talons and their beaks, and they enjoy their meals.

Gerri has been filming the entire eagle attack. He turns and says to Travis, "Man, that was impressive."

Travis nods and says, "Yes, most impressive. I don't see how you can defend against an eagle attack."

"I agree, but we do have the recording. The solution to this problem is out of my lane."

"It will be interesting to see what the skunkworks division of WMA does to solve this problem."

For the remainder of the afternoon and early evening, no significant events are witnessed. All the Klansmen return from their assignments at 7 P.M., and they go to what appears to be a chow hall at 8 P.M.

At 9 P.M., one company marches out from one of the buildings. Each Klansman is holding what appears to be an unlit torch. They march approximately two hundred meters to the center of the encampment. On command, they form a circle and light their torches. A group of six Klansmen move to the center of the circle and plant a cross in a pre-dug hole in the ground. The cross is wrapped in a white cloth, and a Klansman with a torch marches to the center and lights the cross. In two minutes, the cross is engulfed in flames. The six Klansmen retreat to the circle. A command is shouted, and the thirty-plus Klansmen all raise their torches and free hands into a Nazi salute and yell, "WHITE POWER! WHITE POWER! After yelling for a good five minutes and as the fire on the cross is slowing burning out, the Klansmen all get on their knees and shout, "LONG LIVE THE CONFEDERACY!"

The ritual of cross burning is repeated every night by a different company. By 11 P.M., all of the camp lights are out. Travis and Gerri have completed their shift, and they walk back to the exchange area.

Ethan asks, "Did you witness anything new or unusual?"

"Boy did we," says Travis. "This afternoon, we witnessed the eagles destroying two drones. It was most impressive. At 9 P.M., the terrorists engaged in an old-fashioned cross burning. We counted thirty-five Klansmen at the ceremony. We guess that a different company performs it every night.

Reuben adds, "The other two major items that we witnessed were the removing of two large cases from the SUV and the two women who arrived with the big, mean-looking dude."

"The two women appeared to have their hands tied and were under guard." Travis takes out a map and points to a dirt road. "I believe that they drove down this road, which leads to this building on the southernmost side of the camp."

"We need to find out what the building at the southern side of the camp is being used for," says Ethan.

"If I had to guess, it's probably where the girls are being used in sex trafficking."

"Yeah, most likely, but according to Claude, the spotter in Scotland told them that the women were slaves. They were kept locked in. We need to find out if this is true. We have been here two full days; one more day will not yield any additional information. We need to survey the south side where we believe they took the women."

Reuben says, "OK, let's look at the map and figure out the best way to get there."

"We will need to stay clear of roads, paths, and trails. Where was the ATV on the cliffside?"

After the initial discussions, Travis looks at the map using a penlight and says, "We have two choices. One of the most direct ways is to go to the top of the cliffs and go around for about fifteen miles. Two, we go down the cliffs and meet up with Matt and base camp one. Have a good night's rest. Have

Matt break up camp, and we hide in the panel van. He drives around and puts us only ten miles from our observation point."

Ethan, as the team leader, thinks about the two recommendations and says, "We do a combination of the two suggestions. One, we go back to Base Camp One, have a good night's rest and some normal food for a day. As we come in, we break up into two groups, each dressing in our hiking outfits. We lighten our backpacks to twenty-five pounds to look like hikers. Matt drives the rest of the equipment to the south side, finds a camping area, and we meet up there again. I am concerned that some of the forest rangers may be on the take. They will report to Wolf that hikers came in but did not exist."

"Good point," says Gerri.

"I agree," says Travis. Reuben nods and gives the thumbs up.

"OK," says Ethan, "it is now 11:30 P.M. Let's have a good night's sleep, and we'll set out for Camp One first thing in the morning."

Ethan is up at 6 A.M., and he sends an encrypted text using the Iridium satellite phone.

The second-day report reads as follows;

Witnessed eagle training for drone surveillance. Impressive, the drones had no chance of survival. We have video recordings.

Tangos had a formal parade. The battalion is organized as three companies, approximately one hundred men. All are armed with AR-15s and handguns.

Military-type training. Entire battalion runs with backpacks and arms for twenty miles. They are all in excellent shape.

The team witnessed a stretch van with what appeared to be two Hispanic women with their hands tied and wearing ankle bracelets. Indications are they are using women as sex slaves.

Also witnessed the loading of boxes. We were not able to tell what was in the boxes as they were offloaded inside of a closed warehouse. Best guess is that they contain drugs.

About thirty-five Klansmen performed a cross-burning ceremony. The ceremony ended with the group forming a circle around the cross and screaming, "White Power."

Ethan tells Reuben, "Let's break down camp and move to the south side. We need to find out where the women are being taken and what security they have around the slave house. Once we reach Base Camp One, I will call in."

At 7 A.M. the following morning, they are headed back to the top of the cliffs. They reach the cliffs at noon. They are down with all of their equipment by 2 P.M. At 6 P.M., they reach Base Camp One.

Matt says, "Good to see you guys. Had me worried when we could not establish comms with the MANETs. I guess that we need relays between the comm points. The terrain is too hilly and has tall trees. Not good for line-of-sight comms."

"How is the internet?" asks Ethan. "How much bandwidth do we have at the campsite?"

"Not bad, but it's not fiber. The campsite has a dish network. I get ten megabytes down and five megabytes up. We bought the unlimited option."

"OK, I will set up a conference call tonight. We can use the conference line from WMA. Later I can send video and snapshots using a transfer site."

"OK, I have already told the command post at VHF to expect a conference call tonight."

"Did you give them the time?"

"No, I did not know what time you would be in."

"OK, makes sense. Let me send a group text and tell them to be on the conference line at 8:30 P.M."

"Keep in mind that we are one hour behind in Tennessee."

"Yeah, forgot. Thanks. I will make it 7:30 Tennessee time, 8:30 in Virginia."

Ethan sends an encrypted email to the command post: "Setting up a conference call at 8:30 P.M., Virginia time." He sends the email to Brad, Jesse, Rose, Claude, Alex, Jeff, Vinny, and Louie. At 8:28, Ethan calls into the encrypted conference line as the leader. Within two minutes, all participants are on the line.

Ethan says, "Thanks for coming online. All four operators plus Matt are here in Tennessee. We are on a speaker."

"Rose, Alex, and I are at the Command Post on a speaker," says Claude.

The senator comes online and says, "Jeff, Vinny, Louie, and I are in the WMA conference room."

"OK, looks like we have a full house," says Ethan.

He begins the conference call, going through a detailed description of the KKK camp. He describes the double fence, dogs, cameras, and guard towers and gives the number of Klansmen.

Rose interrupts, saying, "Ethan, are you sure that the number is 110?"

"Yes, very sure. They had a formal parade for Wilhelm X. Strassman. That's the terrorist that Wolf killed in Scotland."

"Wow, you are that close?"

"No, the leader is a Colonel. I think it is Wolf. He used a bullhorn to make the announcement."

"OK, understood—go ahead. Continue."

Ethan then describes the extended van that arrived at the site. "Wolf and a large woman came out and inspected the items in a large case. After the inspection, the van drove into a warehouse."

"Any idea what was in the van?" asks Rose.

"Best guess is drugs, but not certain. We would need to break into the camp and physically inspect the contents of the van."

The discussion now turns to the eagles. Ethan says, "Right call on not using the drone for video surveillance." He describes the eagles destroying two drones and capturing a third.

Vinny then comes on the line. "Did the drone operators take evasive actions?"

"They sure did," says Gerri. "They even flew the drone under the trees, kind of nap of the earth. Even made a zig-zag pattern, flew the drones in rapid starts, stops, and drops. They did about anything they could—still, the eagles countered every move and attacked like kamikaze pilots. Killed the drones with one attack. The third drone was captured and taken to the trainer. Frankly, I was impressed."

"WOW," says Vinny. "Wish I could have seen that!"

"Well, you will get your wish; we recorded the complete actions by the eagles. I will upload to the transfer site tonight."

"Great, I will certainly take a look. Thanks."

"Next, we have what appears to be women being held as captives. We think they are being used as sex slaves. On the second day, a white SUV drove up with two women. The women were tied and had ankle bracelets. The man driving the SUV was well dressed, Cargo pants and brown fatigue t-shirt, and had tattoos on his arms. Frankly, he looked like a coyote. The last thing we witnessed was a cross-burning ceremony."

Claude, "How many Klansmen participated?"

"About thirty-five. From the parade that we witnessed, I would say that it was one of the three companies."

Senator Montana says, "Ethan, women being held as sex slaves is a severe accusation. Is there any way that we can conclude with any certainty that the women are being held against their wishes?"

"Sir, we intend to move to the south side and attempt to obtain visual evidence of the building being used for sex trafficking."

Claude says, "Ethan, you and your team need to proceed with extreme caution. The south side has very few places for concealment. Also, from the satellite photos, the building is close to Highway 441. This will mean that there is a high probability that you may be detected."

"Yes, we are fully aware of the dangers, but we think that we need to provide ample proof to allow a judge to issue a warrant for the FBI to conduct a search of the property. However, based on what we have uncovered to date, the KKK camp would not allow a search of the property without a major firefight. Should the FBI attempt to issue a warrant, in my opinion, Wolf would order an all-out gun battle. The KKK camp will not go down without a fight."

"Ethan," says Rose, "if I understand you correctly, you and your team will move to an observation point to take photos and/or video of what we believe is the slave building."

"Yes, we will be moving to an observation point beginning tomorrow. We should be at our selected location the day after tomorrow. It is my opinion that we should have the required information within a maximum of two days."

"Ethan, be very careful. This man—Wolf—is not the average bad guy. He was one of us—remember, he was a decorated Marine. He thinks like us, and he is very clever. He thinks out of the box. We do not have the element of surprise. He knows that we know that he attempted to kill me. The wild card that we have is that he does not know that his spotter, Wilhelm, told us about the nefarious activities that are ongoing at the camp."

"Thank you, Rose," replies Ethan. "We will be extra careful. No actions will be taken to allow the team to be compromised. Our mission is strictly surveillance—we fully understand that."

"Ethan, keep your head down and good luck to you and your team. We look forward to hearing from you in two or three days."

That evening, Ethan transfers over a hundred gigabytes of high-definition still frames and over two hours of video using an encrypted file transfer protocol (FTP) server at WMA. The following morning, the pictures and videos are available at the VHF safe house and at WMA for analysis.

Chapter Thirty-Seven

Physical Surveillance South Side

KKK Camp, Tennessee

On the morning of the third day, Ethan and Reuben leave the campsite. They are dressed as typical hikers and have thirty-pound backpacks. One hour later, Travis and Gerri exit the campground. They also are dressed as hikers. Two hours and thirty-three minutes after leaving the campsite, Ethan and Reuben stop at a rest stop to use the facilities. When inside the facility, a very friendly forest ranger approaches them and asks, "How is your experience on the Mountain Top hiking trail?"

"Excellent," says Ethan. "We have enjoyed our week in the mountains of Tennessee."

"Did you use our campsites?"

"Yes, and like the Davy Crockett song, we also got to know every tree in our one week."

"Yes, we do have a lot of trees. Enjoy your hiking in our wonderful state."

After they are well on their way on the hiking trail, Reuben says, "You handled that interrogation quite well. Do you think he is a paid lookout for the KKK camp?"

"Never know, but we need to be aware that Wolf may pay these rangers under the table. After all, they make minimum wage, and receiving a tip for information is probably seen as no one getting hurt, so WHY NOT?" Ethan and Reuben continue their walk and forget about the incident.

By 2 P.M., Ethan and Reuben reach the campsite where Matt has rented a camping space. Again, the camping space is well concealed and surrounded by woods. As they arrive, Matt welcomes them and says, "The VHF command post has reviewed the data sent and would like to have a conference call tonight at 8:30 EST."

"OK," says Ethan. "Did they say why?"

"No, they just said that they had studied the data and requested a conference call."

"OK, guess we wait for the conference call."

At 3:30 P.M., Travis and Gerri arrive at the campsite. Early that evening, they study the map and discuss the path that they will take to the chosen area. At 8:30 P.M., they call into the conference number.

Claude begins the discussion. "Team, we have reviewed the pictures and video. Great intel. We are concerned that we do not have real-time comms with the team when you are at your observation post. This morning, Rick and Alex left on a vehicle to Nashville. They have six MANETs. Three are camouflaged as tree branches. We would like for a one-day delay in your surveillance and wait until we have real-time communications. Rick knows how to set up the comms. Alex and Rick can bivouac at the campsite with Matt. They would be available should you need help to exfile."

"I can understand the comms," says Ethan, "but why the extra manpower?"

"As I said last night," says Rose, "we are concerned about Wolf. We believe that he will have extra protection around the slave quarters. He will know that this is a serious crime. He may have some extra security. Best to have some assets that can respond in less than two hours. Rick also knows how to operate the drone. Should you run into trouble, we can use the drone to provide a real-time view of the area."

"Have you forgotten the eagles?"

"No, Vinny and Jeff stayed up all night and have come up with a solution. The drone that Rick will launch has a reflecting surface. According to research on the internet, eagles do not like objects that reflect. The downside is that a person on the ground will most likely see the drone. However, at that time, we will be in a retreat mode. The camp will know that they are being surveyed."

"What about the drone being shot down?"

"Not likely. We will be flying it above five thousand feet. A bullet will lose its trajectory at that height, and it will be fighting gravity and will fall back down to earth. The height will also help with the eagles not attacking. Eagles can fly as high as ten thousand feet; however, they have likely been trained to find drones at under a thousand feet."

"OK, so the anti-eagle defense is from the drawing board and has not been tried."

"That's correct, but having only twelve hours, we think it will work."

Vinny, who is on the conference call from the WMA facility in Alexandria, says, "We think it will work. But even if it does not, we calculate that we will have five to ten minutes of excellent video. That should be enough to provide a real-time picture of the areas in question. Secondly, since we will have real-time comms, the drone has been outfitted with the synthetic aperture antenna. Louie also worked overnight and modified the software to detect objects that have the characteristics of an eagle. Should an eagle be detected, the drone will fly to ten thousand feet and get the hell out of the area. The drone has eight blades; thus, the top speed is close to a hundred miles per hour. According to the internet, the top speed of an Eagle is also a hundred miles per hour; thus, we will always retain our distance."

Travis, who has been listening, says, "In theory, this all sounds great, but will it work?"

"Guess you don't know the skunkworks team," says Reuben. "They have never failed us before. If Louie is involved, I bet that it will work!"

"OK," says Ethan, "we stand down one more day and wait for Rick and Alex."

"Good luck, guys," says Rose, "and break a leg."

"Thanks."

On the fourth day, the team studies the maps provided by the Geospatial Satellite Office. The location of the buildings that need to be surveyed is only two miles off of Highway 441. The land around the area to be surveyed is flat with tall birch, basswood, buckeye, magnolia, red maple, and tulip poplar trees.

The grasses growing in the surveillance area are switchgrass and big blue stem. These grasses grow to be three to six feet tall. This is good and bad: good in that they can easily hide and bad because the tall grass will obstruct their view. The ideal solution would be to use the surveillance drone to find the surveillance spot. The problem is the eagles. The team will wait and discuss the problem with Rick.

At 3 P.M., Matt drives to Nashville to pick up Rick and Alex. At 5 P.M., Rick and Alex arrive at Nashville Airport and park in the long-term parking lot. Alex and Rick take the shuttle bus to the terminal, and Matt picks them up at 5:30. They drive back to the long-term parking lot and offload the van, which was driven by Rick and Alex. They leave in Matt's van at 6 P.M. and arrive at the base camp at 8 P.M. They drive to the base camp tent and offload the MANETs and the surveillance drone.

Ethan now debriefs Rick and Alex on the current situation. The fifth day will be used to set up the MANETs and check out the drone.

Rick explains, "We have brought five MANET systems plus the parts to remove the MANET from the current drone and reconfigure it for a physical installation. Two of the MANETs must be used at the endpoints. The remaining four will be used as relays."

"Where do we install the MANETs?" asks Ethan. "And what is the required separation?"

"As you can see, the MANETs have been painted with a camouflage green and brown pattern. They will need to be installed on trees. The higher, the better. The separation depends on any mountain blockage and attenuation from tree leaves. Based on the ground being flat, we will install the relays no more than five miles apart. Thus, we will have five sections that will cover up to twenty-five miles."

Alex, who has been viewing the map, points to the locations where the MANETs will need to be installed. "I recommend that we use the cell towers along Highway 441. We place the first here at the base camp. Next, we place one on the cell tower outside the campsite, skip two cell towers, place the third on the fourth cell tower, and it communicates with the MANET at the surveillance site."

"Won't the MANET frequency interfere with the cell tower signals?" asks Travis.

"Actually," says Rick, "it will not. The MANET frequency has been set in the 5 GHz range. The cell phones use the 700 MHz range."

"OK, good to have some radio blockheads on the team!"

"Thanks, I take that as a compliment."

"OK," says Ethan, "so, who goes where and installs the MANETs?"

Alex takes command. "The MANET here at the campsite needs to be on the tallest tree. Both Rick and I brought the climbing boots with the spikes on the inside. We also have our special climbing gloves and our belts. We will climb the tallest tree that can support our weight."

While Alex has been talking, Rick has been surveying the campsite area. He says, "Take a look at eleven o'clock."

Alex looks at eleven o'clock and says, "Perfect." They walk inside the tent and get dressed and are ready to climb. They will take a rope with them.

Alex and Rick start climbing. When they reach the highest point, Rick pushes the radio button and says, "Clear the drop zone. Rope coming down."

Matt inserts the MANET and battery into a bag, ties the rope to the bag, and transmits on the radio, "Equipment bag ready. Start pulling." Within seconds the bag starts moving up to Alex and Rick.

Ten minutes later, Alex transmits on the radio, "MANET powered up—ready for the test." The green light comes on, and the MANET is receiving.

The next two locations will not involve Alex. Wolf has seen Alex, and it would be taking an unnecessary risk. Rick and Matt will install the MANETs on the cell towers. They both dress in work coveralls. Rick and Alex brought a magnetic sign, which they place on the two van doors. The sign reads "Tennessee Cellular Associates. When you need comms, who you gonna call—TCA!" The installation at the two cell towers goes without any problems.

Rick and Matt drive two miles from the last cell tower installation, and Rick keys his radio. "Base camp, how you copy."

Alex answers, "Base camp, copy."

"OK, coming home."

Rick and Matt drive back to the base camp. They have now established wideband communications for fifteen miles, and the last installation will be at the surveillance site.

As the "comms crew" is establishing the real-time comms, Ethan, Reuben, Travis, and Gerri have been busy designing the surveillance plan.

Ethan says, "Rick, we would like to launch the drone and survey the area we have selected. The plan will be to drive a good ten miles outside the perimeter of the KKK camp, fly the drone to five thousand feet, and slowly bring it over the area to be inspected."

"We are going to use tomorrow to determine the flight schedule for the eagles," says Reuben. "They will likely fly on some random flight schedule, like a round trip around the camp once an hour. This will create a half-hour opportunity to video and record the area of interest. Should the eagles detect the drone, the down-looking synthetic radar will detect them and issue our warning. We will immediately get the hell outta there."

"The Eagles are swift flyers," says Travis. "Are we sure that they will not overtake the drone?"

"Louie upgraded the software," says Rick. "The top speed of the drone is a hundred miles per hour! Research on the internet indicates that the top speed for trained Eagles is about the same. We should be OK."

Ethan, Rueben, Travis, and Gerri are now dressed in their camos. They will walk toward the KKK camp but not enter the property. They will split into the two groups and observe the eagle flight patterns from two different locations two miles from the KKK property perimeter. They arrive at noon.

They transmit on the radio, "Base camp, this is Alpha. How do you copy?"

"Copy, ten-four. Bravo."

"Charlie, Copy."

"Delta, Copy."

They have all established comms from the base camp to a location close to the surveillance point. Base camp transmits, "Team Alligator, I have a patch to the primary and secondary command posts. Please transmit video for check test."

"Roger will do. Stand by." Ethan takes out the video camera and pushes the play button. "Transmitting. Command post, do you copy?"

"Primary CP, copy. Video excellent."

"Secondary CP. Video excellent."

Vinny cannot hold back his excitement. "Hell, of a job, guys. Wish I was there."

"Great job, guys," says Jeff. "Vinny has been more nervous than when his wife gave birth to their first child!"

"OK, guys," says Rose, "you are set. We will be monitoring your surveillance tomorrow. Vinny and Jeff will have the sky watch. They will be able to control the drone from here—great job to all. Tomorrow is a big day. Be careful."

"Thanks, says Ethan, "will do, and thanks to Rick and Alex. They did a great job."

On the sixth day, the four-man team is ready for the most challenging and dangerous part of the surveillance. The two pairs leave with their eighty-pound backpacks and walk for approximately fifteen miles. The last five will be the most dangerous. They will need to move within a half-mile from the building under question. The surveillance spot will be only one hundred meters from the outer fence. One significant advantage that they have is radio communication. At five miles to the surveillance location, the four-man crew takes a knee, and Ethan transmits on the radio, "Request video surveillance from the drone. Is there any unusual activity, should we proceed?"

Vinny, from the secondary CP, says, "Request status of eagles. Will fly drone three minutes after the eagles have completed their last pass."

"Will do," says Ethan. Twenty minutes later: "Fly drone now—eagles completed pass minus three minutes."

"Roger. Drone is gaining altitude and flying toward the surveillance location. ETA ten minutes."

Ten minutes later, Ethan and crew watch the drone head to the surveillance site. At twenty-five minutes, the drone passes overhead and then flies back to the campsite.

Vinny says, "Location has a road with connection to Highway 441. Guard shack approximately half a mile from the road. A guard was seen in the guard shack, and the target building has a single fence. Cameras noted approximately every fifty meters. Two guards at the entrance. Only one building noted; however, there is what looks like a cellar door. Best guess is that there are more rooms underground. Dog houses noted but no guards. Likely that the dogs are in the underground shelter. Any questions?"

"Thanks," says Ethan. "That was a good report."

"We will be online. Any help we can provide—we are ready."

"Thanks, we are now moving to our surveillance location."

The four-man team carefully walks to within one mile of the surveillance location. Again, the team undresses and applies the anti-odor spray. Before pulling up their underwear, they apply Bengay to their bodies. This is to combat any human odor. The Bengay will disorient any smelling dogs. They need to be aware that the Bengay will wear off. They also have the Ozonics anti-odor machine.

Additionally, Rick brought some skunk spray from Virginia. They will only use the skunk spray if they are being tracked. Rick has told them, "It's pretty strong. If you use it, make sure you pinch your nose until you are well out of the skunk range."

As they did on the northern side, they will take eight-hour shifts. Ethan and Reuben take the first shift after they arrive at the surveillance location at 2 P.M. The afternoon is relatively quiet. At 8 P.M., a Ford Economy van drives to the front of the building. The driver and four men step out of the truck. The men are well dressed and are all of age forty or higher.

Reuben whisper, "Johns." Ethan gives him a thumbs up. The still camera snaps pictures as they watch the ongoing arrival of the men. The four men enter the building. The driver is in his late twenties or early thirties and is wearing cargo pants, black Nike tennis shoes, tight golf shirt, and a Titans baseball cap. He has a trimmed black beard and tattoos on his arms. After about twenty minutes, the driver leaves and drives to the gate and Highway 441. For the remainder of the night, a van shuttles Johns to the building, and after some two or three hours, the men leave on the shuttling passenger van. From 8 P.M. to 4 A.M., the team counts over fifty Johns. Travis and Gerri take the shift from 10 P.M. to 6 A.M.

Travis and Gerri come back to the exchange point, and Ethan says, "Get some sleep. Nothing is happening during daylight hours. We will communicate with Rick, Matt, and Alex. We need them to place a stakeout on Highway 441 and find where the Johns are coming from."

"OK," says Travis, "we only need a quick shuteye, and I have some ideas."

At noon on the seventh day, Ethan, Reuben, Travis, and Gerri move back to a location one mile from the perimeter fence. They can now speak freely without being concerned that one of the guards will hear their conversations.

Travis says, "We need to have eyes inside the prostitute building. The issue is, are they being held as sex slaves?"

"OK, let's discuss ideas," says Ethan.

"I believe that we can dig under the fence and move our way to the building without being seen," says Gerri.

"Do we have tools?"

"No, but we can go back to the base camp and appropriate the tools."

Travis asks, "How about we fake a John and try to go in through the front door?"

"That is very high risk," says Reuben. "We cannot just show up and flash some cash and they let him in. This carries a very high risk. Whoever is the John may not make it out."

Alex has been listening on the open conference line. He says, "I am not on site, but I do have a recommendation. If I understand the situation, there is a multi-passenger van shuttling the Johns. Most heavy-duty vans have a high body. Would it be possible to have one of you sneak under the van carriage? You can have some marine rope knots ready to hook the body to the undercarriage. You use this technique to enter and exit the camp. The key is, does the van stop at the guard gate long enough to allow a person to sneak under the van and attach himself?"

"Damn a good idea," says Ethan. "We will need to survey the front gate and see if the opportunity presents itself."

"I have experience in doing exactly this technique," says Alex. "Ethan, you're the team leader on this operation. It's your decision, but I believe I am the most experienced and have successfully performed this type of infiltration."

"OK, I agree. We will stake out the guard shack tomorrow, and go ahead and start your journey to our location ASAP."

"Vinny, are you on the line?" asks Alex.

"Yes, I'm listening."

"OK, can you play back the recording of the slave building and investigate all of the surroundings at the guardhouse?"

"Anything in particular?"

"Yes, we need to better understand the terrain, trees, bushes, tall grass, anything that will assist or create a problem when I attempt to sneak under the van."

"OK, I got it. I will get back to you by the time you reach the surveillance point."

"OK, thanks. As soon as I collect my camos, bug spray, Bengay, etc. I'm on my way. I will also bring some J-hooks to allow the connection to the undercarriage."

Alex makes good time and is at the surveillance location at 2 P.M. He says over the radio, "Hello to the Ritz Carlton. Beds are a little hard, and the bugs bite, but the views are fantastic."

Ethan smiles and thinks, *we will get along just fine. I like his sense of humor.*

Alex then says, "It's good to be in the field and see some action. Can you give me a summary of your findings on the guardhouse?"

"Yes, will do," says Ethan. "We also have info from Vinny. First, our findings. The road has heavy, tall grass surrounding the road that leads to the guardhouse. The road is paved with asphalt. The asphalt has been painted a dirt-brown color. It blends into the ground and looks like a dirt path. There is a potential for a major problem."

"Go ahead. I'm listening."

"The guards have mirrors on eight-foot poles. They are being used to check the undercarriage of all vehicles entering the property."

"Yes, that is a major problem."

"However, the report from Vinny is very informative. There is an electrical substation on the outside of the fenced property." Both Ethan and Alex are thinking the same thing: *Power outage.* They both start planning the steps that will be needed to create a power outage.

"We will need one more day to collect all of the necessary equipment," says Alex.

"Yes, I agree," replies Ethan. "We are also in luck. The communications to the building are by landline. The phone line is using the same power poles that the power lines use."

Ethan calls for a meeting of the three operatives and Alex. He then gives them the plan to infiltrate the slave building. "The photos sent by Vinny have indicated that there is a power substation outside of the fenced property. We will create a power outage. When that happens, the guards inside the property will likely make a call to the power company to restore the power. We will intercept the call and fake the power company. An hour later, we'll show up and fix the problem."

"I recommend that I return to the campsite and gather the required tools and equipment," says Reuben. "Rick and I packed the phone-tapping items and tools to disable the power. We also pack a magnetic sign that says 'Tennessee Valley Power Company.'"

"OK, we will get on the radio and tell Rick and Matt to start collecting all items."

"Whoever recommended that we have real time comms is a genius," says Travis.

"Your Einstein is Rose," says Alex.

Reuben starts his walk back to the campsite. He is traveling light: only him and the radio. He makes record time and is at the campsite in three hours. Reuben keys his radio. "Ethan, I am at the campsite. All equipment has been loaded, and the van is ready. Ready for instructions for when to proceed with the plan."

"OK, stand by for instructions."

Ethan and Alex discuss when would be the best time to cut the power to the "Chicken House." They will use this code name to refer to the slave building. The building looks more like a large Victorian home. It has a front porch that circles around the house. It has three levels with a veranda on the second floor. Windows on the first floor always have the curtains closed, but the windows on the second and third floors have the curtains open. The first floor is approximately five feet above the ground with stairs from the first-floor porch to the sidewalk. The house has a circular drive way with evergreens bushes neatly trimmed surrounding the driveway. Off to the right is a large shed with what appears to be cellar doors. On the side is a large tractor with a front-end loader and a backhoe. Behind the house are two diesel back-up generators.

Alex says, "I believe that the best time to cut the power will be during the day. One, they will want the power back on so that their business is not interrupted when night comes, and two, we can work better with daylight."

"When Reuben arrives," says Ethan, "he will have at least three coveralls for the electrical workers. Who do you recommend goes into the Chicken House? One should be Reuben; he is experienced and speaks Spanish. Who on your team speaks Spanish?"

"That would be Gerri. His last name is Copal. He is a second-generation Mexican and speaks Spanish fluently."

"OK, then our two-man team will be Reuben and Gerri."

Travis, Reuben, and Gerri have been listening to the plan. Gerri says, "If you had not assigned me, I was ready to raise my hand—we need to find out what the hell is going on in the Chicken House. If the girls are being held as slaves, we need to get the HRT to have a raid!"

"Damn right," says Travis. "I will make sure that we are assigned to the HRT. We need to put down those assholes!"

At 4 P.M., all personnel and equipment are ready. Ethan calls Reuben: "Moving to power station now. Expect a call within the next hour,"

"Roger, standing by in ready mode."

Alex, Ethan, Travis, and Gerri carefully move to the power substation. First, they attach the connection to the phone line. They disconnect any comms to the outside world. All calls will be answered by Travis. Within two minutes, they are inside the power substation. They unscrew the panel that protects the power breakers. Alex pulls the main power breaker. The power to the Chicken House is out. Ten seconds later, the backup generators turn on. Two minutes after that, Travis answers a call from the Chicken House.

"Tennessee Valley Power Company. How can I be of assistance?"

"Our power went out two minutes ago," says one of the guards. "Need to have one of your crews come out and fix the damn problem ASAP. We got a business to run. Losing millions if it is not fixed in the next two hours."

"Yes, sir. We understand. What is the address of the property?"

"The address is 4356 Highway 441."

"Sir, you have a large substation on your property. We cannot have a full crew with the proper equipment for another twenty-four hours."

"Look, you asshole, I told you that we need to get this fixed by sundown. If you do not have a crew out here within the next two hours, I will personally go to your building in Pulaski and put a bullet between your eyes—do you hear me, asshole?"

Travis is really smiling, but he puts on a fake nervous answer. "Yes, eh-eh-eh, I will see if I can get one of our swift power crews to your location. It will not be a full-service truck, but the technicians will be the best we have."

"That's a lot better, asshole. Better have them here ASAP. I'm not kidding about the bullet between your eyes. Now, get on the phone and have that crew here ASAP!"

"Yes, sir. I will call the crew immediately."

Heinrich Schmitz, who is the chief maintenance worker at the Chicken House, turns and tells Rodney Gibbenhaven, the second maintenance worker at the Chicken House, "They will be here; I scared the shit out of the candy-ass operator. Bet he believes me that I will put a bullet between his eyes."

"Heinrich," says Rodney, "you know how to get things done. Bet the colonel will soon promote you to corporal."

"Hope so. After the power is back on, you can call the colonel and tell him what a great job we did to scare the shit out of the power company dispatcher."

"Will do. Now, let's see if the dispatcher comes through."

"He will, or his ass is grass!"

Travis calls Reuben, "Done. Go fix the problem."

"On my way."

Forty-five minutes later, Reuben is turning onto the Chicken House road from Highway 441. Gerri is hiding behind a tree; he comes out and flags down Reuben. Reuben stops and signals to Gerri to open the back doors. The coveralls, boots, gloves, and baseball cap are lying on the floor of the van. Gerri quickly dresses as the second electrical employee. Ten minutes later, they are at the front gate. One guard comes out and walks to the driver-side window. The second guard stands at the front of the truck with his AR-15 at a ready position.

The guard looks at Reuben and Gerri, looks in the truck, and tells the second guard to lift the guardrail. The rail goes up, and the guard with the AR-15 signals with his arm for them to proceed. The guard who was at the van window says. "Drive straight ahead. There is a gentleman by the name of Heinrich waiting for you. Drive straight to the house, no fucking around. You have five minutes to get there. Understand?"

"Yes, sir, understood," replies Reuben.

"Fucking assholes," says Gerri once they pull away.

"It's OK. We use their haste to get the power back up to our advantage."

The front guard calls Heinrich on the radio. "Hey fuck head, the power company just arrived. They are on their way to the house."

"Goddamn it, how many times do I need to tell you to not call me fuck head," says Heinrich. "How many electricians?"

"OK, OK, don't need to blow a gasket, but they look legit." The truck has the logo, and they have work coveralls."

"OK, thanks."

Four minutes later, Reuben and Gerri are at the front of the house.

Rodney tells Heinrich, "Looks like you scared the shit out of the dispatcher. They got here in fifty-five minutes."

"Yeah, the squeaky wheel gets the grease."

Reuben and Gerri step out of the van. Reuben says, "Good afternoon, sir. Can you explain the problem?"

"Yeah," says Heinrich, "no fucking power, idiot. Can't you hear the backup generator?"

"Yes, sir. Can you direct me to the main power panel of the house?"

"Follow me."

They go inside the house and take the stairs to the basement, where the main power panel is located. Reuben takes a voltmeter from his equipment pouch and checks for power. He unscrews the panel cover and checks all the circuit breakers.

While Reuben is checking the connections inside the power breaker, Gerri is engaged in discussion with Heinrich. He is trying to distract Heinrich from observing what Reuben is doing. He is politely asking questions about the electrical system in the house, dishwashers, floodlights, any servers or computers, etc., anything that uses electricity.

Heinrich loses his patience and says, "Shut the fuck up—just fix the problem. Any five-year-old can see what the problem is: NO POWER IS COMING FROM THE SUBSTATION! Now, fix the damn problem."

"Yes, sir. Our next step is to drive to the substation. Says here in my work order that you have two hundred-kilowatt transformers. Can you direct us to the substation?"

"Goddamn, do I need to do everything?"

"No, sir, we can find the substation, but for expediency, it will be best if you point us in the proper direction."

"It's too far to walk. It is located near the guard station. Follow me. I have an F-150. Painted red and blue, like the colors of the Confederate flag."

"Yes, sir, we will follow."

As they drive to the substation, Gerri says, "I thought that the guard at the front gate was an asshole. This guy takes the cake, asshole, shithead, and just plain stupid!"

Heinrich drives to the front gate. Reuben and Gerri park in the tall grass next to the F-150. Heinrich points to the right and says, "Take that path. The substation is thirty yards behind that copse of trees."

Thank you, sir. Be just a minute. We will check it out."

Heinrich follows Reuben and Gerri. Again, Gerri will need to create a distraction.

Reuben sees that the main breaker is turned off.

Heinrich sees the breaker in the off position. He shouts, "GODDAMN IT! SOMEONE TURNED THE BREAKER OFF! That's why we have no power. Turn the fucking breaker back on."

Gerri, who is next to Heinrich, then says, "Sir, the breaker will automatically shut off if there is a short circuit; otherwise, the substation transformer will blow up. If the transformer blows up, we will need a crew from Nashville. That will not be today. Maybe one or two weeks."

As Gerri carries on his diversionary talk, Reuben has purposely disconnected some breakers. He reaches in his tool pouch and brings up a breaker. It is burned black, and the plastic around the connections has melted.

"Here is the problem," he says. "One of the breakers burned to a crisp. I have replaced the circuit breaker from ten to twenty amps. Should be OK now. The bad circuit breaker indicates that it is the power to the outside lights."

Heinrich then says, "OK, now I know you guys are professionals. We recently added outside floodlights for better protection. Our colonel insisted that we add protection lights. No one ever thinks about the consequences." Heinrich knows that's not true; Rodney and he have been connecting TV screens, an electric air conditioner, an old boom box, and other electrical appliances. *He believes Rodney, and he caused the problem. It is best if we just shut the fuck up.*

Reuben says, "This may still not solve your problem. It is quite possible that some of the breakers for the inside rooms may need to be replaced. We now need to go back to the main house."

Heinrich is now gaining confidence that these electrical workers are pros—they know what they are doing. The power will be back up tonight for the Johns. They are taking in over $22,500 a night. If the money train stops, the colonel will turn into the angry Wolf. He has witnessed his anger before, and once is enough.

Heinrich jumps back into his F-150. Sure enough, as he drives up, Rodney says, "Most of the power is up. A couple of areas still are dark. We need to go back down to the main breaker box."

Heinrich is now tired of his escort duties. He tells Rodney, his sidekick, "Take over my escort duties. Whatever these guys need, help them out. We need all our power restored by 8 P.M. tonight."

"Yes, sir," says Rodney. "I will escort them from this point forward."

Rodney is forty pounds overweight. The back of his shirt is always untucked, his hair is long and unkempt. Rodney is wearing gray pants that are two inches too long, the bottom hems are frayed. He is wearing black high-top converse tennis shoes. He is trying to grow a beard, but he only has a few strands of whiskers around his chin and cheeks. It seems like he has more hair coming out of his nose and ears than the beard he is trying to grow.

Reuben and Gerri have heard the instructions, "DO WHATEVER THEY WANT." They will use that to their advantage.

Reuben, Gerri, and Rodney go down to the main breaker. They check all of the circuit breakers. Some are not labeled.

Reuben asks, "What rooms do not have lights?"

"Three rooms on the first floor, two on the second floor, and the main meeting room."

Gerri knows what to do. He says, "I will go out and get an extra radio."

Rodney does not know what to do. He needs to escort both. Reuben says, "Go with him. I promise I will stay right here. I'm not going anywhere."

When Gerri and Rodney come back, Gerri has two radios. Rodney is eating a donut. Gerri gives Rodney a radio, and Rodney stuffs the donut in his mouth. Reuben says, "Rodney, you go to the third floor, and Gerri, you take the second floor. I will flip each breaker, and you tell me if the lights go off."

Rodney is in a quandary. Heinrich told him, "Do whatever is necessary get the power back up by 8 P.M." He thinks, *What I should do?* He then tells Rueben, "Wait a second. We are working on some top-secret shit. I need to cover the tables."

"OK, we can wait."

As Rodney is going through the third, second, and first floor. He tells the girls to hide. The Migra (The US Department of Immigration) is inspecting the property. If they are found, they will be shot. President Trout has ordered that all illegal aliens be rounded up and sent to concentration camps. Of course, it is a lie, but that's the best he can do, and besides, the whores don't know shit.

After fifteen minutes, Rodney comes back with a cookie in one hand and the radio in the other. He says, "Tell me what to do, and I will do it. No need to send your tech up to the first, second, or third floors."

Reuben is ready for that. "Rodney, I need a certified electrical technician. We don't know what problems were caused when the main breaker blew. The breaker kicks off when there is an electrical short or one of the circuits is carrying too many amps. The breaker flipping is normal. If it did not flip off, there would be a fire. We need to know what caused the surge in amps and fix it. You can simply tell me if the room does or does not have power. I need my technician to pull out the light switch and check for frayed wires. If they are frayed, we will need to replace the wires and the switch."

Rodney is now looking at Reuben, eating his cookie, crossed-eyed and totally perplexed. He does not want to sound stupid, so he just says, "OK, I understand. You need someone who knows what he's doing. Electricity is not my profession. Go ahead and do whatever—just have all the lights on by 8 P.M."

"OK," says Reuben, "Gerri, start on the third floor. Rodney, you go to the second floor. We split the team and finish this work by 8 P.M. Keep your radios on channel two. I will tell you what to do depending on my work on the main power panel."

Gerri opens the door to the first room on the third floor. It is empty. He sees a walk-in closet. He takes his iPhone and starts a recording application. He opens the door, and two young Hispanic girls are cowering in the corner. Gerri, whose name is Gersian Opal, speaks fluent Spanish. He says, "*No tengan miedo. Yo soy un amigo. Diga me estan aqui como prisioneras?*" (Do not be afraid. I am a friend. Are you here as prisoners?) They answer, "Si," and go on and explain in Spanish that they were taken against their will in Mexico and brought here in chains.

Gerri then tells them that he and his friends will be back to rescue them. They ask if the American president has ordered all illegal aliens to be killed. They explain that their capturers say they are doing them a favor, that the American president has announced that they are an infestation of insects and will need to be exterminated. Gerri feels for them; after all, he is second-generation Mexican, and if not for the fact that he is light-skinned and speaks English better than most of the President's fan club, he would also be classified as a rodent. He tells them, "*Yo voy a volvere y te rescatera de esta pesadilla.*" (I will return and rescue you from this nightmare.) He then places his finger to his mouth and signals the universal sign to keep quiet.

He keys his radio. "Found the problem. We can wrap it up."

Reuben then keys Rodney. "Rodney, we have lady luck on our side. Gerri has found the problem. I am wrapping it up and headed to our truck. Meet us outside."

"OK," says Rodney, "great news. Headed outside."

Once Reuben, Gerri, and Rodney are outside next to the truck, Reuben writes the work ticket so that Rodney can confirm that everything is working. As he is completing the ticket, Heinrich approaches them with two mean-looking German shepherds.

He says, "Don't worry, they will not attack unless I tell them. So, are we finished?"

Rodney says with a proud voice, "All done. Completed the job at 7 P.M. One hour to spare."

"Those are some good-looking dogs," says Reuben. "Good thing they weren't here when we drove up."

"Yeah," says Heinrich, "I had them in the cellar. They were not feeling too good. I think they ate some poisonous shit like a snake or scorpion. They are back to themselves now. I am taking them out for a walk."

"I take it you let them loose inside the fence line?"

"Not all the time. I let the dogs roam free outside the fence line sometimes. They like to chase down rabbits and squirrels. Boy, when they catch them, it's a sight to see. They tear them up into a thousand pieces. Sometimes they eat their prey. I think that is what happened when they got sick."

While Reuben is using up time talking to Heinrich, Gerri sends an alert text to Alex, Ethan, and Travis: "EVACUATE IMMEDIATELY! DOGS WILL BE ON THE PROWL OUTSIDE THE FENCE LINE! Head toward Highway 441. We can pick you up there."

Immediately upon reading the text, Ethan, Alex, and Travis start tearing down the surveillance nest. They need to sanitize all areas.

Once all items are stuffed in their backpacks, they start on their way toward Highway 441. They each take a skunk odor spray can and spray the area. Every fifty yards, they spray again.

Reuben and Gerri start the truck and drive slowly toward the guard shack. In their rearview mirror, they see Heinrich and the two dogs running around, looking for something to chase and kill. The dogs spot a rabbit and start the chase. One of the dogs catches the rabbit as it is fleeing down the rabbit hole. The dog pulls the rabbit out, and the two dogs devour it. It takes about ten minutes to tear the rabbit to pieces and eat half of it.

Heinrich and Rodney laugh at the killing. After the dogs have completed the hunt, they come back to Heinrich and start sniffing the ground. They run in the direction of the surveillance location. They start sniffing and run back to Heinrich and Rodney. They lie down, and with their paws, they frantically rub their nose. Heinrich and Rodney come up to the dogs, and they can smell the repugnant odor of the skunk. They both laugh. Heinrich says, "Guess they met their match."

"Yeah, they ain't having skunks for dinner."

Alex, Ethan, and Travis don't know this, but the rabbit saved the surveillance from being exposed. Had the rabbit not delayed the dogs, they and Heinrich would likely have found the three operatives. Had that happened, then there would have been a gun battle. It's likely that the dogs, Heinrich, and Rodney would have been killed and the surveillance mission would have been compromised.

Chapter Thirty-Eight

Team Meets in Safe House

Vint Hill Farms, Virginia

Ethan, Alex, and Travis walk at a fast pace to Highway 441. Alex keys his radio. "Reuben, coming up on Highway 441. We are at mile marker 125."

"OK," says Reuben, "we are at mile marker 120. ETA to your location six minutes."

"We are directly behind the mile marker. We'll come out when you are on the shoulder."

"Roger, we are on our way."

Reuben, Gerri, Ethan, Alex, and Travis are soon riding in the Tennessee Valley Electrical van. Reuben removed the sign two miles from the entrance to the Chicken House. Rick and Matt have left them, and they are also on Highway 441. They all agree to meet in Franklin, Tennessee. Franklin is a suburb of Nashville and has a large auto plant. Having six men dressed as auto-workers will not raise any suspicion. They meet at a rest stop. Rick and Alex are driven by Matt to Nashville Airport to pick up their van from the long-term parking lot. All seven operators drive back to the VHF safehouse. For the remainder of the investigation, the safehouse will be used as the command post. It is too risky to use the WMA facility in Alexandria. Wolf found Rose once; he could probably find her again. The team decides to take a day off for decompression. Ten days after leaving the VHF safehouse, they gather for a major debriefing.

Chapter Thirty-Nine

ISIS Headquarters

Peshawar, Pakistan, and Chihuahua, Mexico

The intelligence chief of ISIS is not very happy about the incident he had with Wolf. He decides to tell General Nasir Muhammad Abboud that it is his opinion that Rose is still alive. Abd Al-Malik will spin a story that the assassin thinks that he killed Rose but Malik has used his intelligence network to determine that Rose is still alive. The theme will be: "The stupid American Assassin was fooled by the MI6 operative, but ISIS has not been duped."

Malik goes to Abboud and says, "General, our business agreement with the Juarez drug lord Fernandez has steadily declined in the past three months. The word that I get through the grapevine is that Fernandez is apprehensive about continuing his business relationship because of our loss of territory in Syria. Like everyone else, he does not want to back a loser. I suggest that I travel to Juarez and convince Fernandez to continue his business with us."

"Before I approve the plan," says Abboud. "I need a more detailed explanation of your ideas."

"Yes, sir, I will prepare a plan in the next few days and present it to you."

Malik has the reputation of being a detailed planner. He will work on the plan and present Abboud the details within the next two or three days.

When he's finished, he goes to Abboud and presents the plan. "Sir, the situation in the United States is volatile. There is talk of an armed revolution. Should the president of the United States be impeached and convicted, or if he loses the election by a small margin, there is talk of armed resistance. The white nationalists, KKK, and other extremist groups will resist by using arms. I need to go to Mexico and convince Fernandez to buy more weapons from us. We can provide RPGs, armor-piercing rockets, armed drones, small ground-to-ground rockets, and the standard automatic rifles and ammunition. The weapons factories along the Khyber Pass can manufacture any knockoff at ten percent of the price. ISIS and Fernandez are the keys; we can produce, and he can make the distribution and sales. Secondly, the drug epidemic in the United States will continue to grow with the unstable conditions in the United States. Fernandez needs to increase our supply of opium. Perhaps we need to produce opioids. As the population becomes more desperate, they start fighting amongst themselves. The doctors will prescribe more painkillers—opioids. We can also produce marijuana, heroin, morphine, OxyContin, oxycodone, fentanyl, and any type of opioid. Why should the U.S. drug companies grow rich? We can produce at a fraction of the cost and flood the American public with low-cost pain killers. As you have said in the past—give the Americans guns and drugs, and they will kill themselves. "

"As usual," says Abboud, "your plan is brilliant. You have my permission to journey to Mexico and conduct exploratory talks with Fernandez. Also, see if you can find that lowlife Juan de La Toro."

"Yes, sir, I will start with finding Juan. I agree it's a good idea. After that, I will contact Garcia, the drug cartel chief of staff, and arrange a meeting."

Juan de La Toro is a former ISIS fighter whom they used in the attacks on the United States. Juan and an Arab by the name of Rahal were the leaders in coordinating the attacks, After the attack on the Indian Point nuclear power plant, Juan and Rahal escaped to Mazatlán, Mexico. The CIA and WMA tracked them there. The plan had been to have a yacht, owned by a wealthy sheik, transport them back to Pakistan. The combined CIA/WMA team killed Rahal. However, Juan escaped and is now somewhere in Mexico.

Malik remembers that Rahal and Juan worked with a coyote by the name of Esteban Gutierrez. Rahal reported that they had met Gutierrez in the city of Chihuahua, Mexico. Malik decides that he will try and find Juan through the coyote network. He takes a flight from Peshawar through Dubai and nonstop to Mexico City. From Mexico City, he takes a Mexican Airlines flight to Chihuahua. Malik is brown-skinned and speaks broken Spanish and fluent English. He studied at the University of California Berkeley and was three credits short of receiving a doctorate in computer science when he was expelled. He comes from the Wahhabis family of Muslims. He believes in Sharia law and that all infidels should convert or be killed. However, Malik does not wish to live in a desert tent, milking goats and traveling by camel. He likes the opulent life of the West and has a harem of fifteen women. Upon arriving in Chihuahua, he plans to frequent the whorehouses and see if he can gain any information on Juan. Why not? He will be seeking intelligence and enjoying life at the same time.

After two evenings, and visiting multiple whorehouses in Chihuahua, he has gained some valuable information. If he is trying to find a coyote, he needs to integrate himself into the refugee caravans and ask for a coyote there. The coyotes are hovering around the refugee camps like buzzards circling a carcass.

After three days in Chihuahua, Malik changes his appearance. He goes from a wealthy Arab to a disparate Syria refugee trying to seek asylum in the United States. He finds a caravan of a thousand refugees from Guatemala and El Salvador. He has dressed in some old, dirty Mexican *campasito* (farmhand) clothes. He looks the part of an individual who has been on the run for months. He stops men and women and asks, "*Por favor, me pueden decirme donde puedo encountrar un coyote?*" (Please, can you tell me where I can find a coyote?)

Most shake their heads and say, "No se." (Don't know.)

After asking several men and women, one peasant says, "*Preguntale al hombre de pantalons marron.*" (Ask the man in the brown pants.)

Malik thanks the man. "*Gracias.*"

He walks to the man in the brown pants. He says to him in Spanish, "*Caballero*, I am trying to find a coyote by the name of Esteban Gutierrez."

Brown Pants looks at Malik and says in Spanish, "You don't have enough money to hire that coyote. He is very expensive."

"Maybe. I have some money saved."

"Well, in that case, yes, I know where to find him, but I do not give my information away. It will cost you."

Malik reaches into his pocket and pulls out a roll of one-dollar bills.

Brown Pants laughs in his face and says, "You think I am *pendejo?* (Stupid.)

Malik reaches again into his pocket and pulls out two twenties. "*Bastante?*" (Enough?)

"No, it will cost you one hundred dollars."

"OK, I will give you fifty dollars."

"*Esta bien.*" (OK.)

Malik pulls out two twenties and one ten. "OK, now tell me, where do I find Esteban Gutierrez?"

"Not so fast. You think I am an idiot. Give me the money. Then I tell you."

Malik has no choice; he gives him the fifty.

Brown Pants then says, "Gutierrez comes by once or twice a week. I don't know his schedule, but you cannot miss him. He drives a gray F-150. He always has a cowboy hat, boots, and a big belt buckle. The buckle has the Mexican eagle."

"OK, but this info better be good. I know where to find you."

"Fuck you, asshole. If I wanted to get even with you, I simply tell some of the *pachucos* (hooligans) in the camp that you are some rich Arab buying your way to the United States. If I were you, I would not flash that money around. If the wrong people know, you will be dead in five minutes."

Malik gives Brown Pants a worried look.

Brown Pants says, "Don't worry, I will not tell anyone. I may come back and ask you to give me money for protection in the camp."

Malik thinks, *Same scam no matter where you are in the world, money for protection!*

He now must wait at the refugee camp and watch for the F-150 with the cowboy driver. He dresses down and mingles with the peasants. He thinks back to his first four years with ISIS. He spent months in squalid conditions, similar to what he is experiencing in the refugee camps. He tries to avoid too much interaction, but it is apparent to the others that he is not from a Latin America country. None give him any trouble; they have their own problems to attend to.

Finally, on the fourth day, he sees a gray F-150 truck approaching the refugee camp. He waits until the truck stops. A crowd gathers around it. Most speak briefly to the driver and leave. A few take some papers and go back to their chosen location within the camp. A Mexican federal policeman in full uniform walks over, and it is evident that Gutierrez has to pay off the federal police for the right to be in the camp. Rahal told him about the "*mordidas*," or payoffs. This is the way of Mexico: you have to pay off everyone to get things done.

Finally, the crowd thins out. As Gutierrez is getting ready to climb into the driver's seat, Malik greets him. "*Hola amigo.*"

Instantly Gutierrez recognizes the accent. Arabic. Gutierrez made very good money with the Arabs he helped cross the border last year, so he is immediately interested.

"*Hola, amigo, Que pasa?*" (Hello, friend. What's happening?)

Malik tries speaking in Spanish. Gutierrez interrupts him, saying, "Do you speak English?"

"Yes, I do."

"So, do I. Let's try speaking in English. We both know the language."

"OK, English it is."

"What can I do for you? More Arabs to Detroit?"

"No, I am trying to find Juan de la Toro. Do you know him?"

"Maybe. My memory works better when I oil it with money."

Malik is expecting the "*mordida.*" He pulls out a roll of twenties.

Gutierrez laughs. "No way, *cabron* (dumb ass). This type of information is in the thousands."

"I don't have that amount on me, and it would take a few days to obtain,"

"I can wait,"

"OK, how much?"

"One thousand dollars to provide the info you want."

"It will take a few days."

"As I said, I can wait. Where are you staying?"

"Right now, in the refugee camp. I will need to exit and find a hotel. From there, I can have the money wired to me."

"I can give you a ride to any hotel. Where do you want to check in?

"Any hotel, but I need it to have a business center with a high-speed internet connection."

"OK, that would be the Hotel Chihuahua Modera. It is reasonably priced, and they have a modern business center."

Gutierrez calls ahead and makes the reservation.

"Thank you," says Malik.

"I am only doing this to speed up my payment."

"How do I get in touch with you?"

"You don't. I get in touch with you. I will call the hotel tomorrow after 1 P.M. and collect my thousand dollars. Will you be ready?"

"Depends how fast I can have the money transferred."

"Don't give me any of that bullshit. I know that you Arabs have the *Hawala* system. There is a *Hawala* money lender directly across the street from the hotel. You should have no problem getting the money by tomorrow noon!"

Malik thinks, *this guy is smart. I need to be careful not to bullshit him.*

"Yes, you are correct. I will contact the *Hawala* as soon as I check into the hotel."

Gutierrez drops off Malik at the hotel entrance. Malik checks in and immediately walks across the street and arranges for two thousand dollars to be available the next day at the *Hawala*. The next day at 10 A.M., Malik has the money.

At 1:30 P.M., Gutierrez parks his truck in the front parking lot of the hotel. He walks in dressed as a Mexican *caballero*.

He tells the front desk to call Malik. The clerk at the front desk makes the call and points to a phone in the reception area. "*Puedes usar el telfono en el vistibulo.*" (You can use the phone in the reception area.)

Gutierrez picks up the phone and says, "I am in the lobby. Do you have the *dinero*?"

"*Si*, I am coming down."

Malik takes the stairs down to the lobby. He sees Gutierrez and says, "I have the thousand dollars. Now, can you tell me where I can find Juan?"

"First give me the money." Malik gives Gutierrez an envelope with the thousand dollars in it. Gutierrez opens it and counts the money.

"Now, where is Juan?"

"Not so fast, *compañero* (partner). I will tell Juan that you are looking for him. He may not want to talk to you."

Malik looks pissed, and he says in an angry voice, "That was not the deal. I give you a thousand dollars, and you tell me where to find him."

"You are right, that was the deal. I talked to Juan, and he said he was quite happy with his life and that you are nothing but trouble."

"You pig-fucking infidel. Let me have the money back."

"No fucking way, *pendejo!*"

Gutierrez walks away and says, "Stay close to the phone—Juan may give you a call."

Malik is really pissed. It's the second time he's been played for a fool. He has no choice but to wait at the hotel and hope that Juan calls him. After waiting for seven days, Malik has received no call. He decides to go back to the refugee camp and talk to Gutierrez. As he is leaving the hotel, Gutierrez drives into the hotel parking lot with a passenger. The passenger is dressed in a three-piece, five-thousand-dollar suit with a silk tie and patent leather shoes. He has a neatly trimmed bread and jet-black hair pulled back into a ponytail. Gutierrez and his partner walk over to Malik.

"You fucking asshole," says Malik, "you have the guts to come back after you stole the thousand dollars."

The well-dressed man says, "You fucking Arabs never change. Still as dumb as a camel."

"And just who the hell are you, *pendejo?*"

"Well, it's good to know that you know some Spanish. You really don't know who I am—do you?"

Malik looks carefully and says, "Well, I'll be damned. You look a lot different than you did in the battlefields in Syria."

"Yeah," says Juan, "I have a real job now. Got to look really respectful."

"And just what the hell do you do?

"I'm a *chulo*, I find women for the *Norte Americanos*."

"Juan, can we meet somewhere more private? I have some business deals that will make you millions. Are you interested?"

"Yeah, but Esteban here is my business partner. He will need to be included in any deals."

Esteban says, "We have an office on *la Avenia de le Paradiso*." We can meet at 2 P.M. We work at night."

"OK, give me the address, and I'll be there."

"It's 1347-C *Avenia de le Paradiso.*"

On the following day, Esteban, Juan, and Malik meet at the *Avenia del al Paradiso* office.

Juan begins the conversation. "Malik, I want to clear up what happened in Mazatlán."

"OK, what happened?"

"Rahal and I made it there thirty days after the attack on the nuclear power plant. We followed all operational security protocols. Rahal and I found out on the day of the attacks that the asshole Gilliam had left his phone at the hotel in Orange County. This was the reason that the Maryland site was the first to be compromised."

"Why did we never know about the breach in operational security procedures?"

"Remember, at that time, we were being hunted by every law enforcement agency in the United States: city, county, state, and eighteen federal agencies. We knew that our communications had been compromised when Gilliam left his phone in the California hotel. We decided to go completely dark. We were confident that we could make it to Mazatlán. We were attacked when we were on the yacht there, though. Rahal was a true warrior. He died for the Caliphate—*Allah Akbar!* I outsmarted the infidels and escaped via land routes to Monterrey. After my escape, I could not trust anyone. For the last year, I have gone dark.

"Seven days ago, Esteban told me you were looking for me. I staked out your hotel, and using some stolen intercept equipment, we were able to monitor your calls. I had to make sure that you were legit, that you had not turned to the Iranians, Russians, Americans, or Turks."

Malik does not know whether to praise Juan or condemn him. He simply says, "Praise be to *Allah* you are alive!

Juan keeps quiet. He doesn't believe (and never did) in all of this *Allah* bullshit. Finally, he says, "OK, you are here for a reason. Esteban tells me you said that ISIS can provide much-wanted items to the United States that will bring millions to those who get in early!"

"Yes, that's right. It will require the assistance of the drug cartel."

"You mean the Juarez drug cartel?"

"Perhaps. What do you think?"

"Assholes, all of them. They always go back on their word. That goddamn Fernandez is a backstabbing SOB! Remember, he tried to steal the drugs when the freighter docked in Mazatlán."

"Yes, I remember that."

"After I escaped from Mazatlán, I communicated with Chuy, my friend in Juarez. He invited me to a bar in the Mariscal District. The fuckers had set up a trap to kill me. I was too smart. I learned a lot of shit in the battlefields of Syria and Iraq. Staked out the place first. Found that Chuy had set up a trap. I went behind the two assassins and killed both of them with my ISIS-issued Makarova Russian handgun. Later I found Chuy and killed the SOB. So, no way am I doing any deals with Fernandez. Fuck him! Give me a chance, and I will put a bullet between his eyeballs!"

"Let me explain to you and Esteban my idea to make millions from the *gringos*."

"OK, but this better not involve the Juarez drug cartel."

Esteban says, "Let's hear him out; we can always go to Gulf Coast or the Sinaloa cartels."

Malik now explains the current situation in the United States. He explains that the United States is divided into two camps: the pro-Trout and the anti-Trout. The division is about forty-five to fifty-five percent in favor of the anti-Trout populace. "As you know, Juan, the United States citizens believe in guns, guns, guns. They are like drunken sailors—they simply cannot get enough guns. We can satisfy that thirst. We in the Khyber Pass region have thousands of machine shops. We are the world's breadbasket for gun manufacturing. We do not give a shit about licensing. We can build AR-15s, AK-47s, RPGs, rocket drones, and missiles with a range of a hundred miles. If we have a distribution system in the United States, they will buy as many as we can build."

"OK, I'm listening," says Juan. "How do Esteban and I come in?"

"Good question. We need the initial contact with the cartel, similar to what you did when you contacted Chuy and the word went up through Silva and finally to Fernandez.

"But there is more: opioids! The Americans have so much pain that they buy anything. Let me explain. Opioids are a classification of drug that is derived from, or a synthetic version of, opium. What is it that is grown in Afghanistan and Pakistan? OPIUM. We are sitting on a gold mine. Better than a goldmine. Opium comes from poppies and is replenished by growing the poppies in the farmlands. Morphine is the most abundant natural opioid found in opium! It has been used for years as a pain reliever. As medicine advanced, the scientists in the land of the infidels found ways to replicate the effects of morphine to make it stronger or weaker depending on need. Some opioids, like methadone, were developed due to a scarcity of morphine. Here again we can produce enough to kill three times the population of the infidels. The infidels tried to use a form of heroin in an attempt to make a less-addictive drug. But the *pendejos* at the DEA made it illegal to produce. Today in the land of the infidels, opioids are synonymous with pain relief."

Juan now gets it. He says, "Brilliant. We supply the drugs to make them crazy and then supply the guns to kill themselves."

"And as they are overdosing with drugs and killing themselves with the guns, we are getting rich!" says Esteban.

Juan now understands the plan. He says to Malik, "We are in luck. Let us tell you about our business enterprise in America. I believe it may have a connection. We may not need any assistance from the drug cartels."

"I am interested," says Malik. "Go on."

Esteban says, "For the past year, Juan and I have taken young girls ages fifteen to twenty. These girls are taken from the caravans that are moving north to the United States. It is easy money. The girls and their families are dirt poor. They have nothing. We convince them that we will take them on a safe passage to American. We tell them that all Americans are rich and lazy. They all need servants and nannies. We give the families some money, usually two or three hundred dollars, and they are elated. We take the girls north of the border, feed them and clean them up. You might say we are fatting the cattle to get a better price. We take pictures and auction them to prostitute homes. Some homes are better than others are. However, once we deliver the goods, they are out of our hands. This enterprise has been very successful. The initial layout is three hundred dollars for each girl's family and about a thousand for one month to clean the girl and transport her. We get from five to ten thousand dollars per girl. It's good for the prostitute houses. They make about ten to fifteen thousand dollars per girl per month. If the girl is fifteen when she enters the system, by the time, she is twenty, she has made the prostitute house over one million dollars. The beauty of the business is that every year, they are always in need of new supply. It is self-sustaining. We think of it like farming. And it's the world oldest profession."

"What happens to the girls when they grow old?" asks Malik.

"Not our problem," says Esteban.

Juan replies, "Some whorehouses move them to legit house cleaning services, hard labor on the farms, house cooks, and other jobs that start at the low end of the food chain."

"However," adds Esteban, "you need to treat this as a business. We do hear that some of the older girls are being used in snuff movies. These movies are shown on the darknet and can be used indefinitely—they bring in cash for years."

"And these SOBs claim that ISIS is barbaric?" says Malik. "Not even we carry on such atrocities. We just cut their heads off. Quick death, no pain but snuff movies? These people are animals. Not even Sharia law allows this type of treatment of any woman, not even captured Christian women. We simply rape them and give them a quick death. These infidels are animals, satisfied by viewing the death of a woman while performing terrible sex acts no ISIS fighter would do!"

Juan now says, "We have been selling these girls to white-trash neo-Nazi organizations such as the KKK and the White Supremacy Alliance. Recently I was at the camp near Pulaski, Tennessee. The camp is run by some jackass ex-Marine who has turned bitter and believes that the South will rise again. I know he loves Trout because he is always repeating the saying 'Make America Great Again.' You know that Hitler used the same saying in the 1930s: '*Mach Deutschland Wieder Grossartig*'? [1]

Juan continues, "You know that Americans are so dumb, they don't even know that they are following the same steps as the Germans did in the 1930s. They don't even know that "White Nationalism" and Nazi Fascism is the same thing. Americans vaguely know that it had something to do with Hitler and the Nazis, but that's it. They have no idea that the first words of the Nazi anthem were "Germany above all else" which was their version of "America first." And the way Nazis demonized Jews is no different than the way American "White Nationalists" demonize liberals, negros, Mexicanos, and people from shithole countries. Hitler promised to "make Germany great again." And Hitler denounced the newspapers, which exposed him for what he really was, as "*Lügenpresse*," which is German for "fake news." If the German Nazi party still existed today, they would look exactly like the Republican exists now." [2]

"They are perfect customers. Not only do they buy our girls, but also guns and drugs that we haul from the Mexican border to Tennessee. The leader of the camp goes by the name of Wolf. Frankly, he looks like a wolf, always bitching and growling. He has told me more than once; I will buy as many guns as you can smuggle across the border."

[1] Hitler Speech, February 1940.

[2] Oliver Markus Malloy, Inside the Mind of an Introvert

He told me a couple of weeks ago that if I could find cheap opioids in Mexico and transport them to Tennessee, he would pay top dollar," says Juan.

Malik says, "This opportunity sounds perfect. I will journey back to Pakistan and discuss it with General Abboud. As you know, I am a desk jockey. I make plans, use my head and not my muscles. After I devise the perfect plan,

I will be sending some frontline operators. Sounds like this Wolf person will only deal with people who are muscular and threatening. Kind of like you and Esteban. If I go, he will find me weak—a pencil pusher. I think I know who we need to send to negotiate with him."

"Do I know this great, big ISIS asshole?" asks Juan.

"No, he joined ISIS after you left; however, he was the masked fighter who beheaded that shithead *New York Times* reporter. Of course, he was wearing a balaclava so the public would not recognize him. I first need to discuss this with our general and get back to you."

"OK, we will wait for your return. Tell Abboud to get his head out of his ass and get back out in the field. That's what he is good at."

Malik hears Juan's comment, but no way will he tell Abboud to take his head out of his ass! *Abboud would probably shoot me on the spot. He has done worse.*

Malik Returns to Peshawar, Pakistan

Malik takes a Mexican Airlines flight to Mexico City. From there, he has a fourteen-hour flight on Etihad Airlines to Dubai. On the plane, he comes up with a plan. He cannot interface directly with Wolf. Wolf knows him from their encounter in Islamabad. When he returns to Chihuahua, he will have strong and armed jihadists. As the ISIS intelligence officer, Malik has a detailed knowledge of all fighters. He will select two fighters from Afghanistan. They need to be seasoned and experienced with automatic rifles, handguns, and knives. They need to be in their twenties and be experts in the martial arts. They need to have grown up on the poppy farms. He will use these two fighters to interface directly with Wolf. The main objective will be business; however, if the opportunity presents itself, they will kill Wolf.

He arrives in Peshawar and begins to plan the details of the business trip to Tennessee. He goes to the personnel office of ISIS. They have an encrypted list of all fighters who remain alive. He is told that the warrior he has in mind was killed by a missile from a drone. He needs to find some warriors from the list in the personnel department. ISIS has kept a list of these jihadists. They keep the record for the future, for when they again rise and establish their Caliphate. Malik is searching for experienced jihadists who have battlefield decorations and have lived in some Western country. They need to have conversational English. He would prefer that they be light-skinned. It is absolutely necessary they be from Afghanistan and that they know the poppy industry.

The plan is to convince the Tennessee KKK camp that ISIS can produce opioids at one-tenth the price of US drug companies. He searches the personnel files and finds two jihadists who fit the bill. Their names are Kurush Achakzai and Jaihoon Durani. Kurush is twenty-nine years old and comes from the Helmand Province in Afghanistan. Jaihoon is thirty years old and comes from the Afghanistan-Iraq border. Both grew up on poopy farms. and their fathers tended the fields and were also sheepherders. When ISIS was capturing territory in Iraq and Syria, they were decorated fighters. Malik reviews their files, and they seem to be impressive young men dedicated to the Caliphate.

Malik uses the covert ISIS communications systems to contact the two fighters. The message is: "The ISIS High Command has a mission to which you will be assigned. Report to the location stated in these orders." The letter has an address in Islamabad. Both Kurush and Jaihoon report to the address. There they are told to get into a van. The van has standard couch-type seating with no windows. There is a solid panel between the passengers and the driver. At the head of the two couches is a telephone that connects to the driver. The van starts to drive on a paved road, making frequent stops. Horns are sounding, and people are arguing. Kurush and Jaihoon know that they are in the city. After thirty minutes, the van is driving at a steady speed. They are no longer in the city. The speaker on the phone comes alive. The driver says in Dari, "Holy warriors, we will be at our destination in approximately three hours. Should you need a rest break, call me, and I can pull over."

Riding shotgun is Malik. They will only go eighty miles from the Islamabad address. Malik has ordered the driver to drive for three hours to confuse the passengers. After three hours, it is now dark. They arrive at a house with a ten-foot wall surrounding the property. It is more like a small hotel, and Kurush and Jaihoon are treated with respect. The safe house has servants and a guard detail. Malik tells the servant to show the two guests to their rooms.

He says, "Kurush and Jaihoon, get to know Pakistan well. This will be your home until we depart on your holy journey."

Kurush asks, "Where are we going, how long will we be there, and what is our mission?"

"All in due time, brothers. Let us first enjoy our tea and biscuits. Let's not act like those barbaric infidels."

After they drink their tea and Malik has asked both a thousand questions about their ISIS experience, he is now ready to present some aspects of the mission. He simply gives them an overview. He tells them that they will travel with him to a location outside of Afghanistan. They will be trying to set up a route to sell opium. He does not tell them that the place will be the United States. The intention was always to engage Kurush and Jaihoon in a conversation regarding their experience in ISIS; he needs to make sure that he has chosen the right two individuals. That evening, he contacts ISIS headquarters and orders his top assistant to research the backstories provided by Kurush and Jaihoon.

The next morning, Malik's assistant calls back. "Colonel, everything checks out. Looks like you have two of our best fighters. They are smart, aggressive, and love combat. There is one area that we need to be careful."

"Yes, what is that?'

"They may grow impatient. They both love action. The report we have is that Kurush and Jaihoon volunteered for action to deliver drugs. They overcame major odds against them and still defeated the enemy. They are what the infidels call an "Type-A "personalities."

Malik thinks for a few seconds and says, "Well, given all of the other negatives that one can have—I will take the A-type personality anytime. Thank you, Sergeant. *Allah Akbar*."

The two jihadists from Afghanistan and Malik are now ready to discuss the details of the plan.

Malik says, "We are going on a mission to the heart of the devil, the United States. We will first journey to Chihuahua City, where we have an office. There we will meet Juan de la Toro and Esteban Gutierrez. Juan is a former member of ISIS. ISIS worked with him before he was instrumental in moving our warriors to the United States for the attacks on nuclear power plants and seaports. Juan has formed a partnership with Esteban as coyotes."

Jaihoon asks, "What is a coyote?"

"A coyote is the Mexican name for a person who takes people across the US border."

"Are we going to use these coyotes to cross the border?"

"No, we are going to use fake passports to enter. Our fake document department will be producing our passports from some shithole country."

"What is a shithole country?" asks Kurush.

Malik thinks, *I need to start from the very beginning. These jihadists do not stay abreast of the world news.* "The president of the United States refers to any country that is not European as a shithole."

Malik continues. "We will meet Juan and Esteban in Nashville, Tennessee. We are going to a village that has US citizens who are against all citizens of the United States who do not have origins from Scandinavian countries. They are known as white nationalists."

"Since we will have passports from one of these shithole countries," says Jaihoon, "will they welcome us into their village?"

"Good observation. No, it seems that if a person has money or is capable of producing money, the white nationalists will work with them. It is similar to our saying: 'You don't have to like a person to do business with him.' We plan on taking advantage of this belief."

"And why will these white nationalists be willing to do business with us?" asks Kurush.

"They like to make money. We will be representing ourselves as members of the Taliban. That is the same reason why you have been chosen for this holy journey. As members of the Taliban, we will be offering these white nationalists' cheap opioids."

"What are opioids?" asks Jaihoon.

Again, Malik reminds himself, *start from the beginning.* "Opioids are painkillers. Most opioids originate from opium and are packaged as pills or capsules. These opioid pills and capsules have all been placed in glass bottles with safety seals. The labels all look professional. Having the pills and capsules in bottles makes for ease in transporting. We will sell these painkillers to the white nationalist village. These white nationalists will then sell them to the citizens of the United States."

"I don't get it. The people living in the United States buy painkillers? Why, if it is the richest country in the world and they all live in mansions, are they in such pain?"

"You are correct, but to tell you the truth, I really don't know why—the best explanation is that they are people of the devil. *Allah* works in strange ways. This is an opportunity for us to make money and kill thousands of infidels."

"And why will these pills that we provide kill thousands of Americans?" asks Kurush.

"They are addictive. Last year, over one hundred thousand Americans overdosed on opioids."

"Our nineteen heroes killed four thousand Americans on September 11, 2001, and you are telling us that opioids killed over one hundred thousand last year?" says Jaihoon.

"Yes, that is correct. The Americans kill themselves by overdosing. We will supply more potent pills and capsules that they will be able to buy from the white nationalists. In the long term it is a poison pill that the enemy cannot resist. The more they take, the more they want—it is addictive.

Journey Back to Mexico

Two weeks later, they are ready for their travel to Mexico. All of their papers are in order. They have passports and visas from the shithole countries, Niger, Senegal, and Ethiopia. They first travel to Dubai. There they take a United Emirates and Etihad flight to Mexico City and then a Mexicana Airlines flight to Chihuahua City. Malik is familiar with the city. He has communicated with Juan and Esteban to meet at the ISIS facility on the Pan-American Highway outside of the city.

One day after arriving in Chihuahua, Malik, Jaihoon, and Kurush meet at the ISIS facility.

Malik begins the meeting. Introductions are first given. Then Malik explains the plan to Juan and Esteban. He convinces them that they are representing the Taliban. Juan easily believes the story as he knows that ISIS is closely affiliated with the Taliban. The little English that Kurush and Jaihoon use has a clear Dari accent, and Dari is the language spoken in Afghanistan.

Juan asks Kurush some questions, but he has limited English and no knowledge of Spanish. After a few minutes of communicating with Jaihoon and Kurush, Juan tells Esteban, "*Esta todo bien*." (Everything looks OK.)

Malik now tells Juan and Esteban that the Taliban would like to provide opioids to the American white nationalists. The processing plants in Afghanistan can produce as many opioids as the Americans can buy.

Juan asks, "How will the opioids get to Mexico?"

"Juan," replies Malik, "as you know, I am the intelligence chief of ISIS in Pakistan. ISIS has always had a strong working relationship with the Taliban. ISIS will use our connections at the Karachi seaport to transport the opioids to any seaport in Mexico. You will make the arrangements to have them transported from the seaport to your facility in Chihuahua City. Using your knowledge and connections, you will move the opioids to the United States."

"OK, but we want fifty percent of the sale price to the Americans and the expenses to move the opioids to the United States."

"I can give you twenty-five percent, no more."

"Forty percent."

Finally, they settle on thirty-three percent plus expenses.

After the squabbling, Malik says, "Now that we have an agreement, let's proceed to find a paying customer. What we have prepared is a sample package to the white nationalists in Tennessee. I have a package of opioids ready to be shipped from Dubai to Nashville. Moving fifty pounds of drugs via DHL is not a problem. The street value of the opioids is approximately one million dollars. We will give these to the white nationalists as a free sample of our products. Once they see how quickly and easily these opioids can be sold, we have them as return customers. For a street value of one million dollars, we stand to make five hundred thousand, split sixty-six to thirty-three percent as agreed. Juan and Esteban, all you need to do is close the deal and, from that point forward, move the drugs over the border and have them shipped to the customer."

Juan thinks Esteban and he got a good deal. He knows that the KKK camp in Tennessee has a trucking company. The name of the company is The Rebel Yell. The company president is Adolf Wolfgang Schneider (aka Wolf). All Esteban and Juan need to do is tell Wolf to pick up the goods at a *maquiladora*, and the drugs are as good as in Tennessee.

"OK," Juan says, "we are crossing the border next week with some AK-47s and RPGs. Wolf placed an order the last time I was there. We will meet you in Nashville two weeks from this coming Thursday."

Malik will not tell Juan or Esteban that he has met Wolf. He did tell Kurush and Jaihoon. However, he said to them that he outsmarted Wolf and did not pay him the agreed-upon sum of one million dollars. He said that he told Wolf that he had not completed the contract as stated in the fine print. He said to Jaihoon and Kurush that he had learned this tactic from the president of the United States, who never pays his subcontractors but simply tells them, "Fuck off. You did a lousy job. Malik said to Jaihoon and Kurush that it would be best if he (Malik) does not negotiate with Wolf in the future and that they will need to do it. Both Kurush and Jaihoon feel that it is an honor to be chosen to negotiate with the dumbass infidel. They will make Malik proud of them. They are sure that after they successfully bamboozle the idiot infidel, General Abboud will personally honor them.

Chapter Forty

Continuation of Team Meeting in Safe House

Vint Hill Farms, Virginia

The team of Ethan, Reuben, Travis, Gerri, Alex, Matt, and Rick return from the surveillance of the KKK camp. Claude, Rose, and Mateo remain at the Vint Hills Farm (VHF) command post. Vinny, Jeff, and Louie are at the WMA headquarters in Alexandria, Virginia. In and out of the discussions regarding the KKK camp surveillance are Senator Montana and Brad McKinnon. The senator provides a daily briefing to FBI agent Tony Vega, chief of the HRT team. Weekly the senator delivers a status briefing to the directors of the FBI and CIA, Mr. Hector Calvanese and Dr. Margarita Gilford.

Claude decides to continue with the arrangement of having the command post at the VHF location. Wolf is still alive, and he may choose to continue his search for Rose and kill her. The WMA team does not know if Wolf believes that he killed Rose.

The entire WMA camp team is assembled at the VHF safe house to conduct a detailed debriefing. Vinny and Jeff have been tasked with reviewing the still frames and video taken by the Tennessee team. Claude opens the hotwash. "First, to the Tennessee team, a job well done."

The seven members of the Tennessee team and the three members of the VHF team say in unison, "HOOOAH."

Vinny and Jeff hear the "HOOOAH" and follow with their own.

"Ethan," says Claude, "as the leader of the field team, can you provide a detailed report of the findings?"

"Yes, I will provide the findings and will have several members of my team provide details on the areas that they personally performed or witnessed." Ethan provides the statistics on the number of Klansmen, number of buildings, vehicles, road conditions, fenced area, guards, cameras, and watchdogs.

Claude asks Travis to provide the details of the eagles.

"The camp has two eagles, which are being used for drone protection." Travis provides a description of the eagle training and the attacks by the eagles on three drones. He explains that the drones were taking defensive measures, but the Eagles attacked and destroyed them.

Vinny, from the conference line at WMA, comes on the line. "Thank you very much for the video recordings. The measures taken by the drone operators were top notch. The drones being used by the KKK were off-the-shelf DJI drones. We are working with Louie to come up with a foolproof anti-eagle system."

"Good luck," says Gerri. "What we saw was very impressive. The eagles would have destroyed the drones no matter what they did."

"Yes," says Jeff, "we saw where one of the drones went below the tree line and was flying through the trees. The two eagles worked as a team, similar to a wolf pack."

"I have a comment on what we did not see," says Ethan.

"Interesting," says Claude. "Go ahead. What do you have in mind?"

"After we witnessed the parade, we did an analysis of the buildings, both with our own eyes and with the satellite photos. The buildings that can be seen cannot house 110 people. We surmised that there are large housing areas below ground. For example, we saw the thirty-three members of a company exit from one building that was approximately sixty by ninety feet and one story. That's 5,400 square feet of space, not counting walls, etc. No way can you have thirty-three men in a building that size."

Ethan describes the double fence and the four dogs. He takes a break and asks Travis to continue with the presentation.

Travis says, "The camp is approximately twenty miles by twenty miles. It is situated in extremely rough terrain. It does have a valley in the middle that has a large stream with a lake. The area supports both farming and cattle, cows, sheep, and pigs. A good-size area was a garden with tomatoes, corn, and garden plants. It's likely that strawberries, potatoes, onions, and other foods are being grown. The best guess is that the camp is self-sufficient. Power line and phone lines do come into the facility. Noted were backup generators on all buildings. The fuel lines were not seen; thus, the fuel tanks are likely underground.

"Reuben and Gerri were assigned to survey some remote buildings. These outlying buildings are approximately ten miles from the main camp and are about two miles from Highway 441. The buildings are located in a flat land with tall grasses three to four feet tall."

Reuben says, "Having Rick drive to Tennessee with the extra MANETs was a great call. The real-time communications were critical. Also, having Alex come down proved very valuable. Whoever made those calls needs to have a big attaboy?"

"That was Rose," says Claude.

Reuben turns to Rose and says, "Thank you. Excellent call." Then he continues with his detailed findings. "Gerri and I were able to find a suitable location one hundred meters from the main building, a large Victorian building with an attached section. The building resembled the plantation house Tara in the movie *Gone with the Wind*. From that point forward, we labeled it '*the Chicken House*.' It was later determined that the second building is an entrance to an underground facility.

"Based on the analysis of the area around the front guard gate, it was determined that there was a power substation. Kudos to Vinny for his analysis of the video to determine that a power substation was located outside of the fence perimeter."

Vinny, who is on the video teleconference, says, "Thanks, Reuben."

"Upon having received the info regarding the power substation, Alex joined the team. Initially, Alex was going to attach himself to the undercarriage of the van that brings Johns from outside the camp. This approach was abandoned in favor of a power outage."

Ethan says, "Alex arrived at the surveillance point and disabled the power substation. Reuben and Gerri volunteered as the power technicians to repair the problems with the power outage."

Gerri then provides his findings inside the Chicken House. He has some alarming news. "As suspected, the Chicken House is being used as a whore-house. The women are being held hostage." He goes on to describe the living conditions and tells the team that he recorded the conversation he had with two girls who were being held against their will.

He then says, "The girls are afraid that if they are rescued, the Department of Immigration will execute them. The captives have convinced them that President Trout has declared that all immigrants from Latin America are like an infestation of rodents, sub-humans. They will be sent to concentration camps and gassed, similar to the Nazi concentration camps. I told them that it was not true. I told them that I was a second-generation Mexican-American. I do not know if they believed me, but my ability to speak Spanish with no accent gave them some comfort. I let them know that I would return and they must keep quiet."

"What about the guards?" asks Rose. "Will they report the power outage to the main camp? Will they also keep it quiet?"

"Yes, I think so, especially since we were able to repair the power problem. We had lady luck on our side. I overheard our two escorts say that they believed that they had created a power outage. They were using the outside power outlets to connect some personal items. Since we repaired the problem before the evening business 'day,' it was best to keep quiet and not tell the colonel. I got the impression that Colonel Wolf runs the camp with an iron fist."

"Where are the audio recordings?"

"I uploaded all video and audio files to our server in Alexandria."

Travis, who is an FBI agent, says, "Good, we will need this evidence to obtain a search warrant."

At this time, Vinny interrupts the ongoing discussion. "Before I—I mean, we—discuss the KKK camp with the FBI, I need to tell you some disturbing information that Jeff and I found from the video recordings. Jeff is the best man to present these findings."

Jeff now enters the conversation. "Yes, we did find some disturbing information. From the video and still-frame recordings, we found what appears to be a law enforcement officer taking a bribe. On the second day at the main camp, a man who was completely out of place entered the camp driving a nondescript white Chevy Impala. We were able to capture a still frame of the license plate. It is definitely from an undercover auto. He may be legit, truly an undercover cop, but I doubt it."

"Why do you doubt it?" asks Claude.

"Too much money exchanged hands—over two thousand. Wolf handed the dirty cop two stacks of one-hundred-dollar bills. The stacks were wrapped similar to what the bank does, twenty one-hundred-dollar bills."

Travis says, "I will discuss this directly with the director. We can have our internal affairs investigate and see if the Nashville office has assigned undercover agents to the KKK camp."

"If it is an FBI agent," says Gerri, "he sure as hell isn't doing his job. There are major illegal activities ongoing inside the camp."

Matt and Rick were assigned to determine where the Johns were being collected and dropped off once they visited the Chicken House. Matt says, "Rick and I drove our van to a location two miles from the Highway 441 entrance to the Chicken House. We followed the first shuttle van that left the house. To not be detected, we rented a car from a rental facility in Pulaski. We used the van and the rental car to alternate with the tail."

Rick then provides the information on the pick-up points. "The shuttle vans start at the Red Rooster Restaurant and Dinner Theater in Murfreesboro. We did not enter the premises, as we were not dressed in our evening wear. We parked the van a couple of miles from the Red Rooster. There is a coffee shop across the street and one block south from the Red Rooster. The lot is big, over one hundred parking slots, but it was overflowing. It appears that the Red Rooster is a legit business and acts as an entry point for a gentlemen's club."

"Gentlemen's club," says Gerri. "Yeah, that's probably what they all advertise. Look what happened in Florida. Even the owners of NFL football teams visit whorehouses. Problem is, these Johns are not aware that the girls are being held against their will. Then again, they probably don't give a damn!"

Claude says, "Before we submit our written report on the surveillance of the KKK camp, we will need to visit the Red Rooster and take in a dinner theater performance."

"Hold on," says Vinny. "Jeff and I still have some additional reports from the analysis of the recordings."

By now, the team knows that when either Vinny or Jeff say something, they need to listen. "OK, Vinny what's up?" says Claude.

"We have found Juan de la Toro. You know, Rahal's sidekick? He escaped from the raid we conducted in Mazatlán."

"Hold on," says Rose. "You said that we have found Juan. No way that he would be a member of the KKK. They are on opposite sides of the extremes."

"Yes, Jeff and I agree. But what is it they have in common—dinero, moolah, money!"

"OK, what did you see?"

"Here goes. On the third day of recordings, we saw two well-dressed men deliver two women. The women were all dolled up, but they were obviously drugged and under duress. The two men pushed the women toward Wolf. He and a large woman standing next to the SUV examined the two women. The two men appeared to be haggling with Wolf. After about ten minutes, an exchange of money occurred, and the two women were pushed toward two men dressed in Confederate uniforms. Jeff and I used the software personality profile that Louie completed to find the terrorist by the name of Gilliam from the nuclear power attack. To our surprise, one of the two men is Juan. He appears to have changed his occupation. He is now in the sex slave trade business!"

Chapter Forty-One

ISIS Warriors Meet Wolf

Red Rooster Dinner Theater

Juan and Esteban have made arrangements with the Mexican trucking company Los Camionos de Marsico to have them bring illegal goods into the United States. The Mexican trucking company will always pick up electronic auto parts from a GM *malaquidora* plant. Juan pays the Mexican and American inspectors a *mordida* (payoff) to look the other way and simply wave the truck through. The agreement is that no drugs will cross since the DEA controls the drug crossings. DEA agents cannot be bought. The ATF controls the crossing of weapons. The ATF agents can be bought. They surmise that guns are legal in the United States; thus, getting a few bucks under the table is no harm. What's one more gun? The United States already has more guns than citizens.

The arrangement that Juan and Esteban have is that the truck carrying the trailer with the weapons always stops at the Big Wheels Truck Stop on Interstate 64 outside of Nashville. When the trailer arrives, Juan calls the KKK camp and arranges for the shipment of illegal guns and drugs to be made, Esteban has been crossing the Rio Grande successfully for ten years since he was a teenager. He brings Juan with him.

On the day that the truck is to arrive, Juan and Esteban are sitting at the coffee shop. They see the truck arrive and go outside to meet the driver. They thank him, and the trailer is unhooked from the tractor. Esteban pays off the driver, two hundred dollars, and the tractor drives off without the trailer.

Juan calls the KKK camp. "This is *El Bandido*. I would like to talk to Wolf."

The operator is expecting the call. "Yes, sir, I will patch you to the colonel."

Wolf comes on the line. "About time you showed your fat ass. Do you have the order?"

"I do. Can I expect the payment at the agreed location?"

"Yes, I will send my driver with a tractor. He will confirm the shipment and drive off. He will have the payment." The arrangement has been working for the better part of a year. This only works for physical items.

Kidnapped women are different. Wolf places an order, and the product (women) is delivered directly to the camp. Initially, Juan and Esteban had some concerns. Once they were in the camp, Wolf could double-cross them. He could take the women and not pay. Knowing that this might be a problem, the exchanges were made at the Highway 441 entrance. Juan and Esteban had snipers hidden in case Wolf tried to steal the merchandise. After successfully delivering several women, the two sides trusted each other, and the exchanges were made inside the KKK camp. This was done primarily for security.

Juan continues with the phone conversation with Wolf. "You said the last time we met that you were interested in pushing drugs. As I once told you, I have excellent connections in the Middle East, primarily Afghanistan. The Taliban is looking to sell opioids to Americans. Even though they live in caves and tents, they do have televisions and connections to the internet."

"Juan, no way in hell am I going back to the sandbox. Been there and done that—I want no shit with that camel-infected country!"

"Wolf, hold on. Let me finish. You do not need to go to Afghanistan. Afghanistan is coming to you! So, shut your fat mouth and listen to me. I got a deal you cannot refuse."

"Yeah, heard that before. Bet you have a bridge in Brooklyn that you are selling—right?"

Juan is getting a little hot under the collar. He is a lot like Wolf; he does not take any shit from anyone. "Goddamn it, you want to hear my deal or not? I can take the deal to the outfit up in Montana!"

"OK, OK, what's the deal?"

"When you told me that you were interested in drugs and said that you would buy as many as Esteban and I can produce, I contacted my network in Afghanistan."

"What a bunch of goat fuckers!"

"OK, you can call them whatever shit you want. I have a couple of those goat fuckers here in Tennessee. They would like to talk to you directly. Esteban and I will act as the brokers."

"Whoooa, here in Tennessee? No way will I allow them in my camp."

"OK, tell me where, and we can be there."

Wolf thinks for a few seconds and says, "We can meet at the Red Rooster Dinner Theater."

"OK, what day and what time?"

"This Friday. Come at 4 P.M., and Juan, this better be legit. I will have at least ten armed Klansmen inside the theater and another ten outside. You know me—the three Ps: plan, prepare, and practice."

"OK, Esteban, I, and the two Afghans will be there."

Wolf has purposely delayed the meeting with the two Afghans; he wants to check with his paid law enforcement informants before he has the session. He sends a message to his FBI informant for a meeting. His FBI informant is a member of the Drug Task Force. The Drug Task Force is made up of representatives from all of the federal agencies and from the state police. The informant is in an ideal position. He has been assigned as an undercover agent and has penetrated Wolf's KKK organization. He has turned against the task force and has become a double agent. Wolf pays him over two hundred thousand dollars per year. All payments are made in cryptocurrency; thus, it is impossible for any law enforcement to detect or track. The informant has left his payments in cryptocurrency. The account is with the Binance Chinese Exchange. He is using the crypto payments as his savings account when he retires; thus, he is living within his salary with the FBI.

Wolf meets the informant at the Red Rooster; his undercover name is Rock Irwin.

Wolf says, "Rock I have been approached by two members of the Taliban. They claim they will be able to supply me with drugs. Do you know anything about these two goat herders?"

"No, but that would not be unusual. I will need to check at the Drug Force Headquarters and see what I can find. Do you know their names?"

"No, the people acting as brokers would not give me their names. But even if they did, it would not be their true names. You need to check that these so-called Afghans are not some DEA undercover agents or paid snitches."

"I will check. This would be something I would know. As an undercover agent, I would always be told of actors in my area of investigation. This is standard procedure since we would want to work as a coordinated force. I highly doubt that they are informants."

"OK, I would say that they are legit, but you need to poke around and see if you turn up any info."

"Yes, I can certainly do that. I am scheduled to check with the task force tomorrow. I will see what I can find out. If I do find something, I will send you a text using WhatsApp on my burner phone. If you do not hear from me, then I did not uncover any info. The less we communicate, the better."

"Agreed. Remember, I pay you two hundred thousand dollars to provide exactly this type of information."

"Yes, I know. We have been doing business for the last three years, and I have always provided intelligence that has proven true. So, don't give me that bullshit about where my allegiance lies. I go with the money."

For the next two days, Wolf does not hear from Rock. He is now confident that Juan has not set him up with any law enforcement agency.

Juan and Esteban meet Malik, Kurush, and Jaihoon at the predetermined site: The Supreme Buffet located on I-65, thirty miles outside of Nashville. The buffet is located close to a GM auto parts plant. The plant employs over two thousand workers, so blending in with the crowd will lend security through numbers. Malik wants to go over the deal that Kurush will offer Wolf. Kurush has a better knowledge of English. His spoken English is with a Dari accent, but he can carry on a conversation in English. His command of the English language is not good enough to understand two or more individuals speaking amongst themselves, but if the conversation is between himself and the other person, he will understand.

At noon on the day of the meeting with Wolf, Juan, Esteban, Malik, and the two Afghans meet at the buffet. Juan, greets them in Arabic, "*As-salamu alaykum.*" (Peace be with you.) Malik returns the greeting, "*Alaykum As-salamu,*"

Juan and Malik agree that the traditional form of Arabic greeting will be used when talking to Wolf. They both know that Wolf was in the Marines and is familiar with the greetings used in the Middle East; this will only reinforce that Kurush and Jaihoon are from Afghanistan.

After the greetings, Juan asks, "Malik, what do you have in mind? What will you be offering Wolf and the white nationalists?"

Malik turns to Kurush. "Kurush will be the spokesman for the group. I will not be present."

"Are you sure? This is a big deal; I would think that you would want to be directly involved."

"No, Kurush is very capable. Having only members of the Taliban present will give more credence to the discussions."

"OK, let us hear the deal."

Kurush now speaks; he has a deep voice with a distinct Dari accent but has a good English vocabulary. Juan and Esteban are surprised. Juan thinks, *Yes, it is better that Malik not be at the meeting.* "I will first provide a background of myself and Jaihoon. We both grew up on the poppy farms, so we have expert knowledge of the opium trade in Afghanistan. I will tell him that together, as a joint venture, we both can make money. We in Afghanistan can faithfully produce opioids that will be identical to the drugs being manufactured by American, German, and Swiss companies. I will be prepared, if necessary, to provide the cost of manufacturing the drugs. I can clearly show the numbers that these Western companies are charging as much as a thousand percent over the cost of some of these drugs. For example, the drug OxyContin is provided in capsules of fifteen to two hundred milligrams. A bottle of twenty-five of the eighty-milligram capsules will sell at two to four hundred dollars. In Afghanistan, we can produce the same bottle of twenty-five capsules for less than one dollar. If we provide the twenty-five capsules of OxyContin to you for fifty dollars, you see that there is plenty of profit margin for all of us to make money."

Kurush is prepared to go into a detailed description of the drug factories in Afghanistan. If required, Juan or Esteban can discuss the method of transportation of the drugs into the United States.

"Wolf is very smart," says Juan. "He will quickly grasp the opportunity. He will likely jump ahead and start asking for the first shipment. He will probably ask that a sample be provided so that he can test the demand and set the sale price."

"Yes," replies Kurush, "we are prepared for that. We have a sample of the opioids that we can produce. The drugs in the box have a street value of one million dollars. We produced these drugs for under ten thousand. We will not tell him what the costs are—this is what we will need to negotiate."

Juan and Esteban are impressed with Kurush. Juan says, "I am sold; I think we are ready for our appointment with Wolf."

Juan, Esteban, Kurush, and Jaihoon all ride in a four-door Chevy Suburban. Juan tells Kurush, "Wolf is very abrasive and rude. He will immediately test you to see your reaction. If he insults you, you must trade the insult with him. He will test you to gauge your reaction. Depending on your reaction, this will set the stage for any negotiations."

Kurush says, "Kind of like the president of the United States."

"Yes, that's right. I think that is why the president gets along with Petrov and Kim Ku Chu." These dictators do not take any bullshit from Trout. That's why he respects them."

The black four-door Chevy Suburban drives up to the Red Rooster. Juan is driving, so his attention is mainly on the road. Kurush and Jaihoon are scanning the streets and buildings left and right. They see at least six security guards with handguns holstered. Jaihoon sees one sniper on top of the four-story commercial building in front of the dinner theater. Jaihoon and Kurush signal each other every time they identify a security guard.

Juan parks the Suburban, and the four walks to the entrance of the Red Rooster Dinner Theater. The building is a large, modern structure that resembles a movie theater. At the entrance, there is a ticket office, which is currently closed. To the left of the ticket office is a door to the restaurant. The restaurant advertises that it is open from 6 A.M. to 12 P.M. As the four walks toward the theater-restaurant entrance, an attendant comes out and says, "Gentlemen, welcome to the Red Rooster."

Juan says, "Thank you. We are here to meet with Mr. Adolf Wolfgang Schneider."

"Yes, he is expecting you. Please follow me."

The four follow the attendant. They enter the lobby of the theater and turn to the right. They walk down a hallway, and the attendant stops at the third door. "Gentlemen, please enter." The meeting room is named "Alabama." The attendant says, "Please be seated." The four enter and take a seat, there are three carafes. One is a water pitcher, two are coffee, and one is hot tea. The coffee carafes are labeled caffeine-free and regular. Glasses, coffee, and teacups are also neatly placed on the table. The attendant says, "The colonel will join you is a few minutes. Please make yourselves at home."

As the attendant is showing the guests to the meeting room, Wolf, Major Jacobson, and Lt. Colonel Sondermann are watching their guest through the closed-circuit video security system. Wolf says, "Major Jacobson, take two guards and follow our security protocols."

"Yes, sir."

The major exits the room. He signals the two guards who have been waiting outside of the video surveillance room, and they follow him to the Alabama room. The major and the two security guards enter, and the major says, "Gentlemen, welcome to the Red Rooster. We will need to have you remove your cell phones and weapons that you may be carrying, which includes knives and any metal objects." The four compile and place the objects on the table.

Kurush offers an objection: "We will turn off our cell phones, but they need to stay where we can observe them. We have confidential information on them. Should the phones not be where we can physically observe them, there is no guarantee that the data will not be extracted. We also have security protocols."

"OK, but I will need to confer with my supervisor to obtain permission. Before I check with my supervisor, I will have Sergeant Olson wand you for any metal items you may have in your position."

The four guests do not object, and Sergeant Olson wands all four of the guests. The wand alert goes off when it is passed over Juan. He removes the Suburban keys from his pocket. After removing the keys, he now checks OK. The major leaves the room, and the two guards, who are armed, take positions at the opposite sides of the meeting room.

The major walks to the video surveillance room and says, "Sir, we have a problem. One of the Afghans said that the phones will need to stay where he can physically observe them."

"Yes," replies Wolf, "we heard through the video surveillance system. Colonel Sondermann, follow the major into the room and tell them that you are not allowed to deviate from our strict security protocols. Tell them that we cannot proceed with the cell phones in the room."

"OK, Major, let's go." The colonel enters the Alabama room and says, "I am sorry, but we checked with Colonel Schneider, and he said that the cell phones may not stay in the room."

"Let's get to the point," says Kurush. "You are concerned that the phone may have some recording program or that they may explode and kill the people in this room. We can solve the problem one of two ways. We can remove the battery. All of our phones are Samsung phones, which have removable batteries, or we can reschedule this meeting. We will return without our cell phones."

At this point, Kurush turns to the video camera and says, "Mr. Wolfgang, choose either of these two options. If we cannot come to an agreement, then this meeting is over. We will take the opioid opportunity to the white nationalist camp in Montana."

The major and colonel leave the room and walk quickly to the surveillance room. Wolf says, "Smart son of a bitch! We cannot lose face. What do you two idiots recommend?"

"I have a possible solution," says Major Jacobson. "We have some RFI boxes in the storage room. We take the batteries out and place the phones inside the RFI box. The box stays in the room. This will solve the problem."

"OK, this security issue has told us that these Afghans are smart. They are not some shithead goat fuckers! Go ahead and offer the solution. Tell them that your colonel has come up with a workable solution. I will need to have them think that I am equally as smart. I will need this for any future negotiations."

The major and colonel walk back to the Alabama room and present the solution to Juan and company. Kurush says, "You have a smart leader. OK, bring the RFI box, but the box stays in the room."

"Agreed." A third guard walks in with the RFI box. It is an ammo box that was used to carry the .50-caliber machine gun bullets. The batteries are removed from the phones, and the phones are placed in the RFI box. Kurush points to a table. The guard understands and places the RFI box on the table. Both Kurush and Wolf think they have won the opening round of negotiations.

Lt. Colonel Sondermann takes a seat at the table. Major Jacobson walks to the entrance. As Wolf walks in, Major Jacobson yells, "Gentlemen, Colonel Schneider!" The three guards, Lt. Colonel Sondermann, and the major quickly come to attention. Juan, Esteban, Kurush, and Jaihoon remain seated.

Wolf takes a seat at the head of the table and says, "At ease, gentlemen." The camp members come to parade rest. Wolf looks at Sondermann and Jacobson and tells them, "Take a seat."

The discussions now begin. Wolf turns to Juan. "OK, Juan, what cats did you drag in?"

"The last time we talked, you said that you wanted me to bring you some drugs, opioids to be exact. I have with me representatives from the drug trade in Afghanistan. I would like you to meet Kurush and Jaihoon."

"Do they have last names?"

"They do, but due to security reasons, it is best that first names only be used."

"OK, but they best be prepared to convince me that they are the real deal."

"Fair enough."

Kurush now interjects, saying, "Mr. Wolf, I can assure you that as you say, we are the 'real deal.' We also will need to be convinced that you can make sales in America after we provide you with the opioids. If you cannot sell them, you are wasting our time."

Wolf replies. "Listen to me; you are nothing but a goat fucker. Don't tell me how to run my business."

"OK, you pig fucker," says Kurush. "I don't tell you how to fuck your pigs, and you don't tell me how to fuck my goats!"

Wolf thinks, *these two Afghans have guts. Now let's see if they have the products.*

Juan thinks, *this is going well. Good thing I told Kurush and Jaihoon not to take any bullshit from Wolf. So far, so good.* "OK, now that we have made our opening remarks and we understand each other, can we get to the details of the deal we are offering?"

Kurush introduces Jaihoon and asks, "How do I address the two persons with whom we arranged for the cell phone security?"

Wolf says, "If you need to address them, simply call them person one"—he points to Sondermann— "and person two"—he points to Jacobson—"operational security."

"OK, Mr. Wolf and Mr. One and Mr. Two, it is."

Kurush now gives Wolf a summary of the drug trade in Afghanistan. He makes sure that he provides his background of growing up in the poppy fields and indirectly lets the KKK Klansmen know that his father is a leader in the Taliban. After giving his credentials, he asks Wolf to provide a similar briefing on his opioid distribution network.

Wolf then responds, "I don't need to tell you shit. How do I know that you are not some snitch? As a snitch, you will tell the DEA in Washington who we are and what are we doing."

Juan calls for a break; he asks Wolf, "Can we have a private sidebar?"

Wolf agrees, and Juan and he walk next door and have a private conversation.

Juan does not pull any punches. He lambasts Wolf. "What the fuck are you trying to do? I've brought you a golden opportunity to become the biggest opioid distributor in America. If you are trying to fuck up this deal—you are doing a damn good job!"

"OK, OK," says Wolf, "but I don't like those Arabs. I had my share of those shitheads when I was in the Marines."

"First of all, they are not Arabs. They don't speak Arabic. They speak Dari, and they are descendants of the Persian Empire. They have a rich history of being an independent people. Hell, they even knocked the shit out of Alexander the Great. Now, if you don't want to do business with them, then tell me now, and we take our business elsewhere!"

"OK, OK, don't blow a gasket!"

Wolf and Juan walk back to the Alabama room. Wolf has now changed his demeanor, and he apologizes to Kurush and Jaihoon. Colonel Sondermann and Major Jacobson are astonished; they have never seen Colonel Schneider apologize to anyone. This must really be something big!

After the apology, Wolf says, "We have the best distribution system of any white nationalist organization. My organization has roots back to the founders of the KKK in 1865. Indeed, the land where our camp is located originally belonged to one of the founders. My girlfriend's grandfather, seven times removed, was the founder of the KKK and was the original owner of our property. Being so entrenched in Southern life, we have KKK chapters in over 350 cities and towns in the US. Every one of these chapters will be a distribution point for the opioids. All stand to make a profit to sustain and grow our cause."

Wolf goes on for the better part of an hour describing the KKK trucking company and its connections with Juan and other coyotes. He describes the internet research group (IRG), which will advertise the opioids on social media. After the one-hour presentation, Wolf turns to Juan and says, "Your turn."

Juan says, "Kurush do we have some sample drugs that Wolf can use for a trial distribution?"

"Yes, we do have some. We shipped them to ensure that we could close a deal with any organization in America."

"How soon can you have the sample package?"

"We have it stored in a container in Nashville. We will be able to bring the sample drugs by tomorrow."

"Wolf, is that acceptable?" asks Juan.

"Yes, but we will first need to open the box at our own storage facility. We need to make sure that you have what you say you do."

Kurush thinks, *this asshole still does not trust us. He thinks that we may have an IED in the sample box. Then again, I would probably do the same thing.*

The next day, again at 4 P.M., the group meets in the Alabama room. Wolf asks, "Major Jacobson, did we inspect the box?"

"Yes, sir. It has the opioids as advertised. There were two boxes."

"OK, bring them in." Two of the guards have the two boxes on two roll carts. They are open. Wolf, Sondermann, and Jacobson walk over to them and inspect the opioids. They are all in glass bottles. Wolf unscrews one and finds the security seal, and he carefully examines the labeling on the bottles. They look legit. Even the fine print is legit. The manufacturer of the drugs is from a well-known Swiss company.

Wolf still is not convinced that they are an accurate representation of the real drugs.

Kurush can see that Wolf and Persons One and Two are not totally convinced. He says, "Mr. Wolf, we are providing the sample box and all drugs as a gift from us to you. The gift is at no cost. Go ahead and send these drugs to your distribution points. Inside the box is a manifest of all bottles in the boxes. Each type of opioid has a retail price, our price to you and a suggested price that you can sell the drug. As you will see, our price to you will be twenty-five cents on the dollar. We recommend that you sell at half the retail price. This price structure will allow all of us to make money."

"OK, that's a beginning," says Wolf. "We will distribute the drugs to a few selected chapters and also advertise on the internet. We will see what results we obtain. We should have some feedback within seven to ten days. If all goes well, I will contact Juan, and we then finalize the deal."

"Fair enough. At that time, we will discuss the payment schedule."

Juan, Esteban, Kurush, and Jaihoon exit the Red Rooster and drive back to their hotel. On their way back, they discuss the two days of the initial negotiations.

Malik has remained at the Embassy Suites Hotel outside of Franklin, Tennessee. They arrive and meet him in the lobby area. They all go to Malik's suite.

Juan gives Malik a detailed summary of the discussions with Wolf.

Malik who has a master's in computer science from the University of California Berkeley, asks, "Besides the KKK chapters, how will Wolf attempt to sell the opioids?"

Juan says, "He is always using the darknet. He has educated himself. I understand that he uses it to obtain kill contracts. He always brags to me that it is easy money."

Malik is an expert on the darknet. He uses the hotel internet connection to install a virtual private network (VPN) and uses a complex password to log onto the darknet. Within an hour of surfing the darknet, he finds the advertisement by Wolf. He writes some computer code that will allow him to determine the amount of traffic on Wolf's darknet website. He will continue to monitor the activity to determine the demand on the opioids.

By the third day, the website has more than twenty thousand hits.

On the morning of the fourth day, Wolf contacts Juan. The message reads, "Juan, come by the Red Rooster. Come by next Tuesday at 4 P.M. I am ready to discuss deliveries and payment agreements."

Juan responds, "OK, we will be there."

Five days after their initial visit to the Red Rooster, Juan, Esteban, Kurush, and Jaihoon are back in the Alabama meeting room.

Wolf begins the discussions. This time, he is all business, no insults or bullshitting.

"When can you deliver two million in street value of the same assortment of opioids as was in the sample package?"

Juan looks at Kurush, and Kurush and Jaihoon confer in whispers. They are speaking in Dari; thus, Wolf, Sondermann, and Jacobson cannot understand.

Kurush says, "We can deliver in one week. We will sell the opioids to you at thirty percent of the street value."

"You said that you would sell me the drugs at twenty five percent," says Wolf. "Why the thirty?"

"We need the thirty because of the rush shipment. We will need to take the drugs going to France and ship them to you. Our contract with the French has a penalty of five percent if we do not deliver on time."

"All right, make it two weeks, and I agree on twenty-five percent of face value."

"OK, we will require one-half of the twenty-five percent at the placement of the order. That will be $250,000 when you place the order."

"I don't have $250,000 to place the order. I will pay you once I sell the drugs."

"No deal. The sample package should have netted you at least one million dollars. Wolf actually netted two million it was an easy sell. It was intended to serve as a primer. We know that you had heavy traffic on the website. All purchases on your website were via credit card or bitcoins. You should have no problem making the initial fifty percent payment on placement of the order and the remaining fifty percent upon delivery. If you don't make the delivery payment, we stop all orders."

Wolf has no choice but to accept. There will be no written contract. The deal is sealed with a handshake and drinks. The Afghans have cups to drink hot tea, and Juan and Esteban break out a bottle of *El Patron tequila*. Wolf, Sondermann, and Jacobson pull out a bottle of Jack Daniels. Kurush and Jaihoon say what the hell, and they join in and drink a shot of the whiskey.

Chapter Forty-Two

Surveillance of the Red Rooster Dinner Theater

Murfreesboro, Tennessee

The video recordings have identified Juan de la Toro and a second man selling women to the white nationalists. This provides additional evidence that Wolf and the KKK camp are using women against their will as prostitutes. During the surveillance of the KKK camp, Matt and Rick were assigned to follow the shuttle van. It was found that the Johns were being transported to and from the Red Rooster Restaurant and Dinner Theater.

The decision is made to use the drone for continuous surveillance. The Red Rooster Restaurant and Dinner Theater is in Murfreesboro, twenty-five miles from the Chicken House. There is no danger that the eagles will be patrolling the sky above the theater. One day after the initial meeting at the VHF safe house, Vinny and Jeff travel to Murfreesboro to begin the surveillance. They take all of the video, audio, and communications packages. By the third day, the surveillance drone is up and operational. For the remainder of the first week, things are quiet. Vinny and Jeff have been recording the video. They have three drones with video surveillance packages. Each day, the drones are exchanged. Once they have the last recordings, they download the video to a high-speed server. This server is now used to perform the analysis.

On the second week of surveillance, they see some unusual activity. A total of ten Klansmen set up a protective shield around the dinner theater. Six of the Klansmen are on the ground, patrolling the theater. Four take up positions on the rooftops. The rooftop guards all have long rifles. It is obvious that they are acting as snipers.

Jeff, who is viewing the recorded video, says, "Vinny, you gotta see this."

"Looks like they are expecting some visitors," says Vinny.

"Yeah, looks that way. I will do a fast forward and see when the expected guests arrive."

Jeff and Vinny each have an analysis workstation. The recorded video is advanced until they see a black Suburban arrive on the site. Four men exit the Suburban and walk to the dinner theater. Vinny rewinds the recording and opens the profile identification software. As expected, one of the men is Juan de la Toro. The four men walk to the main entrance of the dinner theater. After two hours, the four men walk out of the dinner theater. They all enter the black Suburban and drive out of the parking lot. Jeff and Vinny have analyzed the video taken yesterday, and they decide that they need a "real-time" video. Early the next day, they rent a room at a hotel that is within one mile of the Red Rooster. One MANET relay is installed on a high hill. The hill has a line of sight to both the Red Rooster and the dinner theater. They install the synthetic aperture antenna, which will allow them to intercept the audio from within the dinner theater.

That afternoon, Juan and his three companions again arrive at the dinner theater. The room where the discussions are taking place is on the first floor of the three-story building. The intercept audio is garbled. No real intelligence can be derived.

Jeff says, "If we wait until they are driving away, we can intercept their discussions inside the Suburban."

"That's an excellent idea," says Vinny. "We wait until they are driving away. If Juan and his three amigos are like most people, they will likely talk about their discussions."

Juan and the three companions exit the Red Rooster at 6 P.M. Juan is driving, and the other three take a shotgun and two seats in the back. The person riding shotgun says, "That pig fucker is a lot more amicable. Perhaps after he sees how easily he can sell the opioids; he will be easier to deal with."

"Did you recognize the accent?" asks Vinny..

"No," says Jeff, "but we have the recording. Between Rose, Alex, and Claude, they should be able to identify the accents of all of the passengers."

"I think that one is Juan and the other is a Mexican. He has that sing-song Tex-Mex accent."

Jeff and Vinny communicate with the command post and provide a briefing of their findings.

Claude says, "OK, guys, good job. Come on home. We need to decide our next step."

The team meets at the VHF station safe house.

Claude, the team leader, asks Travis, the lead FBI agent, "Travis, we now have sufficient intel to obtain a search warrant and have the FBI HRT team conduct a raid."

"Normally," replies Travis, "I would say that we have more than enough; however, we are not living in normal times. The FBI has become very cautious since President Trout took office. He has already fired two FBI directors."

Gerri, the other FBI agent, says, "Fuck this shit! We know that those fucking assholes are holding women as slaves."

"I agree," says Alex, "but we need more hard evidence."

Rose offers a solution: "We need to infiltrate the camp and obtain hard data from the camp's central office. We can enter the camp covertly and extract the data from their computers. Also, we need to visit the Red Rooster and check out their procedures for signing up the Johns."

The team agrees that the KKK camp and the dinner theater will require a covert penetration. The dinner theater will be easier since it is open to the public. The KKK camp will require a high level of planning. The plan for the dinner theater will involve Reuben and Gerri. Both speak Spanish and Italian. They will dress as Italians visiting the Nissan plant in Smyrna, Tennessee. The Nissan plant manufactures parts for the Italian company *Magnetic Marelli*. They will dress in their three-thousand-dollar Giorgio Armani Italian suits. Both have dark complexions and will speak English with an Italian accent.

Reuben and Gerri arrive at the ticket office and say, "*Buona sera, madam.*" (Good evening, madam.) They have already purchased their tickets from the internet. The ticket taker scans their tickets and tells the attendant to show them to their table. They are sharing the table with a couple from Memphis. They engage in the usual talk, what do you do, where are you from, what do you think of the U.S., etc.? The couple from Memphis is amicable, and the time passes quickly. At precisely 8 P.M., a comedian comes out and has the crowd rolling in laughter. At 8:20, the show "A Chorus Line" begins.

As the show is taking place, Gerri goes back to the bar and orders a Scotch whiskey on the rocks. He notices that next to the bar is a double door with a sign above it that reads "The Gentlemen's Club." Gerri notes two men walk out and up to the bar. Gerri moves over to the two men and asks, "What does it take to join the club?"

The gentleman with the bow tie answers, "Money and a reference."

"I have the money. Can you give me a reference?"

"I do not know who you are. Can you show me your passport?"

"Yes, of course." Gerri shows him his passport from Italy.

Bow Tie asks, "Is your buddy also going to join the gentlemen's club?"

"Yes, we both are looking for action."

"OK, it will cost you a thousand dollars each for you to use me as a reference. First, I need to know something about you. When we fill out the application, the madam who runs the place will ask me questions. It would be best if we meet somewhere tomorrow, and you can tell me about your life history."

"Yes, of course," says Gerri. "We are staying at the Carlton Ritz in Nashville. We can meet there."

The following day, Bow Tie, Gerri, and Reuben meet at the Carlton Ritz. Gerri gives Bow Tie, a story regarding their work with *Magneti Marelli*. Bow Tie is more interested in the two thousand dollars for his reference for the two applications.

The next evening, Gerri and Rueben go back to the Red Rooster and apply to join the "gentlemen's club." Bow Tie has told them that there is no guarantee that the madam will accept the application. She is very cautious regarding who can join.

Bow Tie tells them, "You will likely need to offer her some money, but don't look desperate. If she says no, just walk away."

The day after the discussions with Bow Tie, Gerri and Reuben walk to the gentlemen's club and ask to see the proprietor. Gerri says, "We have some applications to join the gentleman's club.

The attendant says, "She is not in at this time. She will be in at 10 P.M."

Gerri and Reuben act normal, and Gerri simply says, "Thank you. We will take a seat at the dinner theater and watch the show."

At 10 P.M., the attendant comes looking for them. She says, "Gentlemen, the madam will see you now."

They walk to the gentlemen's club office and enter the reception area. They wait there for thirty minutes. From the attendant's intercom system, they hear, "Gloria, you can send them in."

They enter Gretchen's office, and she says, "Gentlemen, our club is very exclusive. How did you hear about it?"

"We have a friend from our dealings with the Nissan plant," says Reuben, "As you can see from the application, we have been referred by a current member of the club."

"Yes, I can see that Mr. Higginbottom is your sponsor. I understand that you are in Tennessee on business. May I see your passports?" Gretchen looks at the passports. They seem to be in order. "I will need to contact your employer to certify that you are who you say you are."

"Madam," says Gerri, "if you need to confirm with our employer, then we are withdrawing our application. Surely, you understand why our memberships in the gentlemen's club must remain private. We are both married and have families."

"That's strange. I thought you foreigners had five wives and six girlfriends."

"No, you have us confused with Arabs and Frenchmen,"

"I deny your application, but you are welcome to stay for the show."

Gerri and Reuben remember that Higginbottom told them this might happen: "Hang around. She may change her mind."

At the intermission, Gerri and Rueben are having a drink. The attendant from the gentlemen's club comes over and says, "Gentlemen, Miss Gretchen would like to see you."

They walk into Gretchen's office, and says, "Gentlemen, I have changed my mind. I can give a one-week membership for two thousand dollars each. This is not negotiable. Take it or leave it."

Gerri hands Gretchen two thousand dollars in one-hundred-dollar bills, and Rueben does the same. Gretchen says, "Gentlemen, first night is on me. Enjoy the evening."

The next shuttle leaves in fifteen minutes. Gerri and Reuben need to make sure that they avoid contact with either Heinrich or Rodney. They may recognize them as electrical workers. When they arrive at the Chicken House, they are relieved that neither Heinrich nor Rodney are part of the welcoming committee. Apparently, Heinrich and Rodney are part of the maintenance crew. Two ushers show the group of eight men into the lounge. The prostitutes are in the lounge, wearing nightgowns and baby dolls. Gerri quickly scans the women and locates one he thinks is the same woman that he had the conversation with during the electrical outage. Gerri signals to Rueben to take the woman who was hiding in the closet. The house rules are that as soon as you locate your partner, she will be yours for as long as you are at the Chicken House. The two women do not give any indication that they have noted that Gerri was the electrical worker. After thirty minutes of petting, Gerri and Reuben take the two prostitutes to separate bedrooms.

Gerri asks the girl, "What's your name?"

She says, "*Mi nombre es Yolanda*." Gerri and Yolanda now have a conversation in Spanish. Yolanda asks, "*Eres tu el hombre que estabas aqui como el trabajador electrico?*" (Are you the same man who came as the electrical worker?)

"*Si yo soy el mismo hombre*." (I am the same man). Gerri then tells Yolanda that he is not here for sex. He needs to know as much as she can say to him about the routine that is followed by the people who are holding her as a sex slave.

She then tells him, "They think that I do not understand English. I have heard them talk about what they call contingencies. I do not understand what a contingency is, but they talk about their orders. Their orders are —should the FBI attack, they have been instructed to kill all of us and bury us in a ditch, which they have dug with their tractors. I have overheard them say that they must get rid of the evidence."

Gerri now asks her to give him what she knows about the number of guards. Does she know if the leader of the Klan ever comes to the Chicken House?

She tells him, "No, I have never seen their leader. The woman they call Miss Gretchen runs this business."

"Can you tell me anything else?"

"Yes, there have been several girls that disappeared. They claim that they found them work as nannies or house workers, but I think that they used them to record sex scenes where the woman is killed."

"Are you sure?"

"I have not seen these videos, but I have overheard them say that they are on the darknet."

"Yolanda, you need to stay strong. I will be back with the FBI and rescue all of the girls."

"I do not know that much about attacks, but when you do attack, you must make it fast—no siege. If you have a siege, I promise you that none of us girls will survive."

Gerri has now been with Yolanda for over two hours. He takes off his trousers and shirt and roughs them up. He takes his hand and runs it through his hair and makes it uncombed. Then he exits Yolanda's bedroom.

One of the guards says, "I was about to come in and get you. You must have had a really good time."

"Yes, that was really good; take good care of that girl. When I come back, I always want her."

"You got it."

Gerri and Rueben take the 3 A.M. shuttle back to the Red Rooster. After arriving, they exit the parking lot and compare their discussions with the two girls. They are almost identical. They have both been told of the possible killings of all the girls, who will be buried in a ditch.

Reuben says, "They are taking a page out of the Nazi handbook!"

Chapter Forty-Three

Infiltration of the KKK Camp

Near Pulaski, Tennessee

As Gerri and Reuben are surveying the Red Rooster Dinner Theater, the team has been planning for the infiltration of the KKK camp. After carefully reviewing all audio and video recordings, they assemble at the VHF safe house. The discussions begin with Claude providing a summary of the findings to date.

Travis, the chief FBI agent, says, "As much as I hate to admit it, I do not think that we have enough to convince our director to order an attack on the KKK camp."

"Either way," says Rose, "we need to plan for a method to infiltrate the KKK camp and obtain hard evidence. We are still following orders; that is, only physical surveillance. Entering the camp and extracting data from the white nationalist servers would be a physical action." They all know that the intent of the order for physical surveillance does not include entering the property. However, they all feel that they have no choice. After they have their plan fully developed, they will brief Senator Montana and Brad McKinnon. They will have the final say: go or no-go.

The plan will be to have Rose, Alex, Mateo, and Ethan infiltrate the camp at the extreme southern end. This is the same side as the original surveillance, and it has the one-hundred-foot cliffs. Gerri, who is their expert mountain climber, is not part of the team. He and Reuben are busy surveying the Red Rooster. However, the pitons and screws are still embedded in the face of the mountain. All four team members have experience climbing cliffs. The best mountain climber is Rose. She is the lightest, and with her pentathlon background and SAS training, climbing a mountain cliff will not be a problem. The plan has one possible problem. The building that needs to be entered is the one where Wolf and Gretchen live.

The information that has been obtained to date indicates that both are home during the day; however, they both are at the Red Rooster Dinner Theater during the evenings. Gretchen is very proud of her dinner theater and prostitute business. These two businesses bring in revenue equal to the trucking, illegal drugs, and weapons businesses run by Wolf. He spends most of his evenings at the Red Rooster back rooms, where he runs an illegal casino. It started as a group of Klansmen playing poker. Several theater patrons asked to join the poker game, and from there, the business grew to blackjack tables and roulette wheels.

Before the start of the planned infiltration, Vinny and Jeff have been tasked with monitoring the Red Rooster using the infrared cameras. It will be necessary to know where Gretchen and Wolf are at all times. Vinny and Jeff are at a hotel two miles in the direction of the camp. They have also placed two MANETs closer to the camp. This will allow for the drone to maintain a lower altitude and not be detected by the patrolling eagles.

The physical infiltration starts with the team driving to the campsite five miles from the base of the cliffs. The team makes it to the cliffs. Rose puts on the climbing shoes and special gloves. She hooks two one hundred twenty-five-foot nylon ropes to her belt and starts the climb. Twenty-five minutes later, she is at the top of the cliff. She drops down the nylon ropes. Alex ties the heavier braided polyester rope, which will be used by the other team members to climb the cliff. The required equipment, such as digging tools, air darts, and weapons, is pulled up using nylon bags. After all team members and the equipment are at the top of the cliffs, the team begins its march to the southern point of the outer perimeter of the camp.

After several hours of walking through the dense forest, the team is one hundred meters from the fence line. The planned time for the infiltration is between 11 P.M. and 2 A.M. During this time, both Gretchen and Wolf will be at the Red Rooster. First, the team uses a collapsible step ladder to climb and reposition the camera pointing at the location where the team will infiltrate so that it is now pointed in the opposite direction. Anyone viewing the video will not be able to tell the difference. At 10:30 P.M., Alex carefully moves to the perimeter fence. He has the dart gun, which will be used to disable the watchdogs. He throws a piece of raw meat over the fence. He does not have to wait long; fifteen minutes later, the dogs come running over to the meat. As the dogs are eating it, Alex shoots them with the dart gun. They are asleep within ten seconds.

Alex keys his radio. "The dogs are disabled. Move on up."

"Team coming up," replies Rose.

The team quickly starts with pre-planned actions. Ethan and Mateo start digging under the fence. When the hole is big enough for Rose, she slithers under. Ethan hands her the third shovel. Rose starts digging under the second fence. Ethan and Mateo keep digging under the first fence until Alex can also slither through the hole. Alex now helps Rose dig the second hole. Mateo and Ethan slip all of the items that Rose and Alex will need to extract the information from any computer hard drives or cell phones. Included in the articles are Glock handguns, night vision goggles, and a dart gun to disable the dog inside the building to be searched. It is now 11:45. The plan is to have everything completed by 2 A.M. Rose and Alex are dressed all in black, with their faces painted black, and they have on tight-fitting gloves and black tennis shoes. Again, the major problem will be the house dog. Although it is only a house dog, it is a German shepherd and not the friendliest dog to strangers.

The team has a plan to account for this problem. Gerri and Reuben reported that Gretchen rides a motorcycle and that she always keeps riding clothes in a garage next to the Red Rooster. Alex tasked the team of Gerri and Reuben to replace the jacket with a replica.

Before the team arrived at the initial campsite point, Alex picked up the motorcycle jacket from Gerri. The replacement jacket is identical and is slightly worn. Gerri purchased the jacket from the local Harley Davidson motorcycle shop. The jacket will be used when opening the front door of Gretchen and Wolf's living quarters. The dog will smell Gretchen and give Alex enough time to shoot it with the sleeping dart.

At midnight, Alex and Rose are at the front door. Rose has Gretchen's jacket in front of her. She says, "So far, so good. The dog is at the front door; he is only pawing at the door."

"That's a good sign," says Alex. He gives a thumbs up.

He uses the lockpick gun to open the door. He opens the door, and Rose sticks in the jacket, and throws it on the floor. As the dog is smelling the jacket, Alex aims and shoots it with the dart gun. Within ten seconds, the dog is sleeping.

Alex says, "That should be good for two hours."

"I'll start at the back rooms," says Rose. "You start at the front rooms."

Alex gives Rose a thumbs up, and they start their search. Rose finds three computers in the back room. It appears the room is being used as the communications and computer room. She quickly pulls out a LAN cable, attaches the first computer to her laptop, and starts the extraction process.

She keys her radio. "Alex, bring your laptop to the back room. I have located three computers." In ten seconds, Alex is in the back room. He connects his laptop to the second computer and starts the extraction process. Both laptops have hard drives with over one terabyte of storage; thus, all of the data can be extracted. On the window screen is a download ribbon. It shows that the download will take one hour and ten minutes. This will put them at 1:15 A.M. Usually, that would not be a problem, but they still have one additional computer and four cell phones. They now have an estimate for completion at 2:30 A.M. They will need to stay in contact with the team in Murfreesboro to get a status on Gretchen and/or Wolf. At 2:15 A.M., they begin the extraction of the data from the third computer.

Red Rooster Dinner Theater:

It is now 1:45 A.M. and Gretchen goes outside to get a smoke. She lights up, and it is a bit chilly. She goes to the garage to get her motorcycle jacket and retrieves it from the motorcycle handlebars. As she is walking back to the Red

Rooster, she puts on her jacket. It is a little bit tighter than usual. She thinks, *I must be gaining weight. I need to hit the gym and take off some pounds.* After she finishes her cigarette, she looks down at the sleeve of the jacket. Something is not right. She remembers that the jacket sleeve ends were frayed. This is not my jacket! She quickly goes to the garage.

She needs to get to the camp ASAP. She yells to the shuttle driver, "I am taking the motorcycle!" She runs to the garage, finds her helmet, changes her shoes to motorcycle boots, pulls on some gloves, and presses the start button. No response; the batteries are dead. The motorcycle is a ten-year model, and it has a kick-start pedal. She places her right foot on the pedal and pushes down and tries to start the motorcycle. On the tenth try, the motorcycle comes to life—BARRROM, BARRROM. She loves the sound of the Harley Davidson Road Hog. She pushes the motorcycle out of the garage and jumps on it and waves at the shuttle driver.

The motorcycle quickly speeds up to seventy-five miles per hour. It hits the main highway between Murfreesboro and Pulaski and accelerates to over a hundred miles per hour.

Team Hotel, Murfreesboro

Vinny has been monitoring the dinner theater with an infrared camera. He sees the heat from the motorcycle. The red-yellow dot from the motorcycle driver arrives at the main road to Pulaski. Vinny says, "Claude, I got something you need to look at."

Claude takes a look. "Yeah, that's a problem."

"We need to warn Rose, Alex, Mateo, and Ethan that the bitch will be at the camp in thirty minutes. I calculate the ETA at 2:30!"

"Should we call and tell Rose and Alex to abort?"

"Not yet. Let me try something."

Claude picks up the hotel phone and calls the Tennessee State Police.

The call-taker answers, "State police. What is your situation?"

"I just got off of State Road 231 about two miles outside of Murfreesboro. There is a motorcycle traveling at an extremely high rate of speed. It is putting all vehicles on the highway in great danger."

"Thank you for the call. I will notify dispatch immediately."

The call-taker notifies dispatch. The dispatcher keys her radio on the traffic channel. "There has been a report of a motorcycle on State Highway 231, headed south. The motorcycle is traveling at a high rate of speed. It was reported as being two miles outside of the Murfreesboro city line."

Police Car

The trooper in car number 1353 replies, "Roger on the motorcycle. I am five miles outside the Murfreesboro city limits. Will monitor all traffic and see if motorcycle passes this point."

"Roger. Ten-four."

The trooper hides his car behind a copse of trees, pulls out his radar gun, and waits. Three minutes later, he sees the single light of the motorcycle. It is shagging ass. The radar indicates 115 miles per hour. The trooper quickly jumps in his car. He turns on the lights and his sirens. On the motorcycle, Gretchen sees the flashing lights and thinks through her options. *I can outrun this son of a bitch.* After thinking about it, though, she says to herself, "I cannot outrun the radios." She slows down. She will try and sweet talk the trooper to let her go without a ticket.

Team Hotel, Murfreesboro

Vinny says, "Motorcycle is now ten miles outside of the Murfreesboro city limits."

"At the current speed," says Claude, "what is the ETA for the camp?"

"ETA twenty minutes. Hold on, I see a police car chasing the motorcycle."

"How close is the police car?"

"The police car is directly behind the motorcycle. They are pulling over to the curb. They are stopped. Police car now has floodlights on the motorcycle."

The police car and motorcycle are stopped for five minutes.

Vinny says, "Second police car is now behind the first police car. Must be backup."

"Looks like we are OK," says Claude. "Let me know immediately if the motorcycle is released."

"Got it. Will do."

Police Car and Motorcycle Scene

The trooper from the first police car walks to the motorcycle. He says, "License and registration, please."

Gretchen is ready with both. She wants to get going.

The trooper takes them and goes back to his car. He calls in the license number and registration. The dispatcher responds ten minutes later: "License and registration are good."

"Roger. Ten-four." The trooper walks to the motorcycle and asks, "Do you know why you were pulled over?"

"Probably going too fast."

"Do you know how fast you were going?"

"No, probably doing eighty or ninety."

"I clocked you on radar doing 115 miles per hour. Now, I ask you, why?"

Gretchen thinks—*I need to give him a good excuse, maybe play on his sympathies.* She says with a sad face, "My mother is dying and may not live another day. I wanted to be sure and see her before she died."

The trooper has heard them all. All Gretchen had to do was tell the truth. *Maybe I should let her go with only a warning.* "I am going to need to give you a ticket. I will write that you were doing seventy-nine miles per hour in a sixty-five-mile zone. You will not need to go to court unless you wish to contest the ticket. I would not advise that—I have you on the radar."

"Thank you, officer." Gretchen thinks, *Fucking asshole. Hope he writes the ticket ASAP, and I can get out of here.*

The trooper goes back to his car and writes the ticket. The entire incident took forty-five minutes. As the trooper is giving her the ticket, the shuttle passes on the left side. She takes the ticket and drives at a steady seventy-five miles per hour. Two minutes later, she passes the shuttle bus. The driver honks the horn: beep, beep."

Team Hotel, Murfreesboro

Vinny is looking at the police car motorcycle scene. He says to Claude, "Good call." Now we are back on schedule."

"We're not out of the woods yet. The motorcycle at seventy-five miles per hour will arrive before Alex and Rose are complete. Vinny, give me an ETA."

"ETA will be at 2:45. Alex and Rose have indicated that they will be finished at 3 A.M."

"OK," says Claude, "we need to tell Rose and Alex to clear the area by 2:30 A.M.!"

Camp House

Rose, Alex, and Mateo receive a text: "EVACUATE BY 2:30. MADAM EXPECTED AT 2:45."

Rose replies: "COPY."

Alex looks at the download ribbon. It is at eighty-five percent. Time remaining: twenty minutes. It is 2:20. It will be close. Rose looks at Alex and says, "Pack everything and get ready to exfil."

"Roger, packing all items in my backpack."

The time is now 2:30—ten more minutes. At 2:35, they hear the motorcycle—BARROOM, BARROOM.

"We got company." Rose comes over to the housedog, and she extracts the dart. "You go ahead and exfil. I will be right behind you."

"No can do," says Alex. "We both go out together."

They hear a deep woman's voice. "Patrick, Elan, have you guys seen anything unusual?"

"Not a damn thing," says Patrick. "All is quiet at the site."

"Not exactly, Miss Gretchen," replies Elan. "Something was going on!"

Both Patrick and Gretchen look at Elan. "Elan, what the hell are you talking about?" Gretchen asks.

"Early this evening, those two boys from the Carter house came by on the ATVs, and rooster-tailed the wheels to throw mud at us. Look at my shirt. Goddamn kids. I will be glad when I see Wolfgang. Those kids need a good old-fashioned whipping!" Elan goes over to the bench. "You see, Miss Gretchen, this is the shirt I was wearing—mud all over."

"No, you idiot, that's not what I meant."

Patrick says, "Miss Gretchen, we ain't seen nothing!"

Elan continues with a rendition of things he has seen. He says, "Miss Gretchen, you should have seen the two watchdogs this evening. They came around the security fences like bats coming out of hell. Think they were chasing a rabbit! We probably need to check for holes!"

The exchange between Gretchen and the two guards takes fifteen minutes. This is the fifteen minutes that Rose and Alex need. As they are packing their backpacks, Alex stuffs the jacket in his backpack. They quietly move to the rear door; the dog is waking up. It sees Alex's rear end and starts growling. As Alex closes the back door, Gretchen is opening the front door. Gretchen looks at Rufus and says, "Don't tell me you are also a dumbass like Patrick and Elan—it is me, your master, stupid! Rufus stops growling and starts wagging his tail.

Rose and Alex quietly run to the holes in the fence. Mateo is waiting there. Rose and Alex push the backpacks to him and drop on their backs and pull themselves under the fence. Mateo and Alex cover the hole and repeat the process at the outer fence. They keep a low profile and keep their heads down for about half a mile. They quickly reach the top of the cliff. In one hour, they are at the campsite. Thirty minutes later, they are back at the Murfreesboro Hotel.

Team Hotel, Murfreesboro

Vinny says, "Whew—did you guys really have to make it that close? I was sweating bullets!"

"Not to worry," says Rose. "We had everything under control."

Vinny rolls his eyes and says, "Yeah, yeah, I know?"

The team now assembles at the hotel. Claude chairs the meeting. They need to discuss the findings thus far and if any additional actions are required. The first thing they need to do is send the copies of the hard drives, cell phones, and USB flash drives back to Alexandria, Virginia. They need to have Louis Gilbert and his IT team decrypt the data. The hard drives, cell phones, and USB data are packed and sent via overnight FedEx.

Next, the team discusses the women being held as sex slaves. Gerri and Reuben are also in the discussions.

Gerri states clearly, "We must hit the Chicken House with no warning. I don't give a shit what the FBI must have or not have. If we serve the KKK camp with a search warrant or if the dumb ass FBI initiates a siege, the women will be killed. I have a plan. Both Reuben and I get in one more time as Italians. The second time will be even easier. The difference is that we need to be packing when we are in the Chicken House. What I recommend is that weapons be hidden inside the fence line. This should not present a problem. It will be easier than the main camp. There is only one fence, and there are no dogs patrolling the perimeter. Once the weapons are hidden inside the fence line, Reuben and I will retrieve them. When the attack starts, we will be inside and prevent the killings of the women.

Travis, the chief FBI agent, says, "Gerri, I totally agree with your plan. Be aware that if this plan goes south, both you and I will be dismissed from the FBI. We may even be charged with some bullshit crime. Remember, we are going after Trout supporters."

"I really do not give a shit. There comes a time when you need to do what is right! I will not stand by and do nothing like the Germans did in the1930s."

Vinny, who has been listening, says, "I have some information that supports Gerri's idea to hit the Chicken House with no warning."

He turns to the keyboard and bangs away on some keys, and in ten seconds, he is viewing a video. He explains, "This video was taken on the second day. You can see the day and time in the upper-right side of the display." The video rolls for five seconds, and a Chevrolet Malibu appears. It is a standard white four-door. After the car stops, a clean-cut man exits the vehicle. He goes inside the building with the number three. Vinny now fast-forwards the video to one hour later. The same man comes out, and two young men are carrying two packages about two feet by two feet by one foot. They place the boxes in the trunk. The video shows the car driving away, and Vinny stops the video.

He zooms in on the license plates. "Does anyone know who has cars with these plates?"

They all shake their heads—no idea. Vinny says, "FBI undercover agents."

Travis says, "Are you sure?"

"When I first viewed the video, something was not right. First, the car was different. All the assholes living in the camp are driving pick-ups. Second, the man is clean-cut, short hair, clean-shaven, white shirt, and has what looks like a firearm on his hip. I then sent the photo to Jeff using WhatsApp. Jeff's division does work with law enforcement. Jeff sent back a WhatsApp text saying that his contacts identified the license plate. He said that the plates belong to law enforcement undercover car. I guess that the packages are drugs."

The team gives Vinny a thumbs up. Travis says, "Vinny, that was some finding." Vinny feels proud of this contribution to the mission.

Claude now calls Senator Montana and Brad McKinnon. "Sir, we have a situation here in Tennessee."

He explains the situation, and the senator says, "Give Brad and me a day to think about the situation. We need to check the political winds. We will get back to you no later than tomorrow. In the meantime, start planning the attack on the slave house, or what you guys have labeled the Chicken House, and be ready to execute."

"Yes, sir, we will begin our planning immediately."

Chapter Forty-Four

Decision to Attack

Alexandria, Virginia

Immediately following the phone conversation with the team in Tennessee, Senator Montana and Brad McKinnon review the data. A decision needs to be made to attack or not attack the building holding the captured women. They have no reason not to believe that given a chance, the Klansmen will kill the women and bury them in a six-foot ditch to hide the evidence. Both the senator and Brad agree that the attack does not need to be approved. It is what is called exigent circumstances. However, they would prefer that the attack occurs with the approval of the FBI director.

Senator Montana asks, "Have we decrypted the data taken by Rose and Alex?"

"Louie and his team are currently decrypting the data as we speak," replies Brad. "However, even if the data indicates illegal drugs, women being held against their will, prostitution, illegal opioids, and any other illegal activity, it will not be permissible. Any first-year lawyer coming out of law school will claim that it was obtained without a warrant, and he will be right. Rose and Alex entered the white nationalist building without a warrant. This will be seen as breaking and entering."

"OK, so we cannot use THAT data, what else do we have?"

"We do have some good data from the authorized visual surveillance."

"OK, let's go over the data. I will go over it in no particular order. I will simply bring it up as I think about it."

"I will do likewise."

"We did find Juan de la Toro. He is a solid connection to the attack on the nuclear power plant and on FedEx Field."

"What exactly do we have on Juan de la Toro?"

"We have video of him on the yacht in Mazatlán."

"Again, not good enough. He was simply a member of the crew. What else do we have?

Brad thinks for a few seconds and says, "We have the audio recordings of the woman named Yolanda, who is being held as a captive."

"How did we obtain the audio recording?"

"The recording was obtained by FBI agent Gersian Copal. Our agent Reuben Tellez and Gersian faked a power failure and entered the Chicken House. When they were troubleshooting the problem, Gerri was able to record the conversation with one of the women held hostage."

"Hmmm, that's better, but the defense attorney will say that the information was obtained using false pretenses."

"Wait a minute, Gerri and Reuben paid a second visit to the Chicken House. The second time they entered as members of the gentlemen's club. No breaking and entering. All were aboveboard. During the second visit, Gerri again talked to Yolanda. It was during the second visit that Gerri obtained the recording that the girls would be killed to hide the evidence."

"That's perfect. The recordings are all admissible in court. Both parties consented to the recordings."

"Wait, we got more. The recording of the undercover FBI agent."

"Yes, that's good, but it still needs to be confirmed."

Both Brad and the senator think that they have enough to convince Director Calvanese that an attack is warranted.

Brad says, "I recommend that I first talk to HRT Chief Tony Vega and show him the evidence. I will talk to him offline and get his advice. If he says talk to the director, we will. Tony is a straight shooter. If he says to attack on our own, we attack using only WMA assets. We hold back the two FBI agents assigned to the task team."

"OK, I will set up a face-to-face with Director Calvanese. I will ask that he have Tony and that we again meet at the VHF safe house."

"Contact the team in Tennessee and tell to stand down one more day."

Senator Montana contacts the director's office and requests to meet at the VHF safe house. The priority is solid RED. At the beginning of the Tennessee discussions, a color system was agreed to, white for regular, blue for priority, and red for highest priority (must meet ASAP). Within fifteen minutes, the director's office sends a message to the senator: "Meet at 7 P.M. at the prearranged location."

The senator calls Brad and tells him, "We are set for 7 P.M. tonight. I suggested that he have Agent Vega with him."

The Senator and Brad arrive at 6:45. They enter the safe house and wait. At precisely 6:55, the director and Agent Vega drive up in their armored Ford SUV. For security, they do not have the typically armed escort. The four sits around a conference table and exchange friendly hellos and "how are the wives and children?" After ten minutes of informal discussions, the senator says with a formal posture, as he did when he was the chairman of the Intelligence Committee, "Director, we now have some important and disturbing news."

The director says, "Here's hoping that the evidence is consistent with the search warrant that I signed."

"Yes, sir, what we will be presenting is in accordance with your signed warrant."

"Very well. Go ahead. Continue."

Before the meeting, the senator and Brad agreed that the senator would provide an overview and that Brad would provide the details.

The senator lists the five areas where the visual surveillance has provided hard evidence of drugs, opioids, weapons, murder for hire, and women being held as sex slaves. Brad then provides the details of the evidence obtained with visual surveillance. He emphasizes the need to attack the slave building with no warning. Serving a search warrant before entering the property would, with a probability of ninety-nine percent, lead to the inevitable death of the women being held, hostage. Brad, who is a retired FBI agent, knows that the law will allow this type of attack—it is called exigent circumstances.

Director Calvanese is not entirely convinced. If he makes the decision to use the FBI to attack and they are wrong, his job is in the balance. His most disturbing item is not the women hostages; it is the FBI turncoat agent.

He says, Director Calvanese, "Agent Vega, what do you know about the individual identified as an FBI undercover agent?"

"Yes, sir, I have been briefed daily, and I did a quick search of the Nashville FBI agents. The individual identified in the photo is assigned to the Nashville office. He is currently with the Drug Enforcement Task Force."

"So, there is no doubt that he is an FBI agent?"

"That's right, no doubt that he is an FBI agent."

"OK, I will authorize the raid."

"Hector," says the senator, "may I suggest that the president not be informed until after the raid begins."

"Absolutely. Neither the president nor any politicians will be notified of the raid until it is well underway. Agent Vega use your team from Quantico. Do not notify the Nashville SAC until the attack has begun. Inform him of the double agent and have him arrested immediately."

"Yes, sir."

Chapter Forty-Five

The Attack Plan, Chicken House

Murfreesboro, Tennessee

That evening, the team receives an encrypted message: "The attack on the slave buildings has been approved. Agent Vega will join you tomorrow. Have your plan ready to brief Agent Vega. Agent Vega plus six HRT agents will arrive via vehicles from Atlanta. Travel by air has a higher probability of detection. We have arranged for a new secure location. Details will be provided by Agent Vega."

Claude, Travis, and Rose read the message. It is good and bad: good that the FBI has approved and bad because it implies that Washington will take over from this point forward. Every time that Washington gets involved there is a total fuck up. Claude immediately gets on the phone and requests that Brad fly out to Nashville to be there for the discussions.

Claude sends a text: "Mr. McKinnon, we have received the message that the FBI has approved the raid. The message implies that they are taking over. I do not advise that they take command. We need shooters, not desk jockeys. I would recommend that you take the WMA plane and be here when we have our discussions with Agent Vega."

Brad responds: "OK, I will take the WMA plane to Chattanooga tomorrow. Expect me at the airport at 8 A.M. Please have a vehicle pick me up."

"Roger, see you tomorrow."

The team has a preliminary plan. The details will be worked out when the FBI team arrives.

The plan is as follows;

All attackers are wearing night-vision goggles, black clothes, bulletproof vest, bulletproof helmet, black tennis shoes, and skin-tight gloves.

All attackers have communications through their helmet headsets.

All attackers will be instructed first to try and arrest, and kinetic force will only be used if the arrest procedures fail.

At all times, attackers will have the right to protect themselves if their lives are threatened.

Claude will remain at the command post. Brad and Tony will also stay at the CP.

Vinny and Jeff will jam the talk-around frequencies and the microwave back to the main camp. They will monitor the frequencies from the command post.

Gerri and Reuben will visit the Chicken House as members of the gentlemen's club.

Mateo and Rose will cut a hole in the fence and place weapons for Gerri and Reuben inside the perimeter fence.

The shuttle bus will be stopped outside the perimeter. Johns will be arrested by Travis, who will need help from the HRT team members.

The shuttle will be driven by Travis. HRT team members will act as Johns.

Travis and Alex will arrest the guards at the front gate and place flex-cuffs on them

After arresting the guards, they will knock out the power.

If the dogs attack, they will be shot with the dart gun. If necessary, agents will shoot to kill.

Travis and the HRT agents will come on board the shuttle bus at the checkpoint.

Gerri and Reuben will warn all of the girls to seek cover in a closet or under a bed when the first shot is fired.

Brad arrives on the WMA aircraft at the airport in Chattanooga. Rick picks him up in a rented SUV. Brad has brought three jammers, one for the microwave system, one for the cellular network, and one for the camp radios. He also has brought a wiretapping system for the landline connecting the slave camp to the outside world. Rick has been kept in Tennessee to lend assistance to Vinny and Jeff to set up the jammers, wiretaps, and the drone surveillance/communications MANETs. The drive from Chattanooga to the WMA hotel is two hours.

Brad explains to Claude that the command post will need to be moved. There will be more than fifteen members in the attacking team. Having a bunch of civies staying at the hotels is one thing but having seven FBI agents arriving all at once will immediately raise some suspicion. The FBI has arranged for a safe house in the country between Murfreesboro and Pulaski. The seven FBI agents will drive directly to the safe house, and Claude, Rose, and Travis will also drive there and brief the FBI HRT team. Travis suggests that Gerri also come with him. He is also FBI, and he has the best intelligence since he talked directly to the girls being held as sex slaves.

Claude and Travis give Brad a detailed report of the intel. It is what they had already reported, but additional detail is given, for example, the formal parade that determined the number of Klansmen in the main camp, the eagles that protect the main camp, and the visits by Juan and three others to the camp.

At the mention of Juan, Brad asks, "Did we obtain any evidence of what they are doing in the US?"

"Yes," replies Claude, "but it would not be admissible in court. Remember, Juan is a US citizen. We listened to his conversations using the intercept drone."

"OK, but what did we intercept?"

"They are bringing in opioids from Afghanistan."

"Holy shit, they are going big time."

"Yes, and they are using the white nationalists for the distribution."

"With Trout as the president, the white nationalists are untouchable! They are THE THREAT FROM WITHIN."

Claude and Brad decided that it would be best to have the entire team meet at the FBI safe house. Having fifteen special forces operatives meeting in a hotel room would immediately have the entire communities of Murfreesboro and Pulaski asking, "Do we have terrorists in Tennessee?"

Team Tennessee will be Claude, Rose. Alex. Mateo and Rueben from WMA and Travis and Gerri from the FBI. Brad from Alexandria, Virginia, will also join the team. Matt, Rick, Vinny, and Jeff will remain in the area of the Red Rooster Dinner Theater. They have been given the green light to install the wiretap, the drone intercept equipment, the relays for the communications, jammers for the camp radio, and the jammer for the microwave. The team of eight travels to the FBI safe house in two suburban SUVs. Team Tennessee arrives at the safe house at 2 P.M., and the FBI Quantico team is expected at 3 P.M. It is agreed that Claude, Rose, and Travis will provide the briefing.

At 2:45, the Quantico team arrives. The six special agents and Tony enter the conference room. Rose and Alex immediately see Special Agent Brit Singleton. All three have smiles from ear to ear. They shake hands and greet each other with a hearty, "It will be good to be working together again!"

Brit is the typical G-Man, he is tall, six foot two inches, one hundred ninety-five pounds and speaks with confidence. He has a square jaw, blue eyes, light brown hair cut in a crew cut. Brit is wearing the FBI brown cargo pants, golf shirt, and FBI baseball cap. His muscles from his biceps are showing through the short sleeves of the golf shirt.

Tony says, "Yes, I thought you guys would like to get together again." Immediately the two teams trust one another. Brit Singleton was the FBI special agent assigned to the ISIS attack on the Indian Point nuclear power plant. He worked closely with Alex and Rose to successfully prevent the destruction of the plant. He holds both Rose and Alex in high regard. Rose and Alex equally hold Brit in high regard. He successfully supervised the combined team of WMA and FBI agents.

After the introductions, Brad gives an overview of the mission. He then turns the briefing to Claude. Claude introduces himself and says that the briefing will be conducted by him, Rose, and Gersian "Gerri" Opal. Claude provides an overview of the connection between ISIS and the KKK camp in Tennessee. He explains that an individual by the name of Adolf Wolfgang Schneider answered the post on the darknet to assassinate Rose, and WMA set up a "sting" operation to identify the assassin. Claude goes on to explain what brought them to the Murfreesboro-Pulaski area of Tennessee. A visual surveillance warrant was issued by the FBI director, at which time Agents Travis Coolidge and Gersian Opal were assigned to the surveillance team.

Claude now turns the briefing over to Rose. She says, "Before I go through the responsibilities of each of the team members, I would like Gerri to describe the conditions in the slave house, which we have labeled the Chicken House."

Gerri takes the podium and says, "Good afternoon. My name is Gersian Opal, I have been with the FBI for seven years. I have been assigned primarily to provide operational assistance, and the last two years, I have been working out of the Miami Office. I would like to introduce Agent Reuben Tellez. Reuben and I have penetrated the Chicken House twice. From herein, I will refer to the Chicken House as what it is, a sex slave prison."

Gerri goes on to describe the conditions in the slave prison. "Seventeen women are being held against their will. Most are from Latin America: El Salvador, Guatemala, Honduras, and Mexico. However, lately some of the captured women are young blond co-eds kidnapped from American high schools and universities. The blond women are in higher demand; thus, they charge higher rates for their sexual favors."

At this time, the hand of one of the FBI agents goes up. "Gerri, do the captured women stay there forever? What happens when they grow old and are no longer attractive."

"This is the chilling, terrible part," says Gerri. "One of the slave girls with whom I have established a connection told me that when the girls grow older, they disappear. She believes that they are killed for snuff movies that are played on the darknet. She also told me that she has overheard that the guards have been given orders that should the slave building be under siege by the FBI, all of the girls will be executed and buried in a ditch two miles in the woods."

At this time Rose interjects, "After we received word of the snuff movies, the WMA computer department scanned the darknet, and they were found."

At this time, there is a strong reaction by the FBI agents. "When do we go after these animals?"

Gerri finishes his presentation. He describes the interior of the slave building. On the projector is a hand-drawn representation of the building's three floors plus the basement.

After the thirty-minute presentation by Gerri, Rose details the attack plan. "Our technical department, headed by Jeff Jefferson, is currently setting up jammers and intercepts equipment. We are currently monitoring all incoming and outgoing communications from the slave building."

Brit Singleton raises his hand.

"Yes, Brit, do you have a question?"

"Yes, two questions. One, do we use our own radios, and two, do we have a guarantee that our own radio communication will not be jammed?"

"Good questions. One, yes, you use your own radios. The command post will be manned by Claude. At the command post, we have a radio interoperability system that is capable of patching two or more radio nets into one interoperable communications system. Second, the camp uses the radio frequency in the 150 MHz band. The WMA radio will be using the 700 MHz band, and as you know, the FBI uses the new tri-band radios. As long as you do not use the VHF band, you will be OK. We will also be jamming the microwave frequency in the 9 GHz band. This is the frequency of the microwave between the slave building and the main camp. Also, cell phone communications will be jammed. It is imperative that we deny the KKK their ability to communicate. Our plan will rely on our ability to communicate and their ability to NOT communicate. Brit, does that answer your question?"

"Perfectly. I knew that you would have everything covered, but it is important that we all know the comms plan."

Rose now provides the rules of engagement. "All attackers will be wearing night-vision goggles, black clothes, bulletproof vest, bulletproof helmet, black tennis shoes, and skin-tight gloves. All will have communications through their helmet headsets. We will first try and arrest. Kinetic force will only be used if the arrest procedures fail. At all times, attackers will have the right to defend themselves if their lives are threatened."

Rose continues with the sequence of the attack. "After all comms and jammers are in place and ready for the go signal, Matt, Rick, and two WMA techs will be monitoring the road between the KKK camps and the Red Rooster Dinner Theater. When we are sure that both Wolf and Gretchen are at the dinner theater building, Gerri and Reuben will visit the theater and pay a thousand dollars to visit the slave building. Once Gerri and Reuben are in the slave buildings, the next steps will occur in rapid sequence.

First, the command post will give the OK that all is in order. Second, the frequencies will be jammed. The landline will remain operational, but the CP will monitor the traffic. Mateo and I will cut a hole in the fence and place weapons for Gerri and Reuben. The guns will be placed as close as possible to the house with the preferred location at the trash containers. Mateo and I will stay as close as possible to the slave building. As soon as the shuttle arrives with the FBI agents, all attacking personnel will move swiftly to the building and arrest all KKK personnel. Next, the shuttle bus will be stopped outside the perimeter, and the Johns will be arrested by the FBI. Brit, you, Travis, and all FBI agents will replace the Johns riding in the bus. When the bus arrives at the front gate, FBI agents will arrest the guards at the front entrance. The guards will be flex-cuffed and hog-tied. After arresting the guards, Alex will knock out the power. There are two dogs in the camp. We will use darts to put them to sleep. If the darts do not work, we will shoot them.

"Gerri and Reuben will warn all of the girls. When the first shot is fired, the girls will be instructed to seek cover in a closet or under the bed. Be aware that there will be some Johns in the establishment."

"Do we have any questions?" asks Claude.

"Not a question," says Brit, "but I do have a couple of recommendations."

"Yes, go ahead."

"First, I would recommend that once we enter the camp, we exit the shuttle bus and surround the camp. Second, Alex and Ethan should quickly join Rose and Mateo at the outside of the slave sex building. We need to try for complete surprise. We may be able to arrest the Klan members without a shot being fired."

"I agree," says Claude.

Alex and Ethan give a thumbs up.

Chapter Forty-Six

FBI Headquarters

Nashville, Tennessee

Rock Irwin, the FBI undercover double agent, walks into the FBI motor pool. "Hey, Buster, how are you doing, my friend."

"We are just trying to keep maintaining these cars on the road. Wish you guys were not so hard on them," replies Buster.

"What the hell do you expect? We are cops. We need to chase bad guys. Do you have my favorite white late-model Chevy Malibu?"

"No, last night we a got a high-priority request from Washington. We had two agents come by, and they fingered your Malibu for use."

"So, what the hell did they want two cars for?"

"Hey, I am a lowly car mechanic. Beats the shit out me. They just said they wanted big four-doors. My guess is they will be using cars for three or more people."

Rock thinks, *Big undercover cars...more than three people per car. I smell something rotten in Denmark.* He takes the smaller car and drives to headquarters. He casually asks if anything new is going on. He says, "You know, it's been a long time since we did a raid. We are getting rusty. Maybe we need to tell the chief to have some raid training."

One of the agents tells him, "Shut your fucking mouth. If you want training, put in your papers for training in Quantico!"

Rock hears the word Quantico and thinks, *That's it. Quantico has sent some assholes from the Human Rescue Team—who will they be rescuing? The target is the building where they are holding the prostitutes.*

Rock told Wolf that he was playing with fire. Wolf told him to mind his own fucking business that the prostitute business was his girlfriend's, and she knew what she was doing.

Chapter Forty-Seven

The Attack Begins, Chicken House

Pulaski, Tennessee

Vinny and Jeff are ready for the command to jam the frequencies. They have the drone ready to jam the cellular bands, and both have a pair of headsets to monitor the landline. Gerri and Reuben have entered the sex slave building.

Vinny transmits to Claude, "Gerri and Reuben are in."

Claude keys his radio. "Rose and Mateo, proceed to infiltrate and supply the weapons."

Rose and Mateo cut a hole in the fence and proceed for two miles to the dumpster. In forty-five minutes, they are at the dumpster site.

Claude keys Gerri and Reuben's radio/cell phone with two clicks. Click, click. And again, Click, click. That is the signal that the weapons have been delivered. Gerri takes a food tray from the table and wraps aluminum foil around the dish. The guards are busy looking out the windows. Any threat will come from the outside. The six Johns are nowhere to be seen; they are in the bedrooms with the selected girls. Nine prostitutes are still available, but it is early. Gerri and Reuben have selected two girls each. The thousand-dollar payment for each will entitle them to a three-way sex orgy. Both Gerri and Reuben are engaged in foreplay with the girls. They are kissing them on their cheeks, lips, neck, and ears. As they kiss their ears, they tell them, "*Esta noche es la noche.*" (Tonight, is the night.) They tell them in Spanish, "When you hear gunshots, or I yell, 'Hide,' all of you go to your rooms and hide. Barricade the door and hide in the closets or under the beds."

One of the guards comes over and says in English, "Cut the Italian talk. They know English. And also, when the rest of the customers come in, you can have only two girls."

The second guard says, "Hey, Rodney, maybe we change our names to Giovanni and Stefano. These I-Tal-EE-ANS are oversexed."

Rodney says, "Ha, ha, yeah, I always wanted to be a WOP, a real stud."

Heinrich says, "Rodney, shut your fucking mouth. You cannot even handle Betty Sue, and you want a three-way!"

"Yeah, you're right... I need to take care of the Homefront."

Gerri uses the opportunity to talk to the guards about sex in Italy. He wants them distracted. He knows that the assault team will come busting through the windows and doors anytime. While Gerri has their attention, Reuben takes the tray toward the kitchen and quickly goes out and retrieves the two Glock handguns. Both have fifteen-bullet magazines and one other fully loaded magazine. He places the guns in the food tray and quickly goes back inside. Rodney and Heinrich are wide-eyed as Gerri tells them about his sexual prowess.

The second shuttle leaves the gentlemen's club. It is fully loaded. The first shuttle, which drove Gerri and Reuben, has made it back. It is loading up and will leave in fifteen minutes.

Vinny keys the operational channel. "The second shuttle has left the club. It has been filled to maximum. Twelve passengers in total. ETA to intercept point twenty minutes. The shuttle is moving down Highway 441. Travis and Brit, set up an inspection roadblock."

Cars are being stopped, and license and registration papers are being inspected. The shuttle approaches the barrier and stops. Brit asks for the driver's license and registration. He tells the driver that the bus has been inspected and significant mechanical problems were found. It is not safe to continue.

He tells the driver and passengers, "A second bus will be by shortly. All passengers will need to dismount. An empty bus has been ordered. It will take you to your hotels."

Rick and Matt show up in an empty bus, and the Johns start complaining about the five hundred dollars that they paid. They say nothing to the officers, though, as they may be arrested for soliciting sex. They will come back to the gentlemen's club and demand a refund. Rick and Matt have taken all their cell phones. This is standard procedure. They tell them that they will be returned when they arrive at their hotels.

The five FBI agents come out from their hiding places. There are seven agents, counting Brit and Travis.

Claude calls Alex and Ethan. "Bring down the main power and disconnect the landline."

"Roger," says Alex. "Give me ten minutes for the power and two minutes for the landline." The landline was left operational to monitor any traffic that may have useful intel. "Before the assault begins, the landline will be cut."

Red Rooster Dinner Theater

Gambling Casino

Wolf's cell phone keeps getting the bing-bong that messages are arriving. He checks his iPhone. He has WhatsApp messages from some casino workers, one from Gretchen, two from the idiot Heinrich, and one from Colonel Sondermann. He has told them only to use the WhatsApp when they need security. Only the message from Colonel Sondermann has sensitive information. The rest are all bullshit texts. He deletes the BS text messages and finally comes to the text from Rock Irwin. Lately Rock has been seeing a commie behind every tree. Wolf has told Rock to stop with the bullshit messages, but he seems to not let up on his hysteria. Wolf finally says to himself, "Let's see what 'Rock Head' has seen now—probably ISIS terrorists in Tennessee!"

He opens the text—it reads: "Condition Critical, ATLANTA IS BURNING."

Wolf says, "Shit, this better not be another little shepherd boy screaming WOLF, WOLF, WOLF in the camp!"

He tries calling Rock but gets voicemail. He hangs up and decides to call the main camp. "Janet, this is Wolf. Is there anything going on at the camp?"

"No, sir. All is quiet."

"Call Gretchen's camp. I will stay online to see if you can get through."

A moment later, Janet comes back. "Sir, I can't get through. Looks like the microwave is down."

"OK, thanks."

He does not like to call using the regular cell service, but he needs to know the status of the slave building. After five rings, a recorded voice comes on: "Service is temporally not available in this area,"

He then dials the landline. Heinrich answers the phone. "Heinrich, what's going on at the camp?"

Heinrich thinks, *How the hell did he know that the power went out?*

"We just lost power, sir."

"Heinrich, now listen carefully; you are now in condition ATLANTA IS BURNING!" BBuuuzzzz... The line goes dead.

Heinrich looks at Rodney and says, "What the hell is—Atlanta is burning?"

"Beats the shit out of me. The standard operational procedures book is in the front office." Heinrich rummages through the drawer and pulls out an SOP manual. He combs through the manual and looks at what "Atlanta is burning" means. He says, "Holy shit, we are under attack!" He comes out running and yells at the two guards standing at the front door. "Take your positions at the windows! We are under attack!"

Gerri is in the bedroom with Yolanda and Rebecca.

Reuben moves to the food tray, and in one quick motion, he lifts the Glock and fires two shots. He hits Heinrich and one of the guards. Rodney and the other guard run to the back rooms and exit through the back door and to the second building with the cellar entrance. Rodney and one guard escape through the tunnel, which take them to the south side of the camp.

Rose and Mateo, who are immediately outside of the house, keep their heads down. They are taking incoming fire from the two top floors of the Chicken House. Alex, Ethan, Brit, Travis, and the five HRT agents are still a good mile from the house. They hear the gunfire.

Jeff transmits on the radio, "Tangos with women are moving outside of the house. Looks like the women are resisting. The tangos are pistol-whipping the women and dragging them to the northwest."

Brit, Travis, and the five HRT agents all have their night vision goggles turned on and sitting on their eyes. It is not as good as daylight; the trees and leaves, which have stored the energy of the sunlight, light everything up in green.

Brit says, "Team, double-time to the northwest. Jeff, vector me for an intercept ASAP."

"Turn five degrees right," says Jeff. "Go straight."

Thirty seconds pass. "Turn ten degrees left."

Travis and the five HRT agents are in excellent shape, they are covering ground three times faster than the tangos with the women. All agents know that they must overtake the tangos before they reach the ditch of death. Their legs are aching and beginning to feel rubbery, and the fifty-pound backpacks feel like one hundred pounds. Brit gives the command to dispose of the packs but keep the ammo mags, M-16s, and Glocks. Jettisoning the fifty-pound bags gives them all a new life. They are now sprinting. Not even Usain Bolt could have kept up with them. They are jumping over branches, wading through streams, and sliding downhills. Several of the agents' trip and fall. They quickly get up and continue the run. They start sweating, and the bills of their baseball caps are dripping with sweat. Brit is in touch with Jeff, who tells them that they are two minutes from the intercept vector.

Then they encounter a problem: they have come to a cliff. It is fifty feet straight down. The tangos have reached the death trench and are getting ready to shoot seven of the women. Brit signals all to lie prone, take out their M-16s, and aim at the seven Klansmen left to right. With no hesitation, he says, "One, two, three, shoot." It sounds like one BANG. The seven tangos all fall in the trench. The women are all stunned. After a few seconds, they begin crying and thanking the Lord for their salvation. Some are on their knees. They do not know what happened. Some faint and are lying on their backs, sides, and stomachs. Of the seven women, four are from Latin America, and three are blonds from American universities. Brit, Travis, and the five agents go around the cliff and approach the women.

Three of the women still do not understand that there is no longer danger. They pick up sticks and stones and try to protect themselves. Two of the agents yell out in Spanish, "*Somos amigos! No tenga miedo!*" (We are friends! Do not be afraid!)

Brit then realizes that some of the women are blonds, and he yells, "FBI, FBI! We are not going to hurt you!" The FBI agents now provide comfort to the women. They are surprised that three of the women are Americans.

As Brit, Travis, and the five HRT agents are rescuing the captive women, a firefight is occurring at the slave house. An abnormal difficulty arises as the special agents are clearing the rooms: there are friendlies intermixed with the Klansmen. At last count, there are six Johns and six captive women in the bedrooms. There is no record of which rooms are being used. Gerri asks Yolanda, "*Quales habitaciones se usan normalmente?*" (Which rooms are typically used?)

Yolanda answers in Spanish, "The girls all have their favorites." She tries her best to remember which girls are with Johns. The problem is that six are missing. A total of seventeen girls were sex slaves. Seven have been taken by the guards to be shot. They have been rescued. She and Rebecca are with Gerri. Maria and Anna are with Reuben. That leaves six girls unaccounted for. She makes her best guess as to where they may be. Three rooms are on the second floor, and three bedrooms are on the third floor. For the last fifteen minutes, no shots have been fired. The guards will likely be holding the Johns and the girls as hostages. This is what the HRT has been trained for. In Quantico, they have a simulated village with buildings of various sizes and floors. Their training has all been to rescue hostages.

Brit, Travis, and the five HRT agents have now returned to the slave house. Brit confers with Rose, and they quickly develop a plan. They will first go to the rooms identified by Yolanda. Yolanda has told them that they have all been instructed to hide in a closet or under the bed. They hope that the girls and the Johns have done precisely that. The team will use a battering ram to enter the room. A flash-bang will quickly be thrown into the room, and the HRT will enter in a stacked line.

The HRT agents smash the door of the first room, throw the flash-bang in, and enter with their M-16s in the ready position. The M-16s have special lights attached to the barrels that penetrate the flash-bang smoke. They enter the first room but do not find anyone. Two HRT members kneel down and inspect under the bed, and two HRT members kick down the closet door. They find one girl and one John cowering at the back of the closet. The HRT agents yell, "FBI! FBI! Place your hands where I can see them and come out." The girl and the John come out. Both are extremely frightened.

The young girl is blonde, shivering, and crying, "My name is Jessica Anderson, Jessica Anderson—I was kidnapped last year from my high school in Anniston, Alabama."

The man is dressed in only his underpants and t-shirt. He is sweating and stuttering, "P-p-p-please don't s-s-s-shoot. I s-s-s-swear I will n-n-n-never do this again."

In the next rooms, it goes identical to the first. In both bedrooms, the Johns and the girls are rescued. As the HRT team approaches the fourth room, it catches incoming automatic gunfire. The two lead members of the group are hit. Fortunately, all team members are wearing their bulletproof vests and the Kevlar helmets. The vests are the newest in body protection. They have a double Kevlar weave that will stop bullets fired from AR-15 or AK-47 automatic rifles. The bullets hit the vest and helmet. Both team members also receive bullet wounds on their arms. The injuries are not life-threatening, but the two agents are not capable of continuing with the clearing operations. Travis and Gerri take their positions. The incoming fire came from the lounge on the third floor.

Within minutes of the start of the attack, the FBI director informed the Nashville FBI special agent in charge (SAC) of the attack in his back yard. The director explained that his office was not informed before they began due to an informant amongst his ranks. After some smoothing over the reason for the SAC not being informed, the SAC fell in line and agreed to provide the needed manpower for the attack. Brit now has communications with the Nashville FBI SWAT team. The team has arrived in the latest model of Black Hawk helicopters. The Nashville SWAT team commander's name is Thomas (Tom), Kramer. He is a ten-year veteran of the FBI, with the last five years on the SWAT team. Before joining the FBI, Tom was with the NYPD anti-terrorism task force. Tom is a product of a mixed marriage; his father was of German ancestry, and his mother was Puerto Rican. Tom had a brown, olive complexion inherited from his mother and blue eyes inherited from his father. He was a solid six feet and was on the wrestling team in high school. As most FBI agents, he is a no-nonsense, get-to-the-point Type-A personality. As soon as Tom arrives, the FBI agents are conferring with Brit and Rose, as they are discussing the plan to rescue the hostages.

Again, Tom looks at Brit and then at Rose. Brit gives Tom a quick overview of Rose's credentials. When Brit mentions the Syrian operation. Tom says, "Glad to meet you. Your rescue of the hostages in Syria was truly an outstanding feat—my congratulations."

Rose says, "Thanks."

The plan to rescue the hostages is modified to use the Black Hawk helicopters. SWAT team members will rappel down and attack the Klansmen from the roof. The FBI and WMA team members on the ground will place maximum firepower on the third floor to divert the activity from the air. The Black Hawk helicopters have been upgraded with the latest to minimize the noise of the blades. This whisper model is known as the UH-60WA.

Before the start of the attack, the combined FBI/WMA teams meet to discuss the FBI protocol.

Tony Vega, the chief of the Quantico HRT team, begins the discussions. "We first need to attempt to negotiate the release of the hostages without the use of force."

"I agree," says Brit, "but we need to have our agents in place should we have to attack the moment we fear that the hostages are in danger. Standard rules of engagement."

Rose says, "We need intel: who, how many, and where are they. I will task Vinny to fly the drone with the infrared sensors to determine the number of Klansmen. We know that there are six hostages. The difference will be terrorists." This is the first time that the group has addressed the Klansmen as terrorists.

Tom (Nashville SWAT team chief) says, "Before you send up the drone, allow me to radio the helicopter pilot to vacate the airspace."

"Roger, let us know when we can fly the drone."

Tom transmits on the radio, "Elliot, vacate the airspace above the target building."

"Roger, vacating now."

Rose keys WMA channel five. "Vinny fly the infrared package over the target building. We need to know the number of human bodies and their location."

"Roger, the drone is now flying and headed to the target site. ETA five minutes."

The drone reaches the target site in four minutes. At six minutes, Vinny transmits on the radio, "Twelve bodies have been detected. Eight are lying down in a prone position. My best guess is that they are bound at their hands and feet. They all have the same posture. Three bodies are moving near the windows, probably standing guard. The fourth is standing over the bodies.

Rose replies, "OK, good intel. Vinny flies the drone back to home plate. We need to have the airspace clear." She then briefs the team members that there are four Klansmen. Three are near the windows in a defensive position.

Tom says, "We brought with us a 'throw in' phone. We need to first try and communicate with the terrorists."

"When we communicate, have either Gerri or Reuben talk with them. They know two of the terrorists. Might be best to have someone they know."

Brit then says, "Could be good, or it could be bad. They may be pissed off with Gerri and Ruben because they entered as so-called Italians, but I think it's worth a try."

The throw-in phone is a regular intercom phone. It has a two-hundred-foot light cable connected to it. Usually, the throw-in phone is a cell phone. However, currently, the cellular band is jammed. The FBI and WMA do not want the members at the slave camp talking to members in the regular terrorist base camp. The base camp has over one hundred terrorists. The last thing the team wants is two or three companies of heavily armed Klansmen advancing to the slave camp.

The throw-in phone is now connected to the terrorist inside the building. A professional negotiator from the Nashville office attempts to talk to the terrorists. The negotiator asks, "Who am I talking to?"

"None of your goddamn fucking business. Now, get this straight. We are in charge, do you understand?"

"OK, what is your demand?"

"Well, idiot—what do you think?"

"You tell me."

"We want that helicopter you have to land in our front yard and fly us to the Nashville Airport. Have a private jet fueled and ready to fly to Cuba."

"OK, you let go of the hostages, and we can arrange for your departure."

"What, you think I'm stupid? We take the hostages with us."

"How about if we trade you one FBI agent for the hostages."

"No deal. I can let the women go, but I keep four of the men. Once I let the women go, you have one hour to arrange for the helicopter and plane. If you do not have the copter on the ground ready to fly, we will shoot the men hostages."

"OK, give me thirty minutes to have the helicopter at the campsite."

"You have ten minutes. You must think I am stupid; I have seen the copter flying around providing video surveillance."

"OK, you got a deal. As soon as the helicopter lands, you give up the women."

"Just bring the fucking copter—then we see!"

The team decides that the helicopter will hover above the landing site. The demand will be made to release the women. After the women are released, then the helicopter will land. The most likely scenario is that the four hostages will be pushed in front of the terrorists. The fourth terrorist will be doing the pointing and talking—he is likely the leader. The best shooter on the FBI/WMA team will take out the team leader; three additional snipers will take out the remaining terrorists.

However, the team needs a backup plan. Claude, Alex, Ethan, and Rose quickly design one. They will be transported by the second helicopter to Nashville Airport. The plane, which, is available to fly the terrorists to Cuba, is the WMA G650 Gulfstream. Claude and Alex are licensed to fly the Gulfstream. Ethan and Rose will act as the attendants. The oxygen tanks on the plane provide the oxygen to the passengers when losing altitude. The oxygen tanks will be exchanged with the general anesthetic Propofol.

The helicopter that will be carrying the terrorists is now hovering at fifty feet. The FBI SWAT team snipers are all in their positions, and if the opportunity presents itself, the team leader, Tom, will give them the shoot command. The helicopter comes down to twenty feet. Brit shouts over the bullhorn, "Send the women out!" He gets no response. Again, he says, "Send the women out!"

The front door opens, and four women walk out. They are spaced about ten feet from each other. The lead terrorist has done this on purpose. If things go south, he can hold back the hostages not released and gun them down. After all the women, are safe and in the hands of the FBI, the helicopter lands. The FBI snipers start looking through the scopes on the rifle barrels. They aim at the front door. They have each have been assigned a terrorist. It is a full thirty seconds until the door opens. The first male hostage appears, and he is told to stand still. The second, third, and fourth hostages exit and they all stand in a straight line. Now the four terrorists come out and stand behind the hostages. The lead terrorist barks a command, and the hostages form a circle, all facing the helicopter. The four terrorists are inside the ring. The group of eight then duckwalk to the helicopter.

Tom, as the lead sniper, says into his microphone headset, "Stand down."

The group of eight boards the helicopter, and it heads for Nashville Airport.

Brit picks up the radio and calls Claude. "Plan B is operational. Expect company in thirty minutes."

"Roger, we are all set."

Thirty minutes later, the Black Hawk arrives at the Nashville Airport. It lands at the commercial aviation hangar. The Klansman leader smiles and tells the others, "We got our ticket to Venezuela."

Second Klansman says, "Thought you said Cuba?"

"Yeah, that was bullshit. Cuba returns all hijackers to the US. The dumbasses think that we will be returned. When we are airborne, we put a gun to the fat-ass pilot and tell him, 'New plan, we're going to Venezuela.' With all the drug contacts Wolf has in these shithole countries, we will be outta there in days."

The terrorists and the hostages exit the copter and walk thirty yards to the G650 Gulfstream. It is a sixty-million-dollar plane. The terrorists look at the plane and say, "We are flying in style."

As they approach the plane, a good-looking flight attendant welcomes them aboard. She has brown hair, is athletic looking, and would pass for a Maria Sharapova look-alike. Inside the plane is a male steward. He is very professional and tells them, "Welcome to Premier Services Executive Airlines. Please be seated. We will be airborne as soon as you are seated and buckled in."

As the plane starts its taxi down the runway, the airline flight attendant speaks with a sexy English accent. She makes sure that she says, "In case we have a sudden loss of altitude, the oxygen masks will fall from the compartment above your head. Please take the mask and place it over your mouth and nose." She then demonstrates how to place the mask and pull the strings. "Sit back and enjoy the movies and the free music on the plane. We hope you have a pleasant flight to Cuba."

To make the ruse look legit, Tony Vega has pulled some strings and has two F-22 fighter jets come up beside the plane.

The lead terrorists says, "Don't worry. They cannot do a damn thing. What they are gonna do, shoot down the plane?"

After twenty minutes, the plane is at thirty thousand feet. The lead terrorist gets up and puts a gun to Ethan's head. He says, "Get me into the pilot's cabin."

Ethan acts scared and says, "Yes, yes, sir."

As Ethan is showing the terrorist to the pilot's cabin, he clicks his radio two times. This is the signal for Alex to get ready because they are coming in.

Ethan enters the cabin, followed by the terrorist. In a flash, Alex has the terrorist on the cabin floor, and with one solid punch, the terrorist is out cold.

Claude now puts the plane into a sharp nosedive. The oxygen masks deploy, and all of the passengers are scrambling to place them on their mouths and nose. Rose is going down the aisle, shouting, "MASK ON QUICKLY, QUICKLY!" She reaches the last row, sits in her seat, and uses a portable oxygen mask.

The three terrorists think, *What the hell is Sean doing? Fucking idiot. Did he have to kill the pilot when he told him that we are headed to Venezuela?*

Within ten seconds, the terrorists and the hostages have placed their Propofol masks on their mouths and nose. In another twenty seconds, they are asleep. Rose and Ethan quickly use flex-cuffs on the three terrorists in the main cabin. They tie their hands and ankles, and Alex does the same to the terrorist in the pilot's cabin. They then disarm all the terrorists, checking for handguns and knives. They find that all have ankle knife holsters. After that, they strip all the terrorists to their underwear and drag them to the rear of the plane.

After the terrorists are tied, the hostages are given a sponge bath. Oxygen masks are placed on their mouths, and within a few seconds, they are awake. Some think they have awoken from a nightmare. They look at Rose and Ethan with puzzled looks and simply say, "What happened? Where am I?"

Rose and Ethan explain to them what happen and that they are safe. After they realize what happened, they are mostly worried about their wives. Rose simply tells them, "We will only say that you were abducted by terrorists from the gentlemen's club cigar bar."

All four say in unison, "Thank you very much."

She turns and says, "Hope you guys learned your lesson. You can tell your grandkids the day you were kidnapped by terrorists. That will be quite a story."

Ethan and Rose are glad that the hostages have recovered. The plane has turned and will be landing at Nashville Airport in ten minutes. The terrorists are starting to wake up.

One of the terrorists tells Sean, "Guess we are not in Venezuela."

Sean says, "Shut the fuck up. We do not say a word. We want our lawyers. We were framed!"

When the plane lands, Tom has two police vans waiting for the terrorists. There are also four ambulances waiting for the hostages (Johns).

There are twenty-five news reporters, and the CNN, MSNBC, Fox News, and local news vans are starting to show up. As he did in Buchanan, New York, Special Agent Brit Singleton says, "Showtime!"

Chapter Forty-Eight

KKK Main Camp

Pulaski, Tennessee

Wolfgang is pissed at himself and keeps asking himself, "What went wrong?" He thinks over the events that have transpired in the last month. He then thinks, *Goddamn it. It has to be Juan and those fucking goat fuckers!* He needs to protect the main camp. At 11;30 P.M., he leaves the Red Rooster and drives to the main camp. He calls Colonel Sondermann and tells him to have the entire staff assembled at 1 A.M. He calls Gretchen and gives her the bad news. The henhouse is under attack. He believes it is being attacked by the FBI.

"I was able to call Heinrich and give him advance warning, and I did tell him to implement the Atlanta Is Burning option. Then the line went dead."

Gretchen asks, "How the hell did the cops know about what we were doing?"

"Gretchen, I know you are pissed. So am I, but now is not the time to play the blame game. We need to implement our cover-up plans."

"OK, you are right; I will start immediately to destroy all records related to our gentlemen's club customer list. Fortunately, we never implemented a computer-based system exactly for this very reason. We will start burning papers tonight."

"Please shut down the gambling casino. Remove all gambling materials and have them stored in our off-site storage facility. I will have a team from the camp pick up the materials tomorrow and move them to our secret underground bunker."

"Do we know if the henhouse destroyed the evidence?"

"I do not know. As I said, I was able to tell Heinrich to implement the Atlanta Is Burning option."

"Yeah, I just wish we had practiced the option. We had a couple of bitches that were giving us problems. Besides, we really needed to replenish our stock with blonds—they were bringing in twice what the bitches from the shithole countries were bringing in."

"OK, we will know by tomorrow the status of the henhouse. We had some pretty strong escape plans; I only hope they used the cellar escape to get the hell out of there. Gretchen, when you finish with the cleanup, you need to move your ass to the main camp ASAP."

"Will do. I should be there by daylight."

At 7 A.M., the KKK staff meet at the main camp. Wolf opens the meeting. "Klansmen, we have reliable indicators that our prostitute building was attacked sometime late last night and early this morning."

Lt. Colonel Sondermann says, "After Colonel Schneider contacted me via a phone call, we quickly attempted to contact the prostitute house. We tried using our normal microwave, and we found that the frequency was jammed. We tried both cellular and landline. The cellular was jammed, and the landline was cut. I had Major Jacobson drive to within the radio horizon of the talk-around frequency, and it also was jammed. I will now have Major Jacobson provide a summary of what he heard and saw."

Major Jacobson says, "As the colonel said, I drove to the outskirts of the camp. I tried the talk-around frequency and found that it was jammed. I then decided to walk through the woods. Fortunately, I had my night vision goggles. I walked to the hill on the north side and stopped there to see if I could see anything. I witnessed the killing of seven Klansmen. Our camp Klansmen were following orders and were in the process of destroying the evidence. Before our brothers could execute, eh, follow orders, shots and the muzzle flashes were heard and seen from the hill opposite where I was standing. Seven of our Klansmen were murdered in cold blood!"

When the major states that the Klansmen were murdered, the staff members erupt in much anger. "Goddamn feds! They will pay for their atrocities!"

"I also contacted our inside informant," says Wolf. "He said that the attacking team came from Washington."

One of the captains says. "Why did our informant not warn us hours before the attack? Isn't that why we pay him?"

Wolf will now lie. "Our informant did warn us, and immediately sent me a text, as was the proper protocol, then immediately called Janet at the base camp, but she was not able to contact the southern camp. I immediately called the slave camp. Heinrich did answer, and I told him to execute the Atlanta Is Burning protocol. Let's hope that the evidence was destroyed."

"But didn't Major Jacobson just tell us that seven of our Klansmen were murdered?"

"Yes, but there is no reason to believe that the evidence was not also destroyed."

The staff members do not push the point—they all know that the seven prostitutes likely survived.

Wolf now starts with the items that need to be implemented for a defensive position. "There is a strong likelihood that the main camp will either be attacked or that a search warrant will be served."

Lt. Colonel Sondermann says, "I will contact our lawyers in Nashville and ask them to be here first thing this morning. We are taking the necessary steps to challenge any court order. They have no basis for a search. The southern building and the main camp have absolutely no formal connection. The southern building is an LLC and stands on its own. The president and owner of the LLC are listed as Gretchen Miller. We have no connection to the limited liability corporation."

Wolf says, "Captain Baker, what is the status of the weapons and ammunition?"

"We are well stocked; each member of the Klan has been issued an AR-15, AK-47, Glock handgun, and knife. They each have an ammo belt with over five hundred rounds of ammunition for the AR-15 and AK-47. They have five magazines for the Glock and one hundred bullets. In the armory, we have fifteen RPGs, five for each company, with ten grenades for each RPG. We also have ten air-to-ground shoulder-fired systems, with five missiles per system. Also, each Klansman has a bulletproof vest, night vision goggles, and a Kevlar vest and helmet."

"How about snipers and long rifles?" asks Major Jacobson.

"Yes, each company has three trained snipers with a Remington rifle. They are required to shoot every week."

Wolf interjects. "You need to give the snipers additional training. The last time I competed against them, only two of the nine could shoot better than me—and I only train once a month."

"Yes, sir, I will personally see that the snipers receive double training!"

"Have you inspected the battle, trenches?"

"Yes, sir, they are reinforced with sandbags."

"What about the underground storage areas?"

"We are in good shape, enough for one year with no replenishment."

"OK, starting at daybreak, double the guards. We are at DEFCON 1. The attack is imminent."

By 9 A.M., the KKK command staff have been making the necessary movements to protect the camp against a possible attack.

Major Jacobson comes running into the command staff war room. He shouts, "CCN has just now announced a major news break regarding a raid on a house that was holding women as sex slaves."

Wolf snaps back, "Turn the TV to Fox News; that goddamn CCN is nothing but fake news!"

Major Jacobson uses the remote and turns the TV to Fox News. Across the screen is a banner saying: "Breaking news, FBI to have news report any time." The Fox News anchor says that the FBI will be giving a live news release anytime. The morning anchor then says, "Ladies and gentlemen, we are switching to Samantha Givens from our news affiliate in Nashville."

"Good morning, ladies and gentlemen, my name is Samantha Givens with Station KRWD in Nashville. We have recently learned that the FBI conducted a raid on a house in the Pulaski area of Tennessee. The attack resulted in the rescue of women being held as sex slaves. It is our understanding that several hostages were also rescued and that some members of the HRT received non-life-threatening injuries. Hold on a minute, I now see an FBI agent coming to the podium."

The screen now shows a man in his mid-thirties with a square jaw and broad shoulders. He is clean-shaven and is wearing military-style boots, brown cargo pants, and a brown FBI polo-shirt. The polo-shirt shows his muscular biceps and long arms. The FBI man comes to the podium and introduces himself as Brit Samuel Singleton special agent from the Quantico Division.

Brit begins his presentation. "Ladies and gentlemen, beginning last night at approximately 11:30 P.M. local time, elements of the Quantico HRT, the Nashville FBI SWAT teams, and NGA special forces conducted a raid on a White Nationalists terrorist camp. The raid resulted in the rescue of seventeen women being held against their will. They were being used as sex slaves. Thirteen of the women were from Latin America countries, and four were American girls."

At the mention of America girls, the news reporters all start shouting and raising their hands. "Can you tell us the names of the American girls?"

Brit calmly raises his hand and pushes open his palms, signaling quiet. "Please allow me to complete my report, and then I will take questions."

Throughout the gathering of now more than thirty reporters, you could hear the low murmurs: "These girls have to be some of the co-eds that have been disappearing from our colleges and universities."

Brit continues: "We were also able to rescue seventeen hostages. Four of these hostages were being used by the terrorists as human shields. Now for the causalities. Eleven terrorists were killed, and four were apprehended. The four terrorists who have been arrested are all Americans and are members of the Pulaski Chapter of the KKK. The FBI did suffer some non-life-threatening injuries. Two of the HRT team were wounded on the arms and hands, and they are expected to fully recover." Brit goes on for another twenty minutes, providing details of the attack. He finishes by asking, "Now, if there are any questions, I will do my best to answer."

The reporter from the local news radio stations asks, "Sir, the fact that there so many terrorists were killed with no FBI casualties makes it seem like you must have lined them up and killed them in cold blood. Can you tell us how eleven terrorists were killed and only two of on your team suffered only minor superficial wounds?"

Brit grits his teeth and calmly answers the question, "Seven of the terrorists were within seconds of murdering the women. The intel that we had was that they were ordered to destroy the evidence if they were attacked. The raid was carried out as a surprise to prevent the killing of the women captives. My HRT team and I arrived at the death site within seconds of the women being executed. I gave the command to shoot the terrorist before they could kill the women."

The reporter has a follow-up question: "How can we be sure that you aren't just giving us bullshit information. Even the president does not believe the FBI!"

The other reporters tell the reporter from the local Fox News station to shut up and let them get to the facts.

Again, Brit raises his hands, palms out, and says, "Later today, we will arrange for representatives of the news media to visit what we call the ditch of death. This is where the KKK would kill the women that they considered to be of no use to them." Brit also knows that the WMA drone has video of the women being dragged through the forest; however, the FBI will not show the video. The WMA drone and its capabilities are top secret. It is what the Intel community calls "methods and sources." this type of information is closely held; it must not divulge to the general public nor to America's adversaries.

A reporter from Fox News asks, "How can we be sure that the women would have been killed?"

"Our recovery team has exhumed four bodies from the ditch of death. Preliminary reports are that the cause of death was a bullet to the head, execution-style."

Brit now feels that he needs to tell them about the snuff movies. He goes on to explain that this branch of the KKK was recording the killing of women in the act of performing a sexual act. All of the reporters are frantically writing on their notepads. The reporter from the local Fox News affiliate keeps shaking his head. "Fucking lies, all lies."

The CNN reporter asks how the four terrorists were captured without any of the hostages being harmed.

Brit says, "We have some outstanding negotiators, and they earned their paycheck."

As the news presentation is coming to an end, a reporter from the *New York Times* says, "Brit, I want to thank you for your professionalism in successfully managing the Indian Point nuclear power plant attack. Had it not been for your leadership, I probably would not be here today. The raid on the KKK camp was obviously carried out with the same degree of professionalism. You mentioned in your opening remarks that the team was made up of elements from Quantico, Nashville, and an NGA. My question is, can you tell us who the NGA is, and did you have assistance from the NGA during the raid?"

Brit looks at the *New York Times* reporter and says, "Butch, first, I thank you very much for your kind words. I am sure that all of the men and women who participated in the prevention of the ISIS attacks of last year appreciate your sincere thank you. Now, for the second part, it is against FBI policy to provide the names of any agents who perform these dangerous and life-threatening assignments. I believe that all of you can understand why we cannot divulge the NGA entity or the names of the people involved."

"Well, from all of us, and especially the *New York Times*, THANK YOU VERY MUCH."

All of the reporters minus one applaud and say, "Thank you."

Wolf and his entire staff are glued to the TV set. Finally, Wolf says, "Well, we know now what happened."

"Nothing was said about any continuing investigation," says Lt. Colonel Sondermann.

"You're right. I don't think that our mole has broken his cover. I need to talk to him ASAP and try and find out what's going on."

"He mentioned eleven killed, and four captured," says Major Jacobson. "We had seventeen at the camp. Where are the other two?" Jacobson answers his own question. "They escaped via the cellar tunnel. Hopefully, they followed the SOP and pulled the lever for the avalanche behind them to conceal the exit to the tunnel."

"Won't make any difference," says Wolf. "We will never use that building again."

Wolf is now getting depressed. All that he has worked for is falling apart. He needs to stay strong as the leader. They will all key off his personality. He comes back to himself and starts barking orders: "Damn the torpedoes, full speed ahead." They all perk up and start the DEFCON-1 operations. "All men to the trenches, double the guards, shoot to kill. No Goddamn FBI HRT, SWAT Team, Tiger Team, or whatever the hell they want to call it is gonna march in here and arrest us. We fight to the death."

By eleven A.M., all positions are manned. The eagles will be patrolling all day, with only one half-hour break every two hours.

"No goddamn drone will be flying the skies over the camp!" shouts Wolf. "Let the four dogs lose. Keep them hungry and mean."

After he gives the orders, he walks to his house in a posture that Napoleon would envy. Gretchen also needs a pep talk. Her theater, gentlemen's club, and henhouse are all destroyed. They will not survive.

Wolf tells her to cheer up. "I have a plan."

"What, some dumbass plan like the one you had to go chasing that woman who bested you in the sandbox?"

Wolf reluctantly agrees that things started going south in Scotland. Now he is sure that Estella Rose Mathews is still alive and is merely teasing him. She knew from the moment they set up the trap in Scotland who he was. She could have easily shot him any time when he was traveling between the main camp and the Red Rooster. The final piece that fell in place was when that New York reporter asked that FBI Agent, "Who is the NGA?" He now knows it is WMA and Rose is the lead special forces agent! How stupid he has been. He needs to make it up to Gretchen. The collapse of her three businesses is directly related to his arrogance and stupidity.

Chapter Forty-Nine

President Is Briefed on the Raid

White House, Washington, DC

The morning of the raid on the slave camp, President Trout is briefed by the director of the FBI, Hector Calvanese.

"Sir, last night, a raid was successfully carried out against a terrorist camp."

Before the director can say another word, the President interrupts: "God-damn A-Arabs, I thought you killed all those sons of ditches last year when they tried blowing up the New York nuclear plant!"

"Yes, sir, we did kill a boatload; however, these are not Arabs."

Again, the president interrupts: "What, not A-Arabs? Then who? MS-13, immigrants from those shithole countries—who, then?"

"Sir, if you allow me a few minutes, I can explain."

"Goddamn it, Hector, you have already been standing in front of the TV. There is a great special on Fox News. Mary Sue is being interviewed by Sean Hamilton. The interview will be about how great it is to be working with such a smart and intelligent president. Hector, what do you think? Aren't I the most intelligent president ever? You worked for O'Hara and Weed, so surely you know that I am head and shoulders above those two idiots.

"OK, Hector, you're wasting my time. Now, what about that raid on the terrorist camp?"

Hector clears his throat and says, "Sir, last night, the FBI rescued seventeen women being held as sex slaves."

"Yeah, yeah, you told me that. Now, get on with it! You have not told me a damn thing. Hurry up, I am watching a documentary on myself on Fox News. It's an excellent documentary. It's going through all of my accomplishments of the last two years. Damn, I am good. OK, what do you got about some terrorists? If I had my wall, these damn things wouldn't happen."

"Yes, sir, the wall would prevent everything."

As the director is trying to brief the president, there is a news flash on Fox News. The banner reads: "Terrorism in the heartland. The camp is in the Pulaski, Tennessee, area. Seventeen women have been rescued by the FBI."

The president says, "Hector, what the hell is going on? Why have you not briefed me on this raid? By the way, did I authorize the raid? If I didn't, then make sure you say I did."

"Yes, sir, I will."

"Now, about the rescued women, who were they?"

"Thirteen were from Latin America, and four were from colleges and universities in the United States."

"You mean you found the girls abducted from our southern universities of Alabama, North Carolina, and Tennessee?"

"Yes, sir, the ones that have been on all the news channels."

"OK, tell Miss Piggy (Trout has a nickname for everyone), my press secretary, about the four co-eds and have her conduct a press conference. Make sure you give her all of the details on my super-intelligence in solving the case."

"Yes, sir, I will." Hector knows better than to mention the thirteen Latin American women. Trout will probably say something that would be best not to print or discuss at a news conference.

Within two hours, the press secretary, Sandra Honeysuckle, is giving a briefing on the rescue of the seventeen women. Little to no mention is made of the thirteen Latin American women. All attention is given to the four coeds from the American universities.

Gerri and Reuben are watching the press conference. They simply shake their heads and say, "Why did we expect any different?" They and the rest of the team members are proud of what they did and the lives they saved.

Chapter Fifty

FBI Safe House

Outside of Nashville, Tennessee

The team assembles at the Nashville safe house. They conduct a hotwash and discuss the raid on the Chicken House. After the hotwash, they turn their attention to the main camp. The video taken of Juan de la Toro meeting with camp representatives was deemed to be outside the search warrant.

A considerable amount of the activity recorded was legal. Such events as parades, cross burnings, pistol practice, martial arts, running, and other physical activities were considered to be within the scope of the warrant. However, none of these activities rise to the level for the issuing of a search warrant, they are all normal activities expressing their first amendment rights to assemble and express themselves.

They do have the video of the undercover agent meeting with Wolf, and that also was explained as a regular meeting of the secret agent performing his duties. A warrant is requested to allow for the search of the camp, and the request is denied. The judge says that the video taken in Mazatlán compared to the footage taken from the KKK camp is relying on a software application that has not been proven reliable. The judge understands that the personality software profiles are sound and very impressive, but the technology belongs in a Tom Clancy book. Maybe Jack Ryan can use it, but in the real world—it's not good enough.

The team attempted to have the judge issue the search warrant because they know that Wolf will destroy any evidence that is currently in the camp. The best they can do is set up a roadblock at the exit point of the camp and check all vehicles for contraband. The other possibility is that the search of the gentlemen's club and the Red Rooster will find evidence linking the main camp with the slave camp.

The surveillance task authorized by FBI Director Hector Calvanese is still valid. Using this surveillance authorization, the team will need to find some information that will allow them to search the property physically.

Brad McKinnon, being a former FBI agent, has an idea. He says, "Perhaps we can get a pen register on our suspected double agent, Rock Irwin?"

Tom Kramer, who is the Nashville SWAT team leader, is not generally involved with electronic intercept surveillance. He asks, "What is a pen register?"

Brad very diplomatically says, "The term pen registers originally referred to a device for recording telegraph signals on a strip of paper. Obviously, the recording was done by the use of a pen. For example, Samuel Morse's 1840 telegraph patent described such a register as consisting of a device holding a writing device, such as a pen or pencil. The writing device would automatically write down the Morse codes that were being transmitted."

Tom then asks, "But how do we get the digits being dialed?"

Brad now gives a modern explanation, saying, "The pen registers of today are really trap and trace devices. A trap and trace device will show what phone number called a specific telephone number, in other words, all incoming phone numbers. The current pen register will show what numbers a phone called or all outgoing phone numbers. These two intercepts are often jointly referred to as 'pen register' or 'trap and trace' devices to reflect the fact that the same program will do both functions. Today law enforcement agencies use the term 'pen register' to describe both types of devices."

Tom then says, "So, it's an old term that had an original meaning, and the name has been carried through the years."

"Yeah. If you stop and think about it, these types of terms carried over from the old days exist everywhere. For example, 'cc' in your e-mails stands for carbon copy, and 'RSVP,' I bet nobody knows what it really stands for."

"It means 'please respond,' answers Tom.

"It is a French term," says Rose. "It means *Répondez s'il vous plaît*," which translates to 'Respond if you please.'"

Tom says, "Not only did I have a history lesson on pen registers, but I learned that 'cc' means a copy, and I had my French lesson for the month. Thanks, Brad and Rose."

Tom continues: "We already have a wire on Rock's home and cell phones. So far, we have nothing." (Note: a wire has both digits dialed and audio content.)

Brad thinks, *Of course, he will never use his FBI-issued phone.*

Rose, being the diplomat, says, "My experience with persons who are working covertly is that they will always have a second and, at times, a third phone. Some will be burner phones. They will use these phones with fictitious names and billing addresses. We can have Jeff and Louie create a roaming geo-fence to track the FBI-issued phone. We will intercept all cell calls made from within the geo-fence. Then, by process of elimination, we can determine the likely numbers that Rock is dialing. Once we have the numbers, we can look up on a publicly available website which phone company owns the number. The Nashville FBI office can now request a pen register on these numbers."

Brit, who has always admired Rose, not only for her good looks but also for her excellent knowledge of how to catch bad guys, says, "Rose, that's great. How fast can we implement it?"

"Knowing Jeff and Louie, I guess that they already have this capability. All we need is the number of the FBI-issued phone."

Tom says, "Let me make a phone call, and I can get the info ASAP."

Brit then says, "Tom, best to make a radio call. It is more secure."

"Roger will do."

Tom makes the call, and within ten minutes, Rose is calling on the secure line to Jeff and Louie. She tells Jeff the number.

"OK," says Jeff, "we can cross-reference the phone number to the IMSI and should have the GPS on the FBI-issued phone and the geo-fencing within fifteen minutes. I can send you a report as the phone moves and calls within the geo-fence and what calls are being made. The more he moves, the better."

Tom says, "Hold on a minute. What is geo-fencing, and is it legal? "

Rose says with a patience of the Dalai Lama, "Geo-fencing is done all the time by businesses on the internet. For example, let's say you are selling expensive foreign cars like BMW's or Mercedes. You would probably want to know who attended the Foreign Car Show at the Washington Expo Center. You contract with one of the many companies who track all phones in any given area. The area of interest would be, the one block where the Expo center is located. The tracking company will send you the IMSI of all phone numbers that were in that one block area during the show at the Expo Center."

Tom, "What's an IMSI?"

"Sorry, the IMSI stands for International Mobile Subscriber Identity number, every mobile phone has a unique identification number. This number is embedded in the phone. You can change your phone number, but you cannot change the IMSI."

"Oh, yeah I get it, kind of like your DNA, right?

"You got it."

"But isn't this illegal?"

"No, the IMSI is transmitted across the network in the clear. Like the address on an envelope. It gives the phone a unique I.D number so that the phones maybe located. What you do not intercept is the phone number or the content of the call. The geo-fencing simply matches the IMSI to the GPS of the phone and *VIOLA* you have all phones that are "turned on" inside the geographical fence, thus geo-fencing."

Tom, "Thanks Rose, think I will order a geo-fence on my teenage daughters."

Rose looks at Tom, "Really!"

"Only for protection, don't want them in night clubs after midnight. Nothing good ever happens after midnight."

"Yeah, you got a point there."

After Rose finishes her explanation of geo-fencing, she tells the group that the data should start rolling in in about fifteen minutes. "The more Rock moves, the better."

Brit gets on the secure line and calls the Nashville SAC. "Sir, we need to have our prime suspect double agent be given an assignment where he will need to travel."

"Roger will do."

The fact that there is a possible double agent is a very closely held secret. Only the Nashville SAC and Internal Affairs are aware of a potential double agent.

Within half an hour, the target is moving. An automatic report is generated every time the target comes to a different cell tower or when stationary for more than fifteen minutes. The reports start at 10 A.M. The target drives from Nashville to Murfreesboro to Pulaski and on to Trenton. A total of 853 reports are generated. The number of all calls made from all phones equals 12,456. A software program called a "spider chart" come up on the screen. It is evident from the spider chart, which numbers are common. Three outgoing numbers are being made to two numbers. As suspected, the three outgoing numbers are from the unlisted number and burner phones. The numbers being called are listed as being located in the KKK camp. This information is now used to have the warrant include the five numbers as pen registers. After two days of pens being collected, the judge modifies the court order to allow for a physical search of the main KKK camp.

Chapter Fifty-One

Search Warrant

Main KKK Camp

Before the delivery of the search warrant to the KKK camp, Brit tells the members of the WMA that this will be strictly an FBI raid; it would be best if WMA individuals were not caught in the crossfire. Brit tells Claude, Rose, and Alex, "I was able to convince Tom that we should have the three of you stay here in the FBI camp as subject matter experts (SMEs)." Tom then looks at the three and winks. "SMEs can also pull triggers."

Claude then makes a decision. He sends Vinny, Jeff, Matt, and Rick back to the home office in Virginia. Jeff, Matt, and Rick are reassigned to programs providing equipment and services to domestic law enforcement agencies. Vinny is assigned to work with Louie on some R&D programs.

Brad McKinnon calls Claude on the secure line. "Claude, is it my understanding that the FBI has taken complete control?"

"Yes, however, Brit wants us to stick around and provide expert advice. Brit let us know that the decision to jettison WMA operatives was made by the Nashville SAC. Now that everything looks like a piece of cake, they want all the credit for taking down the terrorists. The Nashville SAC wants a feather in his cap. He wants his next assignment to be the SAC in New York, Los Angeles, or Miami."

"Yeah, I get it. Somehow it never changes. It was that way when I was an FBI agent."

"Rose thinks that Wolf still has many rabbits to pull out of the hat! You think we can have Jeff, Matt, Rick, and Vinny on standby in case we need them?"

"I'll see what I can do, but we have quite a backlog, and we will need to reassign them to programs with charge numbers. We need to pay the bills."

"OK, understood. We will do the best we can with the resources we have. Perhaps Rose is wrong, but she's never been wrong before, so only time will tell."

Later that day, Brit comes in the WMA trailer and gives Claude one FBI radio to monitor the activity. Using the radio's interoperability gateway, all members of the WMA team may listen to the activity.

Claude tells Brit, "If you need us, we are standing by."

"Thanks, you have done more than your share; it's time for us to contribute to the battle against these domestic terrorists."

Usually, the search warrants are delivered to the domicile of the target at 4 A.M. The idea is that the target is not prepared for a search warrant to be issued. In this case, the situation is entirely different. The target includes the name Adolf Wolfgang Schneider, and the address listed is that of the main KKK camp. The front gate of the camp has been fortified and has two guard towers with watchtowers above the tree line. The watchtowers are set back to allow a clear view of the front gate. Both towers have .50-caliber machine guns with steel-plate protective shields. It is decided that the search warrant will be delivered at 10 A.M. The FBI will be there in force, fifty armed agents and two armed track vehicles. Each vehicle has an armored .50-caliber machine gun.

Brit and Tom step out of an armored personnel carrier and push the button on the intercom on the side of the front gate.

A voice comes back with a command: "State your name and purpose!"

"This is the FBI," says Tom. "We have a duly authorized warrant issued by a federal court to search your property."

"Who issued the warrant?"

"The warrant has been issued by the Fifth District Court of Nashville and signed by a federal judge."

"A federal judge of which country?"

"The United States of America."

"You will need to process your complaint through our secretary of international affairs. We do not recognize warrants issued by foreign powers."

"And just what country are you?"

"We are the Confederate States of America. Our original capital was Montgomery, Alabama, and it is now Pulaski, Tennessee, home of the Confederacy. You are currently trespassing on Confederate territory, and if you do not vacate the premises in ten minutes, it will be considered an act of war. We kindly ask that you get the hell off our land!"

THE SIEGE STARTS

Brit and Tom decide to have a round-table discussion with Rose, Alex, and Claude. However, they are steadfast that this is an FBI mission. They will only seek advice from the WMA operatives; they are SMEs. Relegating Rose, Alex, and Claude to SME status is a polite way of saying. "We think we can do it, but we may get our ass in a sling and need the rescue dogs!"

Brit begins the discussion. "The terrorists are heavily armed. We could request two hundred-armed law enforcement officers from the ATF, DEA, and state police. In the end, we would prevail, but casualties would be extremely high on both sides."

Tom then says, "We have no choice but a prolonged siege."

"Based on the information we have; how long do we think the terrorists can last without receiving nourishment?"

"Based on the information from the surveillance," says Alex, "they may be able to last indefinitely."

"How is that possible?"

"They have a fully functional farm. The farm has over fifty acres of foodstuffs: tomatoes, potatoes, corn, lettuce, cabbage, onions, and other vegetables. The farm has livestock, bulls, pigs, and rabbits. They also have a solar farm and windmills, which provide all their power. They have existed since the end of the Civil War, completely off the grid. Only in the last ten years have they connected to the outside world. The connection came when Gretchen took over from her father. Later, when she met Wolfgang, the community started moving drugs and human traffic. Now it appears that they are importing opioids from Afghanistan."

Rose then says, "My experience says one thing: we need to cut off the head of the snake. We do that, and the body will die. In this case, we need to eliminate Wolf, Gretchen, and the top two or three of his staff. We do that, and the troops will likely surrender."

Brit and Tom like the idea. Tom says, "I think we have some agents who have experience in Iraq and Afghanistan, and we can use them for the infiltration and kill."

Alex says, "You will need more than just Iraq and Afghanistan experience. You will need some highly skilled special operations soldiers."

"OK, we can review the background of our agents in North Carolina. Last time I was there, a great many of our agents had experience with Delta Force. You know that Delta Force personnel are stationed in Fort Bragg, Fayetteville, North Carolina. Our FBI office is located in Raleigh, North Carolina. Raleigh is only a few hours' drive from Fayetteville.

"Yes, if they are experienced ex-special forces, it will increase your chances of success."

"OK, but this will need the approval of the special agent in charge of the Nashville office. Mr. Stanko Kowalski will likely require the approval of the director."

Brit likes the idea and says, "Tom, you call agent Kowalski, and I will call the director,"

Tom thinks for a few seconds. "The best thing to do is let me speak to the SAC directly. I recommend that you not call the director. It would be best if I speak to the SAC personally and we discuss the idea. I have no reason to believe that he will disagree; after all, this saves lives."

"I agree. I will stand down."

Tom looks at Alex and Rose and says, "One more thing. Let the FBI carry through with this plan. It is best if the idea, planning, and implementation are entirely FBI."

Rose, Alex, and Claude know what Tom is saying: "Keep this to yourselves. It is best if the senator does not call the director."

Chapter Fifty-Two

FBI Plan to Cut off the Head of the Snake

Nashville, Tennessee

Agent Thomas "Tom" Kramer drives to Nashville to discuss his ideas with his boss, SAC Stanko Kowalski. Tom enters the reception area of the SAC and asks Yvette if he can see Mr. Kowalski. Yvette tells him, "Certainly, please have a seat." Yvette has a list of selected people who can come in at any time. She has been directed that the people on the list have top priority if they call or come into the office and to contact the SAC immediately. On that list are the president, FBI director, chief of internal affairs, and two individuals by name, Tom Kramer and Brit Singleton.

Yvette pushes the intercom button and says, "Mr. Kowalski, Agent Kramer is here to see you, sir."

"OK, let me finish up with Agent Holmes and send him in when Agent Holmes exits."

"Yes, sir."

Tom hears the conversation and picks up a magazine on the latest weapons for law enforcement. He is just starting to look at the table of contents when Agent Holmes walks out.

Evette looks at Tom and says, "Mr. Kowalski will see you now."

"Thank you." Tom walks into the office of the SAC.

After some small talk, the SAC asks, "How is the siege coming along?"

Tom answers, "Sir, we have calculated that the siege can last indefinitely. The longer the siege lasts, the more support the white nationalists are getting from the population. Frankly, the president going to his rallies does not help. He keeps slamming the FBI and saying that the deep state is out to get him. Most of his supporters are sympathizers with right-wing tendencies. They equate the white nationalists with being tough on immigration. His rallying call of 'Build the Wall' also does not help. Every day, the number of protesters on both sides grows. Pretty soon, we are going to need the state police to keep the two sides from going to war."

The SAC agrees and says, "OK, you and Brit are in charge, so what do you think we should do, attack the camp?"

"No, that would result in a bloodbath; the white nationalists are armed to the teeth."

"Yes, I have read the reports. They have automatic weapons and RPGs, and is it correct that they have shoulder-fired missiles to shoot down helicopters?"

"Yes, sir. We were able to record the movement of some of these weapons during the surveillance authorized by the director."

"So, what is your plan?"

Tom now has the opening he has been maneuvering for. He says, "Sir, both Brit and I think it best to have a covert team infiltrate the camp and kill the leaders. We know who the leaders are, and based on our intel from the surveillance, we also know where they have their daily briefings and in which buildings they live."

"Let's stop right there. If you are suggesting that the NGA special operations forces undertake the covert mission, this is a non-starter. The answer is NO WAY! Is that understood?"

"Yes, sir, fully understood. I did not come here to ask that we use the NGA agents. I came here to discuss the use of our own covert team. The FBI has an equally, if not better, trained team of special agents who could successfully carry out the arrest or kill."

"OK, I am listening. What are the details of your plan?"

"Sir, between the Nashville and North Carolina offices, we have more than twenty agents with special forces experience. We assign a task force of eight to ten covert agents to penetrate the terrorists' defenses and cut off the head of the snake."

"I like your way of thinking. Yes, I think that with good planning, it has a good chance of success. Have you come up with a name?"

"No, sir. I first needed your permission to proceed. I will need you to contact the North Carolina SAC before I start digging into the files to find agents with the type of experience that we need."

"OK, I will call the North Carolina SAC. There is no reason to believe that he will not offer his full support. I will call the director and inform him of our plans, and I will make it crystal clear that he should not discuss this with the president."

"Yes, sir, good idea,"

"As you know, I am a student of the Civil War. Let's name the covert operation' Cincinnati.' This is in honor of Grant's horse."

"Yes, sir, Operation Cincinnati, similar to the Trojan horse story in Greek mythology."

"Yes, and with good planning, we will also be successful."

Chapter Fifty Three

Operation Cincinnati

Raleigh, NC, Nashville, TN

Tom drives back to the FBI safehouse and informs the combined team that a covert operation has been approved. "The name of the covert operation is 'Operation Cincinnati.' It is in honor of General Sheridan's horse. I also have the approval to have Claude, Rose, and Alex remain in the FBI secure area and provide expert advice. They will only be used if absolutely necessary. All others, including Jeff and Vinny, will need to return to the Alexandria office. Alex will retain one drone with the communications package. When the shooting starts, the WMA team can use their own comms. The Nashville SAC Kowalski has made it clear that this will be strictly an FBI mission."

The first item of business will be to select the individuals who will infiltrate, capture, or kill the leadership of the white nationalists. To decrease the temperature at the outside of the terrorists' camp, the FBI will reduce the guard staff to twelve agents. The agents will now dress in civilian clothes to reduce the signature of a military presence. The search warrant, which has been presented daily, will now be presented every three days. The combination of these factors should result in the protestors losing steam.

After one week, the crowd has only a handful of demonstrators from each side. Now the serious business of selecting the kill team starts. Tom travels to Raleigh, NC, and discusses the mission with the North Carolina SAC. The Tennessee SAC, Mr. Kowalski, has called the North Carolina SAC, Ronald Morgenstern. He tells Morgenstern that agent Tomas Kramer will be visiting his office. Kowalski gives Morgenstern a call and gives an overview of the request. Agent Kramer will provide the details.

Agent Kramer enters the North Carolina SAC's office, and after they exchange some pleasantries, the discussions turn serious. Tom explains the details of the siege and that the terrorists could make it a protracted one. He explains that the longer the siege lasts, the more the population is turning against them. Tom explains to Morgenstern that the Pulaski area of Tennessee was the birthplace of the KKK and that there are many KKK sympathizers in the area. Then he tells him the plan to infiltrate the terrorist camp and arrest or kill the leadership. The plan was developed when it became apparent that the FBI has a large number of former soldiers in Tennessee and North Carolina who have provided their service to the country as special forces soldiers or as FBI agents.

"Mr. Morgenstern," says Tom, "we are looking for agents who were with either Delta or the Seal teams. They have much experience in seeking and destroying the enemy. They have experience in working behind enemy lines. This is what we are looking for."

"Well, you certainly came to the right place. Seems like half of our agents have military backgrounds. I do not know how many have Delta or Seal experience, but that should not be hard to find out. I will put you in contact with our personnel department and authorize you to review the background of all our agents."

Morgenstern picks up the phone and calls the personnel department. "Agent Holyfield, this is your SAC calling. There will be Agent Thomas Kramer from the Tennessee office coming by your office. He will be reviewing all of the personnel files of our agents. He is looking for agents with military backgrounds."

"Yes, sir, I will have a terminal available for his use. All of our personnel files are computerized. They are on a closed network, not accessible from the outside. I will give him a one-day password, and he can review the files."

"Excellent. Come by my office and pick him up," says Morgenstern.

Yes, sir. I will be there in ten minutes."

"Agent Kramer," says Morgenstern, "you are all set. Agent Holyfield will come by my office and show you to the personnel department. After you select the agents for your team, let me know. Good luck!"

"Thank you, sir. After I have reviewed the files, I will have my team member help with the interviews. I will likely need two or three days to complete the select down."

"Of course. Should you need more time, tell Agent Holyfield, and he will contact me for approval."

Tom walks out of the office, goes outside, and calls Agent Singleton. "Brit, I got the OK to review the files. After I review and do a select down, I am requesting your help for the interviews. We need to interview at least twenty candidates to find the best ten."

"I agree. I will be there tomorrow."

Agent Holyfield comes out and greets Tom. "Agent Kramer, I am Agent Holyfield. Follow me, and I will show you your workspace. You can get started on reviewing the files. They are all in a searchable database so that you can quickly find what you are looking for."

Agent Holyfield has a cubicle arranged for Tom, who immediately starts the process of reviewing the qualifications of the candidates. First, he searches for either Delta or Seal team experience. Next, he examines the group for a minimum of ten years of total special forces and FBI experience. This produces a field of twenty-five candidates. Next, he starts reading their files. All have ten years or more of outstanding performance reviews. He is not surprised; if they did not have outstanding reviews, they probably would not have been hired by the FBI. The next step will be the most time-consuming. He needs to take detail notes. He creates a form using Excel program and creates cells with what he considers the most essential attributes: awards, time in Iraq or Afghanistan, special missions, etc. He continues working through midnight; he needs to complete the review of all candidates so that he can discuss them with Brit first thing in the morning.

At 8 A.M., he meets with Brit. They discuss the process. They decide to review the spreadsheet at the Raleigh FBI office. They rank the candidates in three categories: best, passable, and maybe. They make arrangements with the Raleigh FBI personal office to interview the twenty-five candidates. The personnel office comes back and tells them that only fifteen are available. For several reasons, from being on leave to high priority assignments to out of the country, ten are not available. They tell the personnel office to have the fifteen come in as soon as possible. Tom and Brit want to complete the interviews in two days. However, as often happens, the world does not march to your priorities. Only six are available in the next three days. The personnel office does not know when the other nine will be available. Since they have gone this far, they decided to interview the six candidates. Of the six, only four have a strong interest. The other two say that they like the idea of getting back to some action, but they like the new life of not being concerned with jihadists taking potshots at them.

One of the agents who has expressed an interest is a thirty-year-old former Marine. His background is with MARSOC, the Marines Special Operations Command. His name is Willard Sessions. Sessions decides to communicate with an agent he met at his training at Quantico. When he was at the school in Quantico, he met an agent by the name of Rock Irwin. The two hit it off and became close friends. They were both recent FBI recruits, and when they were in the Marines and Army, they were hellraisers. At the Quantico FBI Academy, they roomed together, and on weekends, they rented two rooms, at a cheap hotel on Route 1 in Stafford, Virginia, and went bar hopping and picked up women. At the end of their three months at Quantico, they graduated in the middle of their class.

After Willard has had a few beers, he decides to communicate with Rock using a secure server. The server is at FBI headquarters in Quantico, and it is available for agents to have secure communications.

Willard decides that this sure as hell is top-secret stuff, so he sends Rock an e-mail. The e-mail reads: "Rock, this is Willard aka the Wizard. We have some agents from the Nashville office recruiting agents from the Raleigh office. Either you guys do not know shit, or they are trying to keep the mission undercover. Do you know anything about what is going on?

Rock replies with a short message: "Sorry, I don't know. If I find something, I will let you know."

Tom and Brit interview the six candidates and come up with a dry hole. They are going to need to use their personnel from the Nashville office.

Brit says, "We could always eat crow and use the NGA."

"No way in hell," replies Tom. "My SAC told me in no uncertain terms that this would be an FBI operation."

"OK, then we use members of your SWAT team."

"I do have some outstanding personnel. They may not all have special operations experience, but they have the drive and ambition."

Brit hears the "not all," and he asks, "You said NOT all have special operations experience. How many, when, and how much?"

"My best man would be Sam Sneed."

"You mean like the golfer?"

"Almost. The golfer is Snead with an a; my Sam is Sneed with a double e."

"Who else you got?"

Tom says, "A couple of men pushing forty but in excellent shape. They would make Jack LaLanne envious. They work out two hours a day and run every marathon on the East Coast, and I would like to be the fourth man. I am in good shape, and they respect my command. Also, I am an expert marksman and keep up with my martial arts training."

"If you allowed me, I would like to join the team."

"OK, but only as a planner. I need to staff the covert teams with Nashville agents."

"That's fine. However, I am asking for one thing."

"As long as it makes sense, sure, why not?"

"I request that we include Rose, Alex, and Claude in the planning phase."

Tom thinks for a full minute and says, "Makes sense, but we keep their involvement to 'subject matter expert advice only.' Do not tell my SAC that they are involved in the planning."

"Trust me, you will not regret this. Operation Cincinnati has added some expertise," says Brit.

Rock Irwin Communicates with Wolf

After Rock receives the encrypted e-mail from Willard, he meets with Wolf at a secluded fishing lodge on the Cumberland River. Still unknown to the

FBI team are the tunnels that connect the rooms under the KKK buildings. The analysis performed by the WMA, suggesting the underground chambers is well known. However, the existence of the tunnels has not been confirmed by the WMA nor the FBI teams. Wolf uses one of two emergency tunnels that exit miles from the main camp. The exit is near the southern cliffs of the camp property. After exiting from the camp, he does not find any problem moving throughout Tennessee. The state has thousands of sympathizers to the rebel cause. The election of President Trout has resulted in an explosion of these sympathizers coming out of hiding. They are now proud to say that they are white nationalists and support the KKK.

Rock tells Wolf about the messages from Willard. The FBI is assembling a special operations team to infiltrate the camp. Wolf correctly deduces that the FBI has taken total command and that they do not wish to use Rose and her team. In a way, it is good, and in a way, it is bad. It's good because he can outsmart the FBI team, and it's bad because he is going have to wait to meet up with Rose. Wolf has stopped using the term "bitch" when he refers to Rose. Even though they are mortal enemies, he has gained much respect for her abilities, both physical and mental. If only Gretchen were like her; then they could rule the underworld and become as strong as the Italian Mafia.

Now that Wolf knows that the FBI is assembling a kill team to infiltrate and try and assassinate the top leadership of the KKK organization, he predicts that the attempted assassination and attack will occur simultaneously. This is standard special forces tactics. He will prepare for the battle and give the FBI a major defeat. First, he will slowly move his soldiers to the homes of sympathizers throughout the South. He calculates that he has two to three weeks before the FBI assembles a force strong enough to overtake the camp.

Wolf gathers his command staff in the war room. "Colonel Sondermann, we initiated a controlled retreat last week. Beginning tonight, we will accelerate the withdrawal of our Klansmen to the homes of white nationalist sympathizers."

Colonel Sondermann turns to Captain Albertson and orders him to begin preparing the plan to evacuate his company to the homes of Southern sympathizers. "Company A will use the southern tunnel. It will be vital that we know where each soldier will be hidden. At a later point in time, they will be recalled." The colonel now turns to Captain Montgomery and orders him to begin the process of evacuating Company B. "Company B will start the process immediately after Company A evacuates. Company B will use the northern tunnel. This orderly evacuation should be completed within seven days."

Major Jacobson now stands and barks out an order, "Soldiers of the Confederacy, before your departure, be sure and place the mannequin that resembles you at your post in the trenches."

Captains Albertson and Montgomery reply, "Yes, sir, we will be sure and place the mannequins as we leave."

Colonel Sondermann now turns to Captain Baker. "Captain, as the commander of Company C, the 'Wilhelm Strassman' Company, you have been given the honor of defending our country from the invaders. You and your soldiers will fight to the death. As your leaders, Colonel Schneider, Miss Gretchen, Major Jacobson, and I will remain with you to defend our country. No better honor can be bestowed upon us than to die for our country."

"Sir," replies Captain Baker, "should we perform the cross-burning every night so that it will appear that all three companies are in our camp?"

"Yes," says Wolf, "good point. Continue the cross burning using your men from Company C."

Wolf's plan is beginning to unfold. Within a week, the camp will have only a skeleton crew. All of Company C will be sacrificed. The plan will be that Colonel Sondermann, Major Jacobson, Gretchen, and he will escape through either the north or south tunnels depending on the flow of the battle. The leadership must survive to make America great again with the beliefs of the Confederate States of America.

Chapter Fifty-Four

Operation Cincinnati Plan of Attack

FBI Safe House, Tennessee

Tom, Brit, Rose, and Alex meet at the FBI safe house to discuss the plan.

Tom says, "The kill team will consist of two four man teams and two comms technicians. Based on intel collected, the targets living quarters have been identified as these two buildings." Tom uses a laser pointer to identify the living quarters.

Rose then says, "How old is this intel?"

"The photo is the latest from the Geospatial Intel Satellite Service."

"No, that's not what I meant. How do we know that these are the living quarters?"

Tom sounds a little irritated as he says, "As far as I know, they came from you and Alex. Didn't you infiltrate the home and download the data from their computers?"

Brit steps in and says, "She's right. The fact that they lived there three weeks ago is no guarantee that they are still living there. I can almost guarantee that they are not living there."

Rose and Alex remain silent, hoping that Tom can figure out what the next move should be.

Tom finally says, "Looks like we need updated intel. How do you recommend that we obtain the latest?"

"The only way is to have eyes on the target," says Alex. "Normally, we would deploy our surveillance drone, but with the eagle patrol, that is no longer possible. The only way is to infiltrate to a location where you can survey the buildings. This may take days before you know where the targets live."

Rose interjects. "Before we use your four-man teams to infiltrate the camp, we should try using our watchtowers."

Since the beginning of the siege, the FBI has moved the outer perimeter of the camp to within miles of the KKK buildings. Several watchtowers similar to the towers that were built by the fire service have been erected to provide twenty-four-hour surveillance of the property. High-powered scopes have been installed at each watchtower to allow for the surveillance of movement inside the camp. Tom assigns four two-man teams to conduct twenty-four by seven surveillance of the terrorist camp. From the info collected, the FBI now knows the pattern of life for the terrorists' leadership.

Additionally, the FBI assigns two Black Hawk helicopters to Operation Cincinnati. These helicopters are being flown daily to provide video surveillance of the white nationalist's camp. The helicopters have remained five miles from the KKK camp perimeter. The FBI is concerned about the KKK surface-to-air missiles.

Inside the Camp

Wolf and his staff are not stupid. They are aware that they are being watched. They purposely hold all staff meetings in a building that can be observed. For any movement that they wish not to be observed, they use the underground tunnels. As anticipated, Wolf, Gretchen, and their dog have moved to a more secure building. Unknown to the FBI, the building has an underground tunnel that connects to all the other buildings. The tunnels also connect to the two escape locations at the extreme south and north ends of the camp.

The eagle patrols continue. For reasons unknown to the FBI, the eagles do not attack the KKK drones. The drones have been providing video surveillance of the FBI positions, personnel, and weapons.

FBI Camp

The FBI has moved their command post to a fifty-three-foot trailer. The trailer is fully equipped with communications, including a satellite link to Nashville and Washington headquarters. Daily video conferences are provided to both. Initially, the FBI Nashville SAC and the FBI director participated in the video teleconferences. However, since there has been no change in status, both the SAC and the director have not been present for three weeks. The WMA team has also taken a back seat. They are not allowed to participate in the video teleconferences; however, Brit did arrange for them to have a portable trailer to use as their informal command post. After, and sometimes before, the daily FBI briefing, both Tom and Brit confer with the WMA team. Brit informs the WMA team that the attack will occur sometime in the next seven days. A small team of HRT agents will attack the northern perimeter. They are expecting heavy resistance. After the initial attack, the FBI team will fall back and take a defensive position. As the northern battle is being fought, the FBI will move agents toward the front gate and simulate a frontal attack. Then two FBI insertion teams will infiltrate through the southern perimeter. The two teams of four men each will covertly move to the two buildings where the KKK high command is located. They will attempt to capture or kill Wolf, Gretchen, Colonel Sondermann, and Major Jacobson. When the terrorists' leaders are eliminated, the FBI will ask for the surrender of the remaining 110 Klansmen. If the plan is executed correctly, the FBI has predicted less than six people will be killed, all terrorists. On paper, the plan looks solid.

Inside the Terrorist Camp

Wolf and his staff have seen the movement of FBI agents. The surveillance drones have provided valuable intel. However, the FBI has allowed the drones to fly freely throughout the last thirty days. This can only be interpreted one way: the FBI wants us to know what they are doing. Primarily, the FBI wants it to be understood that they are a superior force. The terrorists have been monitoring the FBI comms. All comms are encrypted, but the amount of traffic is essential. Wolf, Colonel Sondermann, and Major Jacobson are all military veterans. They have learned all of their intelligence actions through US military training. They have as good, if not a better understanding of the importance of intelligence and communications. Whoever has the best intel and controls the communications airwaves will win the battle. Wolf is fully aware that the FBI has the newest in triband radios. These radios work in the VHF, UHF, and 800 MHz bands. When the battle starts, the terrorists will jam all three bands. The terrorists also have radios. These radios operate in the VHF band. Wolf fully expects that this frequency will be jammed. In preparation for the inevitable battle with the FBI, Wolf ordered fifty Family Radio Service radios from the internet. These radios were delivered to the home of a white nationalist sympathizer in the Pulaski area. Wolf had his technical team modify the radio for the ability to transmit at a higher power level. He also ordered from the internet repeaters for the Family Radio Service band. Wolf knows that it is illegal to transmit at this higher power level. He laughs as he thinks, *What the fuck they gonna do, call the FCC and arrest us?*

Wolf does not like to sit back and wait for the enemy (FBI) to take the initiative. He likes to be in control. Like the FBI, he has a plan, but it is different from the FBI's. He wishes that this condition was perpetual. He likes the excitement of a live chess game. In this game, the loser dies. He thinks of the day in Iraq, him against the ISIS sniper; the man with the best and smartest plan always won. This will be no different.

Wolf's plan will be three-pronged. He has ordered that the three KKK video drones be shot down. First, he will deliberately shoot down two of the three drones. He wants the news trucks to see that two of the camp drones have been shot down by the FBI. Within minutes of his drones being shot down, he will order that the FBI's two observation towers be attacked using RPGs. This will make it appear as though the KKK camp's attack is proportional to them losing their surveillance, and that the camp had no choice but to respond in kind.

Next, the third KKK drone will be shot down. Next, he has ordered that the RPG teams fire rocket at the two FBI guard shacks that were erected the first week of the siege. This will be in response to his third drone being shot down.

The Klansmen have been instructed to NOT shoot any of the news trucks or any civilian shelters. This should not be a problem since the FBI has installed barricades one hundred meters from the FBI portable guard shacks. The news reporters and the crowd, which has been standing watch at the front gate, will see that the white nationalist drones were shot down by the FBI. The news will be: "Terrorists retaliate after their unarmed drones were shot down!"

The third KKK attack will be the *crème de la crème*. Wolf knows that the FBI has been flying helicopters for video surveillance. He will wait until one of the helicopters is above the command trailer and have his surface-to-air missile team fire a missile at the helicopter. This action will be seen by the news trucks as a response to all KKK drones being shot down by the FBI.

The sequence of the events is important to make it appear as though the white nationalists are simply reacting to the actions of the FBI.

Chapter Fifty-Five

The Attack Begins

White Nationalist Camp

Wolf, the leader of the White Nationalists, needs all his troops in place at the beginning of the attack. The White Nationalists want to make it appear that the FBI fired the first shot while the camp defended itself. Now, the entire command staff of the White Nationalists is in the war room, and they establish communications with the field units using the Family Radio Service frequencies.

The three Klansmen each control a video-surveillance drone. Meanwhile, two-person teams are ready with rocket-propelled grenades (RPGs) to attack the FBI's perimeter observation towers and guard sheds on the front gates. Three other White Nationalists are snipers, ready to shoot down the drones. The three snipers are prepared to shoot down their own drones pretending that it was the FBI that did it?

The radio communications come alive in the KKK war room. "Sir, we have an FBI Black Hawk helicopter approaching from the south. I estimate that the copter will be directly over the FBI in eight minutes."

The KKK CP responds, "Advise when the copter is directly over the FBI CP."

Five minutes later, the central-observation team transmits, "Copter will be over the FBI CP in two minutes."

KKK CP tells the terrorist-drone operators, "Commence drone flights."

The three-drone operators respond, "Drones are in flight. Expected times to targets one minute."

KKK command post to snipers: "Sniper teams one and two, acquire your designated drone and fire on my command."

Wolf is outside on the observation deck with binoculars listens to the commands from his CP. He stands tall, similar to Robert E. Lee on his horse, Traveler, watching over the landscape of the battle that is to begin

As the terrorists' drones fly over the front gate guard sheds and directly over the news trucks, and the three terrorist snipers have the drones in their crosshairs.

Wolf gives the command: "Fire, sniper teams one and two."

The two drones are easy targets. The drone operators purposely hover the drones at 200- feet above the targets. The two drones explode in mid-air; debris plummets to the ground. Now, all hell breaks loose!

The news reporters direct their portable cameras at the falling debris. By chance, the Fox News camera crew filmed the entire sequence of the flight of a destroyed drone.

Greg Jensen, of the Fox News Nashville affiliate, announces that the "FBI shot down two of the White Nationalist's unarmed drones! Additional activities just occurred at the White Nationalist Camp. These drones were flying daily for the last three weeks, with no apparent harm. The nationalists' drones were likely providing video images of the FBI's positions. We believe that the FBI attack is imminent."

Tom and Brit are in the FBI command post van, watching the surveillance video downloaded from the FBI helicopter, which provided surveillance of the terrorist camp since the siege began.

Tom keys his radio. "Who the hell ordered the shootdown of the two drones?"

The radio channel is silent. Tom keys the radio again. "Who shot down the drones?"

After thirty seconds, one agent on one of the watchtowers says, "Sir, it appears that someone from within the terrorist camp, fired the shots."

Brit pulls down his radio and tells Tom, "Order the copter down to the home base. The recording from the 360-degree camera on the nose of the copter will tell us from where the shots came. We need this info ASAP, and then we need to have a news conference and tell the American public that the shots came from the terrorists."

Tom turns the radio knob to the air channel: "Copter number one, return to home base ASAP."

"Ten-four," replies the copter pilot. "Returning to home base."

As the copter is coming down, the third sniper fires at the third KKK drone. As with the other two drones, thousands of pieces of debris come raining down on the crowd.

One of the spectators wearing a confederate cap yells, "The White nationalist have now lost all of their video surveillance! Now all bets are off—-no telling what the good people in the camp will do now!"

As the debris from the third drone is coming down, the FBI Black Hawk helicopter makes a sharp U-turn, and people on the ground see two flashes. The helicopter's warming lights start blinking, and a pre-recorded voice comes over the intercom system: "Incoming missiles detected, defensive measures will start immediately." Unlike jet planes, helicopters fly at much lower altitudes. The reaction time is much shorter; thus, defensive measures start automatically. As the two missiles approach the helicopter, the helicopter releases flares and strips of aluminum. The two missiles alter their flight path and explode in close vicinity to the aluminum strips. Within seconds of the firing of the first two missiles, someone fires two additional missiles from the ground. Again, the flares and aluminum strips redirect the missiles to the decoys.

The helicopter pilot says, "I'm out of flares; my aluminum bucket is empty. I'm taking evasive actions to prevent a direct hit to my Black Hawk!"

In real-time, national television shows the entire sequence of the firing of the missiles and the defensive measures the helicopter pilot takes. The crowd., that gathered outside the front gate of the camp is divided like the cheering sections of two opposing teams. As the helicopter successfully avoids its destruction, the majority of the crowd cheers, and applauds. They sound like one big rumble of "Give them hell!" and "ATTA boy!" Both women and men gasp-they cannot believe what they see.

Fifteen-seconds later, someone fires the fifth and sixth missiles. There are no flares or aluminum strips. The helicopter pilot appears to be an expert, as the copter flies down at almost ninety degrees and simultaneously makes a sharp left turn. The pilot tries to hide below the tree line, flying his helicopter through the forest like a cruise missile using a flight algorithm based on software showing nap of-the-earth. The missile with a heat-seeking warhead flies to more than 2,000-feet. The missile snakes around and starts flying toward the helicopter. The fifth missile flies to within the kill radius of the helicopter and explodes, damaging the flight controls. The sixth missile now approaches the helicopter. The helicopter is flying low, which limits the evasive tactics it can perform. The pilot tries to make a right turn; however, the controls do not respond. Thus, the sixth missile explodes within the kill radius of the helicopter. The Black Hawk comes down in a ball of flames!

The quarter of the crowd that has not been cheering the helicopter for evading the missiles now starts yelling and cheering, "Serves them right! Fucking FBI, they are trying to take down the president!"

Tom, Brit, and the entire FBI team in the command post witnessed the shooting down of the helicopter. They decide that Operation Cincinnati must start immediately.

Tom keys the special radio channel. "Begin Operation Cincinnati immediately."

Team One: "Ten-four. Commencing operation now."

Team Two: "Ten-four. Commencing operation now."

Tom and Brit had been planning to lead the covert teams; however, due to the drones and the copter being shot down, the plans have changed.

Brit says, "We had a saying in special operations: 'Plan A is only as good as the first encounter with the enemy.' That's why we always have a Plan B and Plan C."

"Well," says Tom, "we are on Plan B. Let's hope that there is no need to go to Plan C."

Greg Jenson from Fox News is now the lead reporter on the news channels. Fox News has been following the events in Tennessee since the rescue of the women being held as sex slaves. The network has five news trucks, and they have been parked around the perimeter of the camp. They want to ensure that all actions by the FBI are recorded and reported to the American public.

Greg Jensen is now hyperventilating as a result of the helicopter being shot down. He says, his voice rising two octaves. "Ladies and gentlemen, what we are witnessing is simply unbelievable. The FBI shot down the ability of the nationalists to conduct video surveillance, and the nationalists simply responded proportionally. They shot down the FBI video surveillance."

The anchor from Washington asks, "Greg, Greg, can you describe the scene where you are?"

"Yes, it is a madhouse, absolute pandemonium, with reporters, armed citizen militias, families with children, kids throwing rocks, motorcycle gangs, and people with signs saying 'The End is Near' and 'John 3:16.' There are Confederate and Nazi flags and a few American flags. Many are wearing red baseball caps. There is absolutely no crowd control. Along a fence, men, women, and children are crouching, shuffling their feet, and trying to get to safety. Families are lying flat on the sidewalk, covering their faces and sobbing. Skinheads in Nazi uniforms are kicking and shoving the reporters from MSNBC. They are yelling, 'You will never replace us.'"

In front of the guard shacks there a field which has been used by the demonstrators, both pro and con White Nationalists. Groups of black-shirted Nazi's have placed a home-made pressure cooker bomb hidden in the bushes. The bomb goes off with a blinding flash, which is followed by a loud bang that sounds like a thunderclap. Fortunately, the blast occurs in a field that was vacated by the frenzied crowd. The only harm is ringing ears and disorientation. The few deputy sheriffs for crowd control also run off when the blast occurs. As the mayhem is raging, Jensen and his camera operator have taken refuge in the news truck. After the dust settles, Jensen comes out of the truck and stops a young man and asks, "Do you think that the downing of the helicopter was the proper response?"

The young man responds, "Cool, man, Cool. I have not seen fistfights and fireworks like these since Charlottesville."

Jensen then tells the anchor in Washington that they need to retreat back inside of the news truck. Things have gotten out of hand, and they are not safe.

Jensen tells the Washington anchor, "Roy, I will continue to report using the cameras installed at the top of the truck." Five minutes later, skinheads wearing Nazi shirts are on top of the truck and destroying the camera and satellite dish.

Jensen can hear the stomping of boots on the roof. He reports, "Hooligans are now on the roof of the truck. I do not know how much longer—" The feed cuts out, and there is nothing but white noise.

Two hours later, the news truck door has been smashed in, all of the electronic equipment ripped out, and Jensen and his cameraman are dead on the street. They both have been clubbed to death.

Inside the KKK Camp

Wolf and the command staff are monitoring all of the major networks from inside the war room. Seventy-two-inch flat-screen displays are showing CNN, MSNBC, and Fox News plus the local Nashville NBC, CBS, and Fox news affiliates. The downing of the drones and the helicopter have the predicted effect. The best that Wolf can tell is that the FBI has been caught completely flat-footed. They were not prepared for the terrorists to take the initiative. A well-known tactic of the FBI is to surround the property and wait for the bad guys out. Usually, this tactic works, but these bad guys are not typical; the white nationalists have a cause, and they are willing to die for it.

Wolf now expects the FBI to send in their kill teams. He is well aware that at least two teams of four to six agents will try to infiltrate the camp and attempt an assassination. After his informant, Rock Irwin told him about the hit teams, Wolf found three members of the Klan that resembled Sondermann, Jacobson and himself. The three doubles wear uniforms with the proper medals, boots, and hats to resemble the three. Wolf makes sure that they are viewed entering and exiting the war room. Wolf will issue one more command, and then he and his two top commanders will exit the war room through the tunnels and execute the battle from a different location.

Wolf will issue the command to have the RPG teams fire the rockets at the guard shacks. This will bring the battle as close as possible to the news trucks and demonstrator crowds, which are now growing as a result of the newscasts. The predicted response from the FBI will be to use the fifty-plus agents and National Guardsmen to attack. He is aware that the attack will come from the northern flank. It is designed as a diversion to allow the FBI "kill teams" to penetrate and assassinate him and his top commanders. Immediately after the FBI attack on the northern flank starts, Wolf will issue a command to jam all of the FBI frequencies. This will leave the FBI without eyes and ears. Wolf knows that this particular battle will eventually be won by the FBI; he simply does not have their manpower and the resources. However, the tactic is to save himself, his top leaders, and two-thirds of his army. He will resurrect his KKK organization in Idaho or Montana, his original roots.

Wolf and his command staff are in the war room, reviewing the downing of the helicopter. All of the top national networks are carrying the ongoing battle on live TV.

Wolf to Colonel Sondermann, "Are the troops on the ground ready to fire on the observations towers."

"Yes, sir, ready on your command

"Colonel Sondermann," says Wolf, "are the troops on the watchtowers ready to fire on the guard shacks?"

"Yes, sir. RPGs are loaded and will fire on your command."

Wolf reviews all of the news feeds and decides that now is the time to blow up the FBI observation towers and guard shacks. "Order the troops to fire the RPGs. Have the two observation towers hit first, quickly followed by the southern shack, and then the northern shack one minute later."

"Yes, sir. Ordering the teams to fire now."

The captain of Company C receives the command to fire. He orders, "Fire at will!"

Julia Reynolds is the new Fox News on-scene reporter. Fox News has contracted with two off duty policemen as security guards. They are carrying Glock .45 handguns and M-16 automatic rifles. Julia is out walking with her guard detail and her mobile camera operator. She hears the SWOOSH of the rocket-propelled missile. She turns to her left, in the direction of the noise, and sees a rocket and the smoke trail. KA-BOOM—the rocket hits one of the FBI guard shack. The camera operator now turns the camera to the smoldering shack.

Julia is preparing to give a live broadcast of the blown-up shack. She then hears the distinct sound of a second missile: SWOOSH. Within seconds, she hears KA-BOOM. The second guard shack has been hit. As Julia is starting her live broadcast, the FBI ground forces surrounding the front gate open fire on the KKK watchtower RPG teams. Thousands of rounds are hitting the two KKK watchtowers. The metal shields being used for protection are pulverized. The entire tower platform is riddled with bullets. Klansmen are seen falling from the watchtowers, their bodies are like rag dolls torn into pieces.

Quickly national guardsmen exit their portable tents and push the crowd control mobile fence links to one mile from the front gate. The combination of the attack on the guard shacks, the destruction of the RPG concealments, and the national guardsmen establishing a new demonstrator line has caused pandemonium, confusion, hysteria, and total chaos.

In the distance, the sound of the two FBI observation towers being hit is heard, "KA-BOOM, KA-BOOM." This only added to the total chaos.

The scene has become a modern-day Battle of Manassas. The fifty-plus news trucks, demonstrators, FBI agents, and National Guardsmen, are now mixed in a cornucopia of humans and vehicles. The re-establishment of the new demonstration line has the demonstrators fighting amongst themselves. The demonstrators are now shifting to favor the white nationalists, half are now yelling insults at the CNN and MSNBC trucks, and the other half are shouting insults at the Fox News trucks. The National Guardsmen are trying to keep the two factions from killing each other.

Julia is in the news truck as it is moving to the new location. The guards remain outside as sentinels. She says, "Ladies and gentlemen, the battle in the foothills of Tennessee has taken on a new dimension. The FBI guard shacks were destroyed by rocket-propelled missiles. The FBI and the National Guardsmen responded with a barrage of automatic small-arms fire. This small-arms fire obliterated the terrorists' watchtowers. I was within two hundred meters of the firefight, and I could see the FBI guards being blown to bits. I also witnessed the terrorists' bodies falling from their watchtowers and riddled with bullets.

Julia now says something unexpected: "Ladies and gentlemen, I can no longer call these white nationalists' nice people.' We need to call them what they are—terrorists. They are the threat from within. If we do not stop these terrorists, this country will become Germany in the 1930s."

White Nationalist War Room

Wolf is delighted with the progress of the battle. He is equally pleased with the news coverage. The downing of the drones has had an even more significant effect than he expected. He now needs to turn his attention to the kill teams that have infiltrated the camp. The battle started in the late afternoon. It is now getting dark. He knows the tactics of special forces. The kill teams will wait until early the next morning and strike. Wolf asks his senior officer, Colonel Sondermann, "Are we ready to jam all FBI frequencies?"

"Yes, sir. The jammers are on and ready to transmit."

"Start with the VHF, UHF, and 800 MHz frequency ranges."

"Yes, sir. On your command."

"Commence jamming."

The colonel keys the radio. "Captain, start jamming the FBI frequencies."

"Yes, sir, started jamming the VHF, then UHF, and then the 800 MHz bands."

Wolf looks at the spectrum analyzer and sees that all FBI bands are jammed.

He is prepared for a nighttime infiltration, and he has positioned several observation scouts in the southern sector, the most likely area of attack. The scouts have been issued thermal blankets to cover their heat signatures.

FBI Command Van

Tom and Brit have communications with all FBI units involved in the battle plan. The communications are being provided by the WMA special radios using the 1-2 GHz L-band. Vinny and Matt have installed a repeater on a high mountain overlooking the KKK encampment.

Tom communicates with Agent Justin Stenson. Stenson is the team leader of the fifteen-man northern attack team. "Agent Stenson begin your attack now. Engage the enemy for two hours, stand your ground, and pull back to disengage. Follow your plan, as discussed in the pre-planning. This is a diversion. After tomorrow, your team will join the main attack on the midsection."

Agent Stenson replies, "Beginning attack now."

The fifteen-man team encounters strong resistance, including small-arms fire and RPGs, and only advances five hundred meters. The team takes cover behind a copse of trees. They are flat on their stomach when they encounter bullets from a .50-caliber machine gun. The heavy fire strips the team of their cover.

Stenson pulls out his handheld FBI radio. "Command post, encountering heavy machine gunfire. Request assistance." The radio has nothing but static. He gets no response. Stenson again keys his radio. "CP, this is Alpha Team One. Do you copy?" Again, he keys his radio. "CP, do you copy?" Finally, he concludes that the radio band is being jammed. He follows protocol and tries the UHF and the 800 MHz radio bands: again, nothing but static. He now needs to follow his orders. He says, "Damn, they told me this might happen. I left the L-band radio in the SWAT team van!" His orders are to advance on the northern flank and engage the enemy. The northern attack is a diversion to allow the infiltration teams the ability to penetrate the enemy defenses and capture or kill the terrorists' high command.

Stenson and his men find a natural trench used by rainwater running down from a hill. The fifteen-man team hunkers down. Stenson orders that the team continues firing at the enemy lines to simulate an attack. Every fifteen minutes, he tries communicating with the CP. After continuously trying for two hours, he pulls back and tries his radio once every hour. He thinks about going back to the SWAT team van and retrieving the L-band radio. However, he would need to expose himself, and he quickly discards the option. After three hours in the trench, it is evident that the enemy will hold a defensive position. He believes that the mission has been accomplished. He hopes that the attack by his team has allowed the insertion of the infiltration teams.

Infiltration Teams

At 4 P.M., two four-man teams are ready to infiltrate the terrorist camp. The teams are called Tiger Team One and Tiger Team Two. The leader of Tiger Team One is Agent Marco Moretti. The leader of Tiger Team Two is Agent Kale Kahale. Agent Moretti is a fourth-generation Italian American. His great-grandparents immigrated to the US through Ellis Island in the 1920s. Agent Kahale is a Hawaiian. He can trace his ancestry for hundreds of years back to the original natives from Asia that settled the Hawaiian Islands. Both started their careers with local law enforcement. After five years in law enforcement, they applied for the FBI and were accepted. Due to their physical and athletic abilities, their FBI superiors recommended that they apply for the elite HRT. They underwent physical and psychological testing. Both passed with grades in the ninety-fifth percentile. Macro and Kale both attended the Special Operations School in Panama, and they completed yearly training at the HRT Quantico School.

Tiger Team One has been tasked with capturing or killing Adolf Wolfgang Schneider and Gretchen Hannah Miller. Tiger Team Two has been assigned to kill or capture Lt. Colonel Klaus Sondermann and Major Roger Jacobson. To maximize the chances of success, the two teams will follow different infiltration routes. Tiger Team One will enter from the west, and Tiger Team Two will enter from the east. Both teams are dressed in camouflage. Both teams have both the tri-band and L-band radios. However, the teams will not use the long-range radio frequencies; they will maintain radio silence. The team members do, however, communicate with each other using a "talk around" frequency. The talk-around frequency is used by radios for direct connection. The jamming signals would need to be close to the radios to be effective. Thus, the members of the Tiger teams have communications amongst themselves but not to the outside world.

All eight of the team members are experts in small arms and long rifles. Both teams have a demolition expert. The demolition experts have Semtex-10, detonators, and fuses. The teams will use the cover of darkness to make the final approach to the suspected buildings.

At 12 mid-night Team One is two hundred meters from the building where Wolf and Gretchen are living. The team is under heavy camouflage and assumes the prone position, lying in tall grass. They use their high-powered binoculars to view the entry to the building. The team also has an infrared monocle to be used for nighttime surveillance.

Tiger Team Two has also penetrated the camp. They are three hundred meters from the building that has been identified as the officers' quarters. Kale and his team are hidden behind some bushes and large tree trunks. They also have high-powered binoculars and an infrared monocle. At 12:30 A.M., they see the person they think is Major Jacobson walking into the building. At 12:45 A.M., Colonel Sondermann walks in.

The radios that Teams One and Two are carrying can communicate in direct line of sight. From the planning phase, it was considered that both teams would arrive at the target buildings sometime between 10 and 12 P.M. The target buildings are within two hundred meters of each other; thus, the two teams can now communicate.

Marco keys channels three and whispers, "Kale, do you copy?"

"Roger. Copy."

"We will coordinate our attacks, 3:15 A.M."

"Roger."

Marco transmits to all eight members: "Set your watches at 1:30 A.M., on my mark."

At five seconds before 1:30 A.M., Marco gives the countdown: "Five, four, three, two, one, mark."

All eight members are now in sync. Now it is a waiting game. They want to make sure that the targets are asleep.

White Nationalist War Room

From the time that the two FBI Tiger Teams arrived at the perimeter of the terrorists' camp, Wolf and the command staff have been tracking the two teams. Wolf has installed observation teams in the predicted routes. They built hunting platforms in trees and camouflaged the walls. The terrorists covered themselves with thermal blankets. The entire walk through the woods was observed by the Klansmen. The terrorists plan is to allow the FBI agents to enter the buildings. Both buildings have been wired with explosives. The fuse and detonator are remotely controlled by a garage door opener.

Infiltration Teams

The teams are now outside the two target buildings. At 3:00 A.M., the two teams communicate via their radios.

Marco says, "Tiger Team One ready. Infiltrate at 3:15."

"Tiger Team Two ready. Will start infiltration at 3:15," says Kale.

Both teams have their rules of engagement. Teams will try and apprehend the subject tangos. Teams have dart guns to immobilize them. The tangos will be carried out firefighter style. Second, if the tangos resist, deadly force is authorized. Bodies are to be extracted firefighter style. Third, should option one and two not be possible, they are to use the Semtex-10 to blow up the building with tangos inside. It is important that video be taken of all actions. All agents have a Go-Pro camera attached to their helmets. They must make sure that all cameras are rolling when building infiltration commences.

At 3:15, both teams approach the target buildings. Tiger Team One reaches the outer wall of the building. They wait for Tiger Team Two to reach the outer wall of their target building. Both teams are at the entry doors. Marco counts down, "Five, four, three, two, one—go!" Team members three and four use a battering ram to break down the door. The door falls back and makes a loud bang. They quickly throw in a flash-bang and wait outside the door for the smoke to clear. As they are getting ready to enter, a loud explosion occurs in the building—KA-BOOM. The blast is so strong that Marco and the three agents are thrown back twenty feet. As they are lying on the ground, a second blast occurs, totally destroying the building.

At the second building, Kale and his team selected the wrong door. The building is long and horizontal. The front and back doors are similar. They have chosen the back door. The back entrance has a reinforcement bar across it. Usually, two quick hits with the battering ram will break down the door. The door's lock gives way with the first hit, however, the reinforcing bar is holding. As they try to break down the door, they hear the loud KA-BOOM from the primary building. All radios are crackling, "RETREAT, RETREAT, it is an ambush!" The fourth member of the Kale team quickly inserts a fuse and detonator into five pounds of plastic explosives and throws the Semtex-10 through the opening in the door. They all run as fast as possible to get away from the coming explosion. They are thirty feet away when a loud explosion occurs. The building is completely demolished. The explosion is so strong that it is evident that secondary explosions occurred. The building was wired as a trap. All four agents have their ears ringing, and they start hearing small-arms fire. They quickly fall into an orderly retreat pattern.

Marco and the three agents on his team are having similar problems. All four are on the ground from the building explosion. Team members three and four bore the brunt of the blast. They were standing at the doorway with little to no protection. Mainly, they are disoriented, and their ears are ringing. Marco quickly accesses the situation and begins an orderly retreat.

Both teams are fortunate that the middle sector is thinly populated with Klansmen. They are all in the northern sector. Agent Stenson and fifteen agents are conducting the diversionary northern attack. The main objective, to capture or kill the terrorist high command, has not been successful. As Marco is retreating, he knows that the terrorists had prior knowledge of the attackers. He does not know how they obtained the intel, but the mole needs to be found!

The members of two Tiger teams make it back to the ground held by the FBI. Four of the eight need medical attention. They are rushed to the hospital and appear not to have life-threatening injuries. Marco, Kale, and two members of the team now have a debriefing with Tom and Brit. They go over the entire mission. They explain every detail, trying to find where they may have been detected. Nothing is out of the ordinary. They conclude that the terrorists must have had all their buildings wired with explosives. The terrorists know that it is only a question of time before they are overrun. The buildings are wired with IEDs to kill as many agents as possible.

Wolf and the Command Staff

Wolf is furious. "We had the assholes dead in our grasp, and we let them get away. Goddamn idiots, all of you. I can do the best planning, practice, and preparation, but if the execution is fucked up—we get shit! Who in the hell detonated the explosives prematurely?" No one answers. "Who detonated the explosives prematurely?" Again, no answer.

Finally, Captain Baker steps forward. "Sir, it was one of my men; I take full responsibility for the mistake."

"Captain, you are at this moment relieved of your duties. You are now Private Baker."

Wolf quickly looks at his troops and eyes a soldier by the name of Rodney Gibbenhaven. Rodney who was one of the survivors from the Chicken House is now dressed in a confederate uniform. His forty-pound beer belly is hidden with his confederate jacket. He has shaved and cut his hair to a suitable length. His "largeness" impresses Wolf. Wolf points at Rodney and says, "You come forward. What is your name?"

"Rodney Gibbenhaven Sir."

"OK, Rodney ah, ah, whatever your last name is, you are now the captain of Charlie Company!"

"Sir, the last name is Gibbenhaven, sir, Captain Rodney Gibbenhaven."

"Captain eh, eh, Rodney, come forward."

"Yes, sir."

"Private Baker, take those bars off your shoulders and pin Rodney."

"Yes, sir."

"Dismissed."

All troops go back to their assigned posts. Captain Gibbenhaven is lost and does not know what to do.

Major Jacobson comes forward and says, "Follow me."

Every person in that room knows that Rodney was the fuckup. He was not paying attention to the orders and had detonated the explosives prematurely. The only one who does not know is the colonel.

WMA Courtesy Trailer

Rose, Claude, and Alex are using a fifty-three-foot trailer within the FBI protected property to provide advice to the FBI. For the past several weeks, the action in the KKK camp has been routine. Both sides are preparing for the inevitable attacks. During this slow time, Claude, Alex, and Rose have used some surplus lumber to build an outside deck with an awning. They found some lawn chairs and a couple of folding tables, and they drove to the local hardware store and bought a portable grill. Most afternoons, they sit out and enjoy the nice days that are plentiful at the base of the Smoky Mountains.

However, in the last twenty-four hours, there has been plenty of action. It is apparent to Claude, Alex, and Rose that the terrorists and the FBI are now engaged in an all-out battle.

The day after the unsuccessful attempt to take out the terrorists' leadership, Brit knocks on the door of the WMA trailer. Claude walks over and opens the door. Rose and Alex are watching the news on CNN.

Brit, who is generally in a good mood, looks beaten and worried. After the typical hellos and good to see you, Brit says, "Things are not going well. Yesterday was a bad day. It seems as if things are going from bad to worse."

Rose has a good rapport with Brit; they have become good friends and seem to have an excellent professional relationship. This rapport was established when they were working together in Buchanan, New York.

Rose says professionally, "Perhaps if we go over all of the facts regarding the terrorists, we can help you." She goes on to give Brit a more detailed explanation of their encounter with Wolf in Scotland. She also tells Brit that Wolf and she had a near encounter when they were both fighting ISIS in Iraq and Syria. Brit has a good understanding of Rose's background, but he was not fully aware of her near confrontation with Wolf in Djibouti, Africa.

The discussion regarding Rose's professional experience leads to Brit providing a complete detailed explanation of all of the FBI actions. He describes the trip to Raleigh, North Carolina, to recruit agents with special operations backgrounds. He describes the plan to infiltrate the terrorists' camp and the diversion attack on the north end. Brit then says in a depressed mood, "The plan to arrest or kill the officers of the terrorist organization ended in failure."

Alex, who has been listening, says, "Brit, yesterday morning, we heard several large explosions. We believed that the FBI initiated the explosions."

"No, the terrorists wired several buildings with explosives." Brit goes on and tells the group the actions that were taken by the infiltration teams. "We were fortunate that the terrorists exploded them prematurely."

"Are you of the opinion that the terrorists were fully aware of the attempt to take out their leadership?" asks Rose.

"It appears that is the case."

"Why do you think that?" asks Claude.

"The terrorists jammed our radio frequencies as the northern diversionary attack was commencing and as the covert teams started their infiltration. The infiltration teams reached their target buildings by midnight. The two teams were in a position to breach the buildings at approximately 3 A.M. As the teams were about to enter the two buildings, both buildings exploded. The teams were saved because it took longer than expected to enter the buildings. Frankly, we were lucky that all eight members of the team were able to escape. One thing that did work was the northern attack. The covert teams escaped because the middle and southern sectors were thinly manned. Based on the amount of firepower that Agent Stenson's team received on the northern perimeter, we calculated that the terrorist moved their troops to counteract our attack."

Rose then says, "Can you go back to your visit to North Carolina?"

"Certainly. Anything item that you would like to go over?"

"Yes, how many men did you interview?"

"I think it was six."

"And why did you interview only six."

"That's all that was left after the North Carolina FBI personnel office queried the candidates and determined their availability."

"And did you interview the remaining six?"

"Yes, but they were not the top candidates, so we decided to use members of the Nashville covert teams."

"Did any of the six have more interest than others?"

"Yes, there was one candidate who was very inquisitive."

"Do you remember his name, and do we have his files?"

"No, we were not allowed to make copies of the files. However, I do have my notes." Brit pulls out his laptop and opens the Excel spreadsheet where he and Tom listed all of the attributes of the candidates that were interviewed.

He shows the spreadsheet to Rose, and she asks, "Do we have the personnel records of the FBI mole?"

"Yes, we are investigating. We have a copy of his personnel file in the command post. Give me fifteen minutes, and I can retrieve it." Brit walks out of the WMA trailer and goes to the command post van.

As Brit is retrieving Rock Irwin's personnel files, Claude, Alex, and Rose discuss the line of questions. Alex says, "I guess that the leak occurred in North Carolina." The fact that Brit and Tom left without anyone being selected probably pissed off an agent—something like, 'We are not good enough, so fuck them!'"

Brit comes back, and they look at Rock's personnel files and the information on Brit's spreadsheet. They see that the interested agent and Rock were at the Quantico Special Operations School at the same time.

Alex then asks Brit, "Why has Irwin not been arrested?"

"Yes, I asked the same question. The answer is that Irwin is an undercover agent. His job is to intermix with the drug dealers, so this is what he is doing."

"What about the video recording?"

"The video was obtained illegally. According to the lawyers, the evidence was very weak. Again, he could claim that it was part of his job. We did check his living standard. We found nothing unusual; he was living within his means."

"Did you check cryptocurrency transactions?"

"Yes, but as you know, we cannot determine the amounts, nor do we know the sender. Using the internet to purchase or sell cryptocurrency is not illegal. We did check his bank account, and no large transactions were found."

Rose then says, "OK, we need to determine if Irwin is passing info to Wolf. We need to have Irwin overhear some intel from one of our agents. Irwin will pass the info to Wolf, and from his reaction to the info, we will know that we have our mole."

"Excellent," says Brit. "After that, we can arrest him!"

"No, we use Irwin to pass disinformation."

Chapter Fifty-Six

Disinformation Campaign

WMA Command Trailer

In the FBI command van, Brit discusses the idea of a disinformation campaign with the on-site commander, Tom Kramer. Brit has brought Tom up to speed on their conclusion that Rock Irwin is the leak. The WMA team has designed a plan to pass the disinformation to Rock. However, Tom will need to get permission from the Nashville SAC to use WMA assets

Tom says, "As far as I am concerned, I have the permission already. This morning, while you were in discussions with the WMA team, I was being reamed by my SAC Kowalski. He said that I had complete control of the situation. If this conflict goes south, he made it known that he was not taking the fall. So, I have a hundred percent control; let's get to the details of the disinformation campaign."

"OK," says Brit, "let's start our planning."

"Let's keep the disinformation campaign on a strictly need-to-know. We can complete the planning in the WMA command trailer."

Tom and Brit enter the WMA trailer. Brit says, "He is on board."

Claude, as the chief WMA planner, has discussed the details of the plan with Rose and Alex. He turns on the projector and brings up a PowerPoint.

He says, "Tom and Brit, shown on this slide are the major elements of the disinformation campaign."

The slide shows the following points.

Need to identify two covert agents and have Irwin overhear a false plan (needs discussion on the covert selection).

WMA will have Vinny and Matt will join the team and bring the communications and surveillance drones. Louie and Jeff have a new design to prevent eagle attacks.

WMA will bring the MANETs to establish communications.

Assuming the ruse works, the FBI will now have eyes and ears. We should be able to re-establish the initiative.

Need to have a plan to take advantage of the ruse (needs discussion).

Claude says, "OK, can we identify two covert agents who have contact with Irwin?"

"I have the two ideal agents," says Tom, "Marco Moretti and Kale Kahale. They were the lead agents for the infiltration teams."

"Perfect. How will they contact Irwin?"

"This, we will need to discuss. A couple of areas would be at the coffee bar or at the gym."

Alex says, "The gym would be ideal. They can be discussing the events of yesterday and be looking at a piece of paper. They lock the paper in their locker and go running. If Rock is really a covert agent, he will pick the lock in no time and read the disinformation."

"OK," says Claude, "that sounds good. We will discuss with Marco and Kale." He turns to the group and says, "Jeff, Vinny, and Louie have been burning the midnight oil. They are ninety-nine percent sure that they have a solution for the eagle problem. The solution is the eagles' strength. You know the saying 'eagle eyes'? Eagles have excellent eyesight. They can spot a rabbit from two thousand feet in the sky. Vinny did some research and found that ranchers out west were losing young livestock to eagles. Did you know that an eagle can lift five times their weight? Also, eagles have been known to fly up to ten thousand feet. When they are flying at these high altitudes, they exert very little energy; thus, they can easily fly thousands of miles. The eagles only need to come down for food."

Rose says, "Claude, get on with the solution. You are starting to sound like Vinny—rambling about all his exploits." (Note, Claude has always been the one telling Vinny to move it on!) Rose laughs and adds, "Guess we got ourselves a Vinny II?"

Claude laughs and gets to the meat of the solution. "The drones have been modified with pulsing lasers. There is a laser on each side. Eagles do not like sharp light; thus, they will keep their distance from the drone. Oh yeah, before anyone asks, the laser light is not visible to the human eye; thus, they will be undetected by the white nationalists' camp."

Both Tom and Brit are impressed. Tom says, "When do we get the modified drones?"

"I made the call early this afternoon," says Rose. "They are on a WMA plane as we speak. The drones and all equipment should be here by nightfall. We can have them operational by early tomorrow. Vinny and Matt will also be here. Jeff and Rick are not available; they have been assigned to a project in Berlin."

"OK, now the major topic," says Claude. "What is the ruse?"

"We need to plan something big," says Tom, "like a major attack. We provide a fake plan to Marco and Kale, and Irwin reads the plan and communicates with Wolf. Wolf believes the ruse and moves his troops accordingly. We attack where his troops are not."

"I like that. It's simple, not too many moving parts that can be fucked up. OK, how soon can we get Marco and Kale?

"We can have them here tonight," says Brit.

Later that afternoon, Vinny, Matt, and the equipment arrive. Vinny is really excited. He says, "I knew you guys could not live without me—I am really looking forward to fooling those eagles. You know they destroyed two of my favorite drones. Goddamn birdbrains, I'll show them tomorrow."

Vinny then goes into his trademark explanation of the newest anti-drone technology. After five minutes, Rose asks him very politely to wrap it up. She is the only one who can tell him to shut up and Vinny will consider it a compliment.

Much to the amazement of the group, Tom is very interested in drone technology and asks Vinny to give him an individual tutoring session on it.

Vinny is ecstatic and goes outside with Tom to show him the drones and all of the packages. The drones will not fly until tomorrow. They continue their discussion until 7 P.M. when Marco and Kale drive up in their Ford SUV.

Planning of the Fake Map

Marco and Kale arrive at the WMA trailer. They know Tom and Brit, but not the WMA special operations agents. They know them only by reputation. They are looking forward to meeting the group. They enter the trailer, and introductions are made. As is customary, only first names are given. When they see that one of the agents is a woman and they hear her English accent, they know who she is. Rose's reputation has grown with every success she has had in special operations. After working with the HRT team in Orogrande, New Mexico, and her heroic actions in New York, her legend has grown so that she is now known as "Wonder Woman."

After the intros, they sit around the table and get down to discussing the overall plan. Tom gives them the summary, and the WMA team provides the details. Alex, who is the most experienced with disinformation campaigns, explains the need to plant the fake map. He gives them some ideas and options. It is best if Marco or Kale come up with what they think will work. After discussing various methods, they agree that the gym locker has the best likelihood of success.

Marco believes that it would be best if they have a sheet of paper that has been torn from a spiral notebook. Make it look as if he was taking notes. They agree on the approach. Kale says, "The agents have mandatory workouts between five and eight each morning. Usually, Irwin is there between six and eight."

The next morning, Marco and Kale are at the gym early; they lift weights and do a light workout. They see Irwin come in, and they find lockers within earshot of him. Rock takes a seat and starts hanging his shirt and slacks in locker number 45. Marco and Kale find lockers close to Rock, numbers 49 and 52.

Marco says, "Kale, I am short on my miles this week and need to run a ten-miler this morning."

"Well, you sure as hell cannot run a ten-miler with your designer jeans," replies Kale.

"Yeah, you're right. Need my running shorts. They are in my locker." Marco starts to take off his designer jeans, and a hand-drawn map falls out of the back pocket of the jeans.

Kale sees the paper and tells Marco, "You dropped a paper." Kale goes over and picks up the paper, and as he is giving it to Marco, he stops, looks at it, and says, "You dumb shit. You know that you should not take notes about our assignments this week."

"If you don't tell anyone, I won't either, and no harm will come of it."

"Yeah, you're right; just make sure you lock it up. You sure as shit do not want to lose the paper running out in the woods." Marco and Kale exit the gym lockers and go for their ten-mile run.

They return from their run, and Marco says, "He bit. The strand of hair that was placed on the locker door is not there anymore. It has been opened!"

Chapter Fifty-Seven

Vinny Flies the Drone over the Terrorist Camp

Vinny and Matt are up one hour before daybreak, and they configure two drones. One drone will be primarily video surveillance. It will also have a MANET to be used as a relay point. The second drone will be used as a signal intercept system and will also have a MANET as a relay point. Both drones have the anti-eagle pulsing lasers. As the sun breaks the horizon, the drones start flying. Vinny has programmed the drones to fly in racetrack patterns. One flies clockwise, and one flies counterclockwise. He first needs to make sure that the anti-eagle system works.

The eagles have been flying solo. They each have a two-hour patrol. As daybreak approaches, the first eagle takes to flight. It flies to two thousand meters and takes only ten seconds spot one of the drones. The eagle circles the drone. With each circle, it comes closer and closer. At approximately thirty meters from the drone, the eagle aborts the attack and flies off to continue with its flight pattern. Two minutes later, it spots the second drone. Again, the eagle starts the attack pattern. The eagle comes within fifty meters from the drone and aborts its attack.

Matt tells Vinny, "The first test passed. Louie and Jeff will be glad to hear that pulsing lasers worked."

Vinny answers, "I think you are right. Let's wait until the end of the day and be sure that the second eagle will react the same way."

"Good idea, but I think we have a solution."

"OK, I am taking the drones to three thousand meters and will place them in stationary positions at the south and north ends of the camp. We need to test our communications horizon."

Matt pulls out a Pelican case with ten of the special XP7A radios/cell phones. The specialized WMA radios will work in both the cell band and the MANET L-band. Vinny has drafted Alex and Rose to help out with the comms testing. Tom also got up early and volunteered to participate in the testing. As they are getting ready to start the test, Claude and Brit come by and says, "Where is my radio?"

Vinny calls all the testers to huddle up and hands them radios with papers attached with the call sign. He gives them instructions of the area where they need testing. Vinny wants to make sure that the comms will not have a blind spot in the area surrounding the terrorists' camp. After one hour of testing, Vinny is satisfied that they have a hundred percent coverage, that there are no blind spots.

"Calling all call signs, he says. "Return to home base."

All members of the test team return to home base.

Next Vinny needs to figure out how the terrorists are communicating. He brings down one of the drones and tells Matt to install the spectrum analyzer on it. The drone with the spectrum analyzer flies off to a stationary position at three thousand meters.

Vinny asks Tom to order a scout patrol at the northern side of the terrorists' camp.

"OK," says Tom, "I should have a scout patrol on the move in ten minutes."

Vinny and Matt monitor the frequency spectrum. As soon as the patrol is within a hundred meters from the camp perimeter, the spectrum analyzer has a spike in the 450 MHz band. Matt tunes the spectrum analyzer to a more precise frequency.

After tuning the spectrum analyzer and obtaining the frequency, Matt checks with a manual from the FCC. He says, "Well, I'll be damned. The terrorists are using the Family Radio Service band."

Tom says, "How the hell are they using that? Those radios have a very low transmit power." Vinny and Matt look at Tom and are shaking their heads.

Tom then figures it out. "Yeah, I get it. They have modified their radios for higher power levels. I am sure that Wolf simply said, 'If the FCC wants to fine me—well, come and get me.'"

FBI and WMA Surveillance

The video surveillance drones provided by the WMA start providing intel immediately. The WMA trailer now becomes the intel base. Vinny and Matt have been assigned two FBI analysts to assist with the video surveillance and to monitor the Family Radio Service frequencies. The FBI analysts are energetic young women who have the temperament to sit at a terminal and analyze the data. Their names are Suzy and Debbie. Suzy is assisting Vinny in viewing the video. Debbie is helping Matt in listening to the intercepted audio. When Suzy determines that a video segment is pertinent, she flags it, and then Vinny further analyzes it. Debbie does likewise with the audio. When the audio is flagged, Matt will further analyze.

Suzy has been viewing the video of the trenches. She says, "Vinny, there's something very unusual with the terrorists in the trenches. I have been viewing this section for the better part of four hours. I have marked every person with a marker. The marker indicates where their arms and heads are positioned. They have not moved for the entire four hours."

Vinny takes a look and says, "Yes, you are right. Let's fly the drone along the entire trench line and mark their positions. We have another six hours of daylight. Let us see what we find. "

After an additional four hours, they have decided that approximately two out of three are dummies. They conclude that there are only thirty-three terrorists manning the trenches. They immediately bring this to the attention of Tom and Claude. They immediately call a meeting of Tom, Claude, Brit, Rose, and Alex. The intel is confusing. What happened to the other seventy terrorists? They conclude that they need more intel. They decide to ask Matt and Debbie for any intel from the audio intercepts. All audio intercepts are strictly from Wolf and his officers.

Matt says, "There is one recording from a Captain Gibbenhaven regarding the need to move his troops to the northern sector. 'That is where the attack…' After the word' attack,' the intercept stops."

Tom and the four men and one woman know what that means. The mole, Rock Irwin, has communicated that the FBI attack will occur on the northern flank.

Tom and Brit make the decision to start moving trucks to the northern sector. This will make it appear that an attack is imminent. The FBI will turn the tables on the terrorists. When the fake attack commences, the Family Radio Service frequencies will be jammed. The drones, which have been provided by the WMA, will act as relays for the radios/phones provided by WMA. These radios operate in the 5 GHz IP spectrum and will not be affected by the terrorist jammers.

The advantage of using the IP spectrum is that regular smartphones may be used. Smartphones need to download the comms app and the encryption key. Each phone has a unique ID. This ID is entered into the comms server; thus, only phones with the app, encryption key, and ID will be able to use the IP network.

Terrorist Camp

Wolf and his command staff are pleased with the progress of the war. They have taken the initiative. All of the media outlets are carrying the news.

Wolf says, "Goes to show you, everybody loves a winner. Our informant has again given valuable information. The attack by the FBI will occur tomorrow at 4 A.M. on the northern side of the camp."

"Yes, sir," replies Colonel Sondermann. "Everything is ready. Captain Gibbenhaven will lead Company C and protect the northern flank."

Wolf looks around at the officers and says to Captain Gibbenhaven, "Captain, do you know your orders?"

Yes, sir, hold the line as long as possible. We will die martyrs. Long live the Confederacy!"

Wolf thinks, *I made a damn good decision getting rid of Baker; Gibbenhaven has guts and will run through a brick wall for me… Reminds me of Wilhelm.*

Wolf shouts, "Captain Gibbenhaven, you are dismissed! Prepare your troops and defend the northern flank!"

"Yes, sir."

Wolf now addresses Colonel Sondermann and Major Jacobson. "Colonel, be at the jammer location at 3:30 and wait for my command. Major, be ready to fly the video drones on my command. I will view the video and direct the battle from the war room. All of the mortars have been set for the northern side. As soon as Company C is overrun, we order that the mortars be fired. This will decimate the enemy. After the battle is fully underway, we exit through the tunnels. Colonel, you and the major use the northern tunnel. Gretchen and I will use the southern tunnel. We meet again at Camp X-Ray in Montana. Good luck and may the dark force be with us. Dismissed."

Both the colonel and major smartly salute and exit the war room. Wolf is confident that the plan will work to perfection. They have carefully planned, prepared, and practiced daily.

Chapter Fifty-Eight

The Final Battle

FBI Command Van

Tom has been appointed the battlefield commander. Thus far, the terrorists have been winning every battle. Most discouraging is that they are winning over the public. Every step that the FBI takes, the terrorist commanders know the FBI battle plan.

However, the tide is about to change. The FBI has identified the FBI mole and planted some disinformation. Tom intends to take advantage of the disinformation; he is planning a fake attack, followed by the main attack. He has at his disposal all four HRT teams plus two companies of National Guardsmen. Each HRT team has twenty-four members for a total of ninety-six FBI agents. The two National Guard teams total sixty-six; thus, the total number for the attacking force equals 166. All of Tom's men are armed with M-16 automatic rifles and Glock .45 handguns. They are each wearing their camouflage cargo pants, long-sleeve brown pullover, lightweight combat boots, Kevlar vest, and helmet. The helmets all have an embedded radio. The radio comms amongst the troops use a "talk-around frequency" channel. Thus, the terrorist jammer will not affect their comms.

Tom will also be assisted by the WMA team. Vinny and Matt, who have joined the team from Virginia, will lend assistance. The WMA techno-gurus,

Vinny and Matt, plus two-assigned FBI analysts will disrupt or destroy the terrorist video surveillance system and jam the Family Radio Service frequencies. After Vinny and crew neutralize the terrorists' ability to fire ground-to-air missiles, Tom will then be able to employ two Black Hawk helicopters to land FBI agents behind enemy lines.

The fake attack on the northern side begins at 4 A.M. The team leader will be agent Justin Stenson. Two hours after the fake attack, agent Brit Singleton will lead the main attack from the south side. Simultaneous to the main southern attack, the two Black Hawks will insert two twelve-men teams. Leading the two teams will be agents Marco Moretti and Kale Kahale.

Tom will direct the battle from the FBI command van. Claude will also be in the command van and provide real-time assistance as the battle rages. Rose and Alex will be at the WMA trailer. The trailer is connected using a fiber cable; thus, all comms and video monitors are available in both the command van and the trailer. The WMA trailer will assume the responsibility of being the intelligence center of the pending battle. Vinny and Matt now have four drones available for video surveillance, communication relays, and a SIGINT intercept system. The terrorists' Family Radio Service frequency will be jammed; however, there is some concern that the terrorists might have backup comms capability. The spectrum analyzer installed on one of the drones will scan the radio horizon from HF to 10 GHz.

A problem that needs resolution is the destruction of terrorist surveillance drones. The terrorists have been flying their surveillance drones along the terrorist property line. The FBI could easily shoot the drones out of the sky; however, they are reluctant to do so based on the bad publicity they got when the terrorist drones were shot out of the sky by the terrorists. If the terrorist drones are to be destroyed, it will need to be clear that it was the terrorists that shot them down. The WMA team has a solution.

The morning of the attack, Vinny and Matt are flying a special drone with a sonic feed horn. The feed horn is shaped like a megaphone used by a cheerleading squad. The feed horn can amplify sound and direct it to any chosen location. Analysis completed by the WMA team has indicated that the likely reason that the eagles do not attack their own drones is due to a unique sound frequency that the drones emit. The eagles have been trained not to attack a drone with this unique sound frequency. Louie, Jeff, and Vinny have designed a drone "package" with a sound system that can generate sounds in the sub-sonic human range.

A WMA drone with the pulsating lasers will approach the terrorist drones and emit a frequency using the feed horn system. The wavelength emitted by the WMA drone will mix with the terrorist drone frequency and result in a new frequency. The idea is that the eagle will not hear the proper frequency and attack the terrorist drone.

Vinny asks, "Matt, is the feed horn system ready for a flight?"

"Ready."

"OK, hold the drone over your head. I will turn on the six motors, After I check out the control panel and all indicators are OK, I will give you the thumbs up and let go. Hold on tight the drone has six motors to allow larger payloads."

"Roger."

Vinny gives the thumbs up. The drone takes flight.

The WMA trailer has been modified with the drone control and comms antennas on the roof of the trailer. Vinny and Matt do not need to be outside. They are viewing the video and GPS location of all WMA drones on the screens. The entire intel team includes Vinny, Matt, Suzy, Debbie, Rose, and Alex. The WMA drone gains altitude and flies to three thousand meters.

Debbie says, "The eagle is approaching our drone. Eagle has now investigated and is flying away from our drone."

"Roger," says Vinny. "I am flying our drone toward terrorist drone number one."

"WMA drone now within the target range of the feed horn frequency."

Vinny turns the WMA drone so that the feed horn is pointing at the terrorist drone.

Debbie says, "Eagle is approaching terrorist drone. Eagle is circling."

"Now the moment of truth," says Rose. "Will this work?"

Vinny, who is usually very talkative, is quietly steering the feed horn. His attention is one hundred percent on the WMA drone, the eagle, and the terrorist drone. The eagle seems to be flying a greater number of circles than usual.

Debbie says, "She looks like she is getting tired."

"No, she is just being indecisive. I need to move our drone closer to the terrorist drone. I think that we are not disrupting the ID frequency to a significant level." Vinny maneuvers the WMA drone closer to the terrorist drone.

Debbie says, "Wow, the eagle is in a diving flight—straight to the terrorist drone!"

The eagle's talons strike the drone dead center. The terrorist drone is destroyed.

The video recording does not show the WMA drone. The recording will be released to the press at the appropriate time.

White Nationalist War Room

Wolf is now operating in the war room with only his two aides; he has ordered Company C to the northern sector to blunt the attack by the FBI, and he has order Colonel Sondermann to man the jammers and Major Jacobson to fly the video drones. Wolf is confident in his ability to jam the FBI communications and to maintain his own comms. He has maintained his ground-to-air missile crews in the ready state. Since the downing of the helicopters, the FBI has not flown any aircraft over the terrorist camp. Secondly, no surveillance drones have been detected over the camp since he started flying the eagle patrols.

Without warning, the video from terrorist drone number one suddenly goes blank, and five minutes later, the video from drone number two goes blank, followed by drone number three. After the loss of drone number one, Wolf is on the radio with Major Jacobson.

"What the fuck is going on with the video drones?"

"Sir, we have no idea, but we are looking into the situation."

"Were they shot down by the FBI?"

"No, sir. We did not hear any gunshots. I am sending a Klansman to investigate. He will be using one of the ATV, so we will have some of the debris within minutes."

As Wolf is discussing the downing of the first drone, the second video feed goes blank.

Wolf is now getting pissed. He yells, "What the hell is going on?"

He reaches for his radio, keys it, and yells at Major Jacobson, "Major, get some drones in the air ASAP. We are blind!" He receives no answer; again, he yells into the radio, "Major, again, what the fuck is going on!" Wolf finally realizes that the radio frequency has nothing but static. He has seen this before in his training with the Marines. He tells him, "We are being jammed."

He thinks about the situation. *I need to remain calm. We need to go to the backup comms plan.* He goes to the cabinet and pulls out a VHF radio. He turns it to channel ten and presses the transmit button. He breathes a sigh of relief when Jacobson and Sondermann answer.

Jacobson tells Wolf, "Sir, the drones are being destroyed by our own eagles."

"Major, says Wolf, "the ID frequency that was your responsibility suddenly stopped working, WHY?"

No answer. Wolf says, "Goddamn it, Jacobson, don't hide behind the radio—answer me, goddamn it!" Still no response. Wolf listens to his radio—again jammed.

Wolf is furious. He has lost control. This is the one thing that he is the most scared of—no control. The enemy now has control of the chessboard. After reflecting on the situation, he thinks, *I need to make the best of the worst situation.* He sees that he has his two aids. They are young and in good physical shape.

He orders them, "Klansmen, stand up."

They both have been viewing the video from the drones that have been destroyed. They answer, "Yes, sir."

Wolf looks at aid number one and says, "Corporal, run to Colonel Sondermann and tell him to be at building number fifty-one in fifteen minutes."

"Yes, sir." The corporal immediately exits the war room and starts running to the Sondermann location.

Wolf then orders the second aid, "Private, run to Major Jacobson and tell him to meet at building fifty-one in fifteen minutes."

The private salutes sharply and exits the war room. Wolf now starts thinking about his next move. He knows that the FBI, with their superior numbers, will soon overrun the camp. He has prepared for the eventuality. The buildings are all wired to explode with tripwires or remote-control garage openers. He will now add a lesson learned while serving as a Marine in Iraq. He will order his remaining Klansmen to become snipers and kill as many of the invading FBI and National Guardsmen as possible. His plan is still to escape through the tunnels with Gretchen, Sondermann, and Jacobson.

Tom Orders Agent Stenson to Begin the Attack on the Northern Side

The terrorist's jammers have been disabled. The FBI can now use their tri-band radios. Tom keys his radio. "Agent Stenson, begin the attack on the northern side."

"Roger. Beginning attack now." Agent Stenson has told his troops, "We are only staging a fake attack. We attack for thirty minutes and fall back. We make it look like the terrorists are too strong. After the first wave, we wait for further instructions."

Terrorist Company C

Company C captain is Rodney Gibbenhaven. Rodney received a battlefield promotion when Captain Baker fucked up. He doesn't even know what the fuck Baker did, and he really does not care. He is now the top dog, big cheese, king of the hill. If he tells any of his thirty-three men to jump, they say, "How high?" He has seen in the movies where the top commander always has a short whip called a crop. He found a short whip that was for the plow horses. He carries his whip and is continuously slapping it on his open hand. He knows nothing about battlefield tactics. What he does know is from movies. He has seen many Civil War battles. Captain Gibbenhaven orders his troops to dig in and defend the Confederacy. He knows an attack is imminent. Gibbenhaven is nervous, and when he is nervous, he always eats. He reaches into his man purse and pulls out a Babe Ruth candy bar. An attack of Union troops is expected at any time. At 4:30 A.M., the Union troops attack. With the first shot, his knees become wobbly. He has a headache. One of the lieutenants comes running up and says, "Captain, the FBI is starting a pincer movement on the right flank. What should we do?

"Pincer, what's a pincer?"

"A pincer means they are circling us."

"Circling? What, like in the western movies when they circle the wagons?"

The lieutenant shakes his head and says to himself, *Idiot. It's each man for himself.*

There is total confusion, uncertainty, chaos, like chickens with their heads cut off. No one is making decisions. Captain Gibbenhaven has locked himself in the crapper. He is throwing up and crying like a baby. He comes running out, shouting, "Private Baker, Private Baker, take command!"

The thirty-three Klansmen raise their rifles and yell, "Captain Baker! Captain Baker!" They keep repeating the chant.

Finally, Private (Captain) Baker goes to the front and, in a very confident voice, starts barking commands. The company immediately takes on a military demeanor. The command structure is restored. The problem is, time has been lost. There are no communications amongst the terrorist units; thus, each group must act independently. The one-hour delay has Company C in the crosshairs of the terrorist mortars.

Major Jacobson, who has command of the mortar squads, gives the order, "Commence mortar fire." There are four tubes; each tube can fire one mortar round every five seconds. In thirty seconds, each mortar fires six rounds, so twenty-four rounds are fired. The twenty-four rounds have a devastating effect on the terrorists. Twenty-five are killed, and eight have life-threatening injuries. Both Captain Gibbenhaven and Private Baker are killed.

The FBI Intel Team Determines the Mortar and Missile Locations:

Within seconds of the terrorists firing their mortars, the WMA video drones quickly zoom in on the four places where they are being fired from. Debbie writes down the first location, Matt writes down the second, Suzy the third, and Vinny the fourth. Vinny keys the National Guard channel and gives the four sites. The National Guard captain quickly gives the coordinates to the firing teams. Within twenty-five-seconds, the four tubes are firing at the terrorist mortar locations. At thirty seconds, the terrorists' mortar tubes go silent.

Next, the intel team uses the drones to start their hunt for the ground-to-air missile locations. This will be a bit more difficult. The missiles are shoulder-fired; thus, they are mobile. However, they must be stored inside of some type of container or shelter. Some shelters are more likely than other shelters. The ground-to-air missiles need to be stored in a refrigerated container since they have a short shelf life. Vinny instructs Suzy and Debbie to look for International Organization Standard (ISO) shelters. He shows them pictures of thirty-, forty-, and 50-foot ISO shelters. They are transportable. They have refrigeration units mounted to ship such items as food supplies and flowers.

After two hours of scanning the camp, the intel team finds eleven ISO shelters. Of the eleven, five have refrigeration units attached. Vinny confers with Tom, the on-site battlefield commander. Vinny recommends, "There are only five. Destroy them all."

Tom agrees. "Give the mortar team the coordinates. I will call and order them to fire."

"Roger will do," Vinny orders his team to obtain the coordinates for all five refrigerated ISO shelters. Within fifteen minutes, they have the coordinates. Vinny calls the National Guard captain. "Sir, I have the coordinates. They are being sent via encrypted message."

"Yes, I was called by the on-site commander. As soon as I have the coordinates, we will fire ten mortar rounds at each location."

In thirty seconds, the National Guard fire teams lay ten rounds on each location. The intel team watches the video from the drones, and all are direct hits. Secondary explosions are noted at the shelters. Some of the missiles are ignited and fly in crazy patterns in the sky.

Matt says, "This would make a great Fourth of July on the Washington Mall!"

Vinny calls the commander. "Sir, all shelters had missiles. There is no longer a missile threat to our helicopters."

"Thank you. Tell the intel crew well done."

"Will do, sir."

Wolf Meets with His Team and Describes the Sniper Mission

Wolf now realizes that he is at a distinct disadvantage. He has no comms, no video surveillance, no mortars, and no ground-to-air missiles. Wolf will now mount a defensive attack like what the jihadist ISIS terrorists did when he was in Iraq. He has ordered that all buildings be wired for remote explosives. IEDs have been installed on all surrounding buildings, and tripwires have been connected across all possible entry points. He has twelve Klansmen remaining. All are equipment technicians, and none are trained snipers; however, they all have received training on long rifles.

Long rifles are issued, and orders are given to hide in the trees and kill as many of the advancing enemy as possible.

Wolf tells the men acting as snipers, "Captain Gibbenhaven was successful. The mortar attack destroyed the invading army. Now we need to delay the advancing enemy. Help is on the way. We will be victorious; our intel has again provided us the force multiplier to defeat the enemy." He knows that it is all a lie, but these troops have no other sources of information.

Wolf now goes to his living quarters to brief Gretchen on the latest status.

He tells her that all is going as planned. He tries to bullshit her, but she knows Wolf for what he is—A LIAR. She thinks, *maybe those pea-brained Klansmen believe him, but I know better.*

Gretchen goes into a rage. She starts yelling at him, "This is entirely your fucking fault! Your obsession with that English bitch has brought nothing but death and destruction!"

Wolf gets equally pissed and tells her, "Shut your fucking mouth! Get the hell out of here. I should shoot you on the spot."

When Gretchen hears that he will shoot her on the spot, she pulls out a Sig Sauer 1911. It is a big gun, too big for her hands, but Wolf knows that she knows how to use it.

"OK," he says, "I really did not mean to say that. It has not been a good day. The feds will likely overrun the camp by tomorrow. Best you get outta here. You know the way. Use either of the two tunnels."

"OK, I already have my backpack ready to go."

She leaves through the southern tunnel. As she is running through the tunnel, she thinks, *I should have shot the SOB. I may live to regret my lack of action.*

Battle for the Camp

Agent Stenson and his fifteen-man team advance from the north. The first thirty minutes, they encounter no resistance. After advancing approximately two miles, they witness death and destruction, including numerous body parts and dead bodies. As they approach one body, it starts moving: the terrorist tries to raise his arm with a pistol. One of the FBI agents has no choice but to shoot the injured terrorist. The terrorist is shot in the head and instant death. The advancing FBI team carefully examines all bodies. They encounter no additional resistance. They continue advancing toward the main terrorist camp.

Agent Brit Singleton advances with the main FBI and National Guard teams from the south. When the advancing team gets within two kilometers from the main buildings, they encounter heavy sniper fire. Progress over the next two kilometers is slow. The sniper fire is not accurate. Bullets are flying high, low, left, and right. Once the FBI team locates a terrorist sniper, it is only a matter of time before he is eliminated.

Brit is in continuous communication with the intel team. The intel team is using the video from the drones to pinpoint the snipers. Brit gets a radio message from Vinny.

"Brit be aware that the terrorists are installing tripwires. Large bags are hidden behind trees or large stones."

"Can you give us the coordinates of any suspected IEDs?"

"Ten-four." Matt transmits from his radio and provides four suspected locations.

"OK, got them. We will proceed cautiously."

Tom decides to send in two SWAT teams via helicopter. The SWAT teams rappel down with no problem. The two teams each have twelve members. Two minutes after landing, the two teams are advancing toward the terrorists' buildings.

Tom says, "SWAT teams, be aware that there is a high probability that the building has been wired for explosives. Proceed with caution."

One of the SWAT team leaders replies, "Roger. We'll clear the area and wait for the bomb disposal teams to arrive."

Terrorist Camp

Wolf decides that now is the time to make his escape. He signals to Colonel Sondermann and Major Jacobson that it is time to go.

All three headed for building fifty-one. They are armed with an AR-15 and handguns and have knives strapped to their legs. Wolf has a .38 short-nose inserted in the back of his waistband. The .38 has only four bullets inserted in its cylinder.

The three men go to the cellar and enter the tunnel. The tunnels have lights on backup batteries. They start their jog to escape through the southern tunnel.

Chapter Fifty-Nine

Wolf, Gretchen, and Terrorist Officers Escape the Camp

Terrorist Camp

The intel team continues finding the snipers using the video from the drones. The FBI and the National Guardsmen use the information from the intel team and eliminate the threat. The advancing FBI force has now reached the building complex. Vinny directs two of the drones to start scanning the edge of the terrorist camp. The terrorists have been escaping; he needs to find the escape route.

Gretchen has been planning on her escape for days. She reaches the end of the tunnel, runs for a hundred meters, goes behind a copse of trees, and uncovers her hidden ATV. She mounts the ATV and pushes the start button, and the engine comes to life—RRROOOOMMM!

Suzy, who has been monitoring the video camera and is scanning the outer perimeter, says with much excitement, "Guys, I have something." Rose, Alex, and Vinny immediately walk behind her and look at her monitor. They see a person mounting an ATV.

Rose says, "No question; that's Gretchen on the ATV. Stay on her. I am requesting a helicopter to take us to this location. We can rappel down to the tunnel exit."

Alex picks up the radio. "Tom, we are requesting a helicopter. We have found the tunnel exit."

Tom responds, "Roger, I will call the aviation squad and release a copter to your crew. I am also sending Brit and three HRT agents. They will be at the helicopter pad in fifteen minutes."

"Ten-four."

Rose and Alex go to the back of the trailer and pick up their "go pack." The go pack has all the equipment and weapons that will be required. This is standard practice in special operations—you need to be ready at a moment's notice. Rose and Alex have worked as a team in previous missions. They operate better than a synchronized Swiss watch.

The helicopter takes them to a location near the tunnel exit. As the combined WMA-FBI team is rappelling down, Wolf, Sondermann, and Jacobson are exiting the tunnel. Wolf, Sondermann, and Jacobson immediately hear the WHOOP—WHOOP—WHOOP of the helicopter blades. They look up and see six special ops soldiers rappelling down the ropes. Wolf and Jacobson draw their Sigs and start shooting at the rappelling figures. The distance is too far for the handguns; they do not have enough muzzle velocity. The bullets fall short of the intended target.

Wolf, Sondermann, and Jacobson agree to disperse. They are very familiar with the area, and they have the advantage. The three select different routes. After fifteen minutes of jogging and running through the woods, Wolf notices that a drone has been following him. He remembers the drone in Scotland. He removes his long rifle from his shoulder and inserts a special bullet for long-range targets. He waits patiently until the drone is visible. He takes aim, and with one shot, he destroys it.

Sondermann also has a drone following his movement. He takes aim with his high-power rifle and shoots the drone out of the sky.

Gretchen follows a dirt path for two miles, she has a four-wheel Jeep hidden behind a hill covered with thick bushes. As she pulls out of the hidden location, the back wheels of the Jeep make a rooster tail.

Vinny must make a decision: he only has two drones left. He aborts the surveillance and keys the radio on the operational channel. "We only have two drones left. Request tasking."

Rose transmits, "Find the ATV and follow the woman to her destination."

"Ten-four. Will do."

One of the two remaining drones finds the ATV. The rider has driven the ATV to Route 441 and is now driving a car. Vinny gives a description of the vehicle.

Tom says, "Abort drone surveillance. State police will take it from here."

The tracking of Wolf, Sondermann, and Jacobson is extremely dangerous. All are hiding behind trees, bushes, and/or rocks. They wait for the agents, and with their high-powered rifles, they are taking shots at Alex, Brit, Rose, and the three HRT agents. Already one agent has been hit. But the steel-plated vest prevented him from being killed. Another agent has taken a glancing bullet to his Kevlar helmet. Fortunately, it was not a direct hit.

Rose keys her radio. "Suggest we abort the chase on Wolf, Sondermann, and Jacobson. We have a tail on Gretchen. She will take us to Wolf."

Tom, as the incident commander, says, "Agreed. Abort the chase."

Chapter Sixty

Rose Finds Gretchen

Nashville, Tennessee

Before Wolf went on that murder contract to kill the Englishwoman, things were running smoothly for Gretchen. She invested her time and money in the Red Rooster Dinner Theater. After several successful years running a legitimate business, she took some bad advice from Wolf and started the gentlemen's club. For the first two years, she was using women who were registered prostitutes from the Tennessee area. Wolf was running his trucking company and was making good money transporting illegal drugs for the cartels. She made a foolish mistake when Wolf convinced her to use illegal women from Latin America. Gretchen knew it was wrong, but her profits more than doubled. One thing led to another, and she started showing snuff movies on the darknet. The snuff movies were moneymakers since you could run the film over and over again. As for the fact that women were killed, she had grown thick calluses, and she simply said, "It's show business. If I do not do it, someone else will."

Now, because of her relationship with Wolf, she is wanted for murder and dozens of other illegal activities. She has made the decision to split from Wolf. After thinking about her breakup with him, she knows that he will never let her leave alive; she knows too much. When Wolf confronted her on the day, she left the camp, she was sure that he was going to kill her. She was ready and pulled out her Sig Sauer 1911 handgun. Wolf quickly became very apologetic and said that she would always be her one and only love, that together they would rebuild their businesses. He was lying, and she knew it; she should have killed him. Now she is convinced that she needs to kill him before he kills her. She knows him like the back of her hand; he will show up at the Nashville Wild Horse Saloon the day after he escapes from the camp. He will likely be meeting with those two assholes Sondermann and Jacobson.

One day after she escapes from the camp, she is sitting on the balcony level of the Wild Horse Saloon. Wolf always has his meetings on the main floor, where it is more crowded. He will likely come in after 10 P.M., with 11 P.M. being the most likely.

Rose, Alex, and Brit have been tailing Gretchen since she escaped on the ATV. For the first twenty miles, they tracked her using the drones. At twenty miles, she stayed overnight at the home of a KKK sympathizer. The evening of the second day, Gretchen drove to Nashville. She parked her car at a public parking lot and entered the Wild Horse Saloon at 7:30 P.M. Since then, she has been sitting at a table for four hours and drinking a beer.

At 7:35, Rose, Alex, and Brit walked into the Wild Horse Saloon. Alex sits at the bar overlooking Gretchen. Brit sits at a table for two on the other side of Gretchen. Rose turns on the bug on her smartphone, makes the screen black, and places it in her purse. She is wearing faded jeans, cowboy boots, and a cowgirl hat.

Gretchen is wearing jeans, motorcycle boots, her denim jacket, no earrings, and her hair combed straight back. She is wearing sunglasses. She has on a Titans football cap, which she is wearing low to cover her eyes. It is evident that she does not want anyone to notice her.

Rose climbs the stairs to the balcony and looks at Gretchen. It feels unreal; she will soon to be face to face with her. She calmly strolls to the table and says, "Mind if I join you?"

"Yes, I do mind. I am waiting for someone."

Rose pulls back the chair and sits down.

"I never said you could sit down. Now, get the fuck outta here!"

"My, my, you need to wash that filthy mouth out with soup."

Gretchen looks at Rose; she thinks, *Good looking with an athletic body, and she speaks with an English accent.* Gretchen starts too tremble and sweat drips down her forehead.

Rose tries to comfort her. "I promise not to pull my Glock if you don't pull your Sig Sauer."

"How the hell do you know I have a Sig in my purse?"

"Just a guess, but I do know that I have a Glock in my belt holster." Rose opens her denim jacket slightly and shows her handgun.

Gretchen now knows who she is. "Are you that bitch—ah, sorry, the Englishwoman that Wolf has been trying to kill for the last year?"

"Bingo. I am the, as you say, the bitch,"

"Sorry, may I call you the English Mrs. James Bond?"

"Close. Jamie will do."

"OK, Jamie, can we rewind and get on a better footing?"

"Of course. Let's have a woman-to-woman talk."

"I would love that. You don't know how long it has been since I was able to have a nice chat with another woman."

Gretchen and Rose start talking about their lives and ordinary things: love, marriage, children, vacations, family, etc. Rose makes up all of her stories, though she does talk about being in the SAS and her service in Iraq. She figures that Wolf has told Gretchen about that part of her life. However, Gretchen is truthful and tells her how she met Wolf and the first eight years. As Gretchen starts to talk about the last two years, it is evident that she has a hatred for Wolf. She blames Wolf for all her troubles.

She says, "Two days ago, when the FBI was outside our doorstep, Wolf came to our residence and was fully intent on killing me. I was ready. As he started his ranting and his face grew a bright red, he started calling me deadweight and saying that it was best that he live his life without me. As he started to pull out his Glock, I already had my Sig Saucer 117 pointed at him. He was startled and immediately showed me his other side—Mr. Jekyll. He can be a Jekyll or a Hyde. The first eight years, he was a Mr. Jekyll. However, in the last two years, he has become Mr. Hyde. Since he was unsuccessful in killing you, he has become a monster. He runs the camp as if he is Hitler. I should have killed him when I had a chance."

"So, why are you meeting with him again?" asks Rose.

"He doesn't know that I am here. Frankly, I have come here on a hunch. He may not come at all. He may be on his way to Montana. But my guess is he will want to lay low here in Tennessee. He has many sympathizers here. He can probably hide out forever."

Gretchen thinks for a moment and then continues. "Why am I here? To kill the son of a bitch. If I do not kill him, he will kill me. I plan to watch him from the balcony. When he leaves, I will follow him. I'll surprise him when he is walking over the river pedestrian bridge. I have a suppressor on my Sig. I can shoot him and drop him in the river. They may never recover his body."

"Let me help you. I also would like to kill the SOB."

"No, this is my job."

"OK, at least I can assist if you need me."

"And how do you think you can help?"

"You can send me a text when you are walking him to the river. That will be your weakest point. You will need to stay close. Too many people will be on the bridge."

"OK, I can send you a text. What is your number?"

Rose gives Gretchen her phone number. "Send me a text—let's make sure it works."

Gretchen thinks, *she will be surprised when my number shows up as restricted.*

Rose's phone sounds the chimes for an incoming text.

Gretchen is looking carefully at her, but her expression does not change, like everybody has a restricted number.

Alex and Louie Actions

Alex and Brit have been listening to Rose and Gretchen's conversation. Alex knows immediately what to do. He calls Louie. "Louie, Rose just now received a text from a restricted number. You need to find that number. Once you find it, you need to install the bug covertly."

"OK, who is the service provider?

Brit says, "AT&T."

"OK, give me five or ten minutes, and I should have the bug installed."

"Thanks, Louie. Just like that?"

"Just like that."

Back to Jamie and Gretchen

Ten minutes after Gretchen sends the text, her phone receives a message: "Upgrade to IOS is available. Recommend upgrade as soon as possible. Upgrade deletes the bug that allows hackers to extract your contact list!"

Gretchen looks at the message. "I can upgrade tonight."

"Can I see your phone?" says Rose. She looks at the message and the info regarding the size of the upgrade. She shows the text message to Gretchen and says, "The update is not a full update. It is a patch. These take only seconds to correct. I really recommend you update."

"Good idea." Gretchen hits the update button. In fifteen seconds, the update (and the bug) is installed.

She says, "Thanks."

It is now 9:55 P.M. Gretchen says, "Jamie, I think it is best if you find another table. Wolf and company will likely be here in the next hour. It's best that we are not seen together."

"Yes, I agree. Remember, if you need help, text me. You may not see me, but I will be close."

"OK, hopefully, I will not need your help."

Rose gets up and walks downstairs and out the front door. Alex follows one minute later, and Brit one minute after that. They all meet in the WMA van. It has been modified with electronic equipment. It has a high-gain cellular antenna, which is inside the luggage rack rails. It looks like any work van used by plumbers or electricians. They are listening to the bug on Gretchen's phone. From 10 to 10:45, nothing happens. The three agents know that the phone bug is working as they can hear the dance music. The intercepted audio has been connected to a filtering system, which allows for voice recognition, and all other sounds are filtered and reduced in volume.

Rose says, "This is better than when I was sitting with Gretchen. I can hear the waiter clearly, and the music is very low in the background."

At 10:55 P.M., Wolf enters the Wild Horse Saloon. The front door attendant recognizes him and says, "Yes, sir, your table is ready." The saloon only reserves tables for VIP guests.

Wolf walks smartly to his table, and at precisely 10:58 P.M., Sondermann and Jacobson enter the saloon. Wolf, Sondermann, and Jacobson are military men. They believe in being punctual.

At 11:15, Gretchen joins the group. Wolf looks at her and says, "I was betting that you had flown the coop."

"You think I am that stupid?' she replies. "My neck is further out on the chopping block than your necks. You idiots got me involved in the prostitute business, but remember, the business is an LLC, and you and Sondermann are the owners and managers. I was the owner of the Red Rooster, a perfectly legit business. They catch me, and I am singing. Get me one of those smart lawyers in Washington like Trout has, and I get out with maybe a slap on my wrist."

Wolf says, "Gretchen, sit down and shut the fuck up!"

For the next hour, the three talk about their plan for the resurrection of the KKK camp in Montana. The convincing victory by the FBI has reversed public opinion. The FBI was on all the major networks, which displayed the drugs, opioids, and counterfeit fifties and hundred-dollar bills, and even Fox News carried the live interviews.

Wolf says, "We are going to lay low in Tennessee for at least three months. Fortunately, we still have supporters who believe in a Confederate America where whites of Aryan descent are supreme."

Colonel Sondermann says, "I have the perfect location in Franklin, Tennessee. It is a farm in the country. The owners of the property will protect me with their lives."

Major Jacobson adds, "I have a cousin outside of Nashville, and he is a Confederate die-hard. He will take me in for any required time."

"OK, we are set," says Wolf. "Go ahead. We leave as individuals. We meet exactly four months from today at Camp X-Ray in Montana. Gretchen and I have some personal issues that we need to take care of; we will follow in fifteen or twenty minutes."

Both Sondermann and Jacobson know what the personal issues are. Wolf is going to kill Gretchen; she has become a burden to the cause.

Wolf now turns into Jekyll and sweet talks Gretchen about their first eight years. He goes on and on about how he will change and that everything is entirely his fault. As always, he has Gretchen eating out of his hand. The hatred that Gretchen had two hours ago has melted like the spring snow.

After twenty minutes of Wolf's best Jekyll imitation, Gretchen has now turned. She says, "Wolf, I have something to tell you that will make you very happy."

"Yes, yes, of course. What is it sweetheart?"

"Before you arrived tonight, I spent the better part of two hours with Jamie, the woman you have been trying to kill."

"Jamie, who the hell is Jamie?"

"The Englishwoman you have been trying to kill. Here, I took her picture when she wasn't looking."

Wolf looks at the picture. The woman in it is dressed as a cowgirl, but there's no question it is Rose Mathews.

Wolf is now pissed. He slowly turns into Mr. Hyde. He is irritable, annoyed, and agitated. He focuses his anger on Gretchen. "Why the hell did you not tell me this earlier? You sat there knowing this and told me nothing? Do you realize that she is probably looking at us from the balcony?"

He grabs Gretchen by the shoulder and pulls her toward him.

"You're hurting me!" screams Gretchen.

Two of the bouncers walk over and tell Wolf and Gretchen, "You must leave."

Gretchen is now scared. "I'm not leaving with him. Call the police."

The bouncers start to dial the police. Wolf jumps up, pulls out his Glock, and says, "Nobody is calling the police. Get the fuck out of our way. He takes the phones from the two bouncers and throws them in his backpack. He pushes the Glock into Gretchen's ribs and forces her out of the saloon.

Gretchen is trying to pull out her cell phone and text Jamie... Wolf tells her," Put the goddamn phone back in your purse. You take it out one more time, and I'll throw it into the river."

Rose, Alex, and Brit have been listening to the conversation. The bug app also has a GPS; thus, they are also tracking Wolf and Gretchen. The one advantage that they have is that Gretchen is putting up a fight. She is resisting Wolf, but he is exceptionally strong and is dragging her. It is after midnight, and Wolf decides to knock her out. He does and then picks her up and carries her over his shoulder. A few people are out after midnight; he simply tells them, "My wife drinks a lot. She is drunk, passed out."

The people passing by all laugh and say, "Poor man has a drunk wife."

Chapter Sixty-One

Rose Encounter with Wolf

Cumberland River, Tennessee

Rose, Alex, and Brit are tracking Wolf and Gretchen using their cellphones. Gretchen's weight is too much for Wolf, so he sets her on a park bench. He ties her hands with his belt, and then he goes to the drinking fountain and uses his hands as a cup and splashes water on her face.

Gretchen starts to stir; she has glassy eyes and is disoriented. Wolf again gives her a pack of lies. He says, "Goddamn bouncers, I had to fight them off They were a couple of black guys who did not like my tattoos with the Confederate flag. Don't worry, I took care of them. I knocked them out with a couple of right hooks."

Gretchen only remembers sitting down with Wolf, Sondermann, and Jacobson. After that, her memory is shut down. She remembers talking to Jamie for the better part of two hours. Then she remembers trying to tell Wolf about her encounter. That is all she can remember. She knows she is in trouble; her instincts tell her so. Wolf is very agitated and nervous. That is not like him. He is walking up and down the sidewalk and looking in every direction. Looking at Wolf and his condition, she now remembers why he is in such a state of concern. She then realizes that she has her hands tied. She asks herself, *Why?*

Her self-preservation instincts take over. She says, "Wolf, are you concerned about the Englishwoman?"

Wolf tries to keep his temper under control as he says, "Damn right I am concerned. How could you talk to her for two hours and then not tell me immediately?

"I tried to tell you, but you were so engrossed with your discussions with Sondermann and Jacobson. You know how you do not want to be interrupted when you are discussing the protection of the camp."

Gretchen pauses for a moment and then continues. "Wolf listen to me. I can give you the Englishwoman on a silver platter, but those fucking bouncers fucked it all up!"

"What the hell you are talking about?"

"If you give me a few minutes, I can tell you everything, but first untie me. By the way, why did you have me tied?"

Wolf thinks very fast and says, "When I started fighting the fucking bouncers, some idiots started throwing chairs. One of the chairs hit you. You were semi-knocked out and started flailing your arms. I tied you up so that you wouldn't hurt yourself."

"I thought you said that the bouncers knocked me out."

"Yes, and the chairs. Now, are you going to tell me about the English bitch?"

"I told her that you and I had a falling out. That I was there to meet you and see if we could work out our problems. She fed me a pile of bullshit. Wants me to turn against you. She said that she can knock you off anytime she desires but wants to take you alive so you can stand trial."

"So, she told you that she could knock me off anytime she desired?"

"Yes."

"What a bunch of bullshit."

"She told me about the time in Djibouti, Africa. She said that you were really pissed when she was the best shooter. She said that you were a mere grunt, a trigger puller, and no brains. If she and you were in a forest, on a mountain, or in a city and there was a fight to the death, ten out of ten matches, she would kill you."

"She said all that?"

"Yeah, said it with a straight face. She said that you had a brain the size of a peanut. To prove it, she said that she completely outsmarted you in Scotland and Tennessee. And that she would do it in Montana if she had to!"

"How the fuck does she know about Montana?"

"Guess she knows a lot about you. That's probably why she outsmarts you!"

Now Wolf is really pissed. He hopes that Rose really is tracking him and that they will meet again at a time and place of his choosing.

Rose, Alex, and Brit

Rose, Alex, and Brit have been listening using the bug.

Alex says, "You told her all that?"

"No, but I should have. That Gretchen is quite a storyteller," says Rose.

"Really—but everything she said was true, right?"

"Yeah, maybe, but I certainly did not tell her that."

Alex says, "She is toying with Wolf. Let's see where she is headed."

"Simple," says Rose, "she is trying not to get herself killed. My guess is she is going to try to set me up! Remember, she does not know that we are listening to their conversations."

"Well, says Brit, "you will be able to add Nashville to that list of you besting Wolf."

"Not yet. The final chapter is not written."

Back to Gretchen and Wolf

Gretchen needs to have Wolf turn his anger toward Rose. She needs to have him cloud his mind with revenge and hostility. Once Wolf is in that stage, she can offer her plan.

"She said that you were a fucking pussy," says Gretchen. "You have other people do your dirty work. You set up Wilhelm in Scotland, and now you are hiding behind Sondermann and Jacobson. You sent that company to the northern sector to protect your ass. Said you did not stand up and fight, that over one hundred men died for you."

"Fucking pussy, fucking pussy, is that what she said!"

"OK, you want to plan to kill the bitch. Let's do it!"

Gretchen knows Wolf—she will remain silent and let him plan the kill mission.

However, she still has not told him that they arranged to have her text Jamie, aka Rose, if she needed help.

Gretchen says in a surprised tone, “Wolf, when I was talking with Jamie, she gave me a number to call if I needed help. I told her that I would not need help and that you would not hurt me. She called her phone number out. As you know, I have a good memory for numbers. I wrote it down just in case I needed it in the future. Here is her number.”

She shows the ten-digit number to Wolf.

“Wolf’s gears now start turning. “Send her a text; tell her that you and I are planning on a new start and that we will be celebrating at the fishing lodge south the Jefferson Bridge. As we are making up for lost time, you will drop some sleeping pills in my blackjack. After our love session, I will sleep like a baby.”

“What location shall I give her?”

“Tell her the building south of the Jefferson Bridge.”

“You mean the fishing lodge with the red roof that looks like a barn? The one on the riverfront?”

“Yeah, that’s it. It is 1:30 A.M. now. We need to be careful walking down to the barn. We will take the long way to ensure that we are not ambushed before then. We should be there at 3:15. Send the text, and let’s go.”

Gretchen has not seen Wolf so happy in months. Gretchen sends the text. It reads: “Wolf and I will be at a red barn two miles south of the Jefferson bridge on the east side of the river. Wait for my three flashes with my flashlight. We should be there at 3 A.M.

Wolf looks at the text and says, “You should add that I will be out cold after our sex orgy.”

“OK,” says Gretchen, and she adds the part that Wolf will be asleep and out cold.

Rose, Alex, and Brit Plan

Rose, Alex, and Brit have been listening to the conversation between Gretchen and Wolf. They are not sure whose side Gretchen is on; it seems that she is now with Wolf.

Alex says, "It really does not matter. We need to assume that she is hostile."

Rose nods. "Yes, she has been sucked into Wolf's orbit again."

"I know the area quite well," says Brit. "It is heavily wooded. I would recommend that we leave now and survey the area. It would be best if we can surprise them as they are entering the lodge. They will not expect anyone as they enter."

"Good idea," says Alex. "Wolf will have his mind on other things."

Rose agrees with the idea. "The plan can be perfected once we arrive on site and survey the property."

All three reach into their go bags and dress all in black. They paint their faces and dress in their lightweight Kevlar vests and helmets. They screw on the suppressors to their Glock 45s and strap on sheaths with their favorite knives. Ross has her trusty SOG serrated combat knife. The knife is strapped below the knee and adjusted to allow her to unsheathe it in one smooth motion and be ready for action. Included in their backpack are night vision goggles.

The team drives their van to a parking lot one mile south of the barn. Without saying a word, they all strap on their night vision goggles. Brit, who knows the area, leads the way through the heavily wooded area. In thirty minutes, they reach the red barn. It is located on the edge of the Cumberland River and appears to be at least forty years old. The building is in reasonably good shape, and the land around the building has been maintained. The barn is actually a fishing lodge owned by a KKK sympathizer. Wolf has befriended the sympathizer and has been allowed to use the building for meetings with drug dealers and his informant, Rock Irwin.

The walls are made of stone with a roof made from big, strong oak planks. Due to the original construction as a winery, the building is in reasonably good shape. Through the years, the river has eroded the land next to the barn. There are only five to ten feet between the river and the backside of the barn. The lodge has two levels. The bottom level has a doorway, which leads to five steps down to the river path. There are signs posted at the front and back of the building: "Private Property No Trespassing."

Rose, Alex, and Brit survey the property. Brit says, "If I recall, there is a dirt road at the front of the property. Wolf and Gretchen will likely approach the building from the road."

Alex takes off his night vision goggles and says, "There appears to be a path to the right." He points out a walking path from the dirt road to the building. The trail is covered with tall grass and has bushes on each side.

"We really do not know from which direction they will approach. What we do know is that Wolf and Gretchen will need to enter through either the front or back door," says Rose.

"We need to be prepared for entry from either the front or rear door," says Alex.

Both Rose and Brit say, "Agreed."

Alex tries to open the front door, and it is locked. He pulls out his lockpick, and in thirty seconds, it is open. Alex quickly goes down to the bottom floor and comes out the back door. He comes around to the front using a wooden staircase.

"The building looks like it is used as a fishing lodge. It is best if we all survey the rooms in case we need to subdue Wolf and Gretchen inside the building," says Alex.

The three enter the building and carefully examine the upper and lower floors. The rooms are nicely arranged with sofas, tables, large refrigerators with freezers, and chairs. The bottom floor has a small stove and kitchen cabinets. It is evident that no one lives there permanently and is used as a fishing lodge.

A plan is quickly developed based on the survey taken. Alex will guard the front door; he will use the bushes and hedges at the front of the building for concealment. Brit will guard the rear entrance; he will use a three-foot stonewall for concealment. The wall is being used as a protective barrier between the river and hikers. Rose will position herself midway between the front and back entrances and provide assistance as required. The team feels that they have a good plan and hope that Murphy is asleep at this early hour.

They do not need to wait long. Fifteen minutes after they are in place, they hear footsteps along the river path. Wolf and Gretchen are walking slowly and carefully down the trail, and Wolf has his head on a swivel and is continuously scanning 360 degrees. They reach the foot of the stairs. Wolf places his finger across his mouth and whispers, "Let's wait here for a few minutes and make sure that we have not been followed." Both listen intently. They hear frogs croaking, owls hooting, nightingales singing, and a few chinchillas scurrying across the walking path. After two minutes of listening, Wolf is satisfied that he is not being followed. As the two carefully walk up the stairs, Rose moves down from her midpoint concealment until she has a clear view of both. She takes off her night vision goggles. The moonlight provides sufficient lighting to see both Wolf and Gretchen clearly.

Wolf reaches into his pocket and pulls out the key. Before he inserts it in the lock, he again does a 360-degree visual observation. As often happens with plans, the unexpected happens. Wolf is six foot three. Brit is six foot two. Wolf's height works to his advantage; Brit's height works to his disadvantage. The added viewing angle for Wolf allows him to see over the three-foot wall.

As Wolf reaches to unlock the door, he quickly pulls out his Sig Sauer 2200 pistol with the suppressor attached and points in the direction of Brit. Brit sees that Wolf has drawn his handgun and quickly falls flat on his belly. Within seconds, two suppressed gunshots are heard, THUMP—THUMP!" Two bullets glance off Brit's Kevlar helmet.

Wolf now has the advantage, and he walks down the stairs in a steady and even pace. His Sig Sauer 2200 is a big, ugly-looking gun. Wolf likes the gun because it not only punches a wallop, but it is made of reinforced stainless steel. He holds his big gun in front with two hands. Gretchen walks directly behind him. He screams, "OK, you motherfucker, if you come out, I just might not kill you!"

Wolf has walked four steps; Rose aims her .45 directly at the Sig Sauer. It makes for an easy target. The stainless steel, the moonlight, and Wolf holding it steady makes it like shooting a duck at the county fair. Rose fires one shot, THUMP! The Sig Sauer is hit directly at its center. The gun flies out of Wolf's hands and lands on the Riverwalk; it has been permanently damaged.

Wolf and Gretchen are entirely taken by surprise. Wolf screams, "What the fuck!"

Rose calmly walks to the Riverwalk, ten feet in front of Wolf and Gretchen. Gretchen now changes her tune. "Jamie—Jamie, thank God. This asshole was going to kill me."

Rose says, "Gretchen, step back. With a shot from this distance, the bullet will go right through this asshole and through you."

As this action is taking place, Brit gets up and staggers around the stone wall.

"Are you OK?" asks Rose.

"Yes, I think so, but I have a headache, and I can still see stars in my eyes."

"You will be OK. Have a seat on the stone wall. Alex is coming and will help in handcuffing these two assholes."

As the conversation between Gretchen, Rose, and Brit is taking place, Wolf is thinking of his next move. He quickly grabs Gretchen, and in the same movement, he reaches behind his back and pulls out his small .38-caliber short-nosed Taurus revolver.

He points the revolver directly at Gretchen's belly and says, "OK, everybody moves back, or I kill this bitch." Wolf is now on the Riverwalk. He walks backward, pulling Gretchen with him. Rose is thinking, *I can probably hit Wolf in the head, but there is no guarantee that Gretchen won't move, and I might hit her. We'll wait it out. He will likely discard Gretchen and run down the Riverwalk.*

Wolf does exactly as Rose predicted. He soon has put fifty yards between himself and Rose. He yells out, "Take your handguns and radios and pitch them into the river—do it now, or I kill this bitch!"

Alex and Rose know that they have extra handguns in their backpacks. They also know that they can use their regular cell phones as radios. Alex, Brit, and Rose pitch their radios and handguns into the river.

Wolf thinks, *now that I have these stupid assholes unarmed, I should shoot them all.* However, his.38 cannot hit the broad side of a barn from fifty yards. He quickly discards that option.

He sees that Alex and Brit are beside Rose. He thinks through all his options. The best option is to kill Gretchen and make a run to freedom. He has been working out, including regular ten-mile runs; thus, he can outrun anyone. Yes, that is the best option.

He tells Gretchen, "OK, smartass, so you were working with your girlfriend. We will meet in hell."

Gretchen starts to protest. "Wolf, Wolf, don't shoot. I was only trying to buy some time. It was always a setup so that you could kill Jamie!

"Doesn't matter. I was always going to kill you. You just gave me an excuse." He fires the .38 twice, shooting her in the belly. Gretchen falls to the ground, and immediately blood starts to flow from her gut. Bullet wounds to the stomach cause significant blood loss; within two minutes, Gretchen is dead.

Wolf pushes her body aside, and like a hundred-meter runner, he starts running north on the river path. He knows the Riverwalk well as he took this path when meeting with KKK sympathizers at the fishing lodge.

Immediately after Wolf kills Gretchen and starts running, Rose and Alex give chase. Alex takes off like a jackrabbit and starts gaining ground on Wolf. Rose is an endurance runner. In high school, she was the best cross-country runner in England. In college, she was a pentathlon athlete. Her best event was the five-thousand-meter run. At half a mile, Alex is winded and starts to slow down; he is now seventy-five meters from Wolf. Alex looks to his left, and Rose passes him. She is running at a steady six-mile per hour pace. At one mile, Rose has closed the gap to the original fifty-meters.

Wolf has been looking back occasionally, and for the first mile, he saw that his pursuers were losing ground and is was now confident that he can reach his parked car and successfully make his escape. After running for one and a half miles, the river comes to some rapids, and the sound of the rushing water is a dull roar, like that of cars on a freeway. Rose is gaining ground, but due to the background noise of the rushing water, Wolf does not know that she has closed the gap to twenty meters. At ten meters, she sees that an incline for the Riverwalk is approaching. The slope leads to a bridge that goes over a small tributary river. The tributary makes a strong confluence where the two rivers meet. As Wolf starts to climb the incline, his running speed falls to a slow jog. Rose quickly gains ground.

Halfway up the incline, Rose is six feet behind Wolf, and with a cat like lunge, she tackles him. The tackle would make an NFL middle linebacker proud of her athletic abilities. Wolf is caught entirely by surprise. With his legs locked up, his body comes down face first on the dirt path. The impact breaks his nose, and it starts bleeding profusely. Rose, on the other hand, cushions her fall by having her head fall on Wolf's legs.

Wolf is startled and disoriented, but Rose is thinking clearly. She quickly lets' go of Wolf's legs and springs up to a baseball catcher's stance behind home plate. She reaches for her Glock but finds an empty holster. She then remembers that she threw it in the river. She knows that having a wrestling match with Wolf will not end up well for her; Wolf has too much upper-body strength.

Wolf has recovered, and he stands up. He regains his composure, and with his left sleeve, he begins wiping the blood from his nose. As he stares at Rose, he actually looked like an angry wolf. His nose is twisted grotesquely due to his face smashing into the dirt path. Now he loses all sense of control, but when he reaches behind his back to withdraw the .38, he finds nothing. The gun was ripped from his back waistband when Rose made the flying tackle. He sneers and snorts like a bull and makes an uncontrolled charge at Rose. As he attacks, Rose smartly steps to her left and grabs the back of his shirt at the neck, and at the same time, she snaps her right leg into the back of Wolf's knee. In one motion, she pulls back with her right hand and steps hard on Wolf's knee joint. Wolf slams on his back like a sack of potatoes.

Rose thinks, *this should do it. When Alex arrives, we can handcuff him.* However, Wolf is not down for the count. When Rose looks back to see if Alex is coming up the path, Wolf is more like a cat; he has nine lives. He quietly rolls over, takes a knee, and charges Rose from behind. He grasps her in a bear hug from behind. He has tremendous upper-body strength and has Rose like a bench vise. He yells in Rose's ear, "Your boyfriend is not gonna help you! You will be dead in thirty seconds!"

Rose does not reply. She thinks, *twenty more seconds, and I will pass out. Think...think... Do something.* Her instincts take over; she kicks her legs up and places them on the path stone wall. With all her strength, she pushes backward. Wolf continues to press harder and harder with his arms. Rose pushes again with all her strength; the two bodies tip over the stone wall and plunge into the confluence of the Cumberland and Chicomack Rivers.

The two bodies slam into the water. Since Rose was on top of Wolf, he takes the blow to the back of his body when the two hit the water. Rose now has the advantage; she is an excellent swimmer and can hold her breath more than five minutes underwater. The average person with special ops training can only hold their breath for two minutes. The push by Rose takes Wolf by surprise. He did not take a deep breath and was nearing exhaustion from three body blows: two from the ground and now one from the water. The plunge by the two bodies takes Wolf and Rose five feet underwater. The most basic instinct takes over: survival. Wolf lets go of Rose and swims to the surface of the water; Rose was prepared for the plunge into the water. She knows that she has the advantage; she was an excellent long-distance swimmer in college. Wolf's muscular body and total weight of 230 pounds now work against him.

However, for a big man, Wolf still is a pretty good swimmer. The body slam into the water has temporally disoriented him. The cold water from the river, though, has heightened his senses. After five to ten seconds, he is ready to fight Rose. He believes that he has an advantage. He looks around and sees her about ten feet from him.

Rose has swum underwater, away from Wolf, and she comes up, takes a deep breath, and dives back underwater. She goes down to eight feet, using a breaststroke, and swims in Wolf's direction. She cannot engage in a water fight on the surface; Wolf is too strong. She grabs him by his pant leg and pulls him down. He has a heavy wool long-sleeve shirt, heavy boots, and light protective vest. The combination of his clothing adds another twenty pounds to his weight. Wolf fights the pull from Rose. He needs to think fast: *She has been underwater for at least one minute. I can take a deep breath and engage underwater. The advantage should be mine.* He takes the deep breath and dives underwater. He knows where she is: she is tugging on his pant leg. He unsheathes his Gerber knife and starts swinging wildly. Rose can tell by the movement of Wolf's leg that he is diving underwater. She lets go of the leg and swims away. She knows that she can stay underwater for five minutes. She figures that at best, Wolf can remain underwater for two minutes. Underwater training in the SAS was routine. She was the best surface and underwater swimmer in her class for both SAS and MI6 training. Another advantage is that she has been underwater for a full minute before Wolf, so her eyes have adjusted better to the conditions.

Immediately after Wolf dives down, she detects the shining blade of his eight-inch Gerber knife and swims away. She also unsheathes her trusty SOG knife, quickly undoes her belt, and ties it in a loop. As Wolf slashes his knife left and right, Rose catches his arm, hand, and knife with her knife. She quickly does a full summersault, and the 180-degree turn catches Wolf's arm in a knot in with her belt. He can now only fight with his left arm. He has now been underwater one minute and forty-five seconds. He wildly throws his left arm at Rose and attempts to surface, but she sticks out her SOG knife and cuts his arm.

Rose has two choices: help him to the surface, in which case she is in danger of Wolf having something in his left hand that could strike her or keep him down for another thirty seconds until he passes out. She can then surface, take him to the shore, and try and revive him using artificial respiration. She chooses the second option. After another thirty seconds, a total of four minutes from the time that she went underwater, she surfaces.

As Rose and Wolf were falling from the bridge, Alex arrived and saw the two plunging into the water. He quickly removed his backpack and shoes, and as he dove into the water, he saw Wolf disappear beneath him. The combination of darkness, water twisters, and whirlpools due to the confluence provides less than five feet of visibility under the water.

After several minutes of frantically searching for Rose, he sees her pulling a body to shore. He swims over to her and helps her pull the body out of the water. He checks for a pulse and asks, "Should we try artificial respiration?"

Rose does not say anything; she has her hands on her knees and is attempting to regain her breath. She has been running on adrenaline and needs time to get her heartbeat back to normal. Alex looks at Wolf and decides to do nothing.

A few minutes later, Brit arrives. He leaps down the stairs to the shore of the river and looks at Wolf. "What happened?"

"He..." Rose replies, panting as she catches her breath, "Also lost the swim match."

Epilogue

The white nationalist movement continues in America. Approximately seventy of the Klansmen from the KKK camp are in hibernation. Their leaders, Wolf, Gretchen, and Colonel Sondermann, were all killed, resulting in a bump in the road. The FBI informant was arrested and is currently awaiting trial.

Major Jacobson is on the FBI's most wanted list and is in hiding with the help of KKK sympathizers.

FBI Agents Tom Kramer and Brit Singleton received most of the praise for their efforts to destroy the Pulaski, Tennessee, terrorist camp. Their efforts resulted in over seventeen women being rescued from forced prostitution and eventual death in snuff films. The WMA operatives, Rose, Alex, Claude, Mateo, and the supporting cast working on covert contracts with the FBI and CIA, and their part in the defeat of the American terrorists are kept under the radar.

Juan de la Toro and Esteban Gutierrez withdraw their supply of drugs and opioids to the Pulaski KKK camp. They continue their work with the Afghanistan Taliban representatives, Kurush Achakzai and Jaihoon Durani. Juan and Esteban have identified hundreds of opportunities in America. Americans love their guns and opioids. As long as there is a demand, there will be someone providing the supply.

The threat from within will continue.

The End